Drew and the Detectives Series

Hollywood Fame and Foul Play

Andrew Pacholyk

author of Scandal Beneath the Skyline

Hollywood Fame and Foul Play
by Andrew Pacholyk MS L.Ac

Editor: BookBright E

ISBN 979-8-9985535-6-1 paperback
ISBN 979-8-9985535-7-8 ebook
ISBN 979-8-9985535-8-5 hardcover
Library of Congress Control Number: 2026906070
Know Publishing, New York, NY

Table of Contents

Chapter 1
Paramount Studios

"Go on," Aisha snapped, catching the rider's reflection in the rearview mirror. "Reach for it. What are you waiting for?"

The car bucked as she floored it, tires screaming against the broken mountain road. Sweat slid down her temple, stinging her eye, but she didn't blink. She couldn't afford to. To her left, the slopes rose wild and jagged, brush clawing at the asphalt as the road doubled back on itself. To her right, nothing. Open air. A yawning chasm wide enough to swallow the car, the bomb, and every bad decision that had brought them here.

The curves came fast and vicious, folding in on themselves like the mountain was trying to trap them. Aisha tightened her grip on the wheel. One wrong move, one panicked grab from the back seat, and this chase would end in fire or freefall. Maybe both.

"What if it explodes?" he asked.

"Then I'm driving this car over the cliff so we trade one horrifying death for another," Aisha said.

Her companion leaned across the back seat and yanked the object free. "Okay, I've got the briefcase. Now what?" he yelled.

Aisha kept her voice steady. One eye tracked the road while the other measured the thin strip of asphalt between her tires and the cliff's edge. "Dial in the password. Slowly. Open it and tell me what you see."

"What's the password again?" he shouted.

"T.A.N.G.O.," she said.

He entered the combination, and the case sprang open. "It looks like a bomb, that's all," he muttered, flipping back the lid. His gaze flicked to the window, already calculating his next move. Then he saw the timer. "It reads 2:25."

"See that brick-like material? That's Semtex. Slowly pull the silver conductor out of it," she said. "Tell me if that stops the timer."

The car hit a bump, forcing the speeding wheels closer to the rocky edge.

"You're driving like a maniac!" the man shouted.

Aisha ignored him, her gaze locked on the winding road ahead. Dust streaked past the windows. The engine choked and sputtered as she shifted gears. "Hold on!" she hollered.

"It's not releasing from the syntax. The conductor is stuck!" His voice cracked now, panic creeping in. He glanced through the gaping hole that had once been the back window. Dark rain clouds chased them up the mountain. "Two minutes!"

"Then we're going to have to ditch the briefcase," Aisha replied, matter-of-fact.

"But we'll lose the one clue that's connected everything in this case!" he shot back.

"Or die trying! We've got a sharp right turn coming up. Get ready to throw the briefcase out your window," Aisha shouted over the roar of the engine as she pressed harder on the gas.

"You better go faster. We're not going to make it!"

Again, Aisha didn't respond. She stayed focused. Stayed the course. Her determination was matched only by her will to live.

"Throw it in 3-2-1!" she yelled.

The man launched the bag out the side window just as Aisha whipped the car into the sharp turn, veering away in the opposite direction. The briefcase caught the wind, sailed over the cliff, and exploded into a massive fireball.

"And…cut!"

The car rolled to a smooth stop.

The frame of the vehicle sat elevated on a cage-like rig, another car mounted behind it. The stunt driver gave Aisha a thumbs-up. She blew him a kiss.

A bevy of girls rushed over, dabbing sweat from her brow, touching up her makeup, gently removing the prop keys from her hand.

"Great job, Aisha," her director called.

She slid on her round black sunglasses and blew him another kiss. "Gracias, Remi."

Remi Harrington was Hollywood's new "IT" director. Tall and distinguished, thirty-something, his dark brunette hair slicked back with pomade as an ode to his famous father. A million-dollar smile complemented his deep green eyes.

"You should be in front of the camera, papi," Aisha replied without looking back.

A cough cut through the air, followed by three more. The nameless actor from the scene with Aisha pried himself out of the back of the car and fell to his knees. He slowly stood and dusted himself off. "Blimey! I don't know how in the blazes you Americans drive on the wrong side of the road. It drives me crazy!"

"Oye, Ollie," Remi called, noticing the man struggle to his feet.

The actor kept coughing. No one rushed over to offer him water, touch up his makeup, or help with his props.

"Matt, get him some water!" Remi shouted to his assistant. "Ollie, you have to pronounce your R's," the director reprimanded. "You're a Brit playing an American in the middle of L.A. What's wrong with you?"

"Bloody hell," the actor muttered, brushing dirt from his shirt.

Aisha watched the exchange. She never liked seeing directors belittle actors. Her gaze followed Remi as he walked away. Then she crossed quickly to her coworker.

"Mi amor, don't worry about all that. You're so gorgeous, no one will be listening to your lines." She gestured from the top of his head to the bottom of his feet. "They'll be too busy ogling over Ollie."

The Brit smiled. "It's a pleasure working with ya," he said. "I've been a big fan of your films from Spain. I'm right glad you're working in Hollywood." His Cockney accent spun through the air like a lively tune from an old-time music hall, carrying the charm and cheek of East London's spirited streets.

Aisha gave him one of her classic smiles, pivoted, and walked away, wrapping herself in a large shoulder shawl.

"That was fantastic." Drew clapped his hands as he approached with a wide grin. They kissed cheek to cheek. "You are a true action star," Drew said.

"Thanks to you," she replied, squeezing his hand.

Drew, who had recently embraced his new role as a full-time detective, could hardly contain his excitement about returning to the bustling cityscape of Los Angeles. The city held a mosaic of pivotal moments that had shaped his journey. At sixteen, he rode his first wave there, an experience that etched a love of surfing into his soul. Years later, the vibrant L.A. arts scene witnessed his evolution from dancer to respected choreographer.

Yet this city of dreams also carried darker memories. These were the same streets he had fled after the mysterious and unsolved death of his beloved aunt, an event that cast a long shadow over his heart and his life.

Now life's winding road had led Drew back to the City of Angels, and he stood at yet another significant crossroads. With a renewed sense of purpose, he was determined to use his skills to help those in dire need, the voiceless and the powerless. He wanted to make a difference, using his knowledge and instincts to solve cases for people who had nowhere else to turn.

Alongside Aisha and their cohorts, Elena, Grace, Israel, Francy, and Debra, they had become well known for solving mysterious and high-profile cases as Drew and the Detectives. They gained a reputation not only as dancers, dubbed the "Sexy Seven" by the hyperbolic press, but also as relentless investigators who unlocked buried secrets and uncovered situations others could not. Their powers of observation, their grasp of cognitive psychology, and their understanding of human behavior were their greatest strengths. As a team, they were unparalleled.

"Did you meet our new client yet?" Aisha asked eagerly.

"Yes, she is a fascinating woman," Drew commented.

He strode across the commissary, his beige khaki pants and shimmering brown Hush Puppies a throwback to an IZOD era that somehow found its way back into Hollywood trends. With two hot coffees in his hands, he joined Aisha at a table where the California sun bathed them in warm, golden light, creating the perfect backdrop for their late-afternoon chat.

The commissary at Paramount Studios was the "grub hub" for actors and actresses between scenes and takes. It was a place where performers came for a warm meal, a hot cup of Joe, or a quiet respite to kick back with an ice cream soda and run their lines. It blended the best of old Hollywood with the energy of a new generation.

"Your director is something else," Drew said. "He's the spitting image of his late father."

"Remi Harrington is a good director, but he has a lot to learn," Aisha confessed. "He's still very raw in his approach. He expects us to know what he's thinking. He assumes a lot." She glanced over and noticed her director at an adjacent table, surrounded by Hollywood starlets of the moment swooning around him.

"He seems to have a temper too," Drew observed.

Aisha quickly changed the subject. "Tell me about our new client."

"Vivienne LeClaire is a mesmerizing movie star from the 1950s. I found her both bewitching and bewildering. She spoke in rhythmic phrases, as if she were reading from a script." Drew made a sweeping gesture from his lips, as though words were lilting from the actress's mouth.

"Really? What did she look like?" Aisha asked, eager to hear a description associated with one of Hollywood's most renowned names.

Drew cleared his throat, already anticipating Aisha's first question.

"Well… she looked good for her age," he began carefully, watching Aisha lift an eyebrow. "I mean it. She had cascading waves of curls falling around her shoulders. Real curls, not the stiff salon kind. And her face…" He shook his head, almost in disbelief. "Her skin still had that porcelain smoothness, the kind that makes you wonder if she struck some secret deal with time itself. And her eyes. Those piercing sapphire eyes didn't just look at me. They went straight through me."

He leaned back and exhaled. "Vivienne LeClaire wasn't just an older woman. She was the kind of woman who walked into a room and instantly reminded everyone else to try harder. She spoke softly. Almost as if she were afraid someone was listening. There was a definite paranoia about her."

"But this is why she called us, no?" Aisha took a long sip of coffee and leaned back in her chair, her long blond hair falling over one shoulder. The fatigue from the day's shoot was beginning to replace her adrenaline-fueled spirit. She slid the wrap into her lap.

"She's convinced someone is following her, listening to her phone conversations, and threatening her life."

"Threatening her how?" Aisha sat up straighter.

"She's been receiving anonymous letters slipped beneath her front door." Drew opened his bag and pulled out a stack of crumpled papers with ominous messages made from cutout letters from magazines and periodicals.

"How original," Aisha muttered, rolling her eyes. *Your days are numbered if you ever tell the truth. It's only a matter of time. I know what you did.* She read the notes aloud.

"She said these words sliced through her like a knife," Drew replied.

"Telling," Aisha said, reading the remaining threats. "What did she do? Did she confess to you?" Her curiosity sharpened. "She doesn't have security? How did she get these letters?"

"She wasn't sure what the letters pertained to. She did admit she'd told plenty of lies during her career. She brushed it off as the 'nature of Hollywood.'" Drew glanced around before sliding the letters back into his bag. "She has a grand mansion in Beverly Hills, yet the large iron gates were open and unguarded. From the circular drive, I could see a house in disrepair, badly in need of a paint job."

Shock crossed Aisha's face. "My God. Not what I expected."

"I rang the bell and was greeted by an elderly gentleman in a tuxedo who looked like he was barely hanging on. He told me the letters had been left at the front door."

Aisha finished her coffee and leaned forward, sitting on the edge of her seat. "What other issues did she have?"

"She explained that 'subtle signs of intrusion began to seep into her sanctuary.' Her exact words," Drew said, mimicking her tone. "A cherished photograph of her receiving an Academy Award was cracked, as if mirroring her fractured peace of mind. The scent of gardenias, her signature fragrance, lingered in the hallway even though she hadn't worn it in weeks."

"It suggests someone has orchestrated an insidious plot to slowly drive her crazy," Aisha said. "Has she gone to the police about this?"

Drew leaned in. "She told me she'd filed several complaints. She feels they were just appeasing her and not really doing anything."

"So clearly, the butler did it," Aisha said dryly.

Drew shook his head. "The police questioned the butler. For several incidents, he wasn't even present, so they ruled him out quickly."

"She wants us to unravel her mystery," Aisha concluded.

"She's a big fan of yours, Aisha," Drew said with a smile. "She was referred to us by Mrs. Belltone in New York." He was referencing their last case.

"Oh, I see." Aisha nodded slowly. "So you feel obligated?"

Drew considered the question. "Yes," he hummed. "A referral is the best compliment. Besides, I'm really curious about Vivienne LeClaire's conundrum." He leaned back, weighing Aisha's words.

"Does she have any idea who could be sending these notes? Does she know what the intruder is referring to?" Aisha raised an eyebrow.

"She was very frank with me," Drew began. "She's lived a very colorful life. She was eager and reckless as a young star. She made questionable choices when it came to relationships, investments, friends, even family." He hesitated. "She's sure she scorned more than a few people along the way."

Aisha lifted her other eyebrow.

"But she can't think of one specific incident that would come back to haunt her like this," Drew concluded.

"Well, it sounds like we have to dig deeper." Aisha shifted in her seat. "Are the rest of the crew here yet?" She was referring to their team.

"Debra and Israel flew in last night. Francy, Grace, and Elena are on the next flight from Miami," Drew confirmed. "We're meeting with Vivienne LeClaire tomorrow." He paused and looked at Aisha with soft, persuading eyes. "She really wants to meet you. She's a big fan."

Aisha scoffed. "She doesn't even know who I am." She rolled her eyes.

"Aisha, you're famous worldwide. You're not just another working actor," Drew said warmly. "You have international appeal."

"You're always good at boosting my ego," Aisha said, blushing as she avoided his gaze.

"I have to agree," a calm voice drifted in from behind them.

Aisha and Drew turned to see an elderly gentleman seated in the far corner beneath a dusty portrait of Rita Hayworth. He sat alone at a two-top, stirring his tea slowly and methodically, as if it were a ritual. He watched her with the kind of focus only someone who had once lit her from the shadows could possess.

Aisha narrowed her eyes. She knew that face. “Oh, hello, mi amor…” She made the effort to stand and greet him.

He was dressed simply, brown corduroy pants with a careful crease down the center, a crisp white BVD T-shirt tucked in like he’d been wearing it that way for decades. A battered gray felt hat rested low on his brow, the brim drooping slightly over his eyes. The hat looked like it had survived a thousand setups and breakdowns, as if it had absorbed the heat of arc lights and the murmurs of secret deals. A small rusted pin clung to the hatband, a faded gold rectangle stamped with “Union 728.”

He rose slowly, removing his hat as she approached, his expression calm and measured.

“You do the lighting for me,” she said. “You lit me like you knew what I was going to feel before I did.”

His mouth turned up slightly. “I didn’t light you. I just gave your light room to breathe.”

She laughed, surprised and almost embarrassed, and pulled out the chair across from him.

“Why don’t I remember your name?”

“Wasn’t mine to give back,” he said, his voice low and dry, tinged with a Southern lilt. “We aren’t the ones people remember. We just make the stars shine.”

He offered his hand. “Harold Keyes. Most call me Keyes, if they need something fixed.”

She took his hand, rough and calloused, but warm and genuine. “I’m Aisha.”

"I know who you are," he said, eyes gleaming. A pause settled between them, thick with things unsaid. The din of the commissary faded into the background. "I was an actor once," he said. "Back in the day. Then one day, poof. My career was done." His fingers tapped against his teacup. "I saw something I wasn't supposed to see. Or maybe I said something no one was supposed to say." The words landed between them like a lead weight.

Aisha leaned in slightly. "This is my dear friend, Drew."

Mr. Keyes studied him, as though deciding whether he should recognize him.

"Not an actor," Drew said with a small smile. "I'm just visiting the set."

Relief softened Mr. Keyes's expression, as though reassured he had not made a mistake or said too much. "Well, you look like you could be the son of Tab Hunter or William Holden."

"Well, thank you. That's a very generous assessment," Drew said, nodding.

"Well, I didn't mean to interrupt. I look forward to bringing you more light in the future." He smiled faintly and tipped his old gray hat.

"I'll see you tomorrow," Aisha said.

☆☆☆

"Madame, can I get you anything before I retire?" the butler asked, leaning closer so Vivienne could hear him.

With her nose buried in a book, she slowly turned to face him and removed her reading glasses. "No, no, Drake. Thank you. Please, go on off to bed." She paused. "And sweet dreams."

Drake lowered his head. His face was a portrait of discretion, angular, unreadable, and aged just enough to command respect without inviting softness. The slightest arch of an eyebrow or the faint narrowing of his eyes spoke volumes, if one knew how to listen. A single silver streak ran through his neatly combed black hair, adding a touch of gravitas that deepened the air of mystery around him. He straightened slowly and nodded in a gentle good night.

Vivienne closed her book and set it on the table before her. She paused, scanning the living room, reassuring herself that she would be all right. It was the story she told herself each night. The comfort never lasted long. Her mind felt like an engine idling in neutral, running nonstop but going nowhere.

Vivienne's illustrious career, once a source of adoration and envy, had drawn a different kind of attention over time. She knew the price of fame all too well, but this felt different, personal, as though the perpetrator held a grudge not only against the icon but against the woman behind the glamour. Shadows seemed to move with purpose, and every creak of her aging mansion felt like part of a symphony of threats.

As night cloaked the city of stars, Vivienne retreated to her private screening room, where the ghosts of her past performances flickered across a worn screen. It seemed to be her only solace, a world she could retreat into and find comfort in. She reached for the manual switch on the ancient cinematograph, settled back into her cushioned chair, and smiled. The film playing was the one that had made her a star, *Velvet Ashes*. Set against the glittering backdrop of 1950s New York, it followed Clara Hensley, a woman cast aside after a scandal she did not cause. She rose from public disgrace to become a dazzling socialite, forced to choose between revenge and reinvention.

The projector's beam cut through the darkness like a beacon, but it was the uninvited silhouette that drew her gaze, a figure looming in the doorway. Her breath caught in her throat, her heart leaping into a frantic tango. This was no longer a vague threat. It was tangible, a predator that had slipped into her world of nostalgia and opulence. "Drake, is that you?" she called to the dark figure in the frame.

Adrenaline pulsed through her. She felt the threat creeping up the back of her neck while she fought to stay calm. "Drake?"

The figure did not answer, only towered in the pitch-black hallway, seeming to grow more menacing with every second.

Vivienne LeClaire, the actress who had once faced cameras and critics with unshakable confidence, now faced her own mortality, the script of her life turning dark with no director to call "cut." "What do you want from me?" she shouted. She noticed the figure swaying slowly from side to side, but it did not advance.

Shaking, she tried to stand, taking her eyes off the doorway for only a moment. A loud sound clapped before her, and she hesitated to raise her gaze to the level of the frame. She was about to scream but swallowed the sound when she heard a door open behind her. "Oh, Drake! An intruder!" she cried, pointing toward the doorway in front of her. The space was now empty.

Drake moved quickly to the front of the screening room. His eyes darted back and forth, surveying the tiny theater for any sign of movement. He brought his index finger to his lips. "Shhhh."

Shivering from fright, Vivienne slowly sank back into her chair and buried her face in her hands. Drake moved toward the doorway. At his feet lay a photocopy of the *Velvet Ashes* manuscript. Slashed across the cover in red ink were the words: time's up.

"Madame, are you all right? Are you hurt?"

Without looking up, she slowly shook her head.

Drake bent down and picked up the manuscript, holding it behind his back to conceal it from his employer.

"Come, Madame. Allow me to give you a sedative." Drake wrapped an arm around Vivienne and helped her to her feet. With careful patience, he escorted her through the neglected house and upstairs to her bedroom at the far end of the mansion.

Chapter 2
West Hollywood

The apartment was a sleek, modern loft tucked away on Huntley Drive, not far from Santa Monica Boulevard, where the hum of traffic filtered through the floor-to-ceiling windows. Sunlight bounced off polished concrete floors, illuminating the minimalist furnishings: a low charcoal-gray sectional, a glass coffee table scattered with oversized art books, and a few abstract pieces that brought bursts of color to the otherwise neutral walls.

"The coffee's ready." Debra emerged from the kitchen carrying a silver tray with three cups. Tiny and sprightly, she drifted across the room like a petal caught on a gentle breeze. Every movement she made was a whisper of elegance. In Drew's eyes, calling her his "petite ballerina" was not just about appearance. It was an affectionate nod to the way she solved problems: light on her feet, swift in her decisions, always dancing just ahead of danger.

Drew and Aisha each reached for a cup. "My morning fuel," Drew said.

"Mi amor, gracias," Aisha said, smiling at her dear friend.

Debra swept her blond hair across her cheeks and bowed gallantly. Her erect dancer's poise made her presence felt wherever she went. "Listen, when are we going to see Ms. LeClaire?"

Drew looked up from his steaming coffee, savoring the pungent taste of caffeine on his tongue. “She’s seeing us at noon.”

“I can’t believe we’re actually going to be working for her,” Debra exclaimed. “Aisha, tell me, how is the filming going?”

Aisha shrugged. “It’s fine. Long hours, a crazy director, and for once, we’re ahead of schedule.”

“That’s a rarity, no?” Debra smirked.

“Yes, but this director is no-nonsense.”

“Well, I can’t believe the movie studio scored you a loft like this,” Debra murmured, her eyes tracing the clean lines and ethereal glow of the open space. “It’s quintessential L.A. That seamless industrial conversion, the lofty ceilings, the light. L.A. architecture always finds a way to turn old warehouses into something effortlessly cool.”

“It was serendipitous that I booked this movie and we signed an L.A. client. It was meant to be,” Aisha said with a smile.

“I don’t see Elena or Israel in their rooms. Did they go out already?” Drew asked, trying to keep track of everyone.

“Go out?” Aisha laughed. “They never came home.” She flipped her cascading honey-blonde hair behind her and, with deliberate grace, traced the air at her side with her long, lacquered nails, each one a perfect curved almond shape in a muted rose tone. The soft click of polished acrylic against her silk blouse sounded both elegant and quietly assertive, as if every movement made a statement before she said a word.

“They went to The Abbey for a drink,” Debra said, shaking her head. “I guess they fell down the rabbit hole.”

“Yes, Alice and the Mad Hatter,” Drew smirked. “And where are Grace and Francy?”

"I'm here," Francy called, stepping out of her room with effortless command. Her sun-kissed, olive-toned skin carried the subtle sheen of an early-morning workout, and every curve reflected strength shaped through discipline and dedication. The green of her sports bra and tank caught the light just so, like shimmering emerald sea foam, framing a silhouette that was lean, powerful, and undeniably energized.

"Are we going to the gym before our appointment?" Drew asked with a smile, offering her a quiet good morning.

Francy's face was framed by dark, softly tousled waves that tumbled to her shoulders, the kind of Italian brunette beauty that carried both warmth and fire. High cheekbones, brushed with a faint blush of exertion, gave her a sculpted yet natural elegance. "As soon as I get my coffee," she said, matching Drew's smile. As Miami's reigning fitness icon and dance leader, Francy was both a force of movement and the grounding core of the group.

"Coming right up," Debra called out, turning on her heels and heading back into the kitchen.

"Grace left early this morning," Francy added. "She said she had to buy the right outfit if she's going to meet her idol."

"Who?" Aisha's head snapped to the side.

"Vivienne LeClaire," Drew answered.

"I didn't think she knew who she was," Aisha said, shaking her head matter-of-factly.

"Grace has a passion for old Hollywood," Drew explained. "She loves the Erté styling, the old-world glamour, and especially the neo-noir detective films from the 1950s." He laughed. "That's what we bond over."

"Oh, they are the best." Debra emerged from the kitchen with another hot cup of coffee for Francy. "The styling was just impeccable."

Francy accepted the coffee with gratitude. "Grace is going to meet us at Vivienne LeClaire's mansion at noon." She took a careful sip before continuing. "Aisha, you're not filming today?"

Aisha leaned back on the sofa and rearranged her tiered skirt over her long legs. "It's a night shoot. My call time is nine. This director doesn't care about the hours, the overtime, or the crazy shooting schedule. He wants what he wants, and that's it."

"Thank goodness you have the SAG union on your side," Debra huffed. "To protect you from crazy directors like him."

"It's that young director with the reputation, right?" Francy asked.

"Remi Harrington," Aisha confirmed.

"He seems like a polished product of nepotism. Another legacy kid with a famous last name and a stylist on speed dial," Francy said. "Too perfect to be real. He embodies the kind of effortless success most people only dream of."

"Well, he's the guy on every magazine cover, the director's name dropped in coffee shop conversations, and the face of a new generation of cinema," Aisha replied.

"I give him points for that," Drew said approvingly. "We love creative genius. Okay, let's hit the gym."

The Sports Connection on Santa Monica Boulevard in West Hollywood was a famous see-and-be-seen health club known for its lively social scene, luxurious amenities, and high-energy cardio classes. It had spawned its own workout culture and often doubled as a singles bar, making it a magnet for celebrities.

Drew, Francy, Debra, and Aisha made their way up to the second-floor workout machines, taking in all the pretty people perched on stationary cycles and the couples paired off, exercising together.

"Are we sure we're in a gym?" Debra peered over the edge of her nose. "This has Miami beat tenfold."

Aisha and Francy were already fending off several men who circled them like sharks. "Aren't you Aisha?" one man asked, extending a small towel toward her.

"No, no. Not me. I hear that a lot," she said, giving him the cold shoulder.

"I have a special workout for you, Italy," another man said, approaching Francy. She pretended not to hear him.

"You girls need a bodyguard," a voice from behind them said. Immediately recognizing her tone, Francy and Aisha quickly turned to find their friend Elena in a wide stance, hands on hips, framed by her ever-present blond pigtails. "You dolls better hit the weights before there's a blockade around you," Elena raised one eyebrow.

The three friends hugged, wishing each other good morning. "I hope you girls had your morning coffee, because I hear this class that we're about to take is a killer." Elena's radiant smile was her greatest camouflage, inviting warmth that masked sharp, streetwise steel. Her Southern ease whispered innocence, cleverly hiding the gritty New York rocker-chic toughness beneath. A natural singer and dancer, she moved through music with electric grace and navigated the gritty pulse of the city even more deftly. Driven and fiercely focused, she was always there to rally her friends through the labyrinth of crime and conspiracy they endured with steely conviction.

"Elena," Drew spotted his friend from across the gym. "You made it." They exchanged kisses, with Debra following suit. "Did you have a nice night?"

"We had a fun night," she replied. "Israel and I started out having drinks at The Abbey, and then we moved on from there," she smiled. "You know Israel. He had to give me the tour of every bar and watering hole in West Hollywood, just to make sure I didn't miss anything."

"And you're still standing?" Debra sang out.

"Do you realize they close the bars at 2am? Can you imagine?"

"That's L.A.," Aisha rang in.

"Of course, Israel found some after-hours party for us to dance at, so we continued our 'welcome to L.A.' event until about 6am."

"And Isra?" Debra asked, referring to Israel by his nickname.

"He conveniently found some trouble to get into, but I made sure we met here at the club at 7am," she grinned, raising one eyebrow again. "He's in the steam room."

"Of course he is," Debra chimed. "Let's get to class."

Israel, the team's living dynamo, burst onto the scene with kinetic energy to spare. In his late twenties, he carried the confidence of someone who was as comfortable deciphering clues as he was flexing muscle, muscle that sat snug beneath the electric blue tank top he wore, which seemed to celebrate who he was. He complemented the vibrant top with neon green athletic shorts and matching chartreuse sneakers, turning heads even before he spoke.

When the moment called for urgency, Israel didn't hesitate. With a sharp grin and muscles tensing like coiled springs, he planted himself beside the group, his voice cutting through the tension. "Not going to class without me!"

The velocity that pulsed around him wasn't just physical. It was the reassurance that every plan, no matter how dangerous, got an extra dose of determination the moment he stepped in. It was in that energy, bright, electrifying, undeniably loyal, that Israel stood out. His ever-buzzing brain, technical prowess, and constant positivity were the spark that ignited courage and action when his detective friends needed it most.

Drew reached out to his friend. "Welcome to L.A. L.A. Land."

"Happy to be here," he smiled, planting a kiss on each one of his friends' cheeks.

"Ready to rock that outfit?" Elena gave Israel a squeeze around the waist, and off the group went.

The fitness studio occupied a central, glass-enclosed space at the heart of the gym, offering a full 360-degree view into its animated interior. Patrons on the main floor could not help but admire the captivating silhouettes unfolding within, an enticing spectacle that added another layer of allure to this notoriously provocative venue, colloquially known as the "Sports Erection."

The room crackled like a movie set under hot spotlights, everyone poised and primed for attention. Each person leaned forward, eyes glinting as they jockeyed for the best vantage point, whether pressed against the floor-to-ceiling windows or perched closest to the elevated stage where the instructor would lead. It felt less like an exercise class and more like a high-stakes callback, every flex and breath an opportunity to stand out. This was Hollywood. The pulse ran fast, the air hung thick with ambition, and the unspoken competition felt as electrifying as the city just beyond the glass.

Drew and the crew pushed their way to the front and center, staring in disbelief at the eager competition around them. "This looks more like a casting call," he whispered. The moment the instructor entered the room, the class gasped in collective reaction. A beat later, the crowd erupted into thunderous applause.

Lexi Vale, the aerobics instructor who commanded every eye in the room, was nothing short of mesmerizing. She wore an electric blue thigh-high leotard that sculpted and celebrated her athletic physique. The look blended fashion and function, echoing the 1980s Lycra staples that defined the era's fitness culture. Beneath it, form-fitting pink leggings glided over every defined muscle, emphasizing the strength underneath. A matching headband crowned her long blonde hair, absorbing sweat while making a bold style statement in true retro aerobics fashion.

"It's a throwback to aerobic chic. I love it," Debra called out over the applause.

"Definitely a look," Elena replied.

Aisha shot Drew a look but said nothing.

Lexi stepped onto the stage and greeted her fans with a quick, knowing smile. She tossed her Hollywood blonde hair behind her and signaled for the music to start. In a heartbeat, she flipped the switch. The retro aerobics vibe ignited the stage, and the sweat machine roared to life.

Chapter 3
Sunset Boulevard

Grace stood before the mansion's front door. Her eyes traced the old, fading clapboards, the weathered paint lifting and peeling with each restless brush of wind. For a moment, she wondered if she had the correct address. She rang the doorbell again and waited.

She gave herself one last glance to ensure everything was in place. The camel-colored pencil skirt she had just bought on Rodeo Drive hugged her hips with the precision of a tailor's dream, its sleek fabric falling cleanly into matching ankle boots that elevated her silhouette. The skirt gathered neatly at her waist, cinched with a wide chocolate-brown leather belt that curved around her frame like an elegant exclamation point. Above it, a crisp white blouse, freshly pressed and delicately structured, was tucked neatly into the skirt.

With a practiced flick of her fingers, she gathered her long rose-pink braids over one shoulder, letting them cascade in soft, orderly coils down the front of her blouse. The color, audacious yet graceful, framed her heart-shaped face with a modern artistry that was impossible to ignore. Her radiant complexion and almond-shaped eyes reflected a quiet confidence as she studied her reflection, not out of vanity, but with the satisfaction of a woman who knew exactly how to dress the part, whatever the role required.

A silent smile tugged at her lips. It wasn't just about fashion. It was strategy, armor, and signature all in one. Grace didn't simply enter a space.

She arrived.

She was meeting one of her idols, after all.

The door opened.

"Yes, miss? Are you one of the detectives?" Drake asked.

Grace smiled gently. "Yes. Yes, I am." It was still hard to get used to her newfound profession.

Drake nodded with a gentleman's ease and pulled open the heavy, brass-handled door, gesturing for her to step inside. As Grace crossed the threshold, the air shifted. A quiet hush settled around her, the kind that belonged only to homes steeped in history, wealth, and just the right touch of scandal. Drake led her through the grand foyer, his steps silent against the polished tile floor, while hers echoed softly, mingling with the ghosts of old conversations and champagne-fueled laughter.

They moved across ancient carpets, Persian no doubt, their once-vibrant reds and deep indigos softened by time and the soles of a thousand shoes, some famous, others infamous. She could almost hear the faint murmur of golden-era Hollywood icons. A legendary actress gliding across the weave in stilettos. A brooding playwright smoking too close to the drapes. The fibers had absorbed drama, decadence, and secrets.

Grace's imagination raced.

Above, the ceiling soared into a dome of opulence, its surface adorned with a sprawling fresco that arrested her mid-stride. It was a celestial tableau of cherubs, goddesses, and sweeping clouds rendered in dreamy pastels, bathed in golden light from a tiered crystal chandelier. Painted by one of Hollywood's many ephemeral, underpaid geniuses, or perhaps, though unlikely, a lost master moonlighting in Los Angeles anonymity. She couldn't tell which, and maybe that was the point. Illusion was the mansion's native language.

Grace took it all in, letting her gaze linger, not only in admiration but in calculation. Every detail in the foyer felt deliberate, chosen to impress, distract, and conceal. She smiled faintly. Whatever secrets this place held were wrapped in velvet, framed in gold, and painted over with centuries of borrowed elegance. And she was only just getting started.

"Wait here, please," Drake said, nodding to Grace as they stopped at the closed doors to the living room. He knocked gently and waited.

"Come, come," came the muffled reply from beyond.

"Madame, Grace, one of the detectives you were meeting at noon, is here," he said, then paused. "Early."

"Oh good. Please, please show her in."

The room was cloaked in darkness. Heavy, floor-length curtains smothered every window, shutting out the faint glow of the city beyond. These were the same windows that once framed a sweeping view of the Hollywood Hills, now hidden behind folds of dusty velvet. The only light came from a single candle flickering on a low side table near the center of the room. Its flame cast long, wavering shadows across the walls, dancing over aged wallpaper and the edges of antique furniture like a memory struggling to take shape. The darkness was not just physical. It was deliberate.

Vivienne LeClaire, the silver-screen siren whose name once evoked enchantment and desire, now murmured a soft "my dear" in the candlelight when she spotted Grace.

Grace couldn't contain her grin. As she approached her idol, she curtsied out of nowhere, then immediately questioned the impulse.

"I… I am so pleased to meet you." The words tumbled out, hovering awkwardly on the tip of her tongue.

"You are such a pretty thing," Vivienne said, warmth and quiet amusement in her voice. "Are all your detective friends as lovely as you and Drew?" The compliment floated through the air with effortless grace.

"I've been a longtime fan," Grace admitted, her cheeks coloring. "I remember seeing pictures of you in that red dress at the *Velvet Ashes* premiere. It's truly your signature look."

Vivienne's expression softened, flattered but also impressed. It had been a long time since anyone in the industry regarded her work as more than a résumé line. "Most people remember the red dress I wore that night, not the keynote."

Grace smirked. "I remember both. Fashion and function."

They shared a quiet laugh, light yet grounded in mutual recognition. Whatever had happened before Drew and the others arrived, whatever fear or shame Vivienne had tried to conceal, began to ease in the presence of someone who remembered her not only for who she had been, but for what she had built.

"You're adorable," Vivienne mouthed.

Grace was too happy to answer. She smiled, wide and unguarded, then turned to the other woman in the room.

"Oh yes, Grace, I must introduce you to my oldest and dearest confidant." She lifted her right arm, presenting her guest. "This is Madame Arquette, my most trusted psychic and medium."

Grace's eyes widened. "How do you do? I am fascinated by the art of foretelling." She nodded politely.

"Yes, quite," Madame Arquette drawled, her voice seeming to rise from somewhere deep within her. "Your aura is very luminous, my dear, if I may be so forward."

Grace detected a British accent, though another dialect threaded through it. Romanian, perhaps? “Oh yes, you may be so forward,” Grace replied lightly before turning back toward her host.

“You must sit down and listen to this,” Vivienne insisted. “Madame Arquette was just about to give me the lowdown.” She eased back into her seat and waved Drake out of the room.

Madame Arquette lowered herself before a crystal ball perched on a three-pronged brass stand. Beside it sat a half-full glass of herbal tea. She lifted it, leaned in, and finished it in two deliberate gulps. Setting the cup onto its rose-colored saucer, she studied the pattern of leftover leaves clinging to the porcelain. A hushed grunt escaped her before her gaze shifted slowly to the crystal.

“The threat is no longer an abstraction. It is real. It is close. And it hungers for the final act of your storied life, Vivienne,” Madame Arquette declared.

Grace froze in her chair.

Vivienne’s petite yet curvaceous figure shifted on the sofa. Grace could not help but notice how her idol carried a deliberate elegance, accentuated by an impeccable fashion sense that showcased trends from twenty years ago as though they had never gone out of style.

Grace was still enamored with her choices. Behind the glamorous façade, though, she knew Vivienne carried a notorious past that only deepened her mystique. Rumors had long swirled about tumultuous affairs with fellow actors and daring escapades that defied the boundaries of polite society. In an era shaped by conformity, Vivienne had been a rebel, unapologetic and untamed. That was what Grace loved most. That was what she remembered.

Vivienne, as if confirming her psychic’s insight, finally released her secret. “He was here. Last night.” Anger sharpened her voice. “He leered at me from the screening room doorway. Hiding in the shadows." Beneath the fury lingered something more fragile, a quiet humiliation at how she had reacted.

"He is here to drive you mad," Madame Arquette said calmly. "I can see it."

"Is he a deranged fan?" Grace blurted out. The revelation thrilled her more than it should have, her mind already racing ahead, piecing together possibilities.

Silence settled over the room.

"What did he look like?" Grace pressed. She had to know.

Vivienne hesitated. "He was a shadow. A shadow from my past."

Grace understood that Vivienne's history was cloaked in secrecy, which only heightened her allure. Tabloids had whispered about connections to powerful figures in the underworld. Others speculated about her true involvement in scandalous affairs. Whatever the truth, Vivienne's life had been marked by controversy and an unrelenting pursuit of excitement.

In some secret corner of her heart, Grace wanted that same kind of danger. That same kind of legend.

"In some strange way…" The words parted her lips before she caught herself drifting too far into the fantasy. She straightened. "Madame Arquette, what else do you see?"

Grace could barely contain her anticipation.

The psychic glanced at her tea leaves once again.

"Vivienne, I see nothing but shadows. They are all around you. You are in for a turbulent time," she warned. "I am going to consult the Tarot." She paused. "Just to confirm."

Grace couldn't contain herself. "I wish Drew was here," she whispered under her breath. She glanced at Vivienne, studying her closely. Grace knew Vivienne was famous for extravagant parties that stretched into the early hours of the morning, where Hollywood elite and socialites from around the world mingled, captivated by her irresistible charm. Vivienne's presence could command an entire room, leaving a lasting impression on anyone fortunate enough to cross her path. Grace could still see that light within her.

"Could this be someone from your past? Someone who has been in the house before and knew their way around?" Grace asked, directing the question to Vivienne.

Vivienne slowly turned her head toward her and paused, as if preparing to deliver the final line of a film. "Darling, half of Hollywood has been through this house."

Madame Arquette cut through the moment with a sharp, deliberate motion, banging her Tarot cards on the table three times, each thud like a gavel sealing fate. Then came the shuffle, rapid and hypnotic, her bejeweled fingers moving with surprising dexterity for someone her age. The motion was neither clumsy nor theatrical. It was practiced. Ritualistic. She never took her eyes off the deck as she split it into two precise halves, then slipped one back into the other with a fluid, seamless motion, like a magician folding time.

The heavy scent of frankincense clung to the dimly lit living room, curling through the shadows between the three women. A melting candle flickered at the center of the table, casting a haunting glow across Madame Arquette's lined face. Light caught on her many rings and the deep obsidian beads of her necklace. She stared at the cards for a long moment, as if listening to them breathe.

Then, slowly and with ceremony, she laid out the first card.

"The Moon," Grace whispered to herself.

The card landed face up, slightly askew, its painted surface gleaming faintly. A wolf and a dog howled beneath a full moon while a narrow path wound into the unknown.

“Ah…” Madame Arquette murmured, her voice rich with accent and something older, something almost ancestral. “The Moon, chère Vivienne. This card speaks in riddles. It warns of illusion, of truths hidden beneath dreams. Not all is as it seems around you. Someone, or something, wears a mask. The path you walk is shadowed, lit only by instinct.” She leaned forward, her dark eyes narrowing. “Trust nothing completely. And trust no one blindly. Even your own mind can betray you under this moon.”

With a flick of her wrist, she placed the second card.

“The World,” Vivienne declared. “Of course it’s the world. That is what I’ve conquered.” A matter-of-fact smile crossed her lips as she settled back against the sofa.

The image radiated harmony: a crowned woman wrapped in a flowing sash, suspended within a laurel wreath. In each corner of the card sat a symbol, lion, bull, eagle, and man.

“Completion,” Madame Arquette breathed. “This is a powerful card, my dear. The World means something is coming to an end. A cycle, a trial, perhaps a long-hidden truth. You are standing on the edge of resolution. But be warned.” She tapped the card gently with her index finger, her nail clicking against the surface. “Completion is not always peace. Sometimes it is revelation. And revelation can be… costly.”

Grace shot Madame Arquette a quick glance. Then came the final card.

“Death,” Vivienne whispered, flinching slightly. Grace did not move.

The card lay flat and final, a skeletal figure on horseback raising a black flag marked with a white rose.

“Ah,” Madame Arquette said, not with fear but with quiet reverence. “La Mort. The card most misunderstood.” She looked directly at

Vivienne. "This is not a promise of death, but a demand for transformation. A truth must die for a new one to be born. Something in your life, perhaps someone, is no longer meant to remain. You will have to let go, whether you want to or not."

She leaned back in her chair, her gaze lingering on the three cards, their painted meanings humming between the women like a vibrating tuning fork.

"Moon. World. Death," she repeated, softer now. "Illusion. Completion. Transformation. You are standing at a threshold, Vivienne. This has been your life. Past, present, future." Madame Arquette's eyes gleamed. "What you choose to carry with you, and what you choose to bury, will shape the woman you become."

The room fell silent again, broken only by the candle's faint crackle and the distant rustle of wind against stained glass.

Behind her calm expression, Grace drew a slow, steady breath.

The doorbell rang. Both Grace and Vivienne jumped in their seats. "That must be my friends," Grace said.

Madame Arquette quickly gathered her belongings. She rose slowly and waited until she heard voices drifting in from the foyer. "I will show myself out the back door," she said as both women stood. Grace thanked her for the experience, while Vivienne simply nodded toward a large bookcase.

Madame Arquette moved with quiet purpose, her layered skirts whispering against the worn area rug as she crossed the room with an ease that defied her years. She passed the candlelit table and approached an old bookcase that spanned nearly the entire far wall. Its shelves were packed tight with leather-bound volumes, obscure occult titles, and dust-coated encyclopedias untouched for decades.

Without hesitation, she reached for a worn, spine-cracked copy of *Les Portes de l'Ombre* and gave it a subtle tug. Ancient hinges groaned as the bookcase shuddered, then creaked open just enough to reveal a narrow passage lined with stone. She offered no dramatic farewell and never looked back. Madame Arquette simply stepped through the opening, the folds of her velvet shawl disappearing into darkness as the bookcase slowly groaned shut behind her, clicking closed like a secret swallowed whole.

Grace's eyes lingered on the now seamless wall. Her voice dropped, almost amused. "I've seen one of those before… in New York."

"Oh, a psychic?" Vivienne asked, her eyes still wide.

"No," Grace replied, a faint smirk playing at her lips. "A hidden exit through a bookcase." Her tone softened, turning reflective. "Last case I worked… different kind of magic."

The double doors swung open with the subtle flair only Drake could manage. Standing stiff-backed in the threshold, he cleared his throat and announced with polite formality, "Madame, your new guests have arrived. Drew and the additional detectives." He faltered slightly over the last words, his gaze lingering a moment too long on Grace, clearly uncertain how to categorize them.

Drew entered first, sharp-eyed and purposeful, a mid-length leather coat cutting across his frame like a blade. His jaw was tight and unreadable, but the clipped rhythm of his steps said enough. He was here on business, and something about the room had already set him on edge. His eyes found Grace briefly, narrowing with recognition, but he said nothing. Instead, he offered Vivienne a single nod and surveyed the space with a glance that measured threat, beauty, and truth in one controlled sweep.

"You are more handsome than when I saw you last," Vivienne said smoothly. "I could tell by your aura that you are a leader. I would even guess… a warrior."

"He's a warrior, all right," Grace agreed, stepping forward to greet Drew with two quick kisses on the cheek.

Aisha followed close behind, calm and composed, her charcoal blazer pressed to perfection. The soft click of her heels echoed her efficiency. An analyst at heart, she was never without a contingency plan tucked into her bag or hidden up her sleeve. Her gaze settled on the remaining candle and the tea cup streaked with leaves, not with curiosity, but with calculation.

Elena entered with her usual quiet confidence, a leather-bound notebook in one hand and the other tucked into the pocket of her coat. Her braided bun was windswept, as if she had come straight from a rooftop chase, and knowing Elena, she probably had. She gave Grace a friendly but curious glance.

Debra arrived next, larger than life in both presence and personality, shifting the energy of the room the moment she stepped inside. Her statement earrings swayed as she walked, and her flannel jacket carried the effortless wear of something chosen as much for style as comfort. She offered Vivienne a warm, brief smile, an unspoken reassurance that they were not just detectives. They were allies.

Israel followed, thoughtful and observant, his hands tucked into the pockets of his dark trousers. He said nothing at first, but his sharp eyes registered everything: the flickering candle, the lingering scent of incense, the faint smudge of lipstick on a delicate tea cup. He nodded toward Grace, a quiet gesture of respect between friends.

Francy came in last, lingering just inside the doorway, a mischievous glint in her eyes as she surveyed the room. Her floral skirt clashed joyfully with the space's dark elegance. The moment her gaze landed on the closed bookcase, her lips curled into a knowing smirk. "Of course there's a huge bookcase," she muttered under her breath, half expecting a pool of blood at the end of it. She glanced at Grace, who smirked back, knowing exactly what Francy was thinking.

The team fanned out instinctively, each taking up space without instruction, veterans of the field and of each other.

Grace shifted slightly, arms crossed. "Looks like the band's back together."

Drew exhaled slowly, finally breaking the silence. "Let's just hope we're all reading from the same sheet music." The sarcasm came easily, his signature brand of dry wit, the kind Elena always chalked up to his New York humor.

Vivienne addressed her guests with a pleased smile. "My dears, our friends from New York, Mr. and Mrs. Belltone, told me I would be awestruck when I met all of you. That, I assure you, was an understatement."

"We were honored to take the Belltones' case," Debra chimed in. "It was actually a very personal case for us as well."

"Oh, I read all about it in the *New York Post*," Vivienne said with a bright smile. "I just knew you would be the right ones for me." Her excitement was palpable.

"Thank you for visiting me the other day, Drew. I hope you were able to understand the depth of my situation and convey it to your friends." Vivienne's gaze moved across the group, greeting each member of the team in turn.

The group listened intently, exchanging small, encouraging smiles.

Vivienne was almost trembling with excitement now. She quickly explained about the intruder from the night before.

"Did he harm you?" Francy asked, stepping forward to reintroduce herself. Her voice was low and calm, but carried the unmistakable edge her friends recognized.

Vivienne let out a soft, dry laugh and lowered her gaze. "Only my ego," she admitted, her words touched with a rueful smile. Her shoulders slumped slightly, a flicker of vulnerability slipping past her practiced poise.

Drew was already reconstructing the scene in his mind. His eyes swept the room again, taking in every shadow, every misplaced object, every door that had yet to be opened.

Before the silence could settle, Aisha stepped forward with quiet assurance, her heels clicking softly against the floor in a rhythm that felt both purposeful and respectful. "I'm Aisha," she said, offering a firm but warm handshake. "Unofficial reality checker. You have nothing to be embarrassed about. You are being targeted. There is nothing to be ashamed of."

Vivienne looked up, her eyes narrowing as recognition dawned. "Wait a second… I know you. You're the new IT girl everyone's talking about."

Aisha chuckled and brushed a strand of hair behind her ear.

"I keep my eye on young Hollywood. The trades are my bible." Vivienne paused, her gaze drifting slightly. "I used to be the IT girl." The words slipped out more quietly, as if memory itself had softened them.

"Used to be? No, Vivienne. You're forever our IT girl." Aisha's tone was sincere but light, perfectly balanced between admiration and solidarity.

Vivienne's lips curved into a fuller smile, the compliment landing on a place she had not realized was still tender. From the edge of the room, Grace caught the exchange with a subtle tilt of her head, something unreadable flickering at the corner of her mouth. Drew remained silent, but the faint twitch at his lip suggested he had registered every word.

Vivienne continued, holding her audience with quiet command as she described the events that had begun to unravel her once secure world. "It started quietly. Anonymous letters slipped beneath my front door, each one a cryptic warning."

Drew, ever methodical, reached into his bag and unfolded several of the notes. Crumpled papers bore ominous phrases, their ransom note style made more disturbing by their childish construction.

"A cherished photograph of me receiving my Academy Award was left shattered," Vivienne went on. "The glass splintered into a spiderweb of cracks across my own smiling face. And the scent of my gardenia perfume lingered in the hallway, even though I hadn't worn it in weeks."

A heavy pause settled over the room.

Grace thought back to the faint trace of gardenia she had noticed in the foyer when she first arrived.

"It wasn't just trespassing. It was choreography," Vivienne said, her voice thick with emotion. "A carefully orchestrated unraveling of my peace of mind, one ghostly breadcrumb at a time." She lifted a gnarled fist toward the ceiling, as if cursing the universe for the cruelty of what felt like an untimely ending.

"Vivienne, is there anyone in charge of your estate? Do you have staff? Security?" Elena stepped forward from the shadows. She smiled gently at Vivienne, who returned the look. Elena already knew the answer, but she was guiding the conversation where it needed to go.

"Drake?" Vivienne called.

The living room doors creaked open. "Madame?"

"Here he is," Vivienne said with a faint smile. "My gardener, my valet, my security." She lowered herself back into her seat, suddenly needing the support.

"That's what I assumed," Elena replied, acknowledging Drake with a polite nod.

Drake stood in silence. His tall frame was as polished as the marble floors beneath him, shoulders squared, spine impossibly straight, like a man trained not only to serve but to disappear while doing so. His charcoal suit was pressed to perfection, marked by a silver fleur-de-lis lapel pin, a subtle nod to a lineage of service that seemed to stretch back generations. Black gloves concealed hands that moved with eerie precision, as though every gesture had been practiced alone a thousand times.

"Drake, is there a way we can get the front gate fixed? Perhaps install some kind of security system?" Elena asked.

Drake did not interrupt. He did not explain. He was the kind of man who opened doors without asking why. "I will defer that question to Madame," he said simply.

"If I may?" Israel stepped forward, quickly reintroducing himself to Vivienne, who greeted him with a bright smile. "With a few quick adjustments, I can set up a strong security system around the outside perimeter. Add a few cameras and monitors, and we can make sure the inside of your home is protected from intruders as well."

"Well, Vivienne, you have the best man for the job standing right in front of you," Drew reassured her.

"Oh, Israel, you would do that for me?" she asked, her voice breathy with relief.

"Consider it done. I'll be here tomorrow at noon to install everything."

Drew leaned forward slightly, his tone shifting into something more measured and investigative. "Vivienne, I need to ask you something." He paused, giving her a moment to prepare. "Is there anyone from your past, professionally or personally, who might have a reason to seek your attention or validation? Someone who felt overlooked, denied an opportunity, or passed over for a role or position they believed they deserved?" He studied her expression carefully. "In short, is there anyone who might still carry a grievance tied to your career or decisions you've made?"

Vivienne exhaled slowly, her sapphire eyes narrowing as she considered the question. "There have been many people in my life, Drew," she began, her voice calm but edged with fatigue. "In a career as long as mine, you inevitably disappoint someone. An audition you don't endorse. A project you decline. A protégé who expected more from you than you had to give." She folded her hands in her lap, golden curls shifting as she dipped her head in thought.

"But immediate reasons?" She shook her head. "Not that I'm aware of. Most of my professional conflicts were years ago, and people tend to move on. Or at least pretend to." A faint, rueful smile touched her lips.

"There was a young actor once, Harold Keyes. Exceptionally talented, but volatile. He believed I cost him a career-defining role after *Velvet Ashes*, though the decision was never mine. He avoided me after that, but his resentment was palpable." Vivienne lifted her gaze to Drew again, steady and unflinching.

Drew and Aisha exchanged a brief look, silent recognition passing between them. They both knew exactly who she meant.

"Beyond him, there are a handful of others who may have felt slighted. But none I would expect to pursue anything so dramatic. At least not unless old wounds have festered more deeply than I realized." She paused, the weight of that possibility settling in.

Grace stepped forward. "Vivienne, I know you introduced Madame Arquette as your oldest and dearest confidant, but do you have any reason to suspect her?" The question left her mouth before she could soften it.

Vivienne did not flinch. "Next to Drake, she is the closest person to me. But you know what they say. A friend who knows your weaknesses can either guard them or use them." She adjusted her dress and crossed her ankles with careful composure. "Yes, the thought has crossed my mind." Her eyes sharpened slightly. "Is there something I should be aware of?"

Without waiting for an answer, she reached for the small bell on the side table and rang it.

The doors opened once more. "Yes, Madame?" Drake asked, stepping inside.

"Did we receive any additional notes today?" Vivienne's voice carried a thread of fatigue now.

"No, Madame." He hesitated. "I believe it is time for your…"

Vivienne raised a hand. "Drake, I know. I know." She turned to her guests with a gentle smile. "My children, I have some flowers to pick in the garden," she said, the lie soft and practiced. It was her way of saying she was going to take a nap.

"Vivienne, before you go, may we take a look around the mansion? We need to make sure you're protected and secure," Drew asked.

"Drew, of course. I trust you completely. You come with excellent references," she sang lightly as Drake escorted her through the massive living room doors.

The room fell quiet, broken only by the ticking of a grandfather clock tucked into a corner of the aging house.

"Let's move slowly. This place hasn't been touched in years," Drew said, scanning the room.

"I don't know about untouched," Elena muttered, pointing toward a set of footprints in the dust leading into the back hallway. "Someone's been here."

Grace lingered behind, her gaze sweeping the room until it settled on the massive walnut bookcase stretching across the far wall. “Good observation, Elena. I think those belong to Vivienne’s psychic.”

Silence settled over the group.

“When I arrived, Vivienne was taking counsel from her psychic, Madame Arquette,” Grace explained. She looked around at their quiet faces. “What, no sarcasm?” She hadn’t expected restraint from them. “When you all arrived, she slipped out through a hidden door in the bookcase.” The words left her mouth almost matter-of-factly.

Aisha and Israel moved closer, their attention sharpening. Israel reached up and tugged at a book. The bookcase did not move.

“Try the one labeled *Les Portes de l’Ombre*. Upper left corner,” Grace advised.

Israel scanned the bookcase again. He found the correct spine and gave it a firm pull. The case clicked, groaned, and swung inward, revealing a narrow corridor swallowed by shadow.

Debra let out a low whistle. “Secret doors. Why does history keep repeating itself with us?”

“We’ve been down this road before,” Aisha said, switching on the flashlight on her phone. “Let’s go.”

The group pressed forward, shoulder to shoulder, their lights cutting through the gloom. The corridor was short, damp, and musty, lined with cold stone and strips of peeling wallpaper that had once been a deep burgundy. At the end hung a heavy velvet curtain that stretched from ceiling to floor. Drew stepped forward and pulled it aside. Beyond it lay the mansion’s private screening room.

Rows of dusty velvet seats faced a blank, decaying screen. The air was thicker here, heavy with stale perfume, mold, and the faint trace of something rotten. Francy’s flashlight swept across the room and stopped at the projection booth. The glass was cracked. Someone had been inside recently.

"This is where it happened," Grace said quietly, stepping down the aisle. "Vivienne told me. She saw him here. The man who threatened her. The man who knew everything."

Aisha moved to the front row and crouched beside an old champagne bottle. The label was worn, and the cork lay discarded nearby. "Someone celebrated something here."

Elena slipped into the booth. "There's still film in the reels. Do we play it?"

Francy nodded once. Elena flipped a switch, and with a slow mechanical clatter, the projector came to life. The screen flickered, then flared into clarity.

A grainy image of Vivienne filled the screen. She sat alone in the room, nervously wringing her hands.

"*Velvet Ashes*," Grace whispered.

The seven detectives stared at the flickering image. On screen, Vivienne suddenly rose to her feet, her younger self alive with restless energy.

"She seems so young there," Francy observed.

"Twenty-nine," Grace answered quietly.

Then, from the shadows behind Vivienne, a man stepped into frame. His face was obscured by light, but something about him struck Drew immediately.

"That's him," Drew said. "That's the guy from your movie set, Aisha. The one who called himself Mr. Keyes. Your lighting guy."

"I think you're right, Drew," Aisha said, leaning closer to the screen. "I need to ask him about his early acting career. There's more to this story."

“The same Harold Keyes Vivienne just mentioned?” Debra asked, surprise flashing across her face.

The film stopped abruptly. Silence swallowed the room.

“Sorry,” Israel called from the back. “But there’s a door back here.” He stepped into view. “It leads directly outside.”

Debra lowered her voice. “This isn’t just a hideout. It’s a trap.”

They moved deeper into the mansion, following the central hallway past ancient sconces and indistinct portraits. Old photographs lined the walls, their once-gold frames faded to a sickly yellow. Their footsteps echoed across warped wooden floors.

“Service kitchen down here,” Israel said, nodding toward a swinging door.

The kitchen was enormous, almost industrial, with rows of rusted stoves, an iron butcher’s rack hanging with long-unused hooks, and a walk-in pantry collapsing under the weight of time.

Elena moved past the bare cupboards, pausing at the only one that still held anything. “Vivienne doesn’t eat much.” She glanced around. “Or Drake is just a terrible cook.”

Outside, they passed through cracked French doors into what once must have been a beautiful garden room. A circular, glass-roofed rotunda rose around them, something out of a fairytale, now overtaken by vines, moss, and the steady sound of dripping water. A single wrought-iron bench sat at its center beneath a wild tangle of overgrown roses.

Aisha reached toward one of the vines, then pulled her hand back. “Poison oak,” she said. “Someone doesn’t want people wandering back here.”

To the west of the rotunda, a narrow path led them to an abandoned swimming pool, a grand, empty rectangle surrounded by sun-bleached chaise lounges and broken statues. The water had long since vanished, leaving behind cracked tile and stubborn weeds.

They reentered the main house and climbed the creaking staircase, dust rising in their wake as they moved down the shadowed hall on the second floor. The bedrooms waited like closed secrets.

Francy pushed open the first door. “Here we go,” she murmured.

The room was frozen in a moment of vanished glamour. An old record player sat in the corner, its needle resting in silence. A shattered mirror leaned against the wall, and a crystal ashtray on the vanity overflowed with lipstick-stained cigarette butts.

Francy narrowed her eyes. “This was a guest room, maybe?”

Across the hall, Drew stepped into a second room and paused in the doorway. The faded wallpaper was patterned with clouds and tiny painted stars. A crib lay on its side near the window, one wheel broken.

He crossed the room, knelt beside a small music box, and wound it. A delicate melody drifted out, soft and haunting.

For a moment he didn’t move. The room felt preserved, not abandoned. As if whatever had happened here had never fully left.

“Vivienne had a child?” Drew looked up from the broken crib.

“A miscarriage,” Grace answered in a whisper.

Drew’s gaze returned to the crib. Something about the space felt less like grief and more like interruption, a life paused mid-sentence. If someone wanted to unsettle Vivienne, this was exactly the kind of memory they would reach for.

Further down the hall, Elena opened the third door and stepped into what looked like a makeshift study. Yellowing blueprints of the mansion were pinned to the walls, covered in notes scribbled in French and symbols she could not immediately identify.

She traced one line with her finger. "Someone was planning something," she murmured, half to herself, half to whoever might be listening.

Aisha joined Debra, who was thumbing through a thick black notebook on the nearby desk.

"It's a scrapbook. Look at this," Debra said with a small smile, holding up an old *Vogue* cover. "LeClaire. It's her."

Aisha's attention drifted to piles of paper stacked in the corner. Her eyes moved quickly over the layers. "Poems, wordplay, solved puzzles… what a collection," she muttered.

"I found a date book," Aisha announced.

Inside were lists of dates and a phrase repeated in red ink: *The death of the author.*

She frowned. "Who was she referring to?"

Drew stepped closer, studying the page. The words didn't read like a threat. They felt deliberate, almost philosophical, like someone trying to make a point rather than simply frighten her.

"Maybe not who," he said quietly. "Maybe what."

Silence settled again, thick and heavy, as if the house itself were holding its breath.

At the end of the hall waited the final door, likely Vivienne's master bedroom. Israel and Aisha paused there together, exchanging a quiet look.

Francy stood at the top of the stairs, peering down into the darkened first floor. "This place was more than a home," she said softly. "It was a theater, an office, and a stage."

Suddenly, Drake appeared at the bottom of the steps. He motioned for Francy to come down. "Hey, everyone. Move it. We're being summoned."

The group descended the grand staircase and met Drake at the door.

"This was left by the intruder last night," he said. "It was on the floor, and Madame did not see it. But I wanted to make sure you had this." He produced a photocopied script of *Velvet Ashes*, the words *time's up* scrawled across it in red ink.

"Someone wanted Vivienne to see something," Drew said quietly, studying the page. "Someone wanted her to remember." His gaze shifted toward the grandfather clock still echoing from the living room next door. "Then let's remember it all before it gets buried again."

Chapter 4
Mulholland Drive

Night shoots were particularly difficult, not only for the actors, but for the entire cast and crew who had to be on location hours in advance to prepare the area. Location shooting was an entirely different beast than working on a soundstage. Permits, regulations, logistics, rules. They all had to be filed, negotiated, and resolved before anyone set foot on site. And this location was especially demanding.

Mulholland Drive was more than a road. It was a spine of dreams, a ribbon of asphalt draped over the bones of hills that both divided and connected the vast, scattered city. Built in the 1920s as a scenic parkway, it was meant to link mountain and ocean, nature and possibility.

To drive it was to inhabit a liminal space. On one side stretched the sprawl of Los Angeles: a tangled web of freeways, the glowing grid of the San Fernando Valley, and the vapor-hazed halo of downtown skyscrapers. On the other rose untamed slopes and wild overgrowth, the road folding back on itself in quiet curves that suggested both loss and renewal.

Here, the myth of Hollywood felt close enough to touch, while the natural world lingered just behind it, breathing quietly beyond the skyline. Mulholland Drive became a threshold. The Hollywood Sign carved into the hillside looked both triumphant and haunting.

But to shut it down for six hours so Hollywood could capture a few exterior shots? That was nearly impossible.

Still, clout could carry you far in this town, and Remi Harrington knew it. So, he worked it. Every angle of it.

Mulholland Drive was now closed to the public so Aisha could shoot her scenes.

Remi stood halfway down the winding stretch where the road crested before climbing again toward the summit. Clad in dark jeans, a navy Polo sweater, and penny loafers, he prowled the pavement like a hamster trapped in its wheel, barking orders with restless urgency.

“Mr. Keyes, angle that top light toward the tree line.” His eyes tracked the beam as it shifted. “Where’s Aisha?” He shot Mr. Keyes a quick thumbs up. “Matt!” Remi shouted to his assistant. “Why doesn’t the car look dirtier? It’s in the middle of a chase, for God’s sake. Get more grime on it. Where’s Aisha?”

Matt darted out from the shadows and, without hesitation, began scooping up dirt and mud with his bare hands, smearing it along the sides of the stunt car.

“I’m here. I’m here, Remi!” Aisha rounded the corner from her trailer, trailed by her entourage of hair, makeup, and wardrobe stylists struggling to keep pace with the action star. She wore the same outfit from the previous day’s shoot, each detail carefully preserved to ensure perfect continuity.

“Okay, sweetheart, I need you in the car,” Remi said. “We’re doing close-ups. Just you and the vehicle.”

Aisha slipped into the driver’s seat of the stunt car and adjusted herself behind the wheel. She shook her head lightly, giving her hair that windswept effect. As she did, she caught sight of Mr. Keyes above, angling his spotlight down toward her.

“Hi, Mr. Keyes,” she mouthed through the windshield.

She tilted the rearview mirror to check her eyeliner, then flipped down the visor to smooth a stray piece of hair into place.

Engines idled as crew members scuttled about, each person wired into the moment. In front of her, a long trailer glinted beneath the studio lights, rigging arms extended, cables pulled taut, camera mounts poised and waiting. On the trailer stood the stunt driver, hands steady on the wheel of a secondary car secured in place. Around him, camera operators, grips, and assistants crouched behind monitors, watching every movement like hawks.

This was no collection of haphazard equipment. It was a moving fortress of technology. A process trailer built to capture motion from exact angles, its wheels humming softly, steel bars locking the lead car into place.

Aisha pressed her foot lightly to the gas, sending a tremor through the frame. Feeling the connection, she lifted her hand and gave a firm thumbs up. No words were needed. The signal crackled across the walkies. They were good to go. The stunt driver ahead nodded, eyes fixed forward.

"Quiet on set," the assistant director called. "This is a rehearsal." The clapboard snapped shut.

Remi's voice cut through the dusk. "And… action."

Aisha's car eased into a tight curve of Mulholland Drive, the asphalt catching the last wash of evening light. Gnarled oaks and thick chaparral arched over the road like ancient sentinels. The climb steepened, tires whispering along the guardrails, as Los Angeles unfurled below them. A sea of lights gathered in the valley, streetlamps flickering awake, headlights threading across canyon roads.

Five cameras rolled, capturing every angle.

Aisha reached the halfway point. The air grew thinner, cooler, scented with sagebrush and dry earth. Over one shoulder lay a sheer drop into a shadowed canyon. She dared a glance across the vista, the city stretching outward in shimmering waves. The Hollywood Sign sat proudly on its hillside. The domes of the Griffith Observatory glowed in the distance. The grid of downtown high-rises sparkled, and beyond them the Pacific faded into dusk.

She almost wanted to pinch herself. Spain's beloved movie star, now becoming an international sensation. She could feel it deep in her bones.

The car crested the peak of Mulholland, and Aisha heard Remi's voice in her earpiece. "Cut." A beat followed. "Brilliant. Bring the car back down."

Then, suddenly, voices crackled through the line. Remi arguing with Blake Derrow, the film's consultant. She recognized Blake's droning tone immediately.

"She didn't do it like that in the studio!"

"She did exactly that," Remi snapped back.

"If she leans back like that, it looks like she's on a leisurely drive, not a car chase," Blake insisted.

"Don't forget who the director of this picture is," Remi shot back.

"Remi?" Aisha pressed her earpiece closer. "Was everything all right with that rehearsal?" The silence that followed made her second-guess asking.

"It was perfect," Remi finally said.

Aisha stepped out of the car and took a long breath. Something about the air felt intoxicating. She gave the cinematographer a thumbs up.

"You don't have to walk back down the mountain. What's wrong with you?" he yapped.

Aisha rolled her eyes. "Thanks, Tomás," she replied without turning around. "That man is unhappy with the world," she added, almost whispering to herself.

She paused, taking in the unique glow of Los Angeles as its lights crept up through the tree line, sparkling like diamonds. The allure of the city sent a quiet thrill through her.

"Aisha," Mr. Keyes called from his perch above. "I have a lighting cue for you." He smiled down at her.

"Mr. Keyes, I have a question for you too."

He signaled to the crew member at the controls to lower the rig. "Aisha, stay forward on the steering wheel when you're going uphill. You keep drifting into the shadows."

"Thank you for that," Aisha said with a smile. "So, I didn't know you were a famous actor."

"Was," he corrected, pulling a face. "It went nowhere."

"That's not true, mi amor. You are a movie star. I just saw you in *Velvet Ashes*."

"Ah, my film debut."

"You had scenes with Vivienne LeClaire," Aisha said, nodding.

"The legend," he replied. "She was something else. That was her breakthrough role." He pulled a comb from his back pocket and ran it through his thick gray hair. "I often wonder what happened to her."

"Do you?" Aisha said lightly. "I saw her today." She watched him carefully, waiting for his reaction.

He stopped combing his hair. "Really?" His expression shifted. "Well, it figures. Two stars of that caliber would know each other," he said with a polite smile. "I hope she's doing well."

"Okay, chatterboxes, let's move," the cinematographer shouted. "I'd like to get home tonight!" Tomás waved his megaphone like a weapon.

"Tomás," Mr. Keyes muttered, glancing at Aisha and shaking his head. "This poor man."

"Aisha, I need you on your mark. Keyes, back to your nest!" The cinematographer's patience was thinning.

As Aisha turned toward her mark, where the car had been reset, she caught sight of her fellow actor. "Ollie," she called, wiggling her fingers in greeting.

Ollie Barrett looked carved from stone, tall, broad-shouldered, with sharp cheekbones and olive skin shadowed by a perpetual five o'clock stubble. His dark hair was thick, just long enough to curl when damp or flatten beneath the heat of studio lights. He carried himself with easy swagger, hands in his pockets, chin tilted slightly upward. "Oye, did ya have a bit of a wander?"

The moment he spoke, the illusion shifted.

He waited for her reaction. "Did ya have a bit of a wander, ya know, a little walk?"

"Mi amor, you are so cute… until you open your mouth. Then I truly do not understand you." She shook her head, laughing softly.

Ollie's accent was unmistakably Cockney, dropped H's, clipped vowels, and a rhythm shaped by the streets of East London. Aisha was still learning to keep up, though she found it strangely charming. He peppered his speech with rhyming slang. "Have a butcher's hook?" when he wanted someone to look. "Dog and bone" when a phone rang. "Trouble and strife" when he grumbled about his girlfriend. The phrases rolled off his tongue as naturally as breath. They were simply part of who he was.

"Hey, Ollie, are you ready?" Remi turned toward the actor. "Remember, you're playing an American. Don't drop your R's," he reminded him, clearly annoyed.

"Ready, governor."

Both actors moved quickly into position, Aisha at the wheel, Ollie in the back seat. The set fell quiet as the crew waited for Remi's call.

"And… action!"

The car lurched forward, tires spinning as Aisha revved the engine a little too hard. She felt her anxiety crawling up her spine. Higher still, as the road climbed toward the summit, fewer houses interrupted the wild ridgeline. The landscape opened around them. At this height, there was space. The world stretched in every direction. From this vantage, the two actors could see the San Fernando Valley to the north, the Santa Monica Mountains rolling west, and the distant darkness of the ocean to the southwest.

Ollie shot Aisha a look of uncertainty as the wheels beneath them wobbled. Aisha glanced left, then checked the rearview mirror. She waited for his line. It did not come. She looked back at him, her eyes urging him to speak. *Say your line.*

"It's not releasing from the… syntax. The conductor is stuck!"

Finally, she thought. Ollie's character was supposed to panic, but this time his fear felt real. He glanced behind him through the gaping hole where the back window should have been. The car continued climbing.

"Two minutes!" Ollie followed with his second line.

"Then we're going to have to ditch the briefcase," Aisha replied, calm and matter-of-fact.

"But we'll lose the one clue that connects everything in this case!" he shouted back.

Aisha barely heard him. Something felt wrong. Ollie's panic no longer looked like acting, and the fear etched across his face made her blood run cold. All she could see was Mulholland Drive stretched beneath a quilt of stars, the city below smoldering with a thousand lights. Aisha held her breath.

Then came a sharp crack, like ice splitting across a frozen pond. Steel cables snapped. One of the suspension arms broke loose. The car shuddered violently.

Aisha's heart leapt. Ahead of her, the long process trailer attached to the stunt car separated in a spray of metal and sparks. Rigging arms twisted outward, cables whipping through the air, cameras tumbling free. The stunt driver stood frozen in shock, hands raised, no longer strapped into his seat.

Aisha's car began rolling backward down Mulholland. Slow at first. Hesitant. Then the emergency tether snapped, and the momentum surged. Faster. Far too fast.

Ollie lunged from the back seat, scrambling forward, his hands fumbling for the console. It was too late. The stunt car broke free, tilting as the rig collapsed behind them.

Aisha's stomach dropped. "No… no… stop." She slammed her palm against the dash, knuckles whitening. The glass rattled. Their world lurched sideways. The car jackknifed, the rear swinging wide, the front tires skidding and screaming against the asphalt.

Then she remembered the earpiece. "Remi, can you hear me?" she shouted.

The cliff edge rushed toward them. Cold air whipped through the open window, sharp as blades. The wheels shrieked as Aisha pumped the brake, her heart lodged in her throat.

"Do something!" Ollie cried.

The car left the pavement and hurtled sideways down the treacherous slope of the Santa Monica Mountains. Its passengers clutched the dashboard, bracing for impact. Towering pines blurred past. Aisha's only hope was that the car might wedge itself between two trunks and stop.

Then she saw it. A massive boulder jutting from the earth behind them. Ollie saw it too.

"That looks like a ski jump and we're going backwards!" he shouted, terror cracking his voice. "We're going to vault right off it!"

Aisha held her breath.

The car slammed into the stone ramp with a violent thud, the undercarriage erupting in sparks as metal scraped against rock. "Hold on!" Ollie yelled.

The angle of the impact shifted their momentum just enough. The car ground upward along the rock face, slowing, shuddering, until its rear wheels slipped past the edge. The back end hovered over open air.

A chasm yawned beneath them.

Aisha forced her eyes open. Pebbles skittered past her window and disappeared into darkness. The car emitted a high, tortured groan, still clinging to earth by shrubs and fractured stone that would not hold for long.

She turned her head sharply and felt her earpiece dislodge. It fell free. Instinctively, she reacted as if she had lost an earring. She watched the small metal clip tumble into the void below.

Ollie's breath rasped against her ear, thick with fear. "Oye, Aisha… grab me. Grab me arm."

She twisted slowly toward him, her legs sliding as gravity pulled at her. The ground beneath the passenger side was gone.

Ollie stretched his fingers toward Aisha, careful not to disturb the fragile stillness holding the car in place. His hand caught her wrist. She pulled with every ounce of strength she had, her skin burning against the vinyl seat.

With a single breath, the car shifted again, swiveling as the back bumper slammed into the trunk of an ancient sycamore. Gravity tugged at them, hungry and patient.

Aisha risked a glance downward. The city lights flickered far below, beautiful, distant, and utterly oblivious to their terror.

"Aisha, we're coming!" Remi's voice echoed up the slope. It sounded impossibly far away. "Don't move!"

"Don't move? Bloody hell," Ollie muttered. His gaze dropped to the floor beside him. A jagged hole gaped in the passenger side, metal torn and twisted, exposing darkness beneath the car. The underside was giving way. "Look," he whispered, nudging her slightly. "The emergency tether."

"What's that?"

"A backup safety line they rig to the bottom of the wheelbase."

"But what's it attached to?"

"Ideally, the stunt trailer," he said, shivering as he bit his lip. "But it isn't now." He paused, listening to the groan of metal.

Aisha turned her head just enough to look at him, afraid even the smallest movement might send them sliding over the edge.

"It might be our last chance," Ollie said quietly. He reached down through the jagged opening.

"What are you doing?" Aisha panicked as more dirt and stone tumbled away beneath them.

"I've got it," Ollie said. Slowly, he pulled the thick, pocked strap up through the gaping hole in the floor. He glanced out through the missing back window, spotting the sycamore tree where the bumper had come to rest.

"If I crawl into the back seat, will you be all right?"

Aisha answered with a quick, breathless "No."

"I'm going to wrap this tether around the tree behind us," he said. Without waiting for permission, he released her arm and crawled into the back seat. The car responded with a deep groan, metal grinding against rock as his weight shifted. Aisha threw her body sideways, trying to counterbalance and keep the car from sliding over the edge.

Ollie's hands trembled, slick with sweat. Aisha kept feeding the tether up through the hole while he gathered it in the back. He shaped the heavy strap into a rough lasso and, on his second attempt, managed to throw it over the thick base of the ancient sycamore. A brief, disbelieving smile crossed his face. Then he realized he had to get back to the front.

He crouched low and stepped carefully onto the passenger seat.

The car groaned again. Metal screamed against stone as it shifted. It slid a few inches, then shuddered to a halt. Suspended in fragile balance, the front end drifted sideways. They hung there, swaying above the void, caught between disaster and survival.

"Don't look down," Ollie whispered, his voice tight.

"I wouldn't dare," Aisha whispered back. Sweat stung her eyes as it ran down her face.

Ollie leaned carefully across the front seat, helping Aisha slide toward the door on what looked like the safer side. Every muscle in his body fought the urge to move too quickly. Then the car tipped again, angling toward the city lights far below.

A sudden surge of resolve shot through Aisha. "Ollie, we have to move. Now." The words tore from her diaphragm. He met her eyes and knew she was right.

"We move or die."

With one final heave, Aisha forced open the driver's side door. They clung to each other, faces inches apart, as they tumbled out of the car and scrambled toward the rock face where it had been perched moments before. Her heart hammered so hard she thought it might burst.

Behind them, the car continued to slide. The tether pulled tight for a brief, desperate second, then snapped the sycamore from its roots. Together they stumbled to the roadside and turned just in time to watch the stunt car tip over the edge, untethered and still moving. Dust burst from its underside as the metal shell dropped into the canyon and exploded into a fireball that lit the night sky. The plume rose above the ridge, a violent reminder of how narrowly they had escaped.

Aisha dropped to her knees, clutching the ground as her hands shook uncontrollably. Ollie crouched beside her, wrapping an arm around her shoulders. Both of them trembled in the stunned quiet that followed.

"Aisha? Ollie?" Remi's voice echoed from behind them.

"Dirty Mulholland," Ollie muttered under his breath.

Chapter 5
Studio City

“Well, she’s not coming out of her room anytime soon.” Debra closed Aisha’s bedroom door, balancing a tray of untouched food in her hands. “All she wants is coffee.” She shook her head, concern lingering across her face.

“She’ll be fine,” Israel said from the corner. “She just needs time to process. Then she’ll be back in front of the camera before you know it.” He sat on the floor, tinkering with his cameras and laser security system.

“Are you trying to get that… LIAR to work?” Debra asked, pursing her lips, unsure what he was actually doing.

“LIDAR,” Israel corrected. “Light Detection and Ranging. The primary function is to create an invisible, high-precision security fence around an area,” he explained.

Drew looked up from the stack of papers he had received from Vivienne LeClaire. The anonymous letters slipped under her front door gave him little to work with. The ominous messages, assembled from cutout letters taken from magazines and periodicals, showed no clear pattern that he could decipher. “I think it’s cool,” Drew said. “It’s the perfect setup for that old mansion.”

“And the cameras are highly sensitive. Think of them as tiny eyes, about the size of marbles,” Israel added.

"Marbles? I thought those were just the packaging the laser lights came in," Debra teased.

"I'll have you know these cameras have depth-sensing capabilities that create a complete laser scan in high definition." Israel sounded quietly proud of what he had built for the movie star's troubled home.

"Nothing will get past those cameras and lasers," Drew assured Debra.

"That's our tech wizard." Debra tucked the rest of Aisha's untouched lunch into the refrigerator. She washed her hands in the sleek, modern sink, then settled onto the couch between Drew and Israel. "Aisha still seems in shock. Her scene partner swears the car was sabotaged."

Israel looked up from his equipment. "What would be the motive?"

"I'm sure they're looking into that," Drew said. "You've got a controversial director, an international movie star, and a film that's pivotal to a major studio." He paused. "There's a lot at stake."

"But why target Aisha?" Debra asked softly, glancing toward the closed bedroom door.

"We may be jumping to conclusions," Drew replied with a small nod. "Let's see what the studio uncovers. Aisha asked me to meet Remi at the OSHA office in Studio City to make sure all her paperwork is filed correctly."

"Ocean office?" Israel asked absently.

"No." Debra clicked her tongue. "OSHA. Occupational Safety and Health Administration."

Israel smirked. "Now who's teasing who? All right, I'm ready." He packed the last of his equipment into his backpack and zipped it shut. "I'm picking up Francy at the gym, then we'll head over to Vivienne's place and set up her security."

Drew tossed his dance bag over his shoulder and strolled toward the red sports car gleaming beneath the California sun. "Need a ride?" he called to Israel as he headed down the sidewalk.

"I'm good," Israel called back. "Francy has her car at the gym. We'll head to the mansion together."

Drew paused, drawing in a slow breath as the late-morning L.A. air carried a familiar scent, one that pulled him straight back to his late teens. Summers spent mastering the waves on a surfboard at Venice Beach with his cousin. Evenings at his favorite aunt's house in the Valley. Those sun-soaked, carefree days surfaced in a vivid rush, lingering just beneath his thoughts.

The S650 red Mustang convertible purred to life as Drew slid behind the wheel and buckled up, sunglasses on, the summer light glinting off the polished hood. He backed out onto the quiet West Hollywood street, easing into the winding back roads that curved through the quirky, electric neighborhood. The city was just waking up, dog walkers, baristas, joggers. Alive, but unhurried.

He turned onto Franklin Avenue, a lesser-known route that let him avoid the chaos of Sunset Boulevard. As the road climbed gently uphill, a whimsical structure emerged through the trees, a storybook castle tucked into the hillside like a secret, framed by towering palms.

The Magic Castle rose like something conjured from another era, a Victorian mansion crowned with turrets and stained glass. Its steep gables and ornate detailing made it feel like a magician's lair pulled straight from a fairytale. Only members or invited guests were allowed inside, but Drew had been there once, a labyrinth of velvet-covered walls, hidden bars, and sleight-of-hand artists who could pull fire from the air. Even from the street, the place hummed with mystery.

Drew passed it slowly, letting the nostalgia settle before accelerating again. Just a few blocks ahead, the road opened to a breathtaking view of the Hollywood Bowl.

Set into the hillside like an ancient amphitheater, the Bowl's iconic white shell arched against a backdrop of golden chaparral and swaying eucalyptus trees. Even empty in the daylight, the venue carried a quiet magic, as if echoes of symphonies and starlit concerts still lingered in the air. Drew had been to shows there many times, strings under the stars, the city lights sparkling behind him like fireflies.

He merged onto the 101 Freeway North, the engine humming as he picked up speed. Traffic was light, rare for mid-morning. The winding road climbed steeply, towering trees and brush rolling past on either side, dotted with homes perched like luxury treehouses. The city hadn't changed much. The names on the billboards were different, and the palm trees looked a little more brittle, but the bones of L.A. remained the same, sun-bleached, cracked, and humming with secrets.

Drew eased his red sports car over the crest of the Hollywood Hills, the summer haze casting a golden wash over the Valley below. The descent into Studio City felt almost cinematic, as if the city itself were setting the stage for a reckoning long overdue. As the car rolled down the twisting incline and the skyline opened before him, the memories hit harder than the dry Santa Ana winds rattling through the canyons.

His aunt, Martha Langley, had lived down there once. She ran a quiet little antique shop tucked between a florist and an old diner on Ventura Boulevard. Everyone loved her. She was kind, sharp-eyed, a chain smoker with a laugh that could cut through L.A. smog. She took him in during the summers of his youth, gave him freedom when his parents would not, and taught him the value of things time forgot. Old watches, vintage radios, war medals with rusted pins. She knew every story they carried.

Then, one August morning, her story ended.

Unsolved. That was the word they used. A police report full of questions, dusty case files, a city too busy to care. She was found behind the register, surrounded by shattered porcelain and unanswered calls. No forced entry. No witnesses. No suspects. Just a broken locket, a bloodstained floor, and Drew, seventeen and heartbroken, watching from the sidewalk as detectives taped off the only place that had ever felt like home.

That day lit a fire inside him. It was why he self-studied criminology alongside his art. It was why he chose this path after dancing professionally. Why Drew and the Detectives even existed. Because if justice could not help Aunt Martha back then, maybe he could bring it to someone else. Maybe that could be enough.

But it never was.

Now, after all these years, Drew had returned. Not just to L.A., but to Studio City. He was here for a different reason, yet the closeness of it all pressed against him, and he still had nothing to go on.

The freeway curved gently, passing the exits for Cahuenga and Barham. To the right, he caught glimpses of Universal Studios' backlot, soundstages rising like giant boxes, the house from *Psycho* peeking out in the distance. He stayed in the middle lane, knowing his exit was just ahead.

Cresting the Hollywood Hills, Studio City opened before him. As he took the off-ramp, the freeway released him into a quieter part of the Valley. Tree-lined streets. Coffee shops filled with writers hunched over laptops. Sound engineers spilling out of post-production houses.

Drew felt the subtle shift, the city behind him, the work ahead. For now, though, windows down and music up, he let the drive stretch a little longer. In L.A., sometimes the journey was the destination.

Drew pulled into the OSHA parking lot and spotted Remi leaning against the hood of his dark blue Aston Martin, letting the sun warm his face. Black Dolce & Gabbana sunglasses hid his eyes, the sharp designer frames matching his sharp demeanor. His short-sleeve Italian button-up, crisp, tailored, and slightly unbuttoned at the collar, looked like it had never known a wrinkle. The soft slate-gray fabric, traced with faint pinstripes, caught the California light. He wore it like armor, effortless yet precise.

"Like father, like son," Drew whispered to himself.

Remi always looked like he had just stepped off a runway or out of a high-concept European film. His signature silver chain glinted against his chest, and a vintage Tag Heuer chronograph hugged his wrist, rare, classic, and unmistakably intentional. Everything about him was curated but never contrived. The man was style distilled into presence.

His hair was cropped short at the sides, with a neatly combed wave on top, slicked back with enough pomade to make him look even more distinguished. He exuded the calm confidence of someone who had spent years on film sets calling the shots and being obeyed. His tan loafers were worn just enough to suggest authenticity rather than affectation, and when he stood, it was with the quiet grace of a man used to being watched.

Remi never rushed greetings. He received them. As Drew stepped out of the car, Remi tilted his chin in acknowledgment. Not a wave, not a smile, just a cool, deliberate gesture, like a seasoned director giving the go-ahead for the next take.

Although Drew had only been formally introduced to him once on set by Aisha, he was surprised to see genuine recognition flash across Remi's face.

"Drew," Remi said. "How are you? How's our star?"

"Recovering," Drew replied. "She should be ready to go back to work in a few days."

"All good, all good," Remi said with a relaxed nod. "Are you sure she doesn't want to kill me?" he added with a wince.

Drew hesitated. Aisha often concealed her real feelings behind a flood of unnecessary words and carefully guarded thoughts. It was not always easy to read her emotional state. "I guess we'll see," he said with a shrug, not wanting to put words in her mouth.

"Aisha told me you two dance together. I could tell she was a dancer by the way she moves. It's funny, with the film called *Final Tango*, she suggested we include a tango in the credits. I told her I'd settle for one at the opening night premiere. So if you both want to put something together, it could be very cool."

"Remi, I think that's a great idea," Drew said, surprise slipping into his voice. "I'll pull it together."

"We're just wrapping a few more exterior shots and finishing the last scenes in the studio, then we're done." He gestured for Drew to follow as they made their way toward the OSHA offices. "It's funny," he said, pausing as he looked around the neighborhood, "there used to be a ton of antique stores around here. This building sits on the foundation of a historic movie warehouse. You could find all kinds of discarded props, wardrobe, and gadgets from old films." A quiet sense of nostalgia settled over him.

Drew noticed the change in his stride as Remi slowed, taking in the hills.

"I remember so many of them along Ventura Boulevard. I used to come here with my father all the time. He loved digging through old warehouses and antique shops. The desk in my office came from one of those little places around the corner that we discovered together." Remi shook his head as they passed through the doors and into the lobby. Before the moment lingered too long, he shifted the subject. "You know how I met Aisha?" he asked, not waiting for an answer. "It was during my father's last film. He directed a project in Spain, and Aisha was the lead actress. I spent a lot of time shadowing him on set. That's when I first saw her work. Her performance left a real impression on me," he added with a thoughtful smile.

"I hope you told her that," Drew said with a smile.

He still couldn't quite pin Remi down. Part visionary, part enigma. Rumors followed him like a camera dolly. Whispers of a Cannes scandal, a film that vanished in post, a quiet studio fallout with a major executive. He was hated by some and revered by others. But he never addressed the stories publicly. He didn't need to. He had that rare kind of charisma that made people fill in the blanks with legend.

Here, in the sun-drenched offices of the Occupational Safety and Health Administration, Remi had a lot of explaining to do. Yet, as always, he seemed slightly above it all. As Drew approached, he couldn't help but wonder if Remi was here to help uncover the truth or if he was already part of a story much bigger than anyone knew.

The air in the OSHA office was thin and stale, the kind that smelled like legal paper and new carpet.

Patricia Morales, the lead investigator, greeted them with a formal nod and escorted Remi and Drew into a white room containing a table and three chairs. Drew had been in enough interrogation rooms to recognize the feeling. Polite words, sharpened knives.

Patricia didn't waste time. She leaned forward, lacing her fingers on the metal table, eyes locked on Remi like a sniper sighting in. "Let's start simple," she said. "Why did a two-ton prop car nearly kill your actors?"

Remi sat across from the investigator like a man rehearsing calm. Crisp appearance, unreadable expression. But Drew knew better. He saw the twitch in Remi's jaw, the silent countdown to detonation.

Remi shifted, adjusting his sunglasses as if they could shield him.

"It wasn't supposed to move," he said evenly. "The rig was locked. Safety confirmed."

"Well," she said, cracking open the file like a coffin lid, "that rig unlocked itself… and flew off a cliff."

Drew didn't speak. Not yet. He watched. Studied, like he always did. But the hairs on the back of his neck stood up anyway.

"We had protocols in place," Remi said, his voice steady. "We had oversight."

"Did you have functioning brakes?" Patricia asked. "Because I've got a safety note here, filed two days before the stunt, flagging cable tension issues. You want to tell me why that was ignored?"

Silence settled over the room. Remi blinked behind his designer glasses, and for the first time he looked like he felt the weight of it.

Drew leaned in, his voice low and direct. "It wasn't ignored."

Remi turned toward him, surprise flashing across his face. Even behind the sunglasses, Drew caught it.

"This is Aisha's written statement covering that night," Drew said, handing over the document. "It details the safety checks, road conditions, and weather. Aisha is thorough. She always has been, whether she's handling logistics or coordinating the team."

"You think I would've run that stunt if I knew it was compromised?" Remi looked at her as if she had three heads.

"I think you were busy chasing your perfect shot," Patricia said coldly. "And two actors almost died because of it." She slid a photo across the table. The twisted wreckage. Tire tracks too close to where the lead actress had been standing.

"And here are the other written statements from the cast and crew who were on set that night, as requested." Remi laid the affidavits on top of her photos. "We are almost finished with the film."

"We don't deal in almost, gentlemen," she said. "We deal in reality. And reality is one wrong bolt away from body bags."

Remi exhaled through his nose, a silent storm building. "What now?" he asked.

"Now," Patricia said, standing, "you shut down every stunt until we say otherwise. You retrain your crew. You resubmit every safety plan. And you pray we don't find this was willful negligence, because then we're talking more than fines. We're talking federal charges."

Drew felt the weight settle over the room, like justice had entered wearing cement boots.

As they walked out, Remi stopped and turned to Drew. "Thanks for speaking up back there. For once in my life, I was at a loss for words, and you saved me."

"Well, I know Aisha is the queen of detail. If she wrote those things, then they were true. She's always thinking two steps ahead. She's not only a master at her craft, but someone who's mastered her life in ways most people never do." That much he knew about his dear friend.

Remi smiled. *"A master can instruct without doing anything. Teach without a word."*

Drew froze in his tracks. It was a phrase he'd heard a hundred times before, usually spoken over a mug of black coffee, a lit cigarette trembling between two fingers, and half-forgotten photographs scattered across the counter of his aunt's shop.

"A master can instruct without doing anything. Teach without a word."

As soon as the words left Remi's mouth, Drew felt it. A strange stillness. Like the air itself had stopped moving. His gaze snapped toward Remi, eyes sharp, as if he'd been yanked out of the present and thrown backward into something buried deep.

Remi turned to him, confused. "What? What did I say?"

Drew hesitated. His mouth opened slightly, but nothing came out. His eyes locked, not on Remi but past him, through him, like he was staring at a ghost only he could see. "That's a phrase my aunt always used."

"Someone said that to me years ago. I never forgot it." Remi smiled, trying to place where he had heard it.

They continued to the parking lot in silence. Remi slipped back into his car and gave Drew a nod goodbye. Drew watched as the Aston Martin pulled out of the spot and disappeared over the hills toward Hollywood.

Now he was on a different mission.

Drew revved his engine and turned left out of the parking lot, heading deeper into Studio City, toward the very street where everything had changed. He drove down Ventura Boulevard, cruising past familiar landmarks now cloaked in time. The diner was still there somehow. The florist was gone. And in the middle stood the old shop, Martha's Place, its windows covered in brown paper, a For Lease sign peeling at the corners.

Martha Langley had a way of seeing people, really seeing them, that went beyond conversation. When clients came into her antique shop, they didn't always say much. Some were regulars. Others were strangers passing through with dust-covered boxes of heirlooms and keepsakes, pieces of forgotten lives wrapped in old newspaper. They left these things behind, sometimes for money, sometimes simply to let go. And she would say, "A master can instruct without doing anything. Teach without a word."

To his aunt, those clients were teachers, even if they didn't realize it. Through the objects they brought in, an old soldier's medal, a cracked porcelain doll, a writer's desk, a locket with initials etched into the back, they revealed something about who they were, what they valued, and what they had lost. They didn't need to explain the story. The item was the story.

She believed people showed you who they were not through speeches, but through choices. What they held onto. What they gave away. What they could no longer bear to keep. That quiet transaction, someone placing a rusted compass or a worn leather-bound journal into her hands, taught her more about the human condition than a thousand conversations ever could.

Drew carried those lessons with him, gifts his aunt had quietly passed down. So the phrase became both philosophy and reminder. Pay attention. Listen to what isn't said. Because some of the greatest lessons don't come with explanations. They come in silences, gestures, and the relics people leave behind.

A warm breeze stirred the dust at his feet, whispering through the cracks in the pavement like a ghost retracing old steps. He stared at the vacant shop, longing heavy in his chest. His thoughts, scattered and half-lost in memory, were pulled back into the present, forced against the sharp edges of reality.

Los Angeles had a rhythm, a way of folding time in on itself and making past mistakes feel current again. It was a city that loved to rewind, to replay old scenes with new actors.

But not this time.

Not if he had anything to say about it.

Chapter 6
Laurel Canyon

Francy adjusted her ball cap against the sun and gave Israel a quick nod as the heavy oak doors creaked open.

Drake stood tall and thin in a black suit, polished to perfection, each strand of hair slicked neatly back. His face remained expressionless, but his eyes held a faint glint of something. Recognition, perhaps. Or caution.

"You came back… and on time," he said, his voice smooth as varnished wood. "Madame LeClaire is indisposed."

"She is expecting us?" Francy asked.

"She is," the butler replied. "But she won't be joining you today. You have the run of the grounds."

Francy and Israel exchanged a glance. That was convenient.

"We'll need access to the perimeter, the interior, and any existing wiring," Israel said, already unslinging a coil of fiber cable from his shoulder.

"Everything is unlocked. Do not disturb the blue parlor," the butler added. Then he turned with a stiff bow and vanished into the mansion's shadows.

"The blue parlor?" Francy repeated.

"I don't remember that one," Israel said with a shrug. "We'll cross that bridge…" He smiled.

The LeClaire estate had once looked like something out of a novel. Ivy-draped balconies, stone gargoyles glaring from every corner, and a fountain that probably hadn't run since LeClaire's last big blockbuster. Now the grounds were overgrown with weeds tall enough to whisper secrets, and the stone walls wept with creeping dampness.

Francy stepped carefully through the brush, scanning for camera angles. "East wall has a blind spot. We should put one near that broken sundial."

Israel grunted in agreement as he knelt by an old conduit box, pulling the rusted door open with a creak. "This wiring is from the sixties. We'll need to replace the whole run to the back entry."

As they worked, the wind stirred the leaves and carried something else with it. An odor. Damp wood. Rotting paper. Francy wrinkled her nose. "Do you smell that?"

"Yeah. Like wet stone and mildew, but sharper."

They rounded the far side of the house, what had once been the carriage wing. Vines gripped the outer walls like desperate fingers. As Israel reached up to secure a small marble-like camera to the soffit, Francy caught something in the ivy. A broken branch? No. Metal.

"Hold up," she said.

She pushed aside a curtain of leaves, revealing a small grate low to the ground, partially buried under soil and creeper. It was old iron, the kind of thing you would miss unless you were staring straight at it.

Israel knelt beside her and switched on the flashlight on his phone. The beam flickered through the slats.

“There’s a tunnel,” he said, his voice low. “It goes under the house.”

Francy ran her fingers along the edge. The grate was loose. Not rusted shut, just loose. “This looks like it was moved recently.”

“Could be how someone’s getting in,” Israel muttered. “That’s about four feet long, wouldn’t you say? They’d have to be small. Or smart. You want to check it out?”

Francy shook her head. “Let’s finish the install, then take another look. After that, we bring this to Drew.”

Israel bent down and attached another small camera to the left side of the gate’s entrance, giving it a firm tug.

As they rose, a warm breeze stirred again, and somewhere deep inside the house a shutter banged shut. Neither acknowledged the shiver running up their spines. They moved quickly, circling the mansion and affixing marble-sized cameras to its most exposed vantage points.

Back inside, Israel installed the first interior camera above the grand staircase. The wallpaper peeled away in swaths, and copied portraits glared down with smudged oil eyes. Francy couldn’t shake the feeling of being watched, and not just by the cameras.

In the west wing, Israel paused beside a set of muddy footprints crossing the marble floor. “These don’t match ours,” he said quietly. “Look at the spacing. Small feet. Maybe a woman.”

Francy stared at them. “Could they be from Madame Arquette?”

“The psychic?” Israel asked. He walked over to the bookcase where they had found her tracks in the dust the day before. “I don’t think so,” he said.

Francy followed the muddy prints to a dark blue curtain and peeled back the soft, dusty fabric. “The blue parlor,” she whispered. “The only room we were told not to enter.”

Off the large living room sat a round space painted in celestial blue. Its windows faced outward toward the Hollywood Hills, the dilapidated pool visible in the distance. Francy hesitated, then held the curtain open just wide enough for Israel to look inside.

"Drew needs to see this," he said, snapping a quick photo of the footprints leading to the room, then another of the room itself, cast in shadow by storm clouds rolling in over the hills.

"I thought it never rained in California?" Francy asked.

"But, girl, don't they warn you," Israel whispered, breaking into song.

"You're too young to know that song." Francy shot him a look.

"You'd be surprised what I know," he said with a smirk.

Outside, storm clouds rumbled with a low, guttural thunder that echoed through the canyon. A strange tingling crept over Francy's skin. "We need to finish outside," she said, pulling the curtains closed, trying to shut out the feeling that had settled over her.

"It feels like we're being watched from the inside." Israel's eyes swept across the massive living room, answered only by the toll of the grandfather clock.

They moved through the foyer and stepped out past the front door.

☆☆☆

The butler moved like a ghost through the hallway adjoining the living room, his footsteps muffled by the thick, moth-eaten carpet that lay just outside the blue parlor. He did not hesitate as he pulled the velvet curtains apart and noticed the muddy footprints. Reaching into his pocket, he produced a white handkerchief and began to mop up the mess.

He stepped inside and looked around cautiously. From the outside, the room appeared undisturbed, the paint flaking in elegant chips, like a portrait aging in real time. Inside, he checked carefully for signs that anything had been moved. The velvet drapes hung open over the tall windows. The heavy furniture remained covered in white sheets, except for one chair in the corner, facing a small hearth.

Vivienne LeClaire sat there.

She was motionless, regal in her posture, as if still hosting a party no one had attended in years. Her hair fell in delicate strands along her cheek. She wore a black satin robe that blended with the shadows clinging to the room. A thick book lay open in her lap, its pages yellowed and brittle, the ink curling with age.

But her eyes were open. Watching.

"You didn't tell them?" she asked, her voice dry but composed. "They were in this room. And I heard them notice the grate outside."

Drake bowed his head. "Yes, Madame. I instructed them not to come in here. They did notice the grate outside, but I thought it best to allow them to finish their work first."

She shifted her gaze toward the darkened fireplace, where the charred remains of something recent still smoldered faintly. The air smelled of sage and scorched linen.

"There's no point in hiding it anymore," she murmured. "They've seen the signs."

Silence hung in the room. Then something shifted.

"He comes at night again, doesn't he?" Vivienne whispered, her voice cracking slightly. "Through the tunnel. Just like before."

The butler said nothing.

Vivienne's hands trembled over the spine of the book. "First it was my jewelry. Then my perfume. Now… my letters."

"They were from your brother," the butler said quietly. "The ones he wrote before the drowning."

Vivienne nodded. Her voice thinned. "He always blamed me. Even after death."

The silence tightened around them.

"He's not here for trinkets anymore," she said at last. "He's here for me. I feel he wants to take me with him."

A sharp crack echoed from somewhere deep in the estate. The butler turned his head slightly, but Madame LeClaire did not flinch.

"He's already inside," Vivienne whispered. "Those cameras will never pick up a ghost," she said softly, almost scornful.

☆☆☆

In the garden, Israel tapped Francy on the shoulder and pointed back toward the house.

"The west-facing camera just went dead."

"Wiring?" Francy asked.

He shook his head. "No. It was clean one second, and then it cut out."

Francy's brow furrowed. "We should take another look at that grate."

Neither of them spoke the thought forming between them.

The camera feed had cut out at 4:13 p.m.

By 4:15, the sky over the estate had dimmed with an unnatural weight, as if dusk had arrived early. But it wasn't dusk. It was the storm pressing down, one the forecast had never predicted.

Francy crouched beside the grate again, flashlight already in her hand. The vines had crept back over it, as if trying to seal it shut in her absence.

“I don’t like this,” Israel muttered behind her, slinging the last of the gear into his pack. “We should call Drew. Get the crew or…” His voice trailed off.

Francy didn’t answer. Her fingers were already hooked under the edge of the iron grate. She lifted. It came free too easily.

“No rust on the hinges,” she said, more to herself than to Israel. “It’s been opened recently. Probably more than once.”

Beneath it lay a narrow shaft, barely wide enough for a person to crawl through on hands and knees. The earth had been packed down from repeated use, and a faint scent of mildew and chlorine clung to the stone walls.

“Smell that?” she asked.

“Pool chemicals,” Israel replied. “Like old, tainted residue.”

They looked at each other. Then, without a word, Francy ducked down and slipped inside.

The tunnel was tighter than it had looked, coffin-tight and colder than expected. The flashlight beam bounced off walls slick with condensation. Every few feet, old metal support brackets jutted from the stone, rusted but intact. The tunnel had been built with intention.

“Someone carved this professionally,” Israel muttered behind her. “Not a drain. Not erosion. This was made.”

“Leading somewhere,” Francy whispered.

Ahead, a faint light flickered, wavering slightly.

They slowed their pace. The tunnel opened into a low chamber. Roots crept through the stone like veins beneath skin. At the far end, a metal ladder rose vertically into darkness. The bottom rungs were wet.

Francy paused, shining her light along the wall beside the ladder. “There. Scratches. Words. Carved by hand?”

She leaned closer, reading aloud.

"She watches through the water.
Do not look upon her face.
Each time seems different, I can tell.
I’ll hide here till I feel it’s safe."

The last phrase caught in Francy’s throat.

Israel turned pale. “I think we should go back.”

A light drizzle began, tapping insistently against the glass pane above. “It’s coming from up there,” Israel said, pointing toward the metal ladder rising through the tunnel ceiling.

Their eyes met, locked in silent understanding. Francy held his gaze for a moment, then looked up at the ladder disappearing into shadow. Without another word, she began to climb.

Overhead, a small square window, no more than three feet by three, shimmered beneath the rain. As the downpour intensified, droplets slipped through the edges and trailed across her face.

“Where does it lead?” Israel called from below, his voice cutting through the darkness.

Francy hesitated. She reached the top of the ladder but could not immediately make sense of what she was seeing. Pressing her forehead to the cool pane of glass, she tried to determine their location.

“Francy?” Israel whispered, uncertainty roughening his voice.

Her fingers brushed a cold metal handle tucked along the edge of the glass. She paused, just for a breath, then pulled. The hatch gave way with a metallic creak.

Without warning, a surge of rainwater burst through the opening, streaked with soot and years of filth. It cascaded down over them, cold and foul, soaking their clothes and stealing their breath.

"What the hell was that?" Israel choked, ducking his head to shield himself from the torrent.

"My bad," Francy mumbled, wiping soot from her lips. But now she felt permission to keep going. She pulled herself upward and emerged into the empty pool.

The tiles were cracked with age, weeds pushing through the joints. The walls were slick. In the far corner, water clung in a shallow puddle, black as ink, reflecting nothing.

"It's the pool!" she shouted back to Israel over the rain now pelting down on her.

Then something else caught her eye.

A man's shoe, black and worn, sat neatly in the shallow end.

Francy froze. "Israel?"

No answer.

She turned back to the hatch. It was closed.

Dropping to her knees, she yanked at the latch. "Israel?"

From beneath the hatch came a sound. Not a voice. Not movement.

Below the estate, Israel stood frozen, staring up at the sealed hatch. He hadn't followed her. He had heard something else, farther down the tunnel behind him.

He descended the ladder and shined the light from his phone into the darkness. A shiver crawled up his spine, like a cold wire threading through bone. He bent quickly, scooping up a handful of pebbles scattered at his feet. With a strained effort, he hurled them upward toward the glass pane far above.

"How the hell do I keep ending up in situations like this?" The thought clawed at his mind as he crouched in the dark, barely breathing.

"Focus." He forced a slow inhale. In. Out. "Just breathe."

His eyes swept the tunnel, walls slick with moisture, shadows pressing in, then snapped back to the glass above. Rain hammered against it in a violent rhythm, each droplet a drumbeat of urgency. A symphony of pressure. Of time running out.

And yet… he wasn't alone. A sound, a shift, maybe a breath, echoed from deeper in the tunnel. His muscles locked tight.

Do I go up? The second half of the question came uninvited. *Or turn back into whatever's waiting below?*

He hesitated, heart hammering hard enough to hurt. Either direction could be a trap.

He swept his flashlight down the tunnel one last time. Nothing. No movement. No one in sight. So he committed to what might be the wrong decision.

He squeezed backward toward the metal grate, its mouth open and waiting. The tunnel narrowed around him, forcing every movement slow and deliberate. One final shove, and he reached for the opening.

A wet hand grabbed his.

His heart dropped.

For a split second, his mind refused to process it. This couldn't be happening. Not here. Not now. The hand gripping his was cold. Human. Real.

Adrenaline surged through him like electricity. His first instinct was to rip free, to scream, but his throat locked shut. No sound came. His thoughts spoke instead. *Who's there? What is that? Did I miss someone following me? Were they already waiting? Watching?*

Every mistake he'd made getting here came flooding back. Every wrong turn. Every second he hesitated. He thought he was alone. He had been praying he was. Fear weighed on his chest, cold and shallow. The rain roared above like a warning. And the hand… it didn't let go.

"Israel, come on! What are you doing?" Francy's annoyed voice rang through the darkness.

Relief crashed over him, though he still couldn't quite believe it was her hand. "What happened to you?" Israel managed to say.

"Come on, let's get out of the rain first!" Francy tightened her grip on his hand, her boots slipping on the wet metal as she tried to pull him up. Rain hammered the street behind her. Water rushed through the rusting grate, soaking Israel's already mud-streaked shirt. He was almost out, almost back on solid ground, when he saw the change in Francy's expression as her grip began to slip.

Francy felt two cold, firm hands shove against her back before she had time to react. She fell backward into the tunnel with Israel.

Her footing vanished. Time stretched. Her arms flailed, breath trapped in her chest, killing the scream before it could escape. She plunged through the open grate, her knee slamming into the concrete edge before she tumbled into the tunnel below, landing hard on something softer than the floor.

"Ow," Israel groaned beneath her, the air punched from his lungs as Francy's weight knocked the wind out of him.

Francy scrambled off him, heart pounding, drenched hair clinging to her cheeks. "Someone just pushed me!" she hissed, whipping her head toward the opening above. “There was someone up there. I felt them!”

Israel coughed and pushed himself upright. “I knew it. I knew I heard something!” His eyes scanned the shadows, his mind already racing.

The sound of boots slapping against wet pavement echoed faintly from above.

Francy didn’t wait for Israel to recover. She leapt for the ledge, hauling herself up with surprising strength. Israel followed close behind, gritting his teeth against the ache in his ribs.

As they pulled themselves through the grate, they caught a glimpse of a figure. Just a flash, dashing toward a truck parked near the front gate.

The figure was dressed in black. Hooded. Lean. Fast. The rain almost erased him, his outline melting into the storm-soaked city. Only the harsh glow of a streetlight caught his silhouette as he yanked open the driver’s-side door and jumped in.

“There!” Francy shouted, bolting forward.

The truck’s headlights sliced through the murk. The engine roared to life, tires screeching as it fishtailed on the slick pavement before rocketing down Sunset Boulevard.

“Go!” Israel yelled, and they sprinted after it. They tore down the sidewalk, rain stinging their faces, lungs burning with the effort.

Francy jumped into the front seat of her burnt-silver Mustang, the rental she had parked nearby, with Israel sliding into the passenger seat. He slapped the dashboard twice, willing the car forward, then pointed down Sunset. “He’s going through the canyon,” Israel said.

Francy’s wheels hit the pavement as they swerved onto the canyon road. The city’s buzz fell away behind them, swallowed by the dense silence of the mountains.

Laurel Canyon twisted ahead, a serpentine stretch of soaked asphalt barely wide enough for two cars to pass, slick as oil. The truck veered sharply, disappearing into the yawning blackness beyond the next curve.

Its headlights quivered through the mist like a ghost, vanishing behind each blind turn just before Francy could line up a clean angle. She gripped the wheel tighter, knuckles pale, tires whining as they bit into the corners. The car fishtailed, then snapped back into line. One eye stayed locked on the flicker of taillights, the other on the canyon's narrow edge. One wrong move, and it was a sheer drop into darkness.

"Left!" Israel shouted over the roar of the engine and the wash of rain. "He's cutting toward Lookout Mountain Drive!"

Francy didn't answer. She downshifted, the engine growling as she swung left, nearly clipping a mailbox. Trees loomed on either side like silent spectators, wet branches scraping the windows as the car tore past.

The truck ahead bucked and jolted, hydroplaning for a heartbeat before smashing through a wooden fence and jerking back onto the road. It was desperate now. He pushed faster.

Francy was faster.

The road narrowed again. One lane now. Old canyon homes flashed by, warm lights glowing behind rain-streaked windows, unaware of the chaos tearing past their quiet lives. The air smelled of wet eucalyptus and burning rubber. They hit a patch of standing water. The car bounced. Francy fought it back under control.

Water cascaded from rocky outcrops in thin waterfalls, flooding the narrow shoulder. Lightning forked overhead, illuminating the chase in split-second flashes. The black truck stayed ahead, a shadowy blur weaving recklessly through the curves, barely holding its lane.

“Keep on him!” Israel shouted over the engine’s roar.

“I am! This guy’s insane!”

Their tires screeched as they hugged a tight curve, the back end flinging dangerously close to the canyon wall. Francy wrestled the wheel, headlights catching fleeting glimpses of the truck as it plunged deeper into the storm-soaked labyrinth.

A rain-triggered rockslide had spilled debris across the road. The truck bounced over it violently but kept going. Francy swerved at the last second, barely missing a massive boulder, the car slamming hard as they landed on the other side.

Francy leaned forward, squinting through the rain-blurred windshield as the car jolted along the muddy canyon road. The truck ahead was still only a blur, its taillights smeared red across the darkness.

“Can you make out the plates?” she shouted over the roar of the engine and the drumming rain. “Anything? The make, model, even a partial number?”

She knew it was a long shot. The downpour distorted everything, and the distance between them shifted with every turn. Still, she held her breath, hoping Israel’s eyes might catch something hers couldn’t. Some detail that would make this ghost of a truck real.

Branches clawed at the windshield, shadows flickering across the glass. The truck’s red taillights flashed around another bend, vanishing for a heartbeat before reappearing on a straightaway. Francy caught a glimpse of the driver, a fleeting reflection in the side mirror. Even through the blur of rain and speed, something about him chilled her.

“Who is that?” she muttered, more to herself than to Israel.

“Whoever it is,” he replied through gritted teeth, “they didn’t want us following.”

Suddenly, the truck cut sharply off the road, kicking up mud and gravel as it tore down a narrow dirt path almost hidden behind overgrown brush and a sagging wooden fence.

“Off-road? Seriously?” Israel cursed, keeping his eyes locked on the truck as it bucked wildly ahead of them over the uneven terrain.

Rain fell in heavy sheets, soaking the canyon in mist and mud. Trees pressed closer, the headlights throwing long, eerie shadows across the path. Somewhere above, an owl cried out, the only witness to the chase unfolding in the darkness below.

Francy clenched the steering wheel, eyes locked on the path ahead.

“Don’t lose him,” Israel said, leaning forward as if he could will the car faster.

“I don’t plan to,” Francy shot back.

The truck made a sudden cut, a tight turn uphill onto a private drive hidden between ivy-covered stone walls. No signs. No lights. Just shadows and fog.

“You wanna go in there?” Francy snapped, adrenaline sharpening her voice.

Israel grinned, eyes fixed on the disappearing taillights. “Don’t you?”

Francy yanked the wheel right.

They vanished into the rain, following the black truck into the haunted veins of Laurel Canyon.

Chapter 7
Wilshire Boulevard

"Your days are numbered if you ever tell the truth. It's only a matter of time. I know what you did." Drew sat stretched out on the loft floor, reading and rereading the threatening notes left at Vivienne LeClaire's mansion. His expression tightened. "She told me these words sliced through her like a knife." The memory weighed heavily on him, the echo of her pain still sharp and unsettling.

Debra shivered. "I can't imagine. I don't know how she can even sleep in that house."

"I think there are many reasons keeping her there," Drew replied.

Both of them turned as Aisha appeared in the bedroom doorway.

"Mi amor," Debra said, hurrying to her side. "How are you feeling?"

Drew studied her face, trying to read the blankness in her stare. "You look… better," he said carefully, unsure whether to trust the fragile calm surrounding her.

Color had returned to Aisha's cheeks, a soft warmth replacing the ghostly pallor that had clung to her after the accident. Her blond hair, once tangled and neglected, was brushed smooth and tied loosely at the nape of her neck. She wore a pale blue sweater that made her seem almost serene, though faint shadows beneath her eyes hinted at sleepless nights and quiet battles she hadn't yet put into words. Still, something about her felt steadier. A quiet resilience lingered beneath the surface.

Aisha stepped into the living room and sat beside Debra. "I'm feeling fine now," she said softly. "But haunting memories are keeping Vivienne from leaving. They tether her to the only place where she still feels connected to what she's lost."

Debra was taken aback by Aisha's astute observation about Vivienne LeClaire.

"Very well said," Drew agreed. His attention drifted back to the messages. At first glance, the threats seemed superficial. A stalker obsessed with a movie star. Yet Aisha's words pushed his thoughts toward something deeper. "Something is off."

The girls leaned in, peering over Drew's shoulder as all three stared at the notes.

"The language in these threats isn't fan-obsessive or sexual," Drew said, pausing as he studied the pages. "It's moralistic. Ritualized."

Aisha nodded. "She told us a cherished photo of her receiving an Academy Award was cracked, like it mirrored her fractured peace of mind."

"And there was the scent of gardenias in the hallway," Drew added. "Even though she hadn't worn her favorite perfume in weeks."

Debra frowned. "I wonder why gardenia is her favorite."

"Days are numbered… only a matter of time," Drew murmured, turning the words over in his mind. "Time. Time. Time." He lifted his gaze slowly. "It's not about danger. It's about reckoning."

The girls exchanged a look, a silent understanding passing between them as a new perspective settled in. Then a sharp crack of thunder split the air, making all three jump. The sound rolled across the sky in a long, menacing rumble that seemed to shake the walls around them, as if the storm itself had come to echo their realization.

Suddenly, the front door burst open.

Aisha, Debra, and Drew jumped, their hearts still hammering from the storm's fury. Francy and Israel stood in the doorway, soaked to the skin and spattered with mud, their eyes wide with something dangerously close to anger. Water pooled at their feet as the wind howled behind them, carrying the sharp scent of rain and something else.

Debra gasped. "Oh my God, are you alright?"

Aisha hurried to the bathroom and grabbed two towels.

Drew said nothing, his mind working as he tried to piece the puzzle together.

"Aisha, you're up! How are you feeling?" Surprise flickered across Francy's face.

Aisha handed them the towels. "I feel alive again," she said. "I'm angrier than scared now." Her eyes moved between them, taking in the mud, the soaked clothes, the tension clinging to them like a second skin. "What happened to you two?"

"We were jumped." Francy peeled off her wet clothes and dried herself quickly by the door. She dragged the towel through her damp brunette hair before collapsing onto the sofa, exhaustion weighing down her limbs.

Israel stayed standing for a moment, shaking his head as if the movement might clear it. He struggled to shape the chaos into words, the car chase, the confrontation at Vivienne's mansion, the way it all spiraled. "We were spooked," he said at last, knowing the words didn't come close but unable to find better ones.

"We met Drake, the butler, at the mansion. He allowed us full access to the house and yard so we could set up security cameras," Francy explained, gulping down the entire bottle of cold water Debra handed her.

"Except the blue parlor," Israel added, unpacking his backpack onto the floor.

"Except the blue parlor, but we went in there anyway." Francy crushed the water bottle in one hand.

"That room off the living room facing the pool?" Drew recalled.

"Hey, that's right, amigo," Israel said, looking up from his inventory count. "Then we found a secret passage under the house."

"I'm not surprised," Aisha said. "Many homes built in the 1920s by wealthy homeowners and Hollywood elites had hidden bars, wine cellars, or smuggling tunnels to conceal alcohol during Prohibition."

"Well, we followed it to the end, and it took us underneath the pool."

"There was an underwater viewing window at the bottom of the pool." Francy tried to sketch it on a piece of paper Israel handed her.

"You mean like an observation window?" Debra leaned over Francy to get a better look at the drawing. "I remember that pool was empty, and not in good condition, I might add."

"Francy crawled out of the window and into the pool," Israel said, demonstrating with his hands.

"Where I found a man's shoe."

"And we found a very strange limerick," Israel confirmed.

"Limerick?" Aisha asked.

"Yes, like a poem or a..."

"Confession?" Israel turned to Francy, searching her face for confirmation.

Francy paused, trying to recall the exact wording.

"She watches through the water.
Do not look upon her face.
Each time seems different, I can tell.
I'll hide here till I feel it's safe."

Francy quickly wrote down the mysterious poem on a piece of paper. A ripple of curiosity and excitement moved through the group.

"Drew, you seem quiet, deep in thought, like you know what that means." Aisha slowly stood, her eyes fixed on him.

The others gathered closer, trying to catch a glimpse of what Francy had written.

"I was doing some research on our client." Drew cleared his throat and sat down. He had everyone's attention now. "Vivienne LeClaire had a younger brother. He was a savant."

"A savant?" Israel asked.

"It's someone who displays extraordinary abilities in a specific area, often while having developmental differences or disabilities," Debra explained.

"Extraordinary abilities? Like juggling while standing on his head?" Israel zipped up his backpack and slid onto the sofa.

"Not exactly," Drew said. "In this case, he was considered a linguistic savant. Someone gifted with language. He might've acted quiet, kept to himself, or had a hard time speaking at times, but when he focused, he showed a natural talent for words, inventive ideas, and poetic phrases built around patterns."

"You said Vivienne had a younger brother." Aisha stressed the word had.

"According to the news stories and tabloid reports I found online, Vivienne's brother drowned in their pool the night her breakthrough film, *Velvet Ashes*, debuted." Drew swallowed hard, struggling to push through the weight of the tragedy.

"That's horrific," Debra shrieked. "What a bittersweet tragedy!"

"Especially since his drowning left behind unanswered questions and a lingering sense that he might've known or sensed something important before his death," Drew admitted.

"Meaning the press thought there was more to the story? That his death wasn't an accident?" Francy asked.

"There was a lot of speculation, since the press kept bringing up stories about the tumultuous relationship the brother and sister had."

"Yes, but come on," Aisha said, clearly agitated. "We all know how the press creates drama to sell stories. We know this firsthand."

"Well, sometimes," Israel chimed in, "those stories can have a kernel of truth."

"Well, if that poem we found in the tunnel under the house was any indication, then it would imply that the brother..."

"Jefferies," Drew supplied.

"If Jefferies did write that poem we found, then it would imply he was afraid of his sister for some reason," Israel deduced.

"When Debra and I were searching the rooms in Vivienne's home, we came across a scrapbook and piles and piles of paper with poems, word puns, and puzzles written on them," Aisha recalled. "Like they were random thoughts."

"That's right." Debra jumped up. "I guess we just assumed they were Vivienne's personal thoughts. Aisha also found a date book."

Aisha remembered its odd contents. "Inside were lists of dates and a repeated phrase written in red ink: *'The death of the author.'* The phrase was written across random dates in different months."

"What author?" Israel asked.

"It's unclear. There was nothing that gave it context. Just the words, *'The death of the author.'*"

"Well, we're not even sure it was Jefferies who wrote that poem in the tunnel. But we do have a bigger problem." Francy stood up. "Someone pushed us down into that tunnel under the house."

"We chased him through Laurel Canyon," Israel said, jumping up, his hands slicing through the air as he mapped the turns and hills.

"Did you get a good look at him?" Debra interrupted.

"Not really," Francy explained. "He was always about fifty feet in front of us. But he was a white guy in a black hoodie, about five-six, and a fast runner."

"He was lean and quick. Oh, and he drove a black truck. A Ford, I think," Israel added, trying his best to recall their assailant.

"We chased him through Laurel Canyon to a private property in the hills," Francy continued.

"Did you recognize the property or the address?" Debra asked.

"It looked like a horse farm," Israel said. "I noticed a large number of stables and fencing."

"My car got stuck in the mud in one of the pastures," Francy said, hanging her head in disappointment.

"Ahh, hence your mud-drenched clothing," Aisha added.

"And you lost him." Debra dropped onto the sofa again, disappointed.

"Did he direct you to that property, or was choosing that route just a spontaneous attempt to escape?"

"It did seem pretty random," Francy answered, still turning the question over in her mind.

"We also found muddy footprints in the house," Israel jumped in.

"Near the blue parlor," Francy quickly added.

Drew stood and began pacing. "Well, clearly the threats and attempts to scare Vivienne LeClaire have escalated since we arrived."

The group nodded in agreement.

A low rumble of thunder rolled through the distant hills, as if in approval. The storm had passed, but its echo lingered in the room, much like the questions surrounding them.

"There seem to be a lot of missing pieces in Vivienne LeClaire's story," Israel said.

"She never told us about her brother," Debra added.

"She never really gave us much information about her past. She either can't remember, or she's trying to forget." Aisha pulled her hair back and sat down.

"I realized something today. *Velvet Ashes* was released by the same studio you're working with now for *Final Tango*, Aisha," Drew revealed.

"You mean Paramount?" Debra asked.

"Yes, but *Velvet Ashes* was filmed on location on Wilshire Boulevard, in a building in Koreatown called Paramount Plaza." Drew reached for his bag. "It seems Paramount used it a lot back in the day for New York or other city scenes because the building was very modern at the time, and the area around it worked perfectly for cityscape locations." He pulled out a tattered old book.

"*The Making of Legendary Films of the 50s & 60s?*" Israel read the title out loud. "Where did you find that?"

"Larry Edmunds Bookshop," Drew said with a smile. "It's one of the few places left for film buffs. It's filled with movie history, rare scripts, behind-the-scenes books, and classic Hollywood memorabilia." He barely contained his excitement. "It's amazing. It's right on the Hollywood Walk of Fame."

"You have to take me there!" Debra exclaimed.

"I found vintage posters of *Velvet Ashes*, and they even had several props from the film. Your lighting technician, Mr. Keyes, also had supporting actor billing."

"There's more to that story. He and I need to have a conversation," Aisha admitted.

"Hey, where are Elena and Grace?" Israel asked, looking around the loft.

"They're following a lead on Vivienne's brother, Jefferies," Drew answered. "Well, it looks like the rain's stopped and the sun's coming back out. What do you say we head over to Paramount Plaza and check it out?"

Francy jumped up. "I think it's a good idea. We can take two cars."

Wilshire Boulevard was often described as a cross-section of Los Angeles itself. Long, sprawling, often traffic-heavy, and constantly changing, it was deeply tied to the city's identity and history. Stretching from downtown LA to the Pacific Ocean in Santa Monica, Wilshire passed through a wide mix of neighborhoods that reflected the city's cultural, economic, and architectural diversity.

In downtown, Wilshire Boulevard felt dense and urban, lined with office towers, historic buildings, and busy intersections. Driving farther west, Drew and the crew found themselves in the heart of Koreatown, where neon signs, restaurants, and crowds of people filled the streets with energy.

"There it is," Debra said, pointing from the back seat.

Paramount Plaza rose along Wilshire Boulevard like a pair of dark sentinels, aloof and watchful, casting long reflections across the street. The twin towers, sleek black-glass monoliths, felt less like ordinary office buildings and more like stage props built for a modern myth, polished to a mirrored sheen. Sunlight glanced off their reflective surfaces, giving them a cool, commanding presence.

"We can park in the garage to your right," Aisha suggested.

The plaza at their base felt ceremonial, a threshold between the human scale of the sidewalk and the towering ambition above.

"There's a real cinematic quality to this space," Debra observed as they crossed the plaza.

"You half expect a dramatic entrance, a limousine door opening, or a character pausing beneath the towers to look up," Israel laughed.

"Yeah, before destiny intervenes," Aisha added.

They pushed through the revolving doors into the lobby of One Paramount Plaza. Sleek and quietly dramatic, the space was defined by dark stone, reflective surfaces, and controlled lighting. Polished floors mirrored the tall glass walls, while clean lines and minimalist design created an atmosphere of power and restraint. It felt deliberate and composed, less welcoming than impressive, like an antechamber to the ambitions housed above.

"The old-timer might know something," Israel said, pointing to a security guard slowly pacing in the sunlight spilling through the large bay windows.

"Excuse me, sir," Debra said, approaching him and reading his name badge. "Hello, Terrell. Could you tell us, is this where Paramount used to shoot movies?"

The gentleman stopped pacing and studied his small audience. His eyes lit up as if he'd been handed a spotlight and invited to regale another group of tourists with the memories he held dear. His age gave him a dignified air, measured movements, a steady voice, and quiet confidence. He carried himself with alert professionalism.

Observant without being intrusive, dependable and reassuring, he seemed like the kind of man whose presence alone made people feel safe. His posture was upright, his gaze attentive, and beneath his no-nonsense exterior was a protective warmth Drew couldn't ignore.

"Oh yes," he said, beaming. "There were many movies made here in this plaza." He removed his hat and scratched his head. "*Into the Moonlight* was filmed right here in this lobby. *Across the Sea* was shot right over there by that fountain," he said, pointing through the window. "And *All the Way Home* was shot right at that front desk. You know the scene where she..."

"That's wonderful, Terrell," Debra interrupted with a smile. "How about *Velvet Ashes*?"

"Oh sure," he said, smiling. "But that was shot in the abandoned part of the building next door." He raised his hand and pointed down a long corridor. "Paramount Plaza is two buildings connected by that central esplanade." He gazed ahead, as if replaying his own memories tied to the film.

"You had to be a very young man at the time. Did you work here then?" Francy asked with a smile, introducing herself.

"Oh sure," he replied proudly. "I was an assistant script supervisor back then. I helped ensure continuity between scenes and kept very detailed notes."

"Did you work on *Velvet Ashes* by any chance?" Drew asked, introducing himself as he shook Terrell's hand.

"*Velvet Ashes*, *When She Left Home*, *Time and Again*. I worked on several of the Vivienne LeClaire pictures. She was a great star."

"We happen to be working for her now," Drew explained, excitement in his voice.

"Are you really?" Terrell's eyes lit up. Tension moved through his body as if she were standing right there in the room. "I'm glad to hear she's still with us. What studio is she with? What are you doing for her?"

"She's not currently filming anything," Drew said sadly.

"It appears she's being targeted by an unknown individual, and we don't yet understand the motive," Debra said, gently guiding the security guard by the small of his back. "As her friends, she's asked for our assistance, which is why we hoped we might find some answers here."

Terrell hesitated, thinking it over. "Targeted how? Hold on…" A wary expression crossed his face, as if something suddenly felt off. "You're not here as some kind of reporters trying to deceive me, are you?"

"Absolutely not," Israel jumped in. He walked over and shook Terrell's hand, then pulled out his phone and flipped through several live images from Vivienne's security cameras.

Terrell raised a hand to his chin, his fingers trailing slowly down his neck. Drew sensed he still wasn't convinced. "As a security watchman, maybe you can make sense of some of these threats Vivienne's received." He reached into his bag and pulled out the notes written on paper.

"This looks serious." Terrell scratched his head and thumbed through the threats again.

"Any idea who would do this or what it might mean?" Drew asked.

"Let's walk," Terrell said, glancing around suspiciously. He led them forward through the long corridor ahead. "Maybe the threats are aimed at her confessing to her brother's murder," he whispered.

Drew and Aisha exchanged a look as they realized the situation was growing deeper.

"People believed she killed her brother?" The shock on Israel's face was unmistakable.

"I don't believe that," Terrell argued, "but many people did. Some people believed her father did it." He shook his head. "There were a few minor scandals around her during her big movie years." He pushed open a pair of doors, leading them out to the plaza.

The Santa Ana winds swirled dust through the air, casting a golden haze over the bright California day, as if the sunshine itself were trying to scrub the sky clean. In sharp contrast, the dilapidated Paramount Plaza stood empty and forlorn, its cracked concrete and faded signage a quiet testament to better days long past. While the sun bathed the world in warmth and clarity, the abandoned building absorbed the light without a trace of life, its hollow windows reflecting a world moving on without it.

"This was the plaza where Vivienne LeClaire slaps her lawyer in the final scene of *Velvet Ashes*! Do you remember?" Again, Terrell couldn't contain his excitement. "There were many script rewrites before they came up with that scene. The director and Vivienne's agent were always arguing over it." He reached for the string of keys hanging neatly at his belt, selected two, and first unlocked the padlock securing the chain across the glass doors. Then, with practiced ease, he disengaged the heavy deadbolt.

Particles danced in the air like memories refusing to settle. Faded movie posters peeled away from water-stained walls, as if even nostalgia had grown tired of holding on. There was nothing glamorous about the place. It was a location that time and the moviemaking industry had forgotten.

The grand, sweeping lobby was still impressive, even after years of neglect. Fading grandeur cast a worn yet dignified air across the space. Israel sensed the weight of memories overtaking their guide as Terrell occasionally paused at familiar touchstones that seemed to carry him back to his youth.

“We should take the stairs,” Terrell suggested. “I don’t much trust the elevators any longer.”

At the far end of the lobby stood a grand marble staircase spiraling upward, its elongated steps framed by a brass railing now dulled with age. “The soundstages and offices were located on every floor except the second floor. That’s where we used to keep all the records, scripts, and production notes for each film we shot here. If someone’s threatening Miss Vivienne, we might find some clues up there.”

Terrell stopped at the top of the stairs and glanced around at the collection of closed doors circling the balcony-like mezzanine. Light poured in through circular, oculus-like opening in the roof’s apex, washing the wide staircase in a bright, almost celestial glow.

Drew let out a low whistle. “This place has the stillness of a mausoleum,” he murmured, the emptiness almost tangible beneath his shoes.

“Are all these rooms filled with archival material?” Aisha asked.

“Yes,” Terrell confirmed with a nod. “Every film that was shot here from 1950 to 1962.”

Francy and Debra reached the top of the stairs. “Wow, this reminds me of the round room Alice landed in when she fell down the rabbit hole,” Debra exclaimed.

Terrell opened the first door in front of them. “It’s been a long while since I’ve been up here. I don’t quite remember how these were organized.” He pushed aside a pile of papers stacked behind the door and flipped the light switch, but nothing happened.

“So, these offices were converted into storage rooms, supposedly?” Francy inquired.

"Supposedly is a strong word. These boxes are labeled by year. That's not storage, that's just chronological clutter," Aisha concluded. "All these boxes and files are marked 1960. When was *Velvet Ashes* released?"

"Ahh, 1952," Terrell recalled. "We may need to go a few doors over." He pivoted on his heels, closed the door behind him, and moved two doors down to his right. "Let's try this treasure trove."

What Drew imagined had once been a thriving movie production office was now a derelict, echo-filled hollow, its cluttered desks and faded call sheets frozen in time. File cabinets were stuffed with papers spilling onto the parquet floor.

"I've got it!" Francy's voice rang out beneath the high ceiling. "*Velvet Ashes*." She pulled a large box from the floor at her feet and opened it slowly. Papers spilled out, yellowed memos stamped and initialed.

"Co-star remains… difficult. Recommend minimizing presence during press," Aisha read from the first paper on the floor.

"Wow. Who was that…" Drew trailed off.

"Harold Keyes," Terrell answered quickly. "'Difficult' is studio code for 'doesn't play along.'"

Aisha and Drew exchanged another look.

"Do you recall how that played out?" Drew asked, pushing a few boxes aside before sitting on the windowsill.

"He was a rising star. A bit full of himself back then," Terrell recalled. "He always questioned certain lines in the script or the reasons behind his character's motivation." He paused, as if replaying the scene in his mind. "But I remember the real drama came at the premiere. He showed up looking disbelieving. He was despondent, defiant, even irreverent. He wouldn't follow directions or sit where he was told." Terrell tilted his head. "I don't think he even went to the film's after-party."

"Check the date," Debra said, her investigative instincts kicking in.

Aisha glanced down at the paperwork. "The premiere of *Velvet Ashes* was June 21, 1952."

"The same day Vivienne's brother died," Drew confirmed.

"So, they trashed Harold Keyes after *Velvet Ashes* was released," Terrell said softly, lowering his head.

"Convenient," Francy whispered.

"They really went after him," Israel said. "In a silent way. Maybe now he's going after Vivienne."

"Harold Keyes is working as my lighting technician on the new film I'm doing," Aisha explained. "We've spoken a few times about his past. He said his acting career ended abruptly." She punctuated the thought with a quiet snap of her fingers. "According to him, he witnessed, or maybe said, something he was never meant to."

"That's a vague confession," Terrell admitted.

"He didn't seem to know Vivienne LeClaire was still alive," Aisha added.

"So, you're not only a detective, but an actress as well?" Terrell studied them with renewed interest. "It's interesting. You all seem to work together so naturally. You move alike, finish each other's sentences. You gel like a dance team."

"Good observation," Francy said. "We're all dancers first. We kind of fell into detective work."

"Oh, the dancing detectives? That's a great gimmick. Well, I was a tap dancer. My twin brother and I had an act," Terrell said with a proud smile. "Thomas and Terrell. We were going to rival the Nicholas Brothers..." He paused. "But sadly, there's only one

Nicholas Brothers." His disappointment was palpable. "Now my twin brother works for Paramount too, in the props department."

"That's wonderful," Drew said gently, noticing the dismay in his eyes. "Our roles in life change over time. It's a natural progression, Terrell. I bet you guys were fantastic."

"Yes," he replied, performing a brief soft-shoe step, "for a moment."

"Here… scripts. Early drafts." Debra looked up from the box she was rifling through. "The director was Clive Harrington. Wasn't that your director's father, Aisha?"

"Yes, it was," Aisha said.

"Oddly enough," Drew added, "Remi discovered Aisha while his father was directing her in his final film in Spain."

"That is quite curious," Terrell observed. "It seems these two situations are unexpectedly connected. Only in Hollywood."

"Whoever is stalking Vivienne LeClaire left a photocopied script of *Velvet Ashes* with the message inscribed in red ink: *time's up.* Would that mean anything to you, Terrell?" Drew asked.

"Well," Terrell said, rubbing his chin as he considered it, "that's interesting. This was Clive Harrington's last film in Hollywood. Soon after, the studio fired him as a director. He only seemed to find work outside of Hollywood after that." He glanced around the room, as if searching for an answer hidden in the dust and files. "Maybe the threat to Vivienne isn't as personal as it is timely."

Drew's puzzling mind clicked. "Then maybe Vivienne isn't just being punished. She's being forced to remember what she erased. We're only twenty days out from the anniversary of *Velvet Ashes* and her brother's death."

"Matters have been escalating," Israel suggested.

"These changes, dialogue cuts, scene swaps, they're all marked 'writer revisions,'" Aisha said, flipping through the files.

"So, it wasn't Vivienne's call," Francy murmured.

"Miss Vivienne was a consummate performer," Terrell said. "But she did what she was told."

Israel lifted a document above his head. "This file has the call sheets. This one's for the night of the premiere."

"Who was actually there?" Drew asked.

Israel scanned the list. "Studio execs. PR. Security. Vivienne arrived late, alone."

"She wasn't even escorted by her co-star, Mr. Keyes?" Debra asked.

Aisha slipped an arm around Israel's waist and leaned in. "Mr. Keyes was scratched off the list."

"Yet the story paints Vivienne as the beneficiary, the survivor who 'inherited' everything," Francy said.

"A perfect red herring," Drew muttered. "Make grief look like greed."

"And power look like coincidence," Israel added.

"Meanwhile, three careers ended that night. Clive Harrington, Mr. Keyes, and Vivienne's brother." Debra shook her head. "That's not coincidence."

"The memos smear Keyes. The scripts mislead. The call sheets quietly contradict the narrative." Drew exhaled slowly. "So, this is about…"

"Control," Debra finished his sentence.

"Yes," Aisha continued, "about how institutions rewrite the past to protect themselves."

"The studio didn't kill them. But it made sure the truth never got top billing," Drew concluded.

Silence settled around them, thick and deliberate, as if the room itself were complicit. The papers in their hands no longer felt like evidence but like artifacts, curated, arranged, and weaponized.

"Somewhere between the scratched-out names and the smiling press photos, the studio had decided who would be remembered and who would be erased." Drew lowered the documents, a cold certainty tightening in his chest. "This wasn't just a cover-up, it was authorship. The tragedy had been edited, the blame carefully miscast, and the ending locked in long before anyone thought to question it."

As twilight settled along Wilshire Boulevard and the city lights hummed to life beyond the glass, one truth emerged with unsettling clarity.

"Terrell, may we borrow these notes?"

Terrell nodded. "Let me get your cellphone number, in case I think of something else."

Drew stacked the papers into his bag and handed Terrell his phone. "Whoever still controls the story might not be finished revising it."

Chapter 8
Boyle Heights

“Why do we always seem to get the morgue and coroner jobs?” Grace said with a huff. “I don’t even like these places. They give me the creeps!”

“Well, Drew thought we did such a great job on our last case that he should send the experts,” Elena explained with a smile. She glanced out the car window and added casually, “Look, Grace, an In-N-Out Burger,” clearly attempting to divert her attention as they passed.

“Well, we’re hitting that place on our way back home,” Grace assured her.

“There’s the USC Medical Center,” Elena pointed out. “We must be close.”

The LA County Medical Examiner’s Office loomed in the distance, a stark contrast to the surrounding university buildings. Constructed in 1909 as hospital offices, the building now served as the public-facing administrative headquarters. Characterized by a blend of Transitional Neoclassical, Beaux-Arts, and Austrian and German Secessionist styles, the facade featured a striking combination of concrete and red brick.

“Look, the door still bears the name ‘County General Hospital,’” Grace commented as they crossed the threshold.

“A touch of nostalgia?” Elena asked.

"Okay." Grace reached for Elena's arm, stopping her in her tracks. "Tell me, what are the questions we need to ask again?" Grace always shivered slightly when she was going into a situation she wasn't sure about.

Elena stopped and looked her in the eye. "We need to learn the cause and manner of death, the time of death, and any statements from the police reports. I'd say that's a good start."

"Yes, but we can't just waltz in and get what we want," Grace argued.

"We can if we put our minds to it. Besides, these are public records," Elena assured her.

Grace pulled her shoulders back and switched on her glowing smile. "Okay, let's go!"

The medical examiner's office smelled faintly of disinfectant and old paper, a place designed to feel neutral but somehow ending up tired. Fluorescent lights hummed overhead as they approached the front desk with confident strides.

At the desk sat a woman with a careful bun pinned at the nape of her neck, silver threaded through dark hair. Her glasses hung from a chain, and her fingers moved with practiced boredom over a keyboard worn smooth by years of forms and refusals. A mug that read *World's Okayest Clerk* guarded the edge of the desk.

Two chairs scraped softly as Grace and Elena stepped forward.

"Good day. I'm looking for an autopsy report," Elena said, calm but edged. "We were told it would be here."

The woman didn't look up right away. "Requests have to be submitted online," she said, reciting. "There's a form. Processing takes about two weeks."

A pause settled between them. The hum of the lights filled it.

"We're only in town for a few days," Grace said, gentler, almost apologetic. "We won't be here in two weeks."

That got the woman to glance up. Her eyes moved from one face to the other, already assembling a polite no, then stopped. Grace's braids caught the light, pink woven bright and deliberate, softening the stark room like something alive had wandered in by mistake.

The clerk hesitated. Her mouth opened, then closed. "Rules are rules," she said, but the words had lost their spine.

Elena leaned in slightly, lowering her voice. "We're not asking for anything complicated. Just to see what's already been written many, many years ago."

The woman's gaze drifted again to the braids, the color reminding her of bubblegum and summer sidewalks, of a daughter who had once begged for the same shade. She glanced to her left, then her right. The hallway behind her was empty. No footsteps. No supervisors.

"Well," she said slowly, fingers curling around the edge of the desk, "sometimes the system is… flexible."

She sighed, a small surrender, and pushed her chair back. "I can give you a few minutes," she added. "That's all."

Relief moved through the space between Grace and Elena, unspoken but shared.

The woman stood, already reaching for a badge clipped beneath the desk. As she rounded the counter, she smiled despite herself, her eyes lingering one last time on the pink braids.

"Follow me," she said.

Walking to another computer, she bent over the desk and asked for the name.

"Jeffries LeClaire," Elena answered quickly. She glanced over at Grace one more time.

The clerk's eyes moved up and down the screen, scanning each name as it appeared alphabetically. "I love your braids," she said without looking up.

Grace immediately knew what had gotten them in the door. "I do them myself," she offered.

"The color is stunning," the clerk said, smiling to herself as she located the file. "Oh, this is an old one. June 21, 1952. The autopsy report lists drowning as the cause of death but notes no water in the lungs, consistent with panic."

"That would be a red flag in my book," Elena whispered.

"How do you die from drowning without water in your lungs?" Grace asked, a perplexed look crossing her face.

"Dry drowning," the clerk said. "It's primarily caused by a lack of oxygen resulting from a vocal cord spasm. It's called a laryngospasm. When water makes contact with the sensitive area of the vocal cords, a protective reflex is triggered, causing them to spasm and forcefully close the airway."

"This prevents water from entering the lungs but also prevents air from entering, effectively shutting off the victim's ability to breathe," Elena said, understanding the mechanism.

"The victim dies from asphyxiation due to a lack of oxygen to the brain and body," the clerk confirmed.

"Time of death is vague, but it says here approximately 7:30 p.m." The clerk looked at the girls. "Did you know this guy?"

"No, we didn't. We…" Grace started.

Elena cleared her throat and interrupted her. "We know his sister. She sent us here. She's still too distraught over her brother's death."

"There are statements here from a Vivienne, the father, and a man named Drake. They're all brief and oddly similar," the clerk said. "You can take a look, but I can't give you much more time. I'm going to take a coffee break, and when I get back, you'll need to wrap this up. Deal?"

"Deal," the girls chorused. "Thank you!"

"This reads like it was written to close a file, not answer questions." Grace's eyes scanned the report.

"Look at this," Elena read. "No struggle marks, no defensive wounds, but also no clear signs he fought the water."

"So, either he went in already unconscious, or someone made sure he couldn't fight."

"Now this is interesting." Grace looked up at Elena. "The brother had a neurological condition common in linguistic savants that could cause sensory overload."

"Alcohol or sedatives were found in trace amounts, dismissed as 'incidental.'" Elena paused, thinking.

"Well, that could be anything," Grace said out loud.

Elena looked further down the page. "Here it says 'Chlorpromazine.' I have no idea what that is."

"It's Thorazine," a voice answered from behind them. The clerk had overheard Elena's question. "It was first available in the early 1950s and was widely credited as the first effective antipsychotic."

"Oh wow, thank you," Grace said.

"I'm studying pharmacology here at USC," the clerk added with a smile.

"The coroner was pressured to release results early due to media attention," Elena read from the notes in the sidebar. "These levels wouldn't kill him, but they'd slow him down."

"Enough that falling into water would be fatal." Grace looked Elena in the eyes.

"Or enough that someone else thought it would be," Elena said quietly. "There's a police report here as well."

"That's not unusual if it's a high-profile case," the clerk said from across the room.

Elena read the information out loud. "The police stated that the pool tiles are slicker than regulation. Lighting near the deep end was poor. There was a decorative ledge that could trip someone entering the pool."

"This isn't a pool. It's a stage," Grace suggested. "And stages are built for appearances, not safety."

"If he didn't swim well, this place would be a nightmare," the clerk added, her interest growing.

"According to these interview notes, the brother avoided the pool and disliked loud gatherings. Vivienne's father often drank near the pool late at night. Drake, the butler, was fiercely protective but secretive."

"In this statement, Vivienne was picked up for her movie premiere at 7:15 p.m. Drake confirmed this."

"So, Vivienne was picked up around the same time her brother was dying?" Grace questioned.

The clerk's curiosity sharpened. She walked over slowly, coffee in hand. "You know, forensic time of death can vary significantly. Often a range is given. Now, you're talking about the 1950s, which by today's standards were rather primitive." She took a sip of coffee. "There could easily be a thirty-minute window of uncertainty, especially if the death occurred in a pool, in the summer, or with other environmental factors involved."

The girls exchanged a glance. They had found the right person to add insight to their investigation.

"Then that gives us about a seventeen- to twenty-minute window," Elena said quietly.

"Seventeen minutes is a lifetime." Grace looked back at the computer screen.

"Long enough to make a death look like an accident," Elena suggested.

Grace took a deep breath. "Or long enough for someone to panic."

"Can I ask you... what is that little icon on the bottom of the page?" Elena pointed to a circular cog wheel at the bottom of the computer notes.

"They are attached notes. Usually filed later. Click on it," the clerk suggested.

"It's a file on Jefferies' therapist." Elena quickly read through the highlights. "Most information could not be disclosed due to patient-physician privilege."

"HIPPA laws?" Grace asked.

"No HIPPA laws in the 1950s," the clerk said, shaking her head. "More of a physician's choice was the norm."

"Well, his therapist suggested Jefferies processed language brilliantly but struggled with social cues. He trusted authority figures instinctively, but when he was confronted with moral choices that went against authority, he would tend to side with the moral choice. In a violent manner," Elena read carefully. "He claimed that he was afraid of disappointing his sister Vivienne."

"Look at this." Grace pointed to the screen. "This says that Jefferies was grappling with a conflict that seemed to consume his days prior to his death." Grace looked up, her eyes widening. "He didn't tell the therapist what the conflict was, but it seemed to involve his sister and someone she was with at the time."

"What? A lover, a coworker, a friend?" the clerk blurted out. She spun a chair around and sat in front of the computer screen. "Let me see that." She looked over the notes. "Wow." She seemed disappointed. "Not much to go on."

"I guess that is why they ruled the case an accidental drowning." Elena shook her head.

"You mean he died outside of the pool, and then somehow he was found in the pool?" Grace asked, a perplexed look crossing her face.

"Correct," the clerk concurred. "Or he fell in the pool, panicked, and spasmed."

"Why would the police let something like this slide through the cracks?" Grace felt a shiver rise through her again.

"Hollywood, doll," Elena stated, matter-of-fact. "High-profile case, rising star's reputations on the line, a famous studio behind it all? It screams cover-up to me."

"I have to agree," the woman added as a ping drew her attention to her phone. "Listen, ladies… my boss just texted me. She's on her way. Which means…"

"I know. We have to skedaddle!" Grace made a motion with both hands. "Okay, we're out of here. And if you want these fabulous pink braids, I'd be happy to do them for you."

The woman smiled, sipping her coffee again and switching off the computer. "I just might take you up on that offer. Thank you," she said.

"No, thank you," Elena replied with a smile. "We're grateful for your help."

Chapter 9
Pacific Palisades

The Pacific Palisades were unnaturally still that morning. They unfolded like a whispered promise between the ocean and the hills. Gatherings of eucalyptus and palms swayed as if keeping time with the tide below. Here, the Pacific was never just scenery. It was a living presence, breathing cool salt air into every dawn. The cliffs rose with quiet confidence, their edges kissed by a low mist that softened the ocean into something painted rather than real. Crew members whispered instead of spoke, as if the air itself might carry secrets.

Aisha stood apart from the others, already in costume. Her wardrobe was immaculate, a cream trench coat, gloves buttoned tight, but her body was tense. She kept glancing toward the director's chair, still empty.

"I can't believe we're back to work," her hairdresser whispered.

Aisha mumbled to herself, low and distant, "Funny place to end a story."

"At least OSHA allowed us to finish the end of the film. Otherwise, this would have all been for nothing." The hairdresser drew a heavy brush through the back of Aisha's blond locks.

"It was only a matter of time before they straightened things out," Aisha assured her.

Ollie arrived next, adjusting his cufflinks with restless energy. He joked with a grip a little too loudly, his laugh echoing longer than it should. “Last scene, last dance. Guess that makes us survivors, eh?”

Lexi Vale stepped onto the set without a word. Her eyes tracked everything, Aisha, Ollie, the camera rigging, the edge of the cliff just beyond the lights. She stopped beside Aisha. “You ever notice how endings always pretend to be neat?”

Aisha didn’t answer.

Remi approached quietly, a script tucked under one arm. He looked tired, worn down even. His loyal assistant, Matt, followed behind, holding his boss’s coffee. Remi’s movements were precise but distracted, like he was following instructions only he could hear. He didn’t greet anyone. Instead, he walked straight to the edge of the set, staring out at the ocean for a long moment.

The assistant director cleared his throat. “We’re ready when you are.” The AD sent Remi a knowing look.

The director nodded, almost absently. “Yes. Let’s not linger today.” Remi had everyone’s attention. No one missed the phrasing. “Okay, here’s the triangle. The scene itself is simple on paper. Aisha’s character has solved everything. Ollie’s character stands exposed. Lexi’s character realizes she’s been used.”

“Okay, people, this is a rehearsal,” the AD called out.

Remi paused. “And action!”

Ollie missed his mark, just barely. Lexi’s line came out sharper than scripted. Aisha didn’t hold her final look as long as directed, her eyes steady and unblinking.

Remi didn’t call cut. He watched as if he were memorizing them. Finally, he spoke. “Good. Very good. Keep that distance.” He gestured not between the actors, but toward the space behind them, toward the cliff. "Some truths don't need witnesses," he whispered, just loud enough for the AD to hear.

Aisha felt a chill that had nothing to do with the fog.

During a lighting adjustment, Lexi found Aisha near the monitors. "He's off today."

Aisha didn't answer. Her thoughts were wrapped around questions she wanted to ask Mr. Keyes.

Ollie overheard Lexi's comment and forced a smile. "Relax. He always goes a bit funny at the end, isn't it? Endings make people come clean."

"Or careless," Aisha suggested. She suddenly spotted Mr. Keyes. He sat in his rigging high above her, looking out at the ocean. "Mr. Keyes, do you have a minute?" She looked up at him, her eyes wide.

"How could I resist that look," he responded as he lowered the rigging to meet her.

"We both worked for Clive Harrington," Aisha said with a smile.

"He directed you in a picture?" The surprise on his face was genuine.

"Yes, in Madrid. It was his last picture before he died."

"I could really say the same thing. I worked with him on *Velvet Ashes*. It was his last picture before his career died. He was fired about a month after the film wrapped." He hesitated, looking down. "Along with me."

"I don't understand," Aisha said, keeping her vulnerable expression.

"Harrington's difficulties began after a leadership transition at Paramount, where he reportedly had trouble adapting to the new studio regime."

"And what about you?" Aisha inquired.

"Well, for me, it was a slow death as an actor. I was dropped from the studio stable of rising stars. I had to do commercials and odd jobs to stay alive." He removed his hat. A sense of shame showed through his rigid exterior. "I witnessed something I did not want to be a part of. Once the higher-ups got wind of this, I was slowly squeezed out of my career."

"What did you witness?" Aisha pressed.

"I've blocked it from my memory for a reason," he said with a nod. "Let's just say I came out of it unscathed. I was able to join the union and still work in the industry years later, behind the scenes."

"Okay, chatterboxes, let's move," the cinematographer yelled. "I'd like to go home today." Tomás waved his megaphone as if it were a weapon.

"Tomás, you don't speak to a star like that," Mr. Keyes replied.

The cinematographer shot back quickly. "Today!"

"I'll be glad when this picture finishes, just so I don't have to deal with that one again." Mr. Keyes tossed his hat back onto his head and gave Aisha's arm a squeeze. "I'll see you at the wrap party," he said with a smile.

Aisha noticed Remi raising his hand.

"Before the last take, I'd like everyone to gather close." Remi's voice was calm, almost gentle. "When you walk away, Aisha, don't look back. Not even for a second. Mentally say to yourself, 'It's done.'"

She nodded, though the line wasn't in the script.

Remi's gaze moved between Lexi Vale, Ollie, and Aisha. "Some stories don't survive being watched." He stepped back, farther than necessary. "To my crew, I am grateful," he said, bowing his head.

The wind picked up. A gull cried overhead, sharp and sudden.

"Okay, people. This is not a rehearsal," the AD called out to the set. "This is for the money shot. Places!" He paused, waiting for everyone to reach their marks. "Rolling."

Remi raised his hand. "And… action."

Aisha delivered her final line and turned away. The camera followed her just as planned. But in the background, for just a second, Lexi noticed something. Remi was no longer by the monitor. No one called cut.

The ocean kept moving.

The scene ended exactly as written.

The wrap party was already being discussed.

Chapter 10
Hollywood Hills

Elena's hands tightened on the steering wheel as she wound through the narrow curves of Beachwood Canyon, muscle memory from countless drives in her early twenties guiding her through the steep switchbacks. City lights shimmered below, distant and glamorous, as if taunting her from a world she'd only momentarily left behind. The canyon walls rose around her, shadows rippling as she edged past gnarled oaks and whispering pines. Her pulse quickened, not from fear but from the familiar thrill of driving through the fabled neighborhood again.

Ahead, the canyon opened into a vantage point that spilled Los Angeles into a glittering panorama. Neon signs and sculpted rooftops stretched like a velvet map, the early evening glow illuminating every building, every star-studded street. Elena slowed, allowing herself a breath to take it in. The view felt electric beneath her skin, and for a moment she let the city's radiance settle into her bones, fueling her resolve.

She guided the car up the long, dark stretch of road, her headlights brushing over quiet homes and tall, shadowed palms. When she rounded a familiar curve, the Hollywood Sign appeared, glowing white against the black silhouette of the hills, a beacon suspended in the dark. The canyon seemed to hold its breath. Elena eased off the gas, letting the sight wash over her, the letters shining above like a quiet, luminous reminder of where she was and why she'd come.

Her sleek black SUV rounded the final bend of the winding road, and the home revealed itself like a shimmering mirage on the canyon's edge. Perched defiantly above a sheer drop, the structure wore a façade of floor-to-ceiling glass, polished concrete, and lightly stained steel, its horizontal roofline hovering like a wing against the starry sky.

A steep, elevated driveway arched like a gentle rampart through a private woodland, leading her closer. At the threshold, a dramatic pivoting glass wall opened, unveiling an entrance courtyard where sculptural curves cast intricate shadows across warm travertine. It felt like a transition from the wild hills of Hollywood into a curated gallery of modern luxury.

"Subtle," Elena mumbled to herself over the jazz music drifting melodically through her car radio.

Elena pulled her vehicle alongside a young man waving at her.

"Good evening," the man said with a bright smile. "Invitation?"

Caught off guard, Elena replied quickly. "It's still in the mail."

The man's smile turned into a grimace.

"Okay, okay," Elena said, rolling her eyes at the whole charade. "This is why I'm bored with Hollywood," she muttered under her breath as she pawed through her purse for the gaudy summons. She pulled it out and presented it with a grin.

"Wonderful," he said, his smile reappearing. "I can valet your car."

Elena gathered her purse and delicate shawl and stepped out of the vehicle.

"Wow," the young valet said. "You look amazing."

Elena answered with a gentle smile. Her suave peach gown swept to her ankles, soft fabric moving in time with the glimmer of her silver shoes as she ascended the winding sidewalk.

Inside, panoramic glazing in the open-planned living room framed Los Angeles like a living screen. Elena stepped onto the terrace, where a rim-flow infinity pool seemed to slice through the cityscape, its edge blending seamlessly into the sprawling valley of lights below. The pool's reflective surface mirrored the amber glow of downtown high-rises and the glittering ribbon of the Pacific highway, an endless sea of light.

"Champagne?" A waiter turned toward Elena, offering a long-stemmed glass alive with fervent bubbles.

Elena suddenly realized there were other people around her. "Oh, yes, sorry," she stuttered. "I was awestruck by my surroundings."

"You'll get used to it… real fast," the waiter assured her, handing over the champagne with a smirk.

"This is just what I imagined one of these wrap parties would be like." Debra slipped a gentle hand around Elena's waist.

"Including the view," Israel added, stepping in to greet her.

Elena turned toward him, looping her arm through his. The three friends embraced, laughing softly as they pulled apart.

"Look, there's Grace and Francy," Israel said, pointing across the room to where their two friends were chatting with a particularly attractive actor. "That guy looks familiar."

"Honey, they all look familiar to you," Debra teased.

The party was in full swing. Laughter echoed across polished marble floors, champagne flutes clinked beneath a mirrored ceiling, and ambient music pulsed from hidden speakers. Outside, delicate string lights snaked through manicured trees, casting warm halos over a cascading fountain and the silhouettes of celebrities drifting through the glow.

"Has anyone seen Aisha and Drew?" Debra asked.

The friends scanned the crowded party, searching for their teammates. "I think they got here early because Remi wanted a photo shoot with the cast beforehand."

"I'm fairly sure Drew drove Aisha here," Israel confirmed.

The music changed, and the space around them quickly filled with reveling partygoers eager to dance and celebrate the end of production. "Well, when in Rome…" Israel shouted over the deep bass as he broke into a dance.

But Drew and Aisha weren't mingling. They slipped away from the crowd and pushed open the double doors leading to Remi's private wing of the house. They moved through the dark hallways of the sprawling modern mansion, guided by a growing sense of curiosity.

"Remi insisted we be here an hour before the party for photographs," Aisha whispered to Drew.

"No one's seen him all evening?" Drew asked.

"He was at the photo shoot in the backyard very briefly, then left the party," Aisha confirmed.

"It's unusual for a man who thrives on being the center of attention." Drew slowed, staring at photos lining the wall. Each framed portrait showed Remi smiling beside one famous celebrity after another.

"Not sticking around after the photo shoot struck me as odd," Aisha said, unease creeping into her voice.

The home's cantilevered lounge, a glass box hovering like a private jet over the edge of the Hollywood Hills, offered a cinematic vantage point. Every inch was curated. Minimalist white furnishings clustered around a sculptural modern fireplace, and recessed walls allowed curtains of light to spill through. Drew looked around the lounge. He could almost feel the electric hum of the city glowing below, framed by slender olive trees and the steel-and-stone terrace jutting out into the void.

Ascending the floating staircase, they reached the master suite, a private retreat with its own glass wall and snug terrace. From here, the entire LA basin stretched outward, from the haze of downtown towers to the shimmering coastline and beyond to the Pacific horizon.

"This is breathtaking," Drew said, his words falling into the subtle, breezy warmth of the Hills whispering through the floor vents, tying them to the rarefied pulse of this modern perch.

"This is the house you'd expect the newest 'it' director to call home," Aisha agreed. "A bold architectural statement perched above the world, all curated elegance, screaming influence, and privacy on a cinematic scale."

"That's one way to put it," Drew said, casting her a glance.

"Remi," Aisha called out. "Where are you? Your guests are missing you," she added, hoping for a response. "Maybe he's passed out," she offered. "He's been under unbelievable amounts of stress."

"Or drunk, or stoned, or coked out of his mind," Drew added with a shrug.

"I know, I know. He has that reputation," Aisha said, shaking her head. "I bet he wanted a quiet moment with a cigar in his private study to celebrate his accomplishments," she added, trying to reassure Drew, though her voice carried a nervous edge.

They stood facing the closed study doors. Without hesitation, Aisha reached for the handle. "Should we go in?" she whispered to Drew. "Remi? Remi… it's Aisha."

Drew stepped beside her, testing the handle himself. He tilted his head, uneasy, unsure what he was sensing. The silence on the other side felt deliberate, almost watchful. Aisha pressed her ear to the door, listening past the pounding of her own heartbeat.

"Nothing. No movement. No voice," she said.

Without warning, she threw her shoulder against the door. On the second hard shove, it burst open, and she stumbled forward, calling out, "Remi, your guests are waiting!"

What they found inside stopped them cold.

The once-pristine study lay in shadow, the only illumination coming from a flickering desk lamp knocked sideways on the floor. Papers were scattered across the Persian rug like leaves in a storm. A shattered crystal decanter bled dark liquor across the floorboards, mingling with something far more sinister.

Remi Harrington was slumped in his Eames leather chair behind his mahogany desk, his head tilted at an unnatural angle, a dark red wound marking his throat. His eyes were frozen wide open, staring past them, past everything. Blood had run down his neck, pooling beneath his collar and soaking into his crisp white dress shirt in a spreading bloom of red. One hand still clutched a Cuban cigar, burned down to ash between his fingers.

To their left, the floor-to-ceiling window shades were drawn shut, hiding the glitter of the city, beautiful, detached, indifferent.

Aisha gasped, her hands flying to her mouth. "Oh my God… Remi…"

Drew stared at the scene before them. The first time he'd seen a body, he'd nearly vomited. The second time, he'd stared until tears blurred his vision. Now, his face remained calm. Inside, though, alarm bells wailed, and only he knew how to quiet them.

Death felt like binary data now, not a life. Each time, the shock faded faster, the detachment tightening. He'd learned to compartmentalize, to ration his humanity. That sense of immunity felt both protective and confining. He knew he should feel something, but each new death pulled him farther from his emotional center, luring him into an abyss of professional stability. He told himself it was what kept him alive, what kept the city alive. But in quieter moments, he wondered at what cost.

Aisha broke his train of thought. "This wasn't a simple killing. This was theatrical. Personal. A message." Her bottom lip trembled, and the rest of her followed, adrenaline racing through her body.

Drew noticed the tears welling in her eyes. He was already moving, his gaze scanning the room. No signs of forced entry. But there was a smear of blood on the doorknob and a footprint near the liquor cabinet, a heel mark as if someone had slipped or been dragged.

Drew moved farther into the room, his polished shoes whispering against the Persian rug. Aisha stood at the aged desk, its surface littered with leather-bound volumes and a toppled award from the Director's Guild. A letter opener lay beside an envelope. An open screenplay rested on the desk, Remi's own. The title page was smudged with blood. One page had been torn, deliberately and violently. A line of dialogue was underlined in red ink:

"You'll never kill the story, but this is your final tango."

"Final Tango. That's the name of our film," Aisha muttered.

Drew looked at her. Her face had gone pale. This wasn't just her director. This was her mentor, maybe even her secret. And now it was her mystery to unravel.

"Remi wrote the screenplay. The killer underlined the words in the story. That can't be random," Aisha said, her voice shaking. "The killer knew this story. That was my line."

A gasp from the study door made them both turn. Grace stood in the doorway, trying to stifle her reaction. Debra pushed the door open farther.

“Another body?” Debra murmured. Her hand lingered on the door a moment longer before she squared her shoulders and stepped inside.

“Drew, Aisha, are you alright?” Francy asked as she and Israel followed close behind.

“We’re alright,” Drew said quietly. “Remi, not so much.”

Francy put an arm around Aisha. Israel moved closer to Drew and whispered in a low voice, “Anything? Knife, shell casings, footprints?”

Drew glanced at him, then motioned toward the slash across the victim’s throat. “A couple of smudged prints here. Looks like they came up behind him with a knife. See this? The angle suggests they were right-handed.”

“Where’s Elena?” Aisha called out.

“Elena’s calling 911. The police should be here soon,” Grace confirmed.

“We all came up here looking for you two,” Francy began.

“I had a sense of dread,” Debra confessed.

“How unusual,” Aisha quipped, trying to push back the stress creeping up the back of her neck.

“There appears to be only one way into this room, and it’s through the doors we’re standing in,” Drew observed.

“The killer must’ve been hiding in here before Remi came in,” Aisha said, following his logic. “There doesn’t seem to have been a struggle. Just an immediate attack.”

Grace moved quietly behind the desk, her gaze carefully avoiding the lifeless figure slumped in the chair. She forced her voice steady as she pieced it together. "Remi was at his desk, enjoying a cigar and going over a script, and then an unseen assailant emerged from behind and slit his throat?" she said, drawing the conclusion aloud.

"Yes, it appears that way," Drew agreed. He paused for a moment, recalling the story Remi had once shared about how he and his father discovered the antique desk. He remembered the way Remi's eyes lit up as he described his father's excitement after stumbling across it in a small, dusty shop tucked away in the Valley. An unexpected find.

Israel turned to look behind him. "Maybe the killer was hiding in there?" he said, pointing toward the wall.

"That's a wall," Francy observed from the front of the room.

But from his angle, Israel noticed something. He glanced around the desk, reached for a tissue from an ornate box, and moved behind the chair. Drew watched as Israel pressed the tissue against the wall. Then Drew saw it too. Israel pushed against an unassuming seam running from ceiling to floor. The closet door clicked and eased open.

"Ah, what a brilliant design," Aisha remarked, stepping forward to examine the recessed structure, careful not to brush her white floral dress against anything.

Drew looked closer. The director's closet resembled a private atelier, every detail whispering quiet prestige and purposeful elegance. Impeccably tailored suits hung from elegant lined hangers, their sharp lines commanding attention. Along the back wall, polished leather shoes stood aligned like prized artifacts, each pair gleaming under soft accent lighting. On a sleek surface rested a meticulously arranged tray of rings and fine watches, timeless pieces displayed with curator-like care. Beside it, built-in drawers concealed additional layers of sartorial armor, offering order and discretion to the wardrobe's core.

"I think we can rule out robbery as a motive," Drew said, turning to his friends with a note of sarcasm.

"There must be some kind of trigger on the floor to open the door from the inside," Francy said, studying the closet and finding no handles on either side.

Israel bent down and spotted a small foot pedal aligned with the edge of the door, a concealed mechanism that released it from the inside.

"That's it," Grace called out.

"So, the killer entered the room before Remi and hid in the closet," Drew said, thinking aloud. "But he was blind. He couldn't see what Remi was doing from behind that door. How would he know when to strike?"

Israel stepped into the closet. "Drew, close the door," he instructed.

Careful not to leave prints, Drew copied Israel's earlier move and grabbed a tissue from the box. He pressed the door shut until he heard a soft click. From inside, he could hear Israel shifting around.

"Absolutely no vantage point to the outside," Israel called back. He stepped on the trigger, and the door quietly released open again. "No way to see anything from in there."

"Maybe he had a verbal cue from outside," Debra suggested.

"You mean someone came into the room to distract him, or made a noise from outside?" Francy asked.

"That's possible," Drew said, following the thought. "If Remi heard someone at the door, or was distracted by someone entering, that could've been the cue for the killer to step out and attack."

"There's half a shoe print above the release on the inside of this door," Israel called out.

Suddenly, red and blue strobes flashed across the hillside, slicing through the stillness of the Hollywood night. The sound of police sirens cut through the quiet of the study.

“They’re here,” Grace said, jumping slightly.

Drew reacted instantly, looking around before rattling off instructions in rapid succession. “Alright, everyone downstairs. I don’t want them thinking we were up here sleuthing around.” He wiped the sweat from his brow. “Aisha and I will stay up here and meet the police.”

The once-vibrant party had dissolved into hushed whispers and confused, frozen guests huddled in small groups from the pool terrace to the limousine circle outside. Security officers stood guard, holding everyone back. Somewhere in the mansion, the DJ had finally shut off the music.

Drew stood near the study door, jaw clenched, arms folded, watching. Observing. Calculating. He’d done this before.

Aisha sat on a velvet chaise in the corner, wrapped in a throw blanket someone had given her. Her eyes were glassy, her fingers trembling around a half-empty water bottle. The glamour of the night had been stripped away, leaving only a woman in shock, smeared mascara, and a haunted gaze.

Detective Jena Singh, a commanding woman in her thirties, breached the top of the steps. Her lean, athletic build and sharp, calculating dark eyes immediately hinted at her South Asian American roots. She carried herself with practiced authority, dressed in a sleek white blouse, leather jacket, and a well-worn detective’s badge clipped to her belt loop.

“Detective Singh,” she announced kindly. “Did you folks find the body?”

“We did,” Drew said. “I’m Drew.”

"Are you both in this movie?" the detective asked. Her warm but no-nonsense approach revealed an empathetic edge.

"Just me," Aisha said, rising from the chaise, still shivering with adrenaline. "I'm Aisha."

"You two found the body?"

Drew nodded. "We were looking for him. He hadn't come out to the party. The door wasn't locked," he explained. "We came in and… saw that."

Detective Singh scribbled something in a leather-bound notebook she'd pulled from her jacket pocket, then turned to Aisha.

"Aisha, you're the lead actress on this upcoming film?"

Aisha nodded slowly. "We just wrapped shooting two weeks ago."

"And your relationship with Remi Harrington?" the detective asked.

She hesitated. Drew noticed.

"Professional," Aisha replied.

Detective Singh raised an eyebrow. "Only professional?"

Drew stepped forward. "Hey, she just found her friend dead. Maybe dial it down a little."

Detective Singh ignored him. "Did you touch anything?"

"We didn't," Drew assured her.

Inside the study, two LAPD officers had taped off the room. The forensic team moved in. Flash cameras fired like lightning, gloved hands dusted for prints, and plastic evidence bags crinkled with every new discovery. A white sheet had been pulled over Remi's body, but blood still seeped beneath it.

Detective Singh turned as a young officer approached, holding two evidence bags.

"Found this tucked into the chair behind the body," the officer said, handing one to her. She avoided looking directly at Aisha.

Inside the bag was a Polaroid of Aisha. Candid. She was sitting in a director's chair on set, laughing. Scrawled across the bottom in red ink were the words: *The star always falls the hardest.*

Aisha recoiled. "What? That wasn't… I've never seen that photo before. What does that mean?"

Singh's eyes sharpened as she studied Aisha's reaction. Then she lifted the second evidence bag. An earring glittered beneath the plastic.

"Aisha, can you explain why your earring, this exact gold hoop, was found beneath the desk near the blood spatter? It matches the one you're wearing now."

Aisha reached for the gold hoop in her ear. She stared at the other one, stunned. "I… this is mine. I wore them tonight. But I lost one earlier. I thought it fell off in the bathroom. I don't know how it got in here."

Drew shot her a look. "You sure you weren't in here earlier? Even for a second?" Detective Singh asked.

She shook her head firmly. "No. I swear."

Singh jotted something down, then leveled her gaze at both of them. "Neither of you is leaving this house."

She turned to the forensic team. "Check all security cameras. I want timestamps. And pull phone records from that phone," she said, pointing to the landline on Remi's desk.

"And who were those five people I saw coming down the steps when I got here? Your friends?" she asked Drew.

"They came looking for us. They were concerned when they couldn't find us. That's what they do. We're a team." Drew smiled, careful not to give away too much.

"Did they touch anything?" Detective Singh interrupted.

"No."

"We're going to have to question all of them," Detective Singh said, turning to a nearby officer as she walked away. "Why don't you both wait downstairs," she added, pointing without looking back.

Drew moved closer to Aisha, his voice low. "Someone's setting you up."

Aisha looked at him, her voice barely above a whisper. "Then they knew I'd come looking for him. Tonight. Here."

They exchanged a look.

"Whoever killed Remi didn't just want him dead. They wanted you framed."

"We'll see you downstairs," Detective Singh called back.

The once-vibrant mansion was now in lockdown.

The music was long gone. The bar was closed. Cast members sat in scattered clusters, still in their designer suits and glittering gowns, murmuring anxiously or texting their publicists. Outside, paparazzi had already begun circling like vultures at the gate. These wolves scented blood.

"How do they find out so fast?" Debra mused.

"They pay," Elena answered.

Drew blended into the scene like a chameleon, weaving through the room with the easy gait of a man who knew how to listen without speaking. His eyes scanned, cataloged, measured. It was his gift. Every guest was a suspect now.

He stopped near a group huddled by the grand piano. Aisha stepped up beside him, quietly identifying each guest.

"Tomás Rivas, the moody cinematographer with a history of fights on set. He never had a nice thing to say to me," she said.

Drew looked up. "And her?" he asked, nodding toward a woman nearby. "Wait a minute. That was our class instructor at the gym," he added, suddenly recognizing her.

"Lexi Vale, a dancer-turned-actress with a suspiciously fast-rising career, and rumors she'd been sleeping with Remi."

Drew rolled his eyes. "And the guy in the suit?"

"Blake Derrow, a bitter screenwriter with two ex-wives and a vendetta against Remi for shelving his last script. He worked as a consultant on our film." Aisha winked. "Okay, I'll leave you to it," she murmured, walking in the opposite direction.

Drew took a breath and eased beside Blake Derrow with a casual smile. "Rough night."

"Worse for Remi, I'd say." The bitter tone rolled off his lips like a viper's hiss, curling through the air with venom in every syllable.

"You and he didn't exactly part ways on good terms, right?"

Blake looked up sharply, eyes narrowing. "What are you implying?"

Drew smiled faintly. "Just curious."

"Did my ex-wife send you?" Blake slurred.

"Which one?" Drew shot back.

"Hey, you're Aisha's friend. I've seen you on set with her. Did she put you up to this?" Blake turned his back and walked away.

From the hallway, Drew heard a voice call out, "We've got something." He followed it.

Detective Singh and a technician were hunched over a monitor as a grainy black-and-white camera feed played footage from just two hours earlier. The timestamp read 9:50 p.m.

The hallway outside the study filled the screen. In the footage, Remi stepped into the room alone. Five minutes passed. Then another figure entered. Tall. Blond. Feminine. Her face was obscured by the camera angle and dim lighting.

Detective Singh paused the footage. "Is that her?"

Drew pressed himself against the door frame, his shoulder grazing the wood as he leaned in. He could hear his own breath, each shallow inhale threatening to betray him. Through the thin barrier, voices carried from the other side, words he wasn't meant to hear, pulled into the hush by the door's subtle resonance.

"Keep watching," the technician said. He sped up the recording, another ten minutes passing in seconds. "The woman leaves, but something's different."

"She's wearing a red shawl," Detective Singh said quickly.

Drew realized immediately it was the deep crimson covering Aisha had worn earlier in the night, before she'd noticed it was missing. The kind of bold, memorable color anyone could associate with her in a crowd.

Detective Singh turned to the technician. "Zoom in on her hands."

The technician enhanced the frame. On her left hand was a ring, large and distinctive, a chunky emerald stone set in gold.

Singh nodded. "That's not just a fashion statement. That's a lead."

"Keep watching," the technician urged.

Suddenly, the image vanished. Static snow filled the screen.

"What happened?" Detective Singh said sharply. "Looks like the feed was cut!"

Chapter 11
Atop The L.A. Skyline

The glass house clung to the hillside, all sharp angles and transparency, its walls revealing more than they concealed. Blue and red strobe lights flashed silently across the hills.

Drew moved immediately. He had heard enough from the conversation at the door and quickly returned to Aisha, who sat apart from the others, trying not to unravel. He leaned close, lowering his voice. "Detective Singh just reviewed surveillance footage from outside the crime scene. A blond woman went into the study to talk to Remi around 9:50 p.m. When she came out, she was wearing your shawl. The only clear detail was a chunky emerald ring on her left hand."

Aisha looked up, startled. "Then… they were trying to 'be me?'"

Drew nodded. "That seems to be the plan. Make it look like you were the last person seen with Remi alive." His gaze flicked toward the other cast members. "But then the feed cut out. No more footage. Someone must have disabled the security system."

Israel and Francy crossed over to them. "Sorry, Aisha, the officer was asking us a lot of questions," Israel said, slipping an arm around her.

"You're shivering," Francy said, taking Aisha's hand.

"Just the adrenaline," Aisha replied, her eyes blank.

Drew leaned in closer. “We think someone is trying to frame Aisha for Remi’s murder,” he whispered, filling them in on the detective’s insinuations.

“Aisha, who do you think would do this? What would their reasons be?” Israel asked, looking at her, perplexed.

Aisha only shrugged. Then she took a long inhale and began piecing things together. “I left my shawl behind the bar with the bartender. I looked around for Remi, then made a trip to the powder room. I think I lost my hoop earring in there.”

Drew and Israel exchanged a glance. “Francy, can you track down the bartender?”

She scanned the room, searching the crowd, most of whom were still waiting to be questioned by the police. “I’ll check it out.”

“Here’s Grace,” Drew said, motioning for her to join them.

“The officer asked me the stupidest questions,” Grace said as she joined her friends. She tossed her pink braids over her shoulder and smoothed her flowing party dress before sitting beside Aisha.

“Watch her,” Drew told Grace, signaling for her to stay with Aisha.

Grace nodded as Drew and Israel turned and headed toward the patio. The lights glowed low against the Hollywood skyline. The guests, fewer now and more restless, stood scattered with drinks in hand, some whispering, some crying, all waiting for permission to leave. The glamour had faded into tension and silent calculation. Everyone wondered who the police would question next, or worse, arrest for Remi’s murder.

Drew and Israel stepped onto the patio, their presence quiet but purposeful. “We’re not looking for guilt. We’re looking for a ring. Big emerald stone, gold setting. Something you’d wear to be noticed. Left hand.”

Israel nodded, scanning the crowd. They split up.

☆☆☆

Aisha fidgeted in her chair. "Come on, Grace, I can't sit here any longer."

The girls made their way back toward the expansive living room. Aisha spotted Lexi Vale in a shimmery white backless gown emblazoned with flowers. She sat on a chaise with a glass of rosé, her phone clutched like armor.

"Lexi. Hey." Aisha smiled and sat beside her. Grace hovered nearby like a bodyguard. Lexi looked up, instantly suspicious.

"Oh. Aisha. This is… tragic." Lexi tilted her head forward, drawing her long blond hair to one side and stroking it like a security blanket.

"You worked with Remi before, didn't you?" Aisha asked.

Lexi smiled thinly. "Yes. I was in his Sundance film. I had a more substantial role in that one. I auditioned for this film, for your role, actually. But Remi said I had 'presence but no power.' What a gentleman. My chakras were just off that day."

"So that's why you teach cardio classes at the gym?" Grace said.

"And model, and maintain a large social media presence," Lexi replied without missing a beat. "It's my karmic duty."

Aisha glanced at Lexi's hands. Empty. No rings. But a jewelry case stuck halfway out of her purse. She took in the white floral dress, the style that seemed to be everywhere in Hollywood this season. "Have you seen my red shawl by any chance?"

Before Aisha could press further, Lexi tossed out a barb.

"But are you okay though? You were close to Remi, weren't you? Like… close-close?" A faint edge of sarcasm curled at her lips.

Aisha didn't answer. Lexi stood and walked away.

"You were… close-close to your director?" Grace asked, her right eyebrow lifting.

"Don't mind her," a voice whispered behind Aisha. She recognized the accent immediately.

"Ollie." Aisha turned to her co-star. "Where have you been?"

"She's right jealous of you, you know," Ollie said, taking Aisha by the arm and placing both hands on her shoulders. "Don't let her dig those heels into ya, that chippy."

"Oh, that chippy… doesn't bother me." Aisha gave him a half smile. "Grace, this is my co-star, Ollie."

Grace offered a flirty smile to the British heartthrob.

"Come on, Grace. I want to talk with Remi's assistant, Matt." Aisha glanced toward the balcony. He stood there, gaze fixed on the view, listening more than he let on. "Matt Valen works as Remi's personal assistant."

"Worked," Grace corrected. She just had to say it.

Matt was lean, slightly underfed, and of average height, with narrow features and tired hazel eyes that missed nothing. His short brown hair and muted, practical wardrobe helped him blend into the background, exactly where he had learned to survive.

"Matt always moves quietly, organized to a fault, always one step ahead of Remi's needs," Aisha whispered to Grace. She could sense his wounded soul even from a distance.

"Aisha," he said, turning toward her. "What are we going to do?"

Outwardly, Matt was soft-spoken, calm, and endlessly reliable. He handled the chaos around Remi with a serene professionalism that made him seem almost invisible. "The press is going to have a field day." He took a deep inhale, then released it slowly. He rarely complained and never sought attention, giving the impression of someone fully dedicated to supporting a genius.

“I’m so sorry for your loss. I know you’ve been with him from the start.” Aisha reached for his outstretched hand and held it tight.

“Oh my God, this means I have to find a new job.” Fear transformed his face. He ran his fingers through his hair. “Aisha, what am I going to do?”

“First, you’re going to breathe. Keep doing that. Deep breaths. You’re in shock.”

“Shock?” Matt replied. “I’m angry, sad, pissed off, confused. Who could have done this?”

Aisha remembered that Matt had grown up in a home where perfection was mandatory and praise was rare, shaping him into someone who equated worth with usefulness. “We’re going to learn the truth,” she replied softly.

“He could be a real pain, but he was all I knew.” Matt collapsed into the chair beside them, shaking from the sudden weight of it all.

Grace watched their interaction quietly. Something about the people in L.A. confused her. They smiled easily, spoke smoothly, said all the right things, yet she couldn’t tell where the truth ended and the performance began. Maybe it was her. Maybe she was overthinking it. Still, the feeling lingered, a quiet sense that everyone was playing a part she hadn’t been given the script for.

☆☆☆

Drew neared the fire pit, where one of the producers, Georgia Lynn, paced back and forth. She was drinking something brown and strong. Her nervous pacing was punctuated by an eye twitch that flared intermittently as she walked. She kept checking her watch.

She appeared to be a woman of Asian descent, likely in her mid to late fifties, with a slender build and a height very similar to Aisha's. Her hair was bleached blond, almost icy. Her features reflected her heritage, high cheekbones, an angular jawline, and slightly almond-shaped dark eyes. In contrast to her pale hair, her eyebrows were noticeably darker. She wore a white floral summer dress similar to Aisha's.

She looked up and recognized Drew.

"You're Aisha's friend," she said matter-of-factly.

Drew nodded. "What happened to your big, bold, beautiful ring?" he asked, cutting into her thoughts, fishing for a reaction.

She froze. She looked down at her right hand, where a thin silver band rested, then laughed tightly. "What ring?"

"Oh. Thought I saw something earlier. Emerald stone. Gold band. Looked vintage."

"Not mine," she replied sharply.

Drew held her gaze. She shifted uncomfortably.

"I'm sorry about Remi," he said.

"I need a cigarette. Harvey is going to be hysterical." She hurried off.

Drew watched her go, eyes narrowing.

Aisha made her way to the back of the house and stepped into the guest powder room. She shut the door behind her, breathing hard.

She pulled out her phone and opened the photos from earlier that night, the photo shoot taken at the beginning of the party. She zoomed in and scanned the faces. There was Remi, right in the center.

Her fingers moved closer, searching the details, lingering on hands and jewelry.

"There."

On Lexi Vale's left hand sat a large emerald ring. The same hand that had been conveniently empty now.

Aisha's stomach dropped. Realization slammed into her, followed by a sharp rush of fear.

☆☆☆

A forensic technician Elena remembered seeing earlier passed by and motioned to her. "Detective Singh is ready to speak with you now," he murmured. Without further explanation, he guided her up the dimly lit staircase and ushered her to a quiet landing just outside Remi's study. She settled into a chair in the shadowed hallway.

The technician slowly opened the study door wider as Elena leaned forward to catch a glimpse inside, her breath catching between anticipation and hesitation.

The forensics team was still examining the room. Detective Singh stood in the doorway of the closet behind the desk. They had found the secret door. Elena leaned farther forward, watching the detective sweep a flashlight across the area behind the desk. Her meticulous movements reminded Elena of herself. From the detective's body language alone, Elena could tell something didn't sit right.

"Wait here. She'll be right out." The technician stuck his head out of the study, then partially closed the door behind him.

Elena listened closely.

"Detective, we ran the partial shoe print we found by the liquor cabinet and inside of the closet door through our database."

"Let me guess. No matches in the system," the detective replied.

"Not even close. It's a size twelve men's boot. Lug sole. Expensive, the kind worn for fashion, not hiking."

"So, she wasn't alone in this room. Or whoever was wearing the shawl had help." Detective Singh walked toward the broken decanter on the floor and crouched down.

"Also… the blood on the side of the desk? It's not from the throat wound," the forensic technician said. "The blood types are different."

Singh looked up. "Say that again?"

"It's smeared, like someone gripped the desk with a bloody hand. But the angle's too low for Remi. Looks like someone crouched or knelt there and bled. Maybe cut themselves. The blood on the doorknob matches the blood on the desk. We've got a sample. We're running it now."

Elena rose slowly, careful not to draw attention. She had heard enough. A profile was forming; she could feel it. Quietly, she slipped back downstairs to inform her friends.

Detective Singh turned toward the closed window in the study. She lifted the rigid, floor-to-ceiling curtain and pushed the window open from the inside, leaning out slightly. No signs of tampering. But below, a balcony railing jutted outward, close enough to reach.

"That looks easy to jump to, or from, doesn't it?" she asked the technician.

"We've got a second person," Detective Singh said, still staring into the darkness. "Male. Injured. Expensive shoes. And smart enough to avoid every camera."

Drew found Aisha leaving the powder room. She stood near a wall of abstract paintings, trying to steady her breathing. Drew noticed how pale she looked. "Are you okay?"

"Lexi Vale had the ring. I saw it in the pre-party photos. She's hiding it now."

Elena came up behind them. She nodded subtly toward the top of the stairs, where Detective Singh was speaking in hushed tones to another officer. "They found a man's footprint in the study. Size 12, designer boot tread. And blood that didn't match Remi." Elena did all she could to steady her breathing.

"Lexi's not working alone," Drew told her. "Did she have your shawl on in the pictures?"

Aisha shook her head. Her eyes widened. "So, this was coordinated. Someone staged this to lure Remi into his study and kill him. There was someone to play 'me' and someone to finish the job."

"I think we should withhold this information about Lexi until we know more," Drew whispered to his friends. He glanced over his shoulder at Detective Singh, who was questioning Israel. "She doesn't know who we are, and as far as she's concerned, we're possible suspects."

The two girls nodded in agreement.

"By the way, I ran into one of the film's producers, Georgia Lynn. She seemed nervous, and she said to me, 'Harvey is going to be hysterical.' Who's Harvey?" Drew asked Aisha.

Aisha shook her head. "Harvey Goldstein is the head of the studio. He's the one who green-lit this picture. I can't believe he doesn't know what's going on. He has his ear to the ground in Hollywood."

"I would imagine he does," Elena agreed.

They scanned the room again. Guests were being allowed to leave one by one after interviews and bag checks. Lexi was still there. They noticed Francy walking through the living room, a partial smile on her face.

"Okay, I was talking with the bartender." She pulled her brunette hair up and wrapped it with an elastic band. "He remembers collecting Aisha's shawl and tucking it away in a corner beneath the bar. But then Remi stopped by for a cognac, saw the shawl, and took it upstairs with him."

"Either he recognized it as Aisha's shawl, or he didn't want any clutter under the bar," Elena suggested.

Drew turned and saw Detective Singh coming their way. She cleared her throat and curled a finger in Elena's direction. "Looks like you're up, girl," Drew reassured her. "We'll be out on the terrace." He grabbed Aisha and Francy by the arm and escorted them outside.

The trio made their way onto the terrace. The crowd had dwindled to just a handful of partygoers still waiting to be interviewed.

Drew spotted Mr. Keyes sitting alone, a beer in his hand. A distraught look was etched across his face, as though he had seen Hollywood at its worst more times than he cared to remember.

Aisha quickly noticed Tomás Rivas, the brooding cinematographer with callused hands and a makeshift bandage on his palm. He was nursing a drink with his left hand; his right wrapped in a bar napkin.

Drew noticed it too, casting a long glance in his direction. "Aisha, let's talk to Tomás. Francy, hang back and observe his behavior."

"Will do," she answered, staring out over the railing, mesmerized by the glittering glow of Los Angeles below.

They found Tomás alone, leaning against the glass railing, trying to smoke a clove cigarette with one hand while struggling with the bar napkin wrapped around the other.

"Rough night." Drew approached slowly.

Tomás responded without looking. "You can say that again." He took another long drag from his cigarette and turned to see who he was speaking to. When he saw Aisha, his expression shifted. He avoided her gaze and turned back to Drew.

"You're impeccably dressed in that dark blue three-piece suit and brown Oxford shoes. I love your look," Drew said. "Is your hand all right?"

Tomás flicked ash from the tip of his cigarette, ignoring the compliment. "Cut myself earlier. Champagne glass in the kitchen. Are you a doctor?" he asked, hesitating.

"No," Drew replied with a half-smile.

"Perhaps a lawyer then?" A glint of hope entered Tomás's voice. "Remi owed me money," he said darkly. "Now I guess I'll never get that back." He slowly turned to Aisha. "And it's your fault."

"My fault?" Aisha said, shock in her voice.

"He was always trying to impress you. Your first day on set, he insisted on bringing you flowers. Do you remember that?"

"Of course I do," Aisha said. "I walked into my dressing room and it was filled with flowers." She smiled at the memory, at how it had made her feel. "From wall to wall."

"Well, he didn't have the money for that impulse buy, so Remi came to me to pay for it. And of course, being the fool that I am, I gave him $1,500 to fill your dressing room with the most fragrant flowers he could find."

Now, with the memory tarnished by the man's words, all Aisha could do was bow her head humbly.

Tomás turned, dropped the remnant of his cigarette, crushed it against the pavement, and walked back into the house, smoke trailing behind him like a veil.

Aisha exhaled. “That was revealing.”

Drew watched the fading ember of Tomás’s cigarette burn out on the stone floor.

Israel spun around to face Aisha and Drew, confusion written across his face. “Guys, Detective Singh just talked to me. She said they were looking at all the men’s shoes. She said ‘boots,’ actually, and they’re checking belongings too. I only told them I had my wallet. Then she wanted to know our relationship.”

“And?” Aisha asked, her voice tense.

“I said we were longtime dance partners,” Israel replied with a shrug. “She wanted to know why we were there and why we’d been upstairs near the crime scene.”

“And?” Aisha pressed, unable to conceal her unease.

“I told her we were looking for you,” Israel said, matching her urgency. “That was our reason for being there.”

“Aisha!” a voice called from behind her.

She turned to see her producer, Georgia Lynn, striding toward her, concern etched across her face.

“What did the police say?” Georgia asked urgently. “Did they tell you anything else about Remi? Do they know who killed him?”

Aisha closed her eyes, her chest tightening as the questions pressed in from every side. Her thoughts raced, colliding, leaving her momentarily speechless. She couldn’t summon the strength to respond.

“They said I was free to go,” Georgia Lynn continued, lowering her voice. “But the detective will be at the office tomorrow to follow up with Harvey.” She hesitated, then added, “Harvey wants you there as well.”

“Why?” Aisha asked, the word escaping in a breathless gasp.

"He has a new script," Georgia said. "Another film he wants you to read for."

The world seemed to tilt beneath Aisha's feet. In that moment, she felt as though she were trapped on a runaway train, moving too fast with no clear way to stop.

"Here comes that detective," Georgia whispered, gathering herself as she kept walking.

Drew and Israel turned to see Detective Singh and a police officer approaching.

"How are you three getting along?" the detective asked, her gaze dropping to Drew's shoes.

"Did Aisha's red shawl turn up?" Drew inquired.

"I thought you had it, Aisha," Detective Singh said.

Aisha took a breath, then smiled. "No, Detective. And I don't have a certain ring that's been discussed either. But I knew who had it at the beginning of the night."

"Yes, we know Lexi Vale owns the ring, but she said she lost track of it during the night. It seems like an awful lot of props were passed around during these events." Detective Singh flipped through her notebook, reviewing a list of items she had written down. "So why were you and your friends questioning the guests?" She waited for an answer. "Several people we interviewed said you were asking inappropriate questions."

Drew offered a faint, apologetic smile. "Inappropriate might be a stretch." Israel and Aisha smiled along with him, as if on cue. "We're in Los Angeles supporting our friend. Aisha is in the middle of this situation. When something happens to one of our friends, we instinctively try to understand what happened and who's involved. I suppose curiosity got the better of us."

"I want answers too," Aisha said, nodding. "Remi was my friend and my director. It was my first picture in Hollywood with him. I owe him a lot. So yes, I've been asking questions."

"I'm sure you understand that," Israel added.

Detective Singh raised her chin, pressing her lips together. She handed each of them her card. "When something comes up, and I know it will, give me a call or text."

Detective Singh studied Drew for a moment longer than necessary, her expression unreadable. Then she closed her notebook with a soft, deliberate snap and slipped it into her coat. "I think I have enough for now," she said. "Enjoy the rest of your evening."

She turned and adjusted her jacket. "And by the way," she said evenly, "I'll be pursuing another theory."

She paused at the door and added, without turning back,

"One that has nothing to do with the guests."

Chapter 12

Sunset Plaza

Harvey Goldstein's office was a monument to control.

The president of Paramount Studios kept it pristine, almost serene. Every inch gleamed: glass walls, walnut shelves, a meticulously organized bookshelf, and a single framed photograph of the old Hollywood sign back when it still read *Hollywoodland*. Before it was cleaned up and sanitized for postcards. In the photo, the sign looked cracked, weather-beaten, dangerous. He liked it that way. It reminded him how he'd fought his way up from the mailroom, sorting envelopes and fetching coffee, to junior executive, then agent, then agent to the stars. And now, at last, he sat where the legends once did, at the head of Paramount Studios.

From the thirty-sixth floor of Sunset Plaza, Los Angeles sprawled beneath him, a grid of dreams and delusions. To most people, the view looked chaotic. To Harvey, it was order. He'd spent twenty-five years imposing it. Yet everything else in his life hummed at a dangerous frequency: a blur of noise, neon, and notifications, the pulse of the city wired straight into his veins. Alarms screeched. Phones buzzed. Thoughts collided midair like sparks in a storm. Every second was a sprint, a caffeine-jacked dash through traffic, deadlines, and conversations that overlapped like competing radio stations. The air felt electric, charged with adrenaline; time folding in on itself. Harvey chased the next thing before the last one had even landed.

At seventy-two, he still carried himself like a man with decades left to burn. Broad shoulders, a runner's posture, eyes that could read a person faster than a résumé ever could. The only thing that betrayed his age was the silver at his temples, and even that seemed deliberate, cultivated like a brand.

A young assistant knocked on the door.

"Mr. Goldstein, Aisha's here for the read-through."

He didn't look up.

"Tell her I'll be there when I'm ready."

The door closed softly. Harvey returned his attention to the folder on his desk, a new script, anonymous and unpolished, but with something raw in its bones. He could smell potential in writing. It was a curse as much as a gift. He traced a line of dialogue with one finger, thoughtful, almost tender. Then, with a small sigh, he closed the folder and locked it in his desk drawer.

The office intercom buzzed.

"Mr. Goldstein, you've got the network on line two."

"Tell them to wait," he said.

He stood and walked to the floor-to-ceiling window, staring out over the haze-shrouded hills. Below him, a billboard for the latest studio release, *The Final Tango*, one of his biggest films, screamed in twenty-foot letters: Starring Aisha Qandisha. Her face smiled down from it, perfect and ageless.

He smiled back, faintly. In his mind flashed the actress who had carried him to the head of Paramount. Vivienne LeClaire. He was grateful for her.

He remembered when she'd first walked into his office, all nerves and hunger, clutching a headshot and swearing she would change everything for him. Maybe it had. For her, it meant immortality. For him, it meant power. And power was all that mattered in the end.

The phone rang again, three quick buzzes.

Harvey pressed the button without turning.

"What?"

"Mr. Goldstein, it's Georgia Lynn. She says the press are waiting. They want a quote."

"Tell them I'll give them one after I have some facts, not before."

He turned back to the window.

"Success isn't about what's fair," he murmured, half to himself. "It's about who gets there first."

That was his truth, the line that had followed him through every boardroom and every scandal. They printed it in trade magazines now, attributing it to "the legendary Harvey Goldstein." He never corrected them.

He adjusted his cufflinks, platinum, understated, expensive, and checked his reflection in the glass. Everything about him was still precise. Unyielding. A man who didn't bend for anyone, not even time.

The phone rang again, three quick buzzes. Harvey pressed the button, annoyed this time.

"What?"

"A Detective Singh is here to see you."

"Who?"

"Detective Singh, the detective assigned to Remi's murder," his assistant whispered into the phone.

"I'm coming out," he barked. "Send everyone to the conference room."

Finally, he picked up the script sitting at the center of his desk and tucked it under his arm. "Let's go make another star," he said aloud, then walked out.

The conference room hummed with quiet tension. Assistants lined the walls, clutching tablets and coffee cups like shields. Harvey walked in and took his place at the head of the long glass table. His suit was dark charcoal, his expression unreadable. A faint tan from weekend tennis softened nothing. He held command of the room. He nodded to the eager crowd awaiting his every word.

He flipped through a stack of storyboards in front of him, each page landing with a flat slap that echoed like judgment. To his right, a young producer shifted nervously.

"I really believe this could be the next big thing, Harvey. It's raw, emotional, it's got heart," the young blood said, trying to sound confident.

Harvey cut him off. "Heart doesn't sell tickets. Faces do." He didn't look up. The producer deflated instantly. Harvey finally set down the storyboards, steepled his fingers, and studied the room. His blue eyes swept across his team, calculating, appraising, always two steps ahead.

"This is the face that will sell our next movie." Harvey turned to Aisha and grasped both of her hands.

Aisha had pulled herself together, every trace of earlier chaos replaced by poise. She had convinced Drew to accompany her, partly for insight into the head of Paramount and partly for her own peace of mind. She smiled at Drew, then turned back to Harvey, glowing in a mid-calf crimson dress that caught the daylight like flame. Conversations paused. Eyes turned. With a slow, confident smile, she greeted Harvey, the picture of composure and quiet power.

"My dear, I want to express my deepest condolences. I'm truly sorry that your first production with us was shadowed by such a tragedy. The loss of your director is profound for all of us. Still, I'm grateful that, through your resilience and the team's dedication, the film is complete and safely in the can."

Aisha smiled gently.

Harvey turned to face the room, his voice cutting through the uneasy silence. "We will get to the bottom of this," he said, steady and resolute. He acknowledged the detective. "Detective Singh has completed a full investigation of the scene. And my producer, Georgia Lynn, a witness and my trusted confidant, will be working alongside the detective to uncover the truth behind this terrible event."

An agent at the table reacted quickly. "Yes, but Remi is dead. Shouldn't we consider delaying the film? Take the time and move the release date closer to the end of the year?"

Harvey leaned across the table and lowered his voice. "Let me tell you something about this business. Everyone's waiting for their break, their big discovery, their moment. But this town doesn't reward patience. It devours it. You wait too long, someone hungrier comes along. You play it safe, they forget your name. Out here, the spotlight burns hotter than the sun, and it doesn't care who it blinds or who it leaves in the dark."

Harvey paused, measuring the room for a reaction. "Remi wanted to make something beautiful. He did. We all did. But beauty doesn't last in this town, not unless you fight for it, not unless you bleed for it. And sometimes… even that's not enough."

He paused again, scanning the faces around the table. Fear, guilt, ambition burned in their eyes.

"So yes, Remi's gone. But don't fool yourselves. This isn't just tragedy. It's a mirror. It shows us what we are, what this business turns us into when the cameras stop rolling. Success isn't about what's fair. It's about who gets there first."

Silence followed. The line landed heavy, the kind people scribble into notebooks and repeat later at industry mixers as "classic Harvey."

He slid the storyboards back across the table. "You've got potential here. Tighten Act Two, find me a male star, and maybe we'll talk. Now get out of here."

His staff moved quickly, wordless, gathering their things and filing out. When the door finally closed, only Aisha, Detective Singh, Georgia Lynn, and Drew remained.

Harvey's attention shifted to Drew. "Who are you?"

Before Drew could answer, before Aisha could step in, Detective Singh spoke. “This is Drew. He’s a detective. He’s working with me.”

Drew froze. Aisha squeezed his hand, grounding him. Harvey studied him in silence, eyes scanning and measuring, trying to figure him out in thirty seconds or less.

“He’s a well-known detective,” Singh continued, steady and direct. “I brought him in on this case. I’ll have a report for you on your director’s death.”

She stood firm, meeting Harvey’s gaze without flinching. Even so, she could feel him shutting the conversation down, closing doors before she could push further.

“Please leave the report with me,” he said. His eyes flicked back to Drew, searching for something, a tell, a weakness, anything. Then he turned to Aisha. “My dear, I have a new script for you. Take it home. Read it over. Let me know what you think.”

She accepted the script quickly, thanking him as she took it from his hands.

He turned on his heels, already moving toward the door, his mind on the next meeting. Behind him, the room exhaled a collective breath, the kind you only take after surviving a storm.

Georgia Lynn stepped forward, claiming the center of the room as though she were about to make a grand declaration, then stopped cold. Her breath caught. Her eyes flashed with unspoken thoughts. She began to pace, heels striking the floor in a sharp, restless rhythm.

Drew watched her closely. Nervous energy radiated off her, every stride betraying the storm inside. And there it was again, the twitch. A quick, involuntary blink at the corner of her eye, pulsing like a tell she couldn’t control. Again, she checked her watch.

She looked at Drew and pointed. "That's why you were asking me questions at the wrap party? Because you're a detective?"

Drew anticipated her approach. He lifted his hands slightly, a calm half-smile forming. "Hey, don't take it the wrong way. I wasn't grilling you," he said, his tone easy, almost casual, trying to disarm her. "You just looked so upset that night. I was checking in, trying to make sure you were okay."

He let the words settle, his eyes softening. "Sometimes people notice things when they're under stress, things they don't even realize are important. But honestly, Georgia Lynn," he said with a small shrug, "I was more worried about you than anything else."

"Does Aisha know she's being followed by a detective?" she asked, matter-of-fact.

Before Drew could answer, Aisha spoke. "Of course I know. He's my dearest confidant and friend." She pulled out her bright red lipstick, reapplied it carefully, then dropped it back into her small purse and snapped it shut with intention.

Drew confirmed with a nod.

"Why were you asking me about a big ring?" Georgia Lynn shot Drew a side-eye glance.

"I was just making small talk," Drew assured her. "Your ring looked vintage. I'm into that."

Drew held her gaze. She shifted uncomfortably.

"I need a cigarette. Harvey is going to expect me in the next meeting." Georgia Lynn ran her fingers through the bleached blond strands falling across her face, then turned to Detective Singh. "Can you give me the bullet points about the case?"

Detective Singh raised an eyebrow. She knew Georgia Lynn was largely disinterested, concerned only with carrying the facts back to her boss.

"Well, a famous director gets his throat slashed in his own home during the party celebrating his finished film. Two suspects. One male, one female. Time of death between 9:50 and 10:00 p.m. No match in our records for the blood found at the scene, and no weapon recovered. The suspect exited through a window onto the adjacent balcony. There was also a red shawl, an emerald ring, and a gold hoop earring involved."

Georgia Lynn stood there with a blank expression, trying to process everything she had just heard. The weight of the facts finally settled over her, and she shuddered.

"Please get me your report."

She turned on her heels and hurried out of the office, her words trailing behind her. "Harvey needs me in a meeting, so please get this done," she said as she strode out of the room.

Silence settled over the conference room, as if the air itself had been vacuumed away. Every sound, the hum of the lights, the faint creak of the floorboards, seemed to disappear. Drew didn't move or speak. The silence pressed in around them, heavy and deliberate, like the moment before a truth finally broke the surface.

"So, I know who both of you are," Detective Singh said, abruptly breaking the silence.

Drew and Aisha exchanged a glance.

"It's funny. When I arrived at Remi's house and saw the seven of you together, I thought you were actors I recognized. Then, as the night went on, I realized I'd seen you in the New York papers about that international shipping case involving Richard Belltone. We were cleaning up the riff-raff that had infiltrated his L.A. port."

Drew and Aisha felt their composure settle into something calmer, more controlled.

"It was important for me to get my point across to Harvey right away. When he asked who you were, I thought it would be better coming from me."

"Well, I appreciate the save," Drew said with a smile.

"I'll admit, Aisha, I wasn't sure about you at first. I didn't know if you were a plant, an assassin, or just a jealous girlfriend caught in the wrong story. But the more I went through the evidence, the clearer it became. You were either being set up, or you just got tangled in a series of very strange circumstances." Detective Singh tucked a strand of brunette hair behind her ear as she pulled a leather-bound notebook from her jacket. She motioned for Aisha and Drew to take a seat.

Aisha nodded gently.

"I'm not sure what you and the detectives have pieced together, but I'm hoping we can share information."

"It would certainly help," Drew said with a smile. His guard finally dropped. He was a good judge of character, and there was something undeniably genuine about Detective Singh. He knew it wasn't easy to land a high-profile job like this, especially in a city steeped in racism, misogyny, and quiet gatekeeping disguised as tradition. She had worked hard to get there, and Drew had always rooted for the underdog.

"As far as I can tell, two people were involved in Remi's murder," Detective Singh said. "A woman who entered the room, and a second person, a man, injured, wearing expensive boots. He was clever enough to avoid every camera." She paused, watching carefully for any reaction to her deduction.

Drew shifted in his seat, his jaw tightening.

"There was a woman who entered the study, stayed for ten minutes, and then left wearing a red shawl. She had an emerald ring on her finger," Detective Singh explained.

Drew nodded, quietly confirming the information he had overheard earlier when she and her technician were speaking by the door.

Aisha leaned forward, her eyes narrowing. "How do you know the man was injured?"

Singh met her gaze. "Blood. A different type from the victim's. A few drops near the door and on the corner of the desk. The lab ran tests, but there was no match in the system."

Drew frowned, glancing at Aisha. "And those boots, you said they were expensive. What kind of expensive?"

"Custom leather. European make," Singh replied evenly. "Not the kind you buy off a shelf."

Aisha crossed her arms. "So, someone with money. Or someone who wanted to look like they had it."

Singh nodded, a faint smile tugging at her lips. "Exactly. Either way, whoever he is, he's careful. Too careful."

Drew exhaled slowly. "Careful people make mistakes eventually."

"But what was the motive?" Aisha asked.

"Love, lust, jealousy, greed, money, revenge, anger, power, control," Detective Singh rattled off.

"Usually stemming from intense emotions, personal gain, relationship conflicts, or financial disputes," Drew added.

Singh nodded. "But this was calculated. The precision of the execution, and the choice of target, tells me it was planned."

Aisha spoke up. "Any one of those motives could apply to Remi. He was a powerful force in the industry, from a reputable family, with plenty of personal conflicts and confrontations."

"That's why we need to pare down the suspect list," Detective Singh said.

“Have you figured out how the killer got into the room, behind the victim, without him noticing?” Drew asked, his voice barely above a whisper.

“He could have been hiding there beforehand,” Detective Singh said, thinking out loud. “There was a hidden closet behind the desk,” she added. “Or the woman could have come in, gotten behind him, and slit his throat. But with that kind of force, my bet is on the male.”

Drew hesitated to respond. He thought it best to measure what he revealed. Aisha didn’t look up from her script.

Detective Singh removed her coat and hung it on the back of the chair. Drew leaned against the table, fingers drumming impatiently. Aisha, torn between her new script and the conversation, felt her mind drifting back to the sight of her director’s final moments.

“Let’s go through this systematically,” Singh said. “Why would someone want Remi dead? Forget who for now. Just motives.”

Aisha tapped the table as if performing Morse code. “He was charming, connected, maybe too much for his own good. Love. Jealousy. People envy what they can’t have.”

Drew nodded. “Romantic drama? Sure. But this was clean, calculated. Not the type of crime of passion you’re imagining.”

“Calculated doesn’t mean emotionless,” Singh replied. “Sometimes emotions are exactly why people plan so carefully.”

Aisha frowned. “Could be financial. He had money. Investments, deals we haven’t fully traced. Someone could profit if he were gone.”

“Or someone was trying to cover a loss,” Drew said. “Embezzlement, insider trading, maybe even a missing client account.” He leaned closer. “Remember those expensive boots? Whoever wore them wasn’t some…” Drew searched for the word. “They moved in the same circles Remi did.”

Singh rubbed her temple. “We need to consider personal grudges too. Old friends, family disputes, former employees. People who felt wronged. Revenge doesn’t need a motive the rest of the world understands.”

Aisha nodded slowly. “So, we’re looking at three broad categories: emotional, financial, and professional. But each of those overlaps. Someone could want him gone for more than one reason.”

Drew tilted his head. “And that’s what makes this messy. Everyone we talk to has plausible reasons, but none of them point directly to the person who did it.”

Singh’s gaze sharpened. “Exactly. That’s why we keep digging. Every little hint, every interaction Remi had in the past month, it’s all a thread.”

Aisha tapped the table again. “There’s the blood near the corner of his desk. Not his. Could it connect to any of these motives? Threats? Fights? Someone got hurt before he did.”

Drew glanced at Singh. “We’re chasing ghosts. And one of them is smart enough to leave no trace.”

Singh turned toward them. “Then we force them into mistakes. We don’t solve this with what we know. We solve it with what they can’t hide.”

Drew leaned back. “We wait for the shadow to slip. And meanwhile, we map motives, suspects, and pressure points. We make the room smaller for them.”

Aisha’s fingers stopped drumming. “And the closer we get, the more dangerous it becomes.”

Singh’s eyes narrowed. “Exactly. That’s why we keep our cards close. No guesses, no shortcuts. Every lead, every conversation, every secret, it’s a step toward the truth.” Her voice turned firm.

"Here's how we move forward. We can't chase everything at once, so we divide responsibility."

Detective Singh stared out the window for a brief moment. "I'll handle the broader investigation. Interviews, surveillance, anything that tracks movement around Remi. I'll also have my team look into finances. Every transaction, every account, every tiny wire transfer that seems off."

"What do we do?" Aisha asked, looking directly into the detective's eyes.

"You follow up on motive. Start with the people closest to Remi. His friends, colleagues, anyone with access to his personal life. Ask questions, probe, and pay attention to what people aren't saying."

Aisha's fingers hovered over her phone. "I'll start with his messages and recent contacts. Social circle, coworkers, anyone who might have a reason to hurt him."

"Exactly," Singh said, her gaze hardening. "We're not looking for certainty yet. We're mapping possibilities. Every lead is a thread. Follow it carefully. Push and prod, but don't scare anyone off."

Aisha's phone vibrated softly in her hand, the sudden pulse cutting through the haze of her thoughts. She glanced down, expecting another message she wasn't ready to read.

"The Los Angeles Times has posted an obituary for Remi."

"I can read it to you both," Detective Singh volunteered

Obituary

Remi Harrington, Rising Hollywood Visionary, Dies at 32

Remi Harrington, a rapidly ascending filmmaker whose distinctive style and precocious talent drew comparisons to some of cinema's greatest auteurs, has died. He was thirty-two.

Harrington emerged as one of Hollywood's most electrifying young voices, earning industry-wide attention after his directorial debut, *The Glass Veil*, premiered at the Sundance Film Festival to standing ovations. The film sold to a major distributor within forty-eight hours, an extraordinary accomplishment that immediately positioned him as a serious creative force. Though early in his career, his name began appearing alongside those of seasoned veterans, not as a novelty, but as a peer.

Born into a family steeped in film tradition, he was the son of Oscar-winning director Clive Harrington, but Remi quickly proved he was more than his pedigree. His work blended old Hollywood elegance with contemporary thematic urgency, weaving vintage visual palettes with explorations of identity, mental health, and social upheaval. Critics praised his "hypnotic eye for composition" and his "emotional precision beneath aesthetic control."

His newest action film, *The Final Tango*, scheduled for an early release, had already generated significant anticipation. Early viewers described it as Harrington's boldest and most vulnerable work, one that now reads not only as an epitaph but as a haunting prediction. The title, once regarded as a gritty metaphor, has taken on a solemn resonance that the industry is still struggling to process.

Chapter 13
Griffth Observatory

"Grace, did you phone the mansion to tell them we're coming?" Israel asked for the third time.

"Israel, I think your short-term memory is gone," she said with a snicker. "Yes, I spoke with Drake, and they're expecting us."

The Uber driver pulled up in front of the iron gates and leaned out the window, searching for the street address.

"Yes, this is the place," Israel confirmed. "I know, it's a work in progress," he added, reassuring the driver as the pair stepped out of the car.

Drake was already waiting, meeting them at the door and escorting them inside. "Madame is in the blue parlor. She would like you to join her there." He stared down his nose at them before adding, "I know you remember where it is."

"Drake, any more threats or problems?" Grace asked.

"I'll allow Madame to give you that information," he replied.

Grace and Israel exchanged a look as they moved through the living room and passed through the blue velvet curtain leading into the fabled room. They entered cautiously, scanning their surroundings. From the outside, the room appeared undisturbed. Velvet drapes were drawn open over the high windows. The heavy furniture remained covered in white sheets, except for one chair in the far corner, positioned toward a small hearth.

In it sat Vivienne LeClaire.

She was motionless, poised, as if in meditation. Her hair was pulled back and tucked beneath a black handkerchief. A black satin robe draped around her like ink poured slowly over skin, glossy and controlled, clinging just enough to suggest intention rather than accident. A thick book lay open in her lap, its pages yellowed and brittle, the ink curling with age. Her eyes remained fixed on the hearth.

"You found out about my brother, didn't you?"

She delivered the line quietly and deliberately, charged with the feeling that something irreversible had just slipped into the open.

"Yes, Vivienne, we did," Grace said gently. "We understand it must have been very painful."

"What was more painful was that he died on the same night as my greatest triumph," she said, clutching her heart, still staring into the fireplace. Then, slowly turning her head toward them, she added, "It's as though the universe demanded a balance, and in taking him, it taught me that joy and grief are sometimes forged in the same flame."

The duo stood speechless.

She shifted her gaze toward the darkened fireplace, where the charred remains of something recent still smoldered faintly. The air carried the scent of burnt orange and photo paper.

Grace understood what was happening. She exchanged a glance with Israel and stepped forward. "After so many years of love and memories, it's understandable to feel the loss deeply. But it's also okay to allow yourself moments of peace now."

Silence hung in the room.

"All the rituals you do will not bring your brother back," Grace said softly, her voice matching the mood.

"But he is here. Haunting me. Visiting me in the house, leaving me signs." Her voice trembled. "I know it's him, not some… jilted actor or ex-lover. My brother wants me to reveal the truths."

"What truths are these, Vivienne?" Israel asked, cutting straight to the point.

Vivienne whispered, though her lips barely seemed to move. Grace noticed her hands trembling over the spine of the book resting in her lap.

"First it was my jewelry. Then my perfume. Now… my letters. They were from my brother," she said quietly. "The ones he wrote before the drowning." Vivienne nodded faintly, her voice growing thin. "He always blamed me. Even after death."

"Did your psychic, Madame Arquette, tell you that?" Grace asked, raising an eyebrow.

Vivienne did not reply.

"May we see your brother's letters?" Grace lifted her hand, almost commanding Vivienne to share her brother's words.

Vivienne hesitated, then slowly flipped to a page in the book, revealing three letters written in ink on yellowed, crinkled paper. She handed them to Grace, who read each one aloud.

You told me
it came from nowhere.
Nothing ever does.
I heard another voice
under the polish.
It wasn't yours.
It wasn't his.

Grace flipped to the next page:

He said he fixed it.
You said it needed fixing.
Some hands take,
then call it shaping.
I recognize the difference.
Someone will be missing
when the cameras roll.

Isreal caught Grace's eyes as she flipped to the last letter:

There is a name
no one is saying.
That's how I know it matters.
If this goes quiet,
remember why.
I won't be here
to remind you.

Vivienne sniffled. "My brother was a brilliant but unstable savant, obsessed with authorship, control, and legacy."

"Do you understand their meaning?" Grace asked.

Vivienne did not reply.

"Who else has seen these?" Israel asked.

"Just Drake," Vivienne said dryly. "After my brother's death, I found his datebook, and in it was one phrase, written obsessively: 'The death of the author.'"

"The quote from Barthes?" Grace asked. "How does it go?"

Israel shrugged. "Who?"

"Barthes wrote, 'The birth of the reader must be at the cost of the death of the author.' It comes from his 1967 essay," Vivienne recited, her eyes fixed on the hearth.

"But Barthes wrote that fifteen years after your brother's death," Grace said, thinking out loud. "So your brother couldn't have been referencing Barthes."

"It felt poignant to me because those were words my brother had formulated years before. My brother Jeffries used to say, 'Stories don't belong to the people who create them.' He would say, 'Meaning only exists once it leaves the author's hands and reaches the public eye.'" Vivienne gently brushed a piece of graying hair back beneath her handkerchief. "At the time, I dismissed it as grief, or madness. Now the phrase has resurfaced, not as philosophy, but as a signature."

Vivienne leaned forward and picked up another note lying near her feet.

"When did you receive this note?" Israel asked sharply.

"The day you came to install your security cameras. It was sitting on the fireplace mantel. My brother knew where to leave it to get my attention." Vivienne pointed to the stone hearth in front of her, her eyes wide with fear.

"I saw muddy footprints outside this room the day Francy and I came to install your security system. He was one step ahead of us." Israel shook his head in disbelief.

"Well, ghosts don't leave muddy footprints, Vivienne, so I don't think it was your brother behind this note," Grace said gently. "I think someone is trying to tell you something."

Vivienne's hands trembled as she slowly passed the note to Grace. "The style matches the other notes. Letters cut out of magazines and books. 'THE DEATH OF THE AUTHOR. Griffith Observatory. 7:30 p.m.'"

"My brother Jeffries used to love it when I took him to the Griffith Observatory. We went all the time. Planetarium shows. Narrated skies."

"Would you say this was common knowledge, Vivienne? Did other people in your circle know Jeffries liked the planetarium?" Grace pressed, searching for a connection.

The actress paused, tilting her head as she reached back into memory. "Well," she said hesitantly, "*Photoplay Magazine* did a little story about me taking Jeffries on an outing to 'see the stars,' as it were. It was rather a puff piece about the two of us." She laughed softly. "I wasn't even famous then. It was just a publicity stunt my agent arranged to get me in the papers." She glanced down at the book in her lap, searching for the article among the pages, but found nothing.

Israel understood immediately. "The observatory. A place where someone else tells you what you're looking at."

Grace nodded. "And where authorship disappears." She leaned toward Vivienne. "Israel and I are going to follow up on this clue and go to the Griffith Observatory."

☆☆☆

The road began in shadow, curling upward from the base of Mount Hollywood like a quiet promise. The Uber driver's headlights swept across chaparral and pale stone, the city falling away behind them in a widening breath of light.

"I love this ride," the driver confessed. "It's most beautiful at night."

Each turn of the road revealed another slice of the skyline through the trees, another shimmer of windows and street lamps like delicate fireflies on a mission, until the world felt suspended between ground and sky.

With the ascent, the air cooled and thinned, carrying the faint scent of dry grass and eucalyptus. The city's noise dissolved into a low, distant murmur, replaced by the whisper of wind brushing the hillside. The observatory remained hidden for most of the climb, as if it preferred anticipation, allowing only fleeting glimpses of its white geometry through the darkness, luminous and unreal, like a thought you weren't ready to reveal.

Then the road straightened, and the summit opened. Los Angeles glowed below, an endless constellation pressed flat against the earth, its hum softened by distance as they reached the top.

The Griffith Observatory stood revealed, bright, serene, and monumental. Its white façade glowed beneath carefully placed lights, radiant against the velvet night. The domes rose with quiet authority, smooth and celestial, as though they had grown there naturally, shaped by the same forces that shaped the stars they watched. Stone terraces stretched outward, welcoming and still, their edges framing the vastness beyond.

"It's Art Deco," Grace cooed, poking her head out the back-seat window. "Look, the Hollywood Sign. Gorgeous!" she exclaimed, staring up at the mountains behind her.

From the summit, the city spread in every direction, a sea of light breathing slowly below. Streets traced delicate veins of gold. Skyscrapers pierced the darkness like distant beacons. Above it all, the sky deepened into a rich indigo, the stars faint but present, holding their ancient vigil. The observatory felt like a threshold, part earth and part sky, a place where time slowed and the immensity of the universe pressed gently against human wonder.

"You have arrived," the driver said with a smile.

All Israel could do was nod, overwhelmed by the view before them. He stepped out of the car with Grace, and then reality settled back in. "What's to say the person who left the note at Vivienne's would be here tonight? There wasn't even a date on it."

"The hour must have some significance," Grace said, scanning the scene slowly.

"Vivienne really believes it's her brother haunting her." Israel still couldn't understand how their client failed to separate physical threats from the ghostly presence that haunted her mind.

Grace glanced at him, her expression thoughtful.

"Belief is more powerful than we give it credit for," she said quietly. "Once an idea takes root, especially one tied to guilt, fear, or grief, it doesn't stay abstract. The mind gives it shape, weight, and presence. After a while, it stops feeling like a thought and starts behaving like reality, something that reacts, follows you, threatens you. To the person living inside it, the difference doesn't matter anymore. It becomes real."

They stopped in awe before the grand structure. Crowds of all ages moved through the palatial park, taking in every detail.

"If you think this is impressive, you should see the city from the terrace," a young boy remarked as he passed by with his father, clearly amused by the starstruck expressions on Grace and Israel's faces.

The detectives moved through the hushed corridors of the Griffith Observatory. Though crowded, the visitors were absorbed in wonder, surrounded by 1930s stylization that continued to tell an evolving modern story. Their footsteps echoed softly against marble floors worn smooth by decades of curious wanderers. Glass cases glowed with quiet knowledge, planets suspended in light, constellations mapped like secrets waiting to be told.

Then, just ahead, a simple sign caught their attention. Grace pointed to the words: *Terrace*, its arrow aimed toward the night. It felt less like a direction and more like an invitation.

The doors opened to a rush of cool air, and the city revealed itself all at once. The terrace stretched wide and open, framed by pale stone and low railings, as if designed to disappear and let the view take command. Below, Los Angeles spilled outward in every direction, a living constellation of gold and white lights. Streets traced glowing paths through the darkness, cars moving like slow-burning sparks, the city breathing in a quiet rhythm. In the distance, downtown rose in sharp silhouettes, towers cutting into the night sky, while the Hollywood Sign hovered faint and iconic against the hills.

"I could easily live here," Israel mouthed, the thought lingering unspoken beyond the movement of his lips.

On a public plaque near the terrace door, someone had written, neatly and deliberately, in black marker:

THE DEATH OF THE AUTHOR
THE DEATH OF THE AUTHOR
THE DEATH OF THE AUTHOR

"Someone is trying to be clever," Grace said. "This is something else."

"What?"

Grace swallowed. "A eulogy. A private protest, maybe?"

Israel frowned. "For who?"

She shook her head.

She ran her finger just above the stone, careful not to touch the ink. "Whoever wrote this isn't killing the author. They're mourning one."

Israel looked past her, scanning the tourists, the couples, the children running between telescopes. "So why scare her?"

Grace turned to him. "They're not scaring Vivienne." She paused. "They're dismantling her."

Before Israel could respond, Grace's gaze locked onto someone standing near the far railing. Still. Watching the city, not the sky. The figure turned for a moment and recognized her. They held each other's gaze.

Israel noticed. "Who's that? He looks like he knows you."

Then the figure mouthed the words slowly and calmly. "She never knew who created her." He ran.

"Hey!" Israel shouted.

They bolted after him. Footsteps rang against the stone as they sprinted through the crowds. Tourists gasped and scattered. The figure vaulted a low wall and disappeared down the service stairs.

Israel and Grace followed, their breaths short and sharp, the city flickering through metal slats as they descended.

"This is planned," Israel said between breaths.

"Yes," Grace replied. "And personal."

The staircase continued downward, past the main level of the observatory and below, where grassy knolls cradled the base of the towering structure. They burst out at the bottom of the service entrance.

"Empty," Israel whispered, surprised.

They pressed themselves against the rough stone base of the observatory, heart pounding so violently they could swear the sound echoed beyond their body, giving their position away. Israel risked a glance around the corner. Nothing yet. Only the dark outlines of the domes shifting slowly in the moonlight high above.

"Keep moving," he muttered to Grace, breath coming in sharp, ragged bursts.

They broke cover, darting along the curved walkways winding around the observatory's perimeter. A warm breeze drifted past, carrying a faint trace of salt from the nearby Pacific. Grace stayed close behind. Up ahead, a broad grassy slope rose toward the road leading back to the main building.

"What just happened?" Israel asked, slowing to catch his breath.

Grace bent down, noticing a folded paper lying on the ground.

Israel watched as she opened it. Not a note. An old film program, yellowed and creased, the kind handed out on opening nights.

"*Velvet Ashes*," Israel read aloud.

One name in the credits had been violently scratched out. Not replaced. Just erased.

Grace closed her eyes. "This isn't about revenge," she said.

Israel looked at her, forcing his breathing to steady. "Then what is it?"

She lifted her gaze to the observatory, glowing above them like a monument to borrowed stars.

"It's a protest," she said softly. "By someone who knows what it means to be brilliant and unheard."

Israel's voice dropped. "You think they're dangerous?"

Grace considered the question carefully. "I think I know who that is. No," she corrected herself. "I think they're grieving. And grief," she added, "doesn't care who it terrifies."

"Who was it?"

"I think that was Remi's assistant, Matt. I only met him at the wrap party, right after Remi's death. He seemed very distraught then."

"But…?" Israel sensed her hesitation.

"I remember thinking at the time that people here often say one thing while hiding something else beneath their words."

“Why would Remi’s assistant be involved in our other case? What’s the connection?” Israel asked.

“He mouthed a message to me upstairs,” Grace whispered. “He said, ‘She never knew who created her.’”

“Created her? Who? Vivienne?” Israel shot her a curious look.

They stood along the side of Mount Hollywood, the Griffith Observatory now revealed from a sharper, unfamiliar angle, less grand and more watchful, as if it were observing them in return. The city unfurled below in a restless sprawl of light, beautiful enough to distract, dangerous enough to deceive. Whatever truth they were circling felt closer now, no longer distant but deliberately withheld, hovering just beyond reach. In that suspended moment, with the observatory at their backs and the city breathing beneath them, it was impossible to shake the feeling that the next step forward would change everything.

Chapter 14
Malibu

The road to Lexi Vale's Malibu bungalow twisted along the Pacific Coast Highway, the late afternoon sun turning the ocean into a sheet of hammered silver while the opposing cliffs rose in sun-bleached slabs. Aisha drove her baby blue convertible, one steady hand guiding them along the coastal curves, the other tapping her polished nails anxiously against her thigh. Drew sat beside her, scrolling through notes on his tablet, while Debra rode in the backseat, sunglasses perched low, arms crossed as if bracing for impact and the quiet anticipation of whatever waited for them at the end.

"Lexi Vale," Debra muttered. "Hollywood's favorite trouble magnet."

"She's also one of the last people who saw Remi alive," Drew reminded her. "And she worked on *The Glass Veil* before she was even born, according to her, anyway."

Aisha snorted. "Her TikTok account claims she's Remi's 'spiritual successor.' Whatever that means."

"It means she's going to be dramatic," Debra said, "and probably disillusioned."

Drew lifted a brow. "Then this should be interesting."

They pulled up to Lexi's bungalow, a small glass-and-cedar hideaway perched above the cliffs, the kind of place designed for influencers who wanted to pretend they lived simply. Bougainvillea spilled down the railings, and wind chimes tinkled in the warm Pacific breeze. The door was already cracked open.

"That's not ominous," Aisha murmured.

Drew motioned for caution as they stepped inside.

"Lexi, it's Aisha. Are you here?" The same feeling came over her now as when she had burst into Remi's office. She was almost hoping she wouldn't find the same outcome. "Lexi? It's Aisha. Your door was open."

The interior was a curated chaos of vintage posters, fairy lights, and half-packed suitcases scattered across the floor. At the center of it all, Lexi Vale sat cross-legged on the sofa, wearing oversized sunglasses and an expression that shifted between terrified and theatrically serene.

"You're late," she said, not looking up from the matcha latte she was stirring. "I was about to cancel for spiritual reasons."

Debra lowered her sunglasses. "We're twenty minutes early."

"Well," Lexi said with a sigh, "my intuition clock runs fast."

Drew stepped forward gently. "Lexi, we're here to ask a few questions about Remi and the night of the wrap party."

Lexi held up a hand. "Before you start, I need to make something clear. I adored Remi. He was a visionary. Intense, demanding, occasionally screaming, but a visionary."

"Witnesses said you argued with him during our photo shoot," Aisha said.

Lexi's tattooed eyebrows shot up. "Oh, honey, that wasn't an argument. Aisha, you were there. That was Remi being Remi. He accused me of 'compromising artistic integrity' because my improv didn't match his 'emotional color palette' during our last scene." She made finger quotes with a flourish. "He was dramatic that day."

"And you?" Debra asked.

Lexi removed her sunglasses, revealing eyes rimmed with smudged mascara. "I'm expressive." She paused, a flicker of recognition crossing her face. "I remember both of you. You took my class at the gym," she said, smiling proudly. "And I've seen your cute face on set with Aisha," she added, flirting with Drew.

Drew took a seat across from her. "We're not here to accuse you of anything. But we need clarity. You went up to Remi's office during the party, around 9:50 p.m.?"

Lexi hesitated.

The air shifted.

"I never saw Remi again after the photo shoot," she whispered. "Besides… I was scared. Not of the situation. Of someone else."

Aisha leaned forward. "Who?"

Lexi swallowed. "There was… someone watching me. All week. On set, outside my classes at the gym, even here. I kept seeing this figure, dark clothes, a hoodie pulled low. Always just far enough away that I couldn't be sure."

Drew's pulse quickened. "Did you tell anyone?"

"I told Remi." She twisted her hands, the bravado slipping. "He told me to embrace it. Said paranoia would 'feed the performance.' He thought I was being dramatic." She paused. "I thought I was being dramatic."

Debra's gaze sharpened. "And now? Are you being dramatic?"

"Now," Lexi whispered, "I think whoever was watching me wanted to scare me."

Aisha exchanged a look with Drew. "Then why?"

Lexi reached behind the sofa and pulled out a small envelope. It was cream-colored, its edges curled and smudged with red ink. "I found that on my doorstep this afternoon." Inside was a single photograph. "It's a still of me from *The Glass Veil*." She gently pulled out the image.

Debra intervened, encouraging Lexi to drop the photo into her scarf. Drew handled it carefully as he read the inscription scribbled across the bottom in red ink: "*The star always falls the hardest*." His face changed. Drew felt the temperature in the room shift.

Aisha exhaled shakily. "That's what was written on my picture we found at Remi's. This is the same kind of candid photo Detective Singh found of me," she confirmed.

Lexi froze. "Oh, Aisha, do you think someone is stalking us because of the movie? Maybe someone wants the entire cast dead. Look what happened to you and Ollie."

Drew carefully placed the image back in the envelope and wrapped the clue in Debra's scarf, slowly handing it to her for safekeeping.

"Tell me about that big chunky emerald ring you wore for the promo pictures," Aisha said, reminding her.

Lexi paused, took a long breath, then released a slow exhale. She lifted her matcha latte for a thoughtful sip. Drew watched as her expression shifted, the unmistakable spark of an idea coming to life.

"Honestly, I didn't find it so much as it… found me. I was wandering down Melrose, no real destination, just following whatever vibe pulled me, and I drifted into this little shop that smelled like old incense and sun-warmed velvet."

"Really?" Debra couldn't wait to hear this story.

"I wasn't even looking at the jewelry, I swear. But then I felt this tiny, cosmic nudge, like the universe was tapping my shoulder. And there it was in this dusty glass case, glowing at me like it had known me in a past life or something."

"I bet it did," Aisha echoed Debra's sentiment.

"I tried it on, and boom, instant soul connection. It was like, 'Oh hey, you're my person.' So obviously I had to take it home. I mean… who am I to argue with destiny?"

Drew intervened. "You wore the ring for the photo shoot at Remi's, and then you took it off. Why?"

Lexi went quiet again, her gaze drifting as if she were watching thoughts float by on some invisible cosmic breeze. A long pause stretched before she finally blinked back into the moment. She frowned softly, the wheels turning in slow motion. "Ummm… well, lots of people were drawn to it. All night, people wanted to try it on. That's when I knew it wanted to release me."

"What wanted to release you?" Drew encouraged an answer with his eyes.

"The ring. Clearly, it wanted a new owner."

"Clearly," Debra grunted.

"Okay, so… I remember someone from the crew wanted me to show the ring to Remi," she said slowly, as if pulling each word from a distant cloud. "They said something about how he'd appreciate the energy, or the symbolism, or… something. It all felt very important at the time. So, I gave it to them to show Remi."

Drew leaned in. "Right, but who was it that asked you? Who did you give the ring to?"

She squinted at nothing in particular, then let out a gentle sigh. "I can totally see their aura in my head, but their actual face? Or name?" She shook her head with a dreamy little laugh. "Nope. It's just… gone. Like the universe hasn't decided to give that part back to me yet."

Debra was tired of the show. "Listen, this is important. We're trying to find out who killed Remi. Can you ask the universe to oblige, please?"

Lexi made a face and closed her eyes. The silence practically sent Debra into a tailspin.

"Nope. It's not there. So sorry," Lexi said with a sigh.

Debra walked away.

"Okay, Lexi, if the universe decides to give up the information and the aura becomes clearer, will you please text me?" Aisha smiled, knowing she wasn't going to get any more plausible information out of her co-star.

Lexi nodded, as if the universe had delivered the message.

"We're going to take this photo and see if our detective friend can get any prints off it." Aisha nodded as though she were telling her, not asking. "And lock your door when we leave," she added.

The trio walked down the driveway to the car, looking around at the property. "Well, they know where she lives. They delivered the threat right to her door," Debra said, pulling her Dior scarf up over her hair.

"Something about this doesn't make sense." Drew rubbed the back of his neck. "It's the same message you received, Aisha."

"Only not directly," she added.

"It's almost as if the killer was fishing for information. Why send the same message to two people?"

Drew stepped closer to the edge of the cliff and looked out at the ocean stretching wide and indifferent before them. He squinted against the soft shimmer lifting off the water. It was the Golden Hour, arriving gently, as if the sun hesitated before its final descent. The light turned warm and deliberate, spilling honeyed tones across everything it touched. For a suspended moment, the world felt more forgiving. More cinematic. As though time itself had agreed to pause and let everything look beautiful before the light gave way.

Below them, the ocean shifted restlessly. Choppy waves gathered in the onshore breeze, the surface flickering like a signal trying to be understood.

Aisha hugged her waistcoat tighter.

"If he wanted to scare me, he could've just sent it again." She gestured toward the cottage behind them. "This, this feels like something else."

She unlocked the car but did not open the door.

"Or someone else," she added. "Maybe it wasn't meant for her at all. Maybe he wanted us to see it."

The idea settled between them, heavy and unwelcome.

Aisha felt a prickling at the back of her neck. The wind had not changed, yet something in the air felt altered.

"Do you think he knew we'd come?"

Drew did not answer immediately. His focus had shifted to the narrow footpath cutting along the cliff's edge, the same one they had passed on the way up.

Overgrown. Unused.

Or so they had thought.

"Someone's been down there," he said quietly. "The grass is flattened. There are fresh tracks in the sand. There were no tracks when we went inside."

Debra frowned. “You noticed that path when we came in?”

“Yes. I noticed her pink car in the garage. The latch on the side gate wasn’t fully seated. Her welcome mat was upside down.” Drew’s voice stayed even, almost clinical.

Debra glanced back at the path. “You mean someone was watching?”

Aisha’s heart thudded. “Watching her house? Or watching us?”

Debra exhaled sharply. “Either way, we’re not staying here. We’ll have one of Detective Singh’s local officers sweep the place. Maybe pull security footage from the road intersection.”

But Aisha didn’t move. Her gaze remained fixed on the narrow cut in the grass along the cliff. A sudden certainty tightened in her chest.

“He wasn’t fishing for information,” she whispered. “He was confirming something.”

Drew turned toward her. “Confirming what?”

“That I got the first message.” Her voice wavered despite her effort to steady it. “And that I’m still alive.”

Silence pressed in around them.

Then something split the quiet. A sharp metallic crack, abrupt and wrong.

Drew’s hand clamped onto Aisha’s shoulder. “Get in the car,” he ordered, eyes scanning the tree line along the cliff. “Now.”

Aisha yanked open the driver’s door, her pulse hammering. “Was that…?”

“Not a branch,” Drew said. His focus sharpened. “Someone’s here.”

Debra felt it too. The weight of unseen eyes. The cold, creeping certainty.

The killer wasn't sending messages anymore.

He was watching for the response.

A gull cried overhead. The wind shifted. The wind chimes along the cottage porch erupted into a violent clatter, no longer delicate but frantic, as if even the Malibu breeze had turned against them.

Aisha slammed her door just as Debra and Drew scrambled into the back seat. The engine roared to life, but before she could throw the car into reverse, Drew caught her arm.

"Wait. Don't move yet."

Aisha froze. "What? Why?"

Drew's voice dropped. "Look at the side mirror."

Her eyes flicked toward the glass.

"Because someone's standing behind the car."

Debra leaned forward, squinting into the dim light. "I don't see anything."

But then Aisha saw it.

A flicker of movement. A shadow where no shadow should be. Tall. Still. Watching.

The figure didn't step closer. Didn't back away. It simply stood there, as if weighing them.

"Aisha," Drew whispered, his grip tightening, "when I say go, floor it toward the bend. Hard right. Don't look back."

Debra swallowed. "What if he—"

"He won't catch us," Drew said.

In the open air of the convertible, the breeze did nothing to soften the rigid line of his jaw.

The shadow shifted. Barely perceptible. Enough.

"Now!"

Aisha slammed the car into gear. The tires shrieked against gravel, stones spraying as the vehicle lunged forward. The cliffside blurred. Her pulse pounded in her ears.

Despite herself, she twisted in her seat.

For a single second, the figure stepped fully into view.

A dark coat. A hood pulled low.

And something glinting in his hand. Metal. Rectangular. Almost like a phone.

Then he turned and disappeared down the cliff path.

Aisha's breath came in shallow bursts. "He wasn't trying to block us. He wanted us to see him."

Drew nodded, his expression hardening. "And he recorded us leaving."

"But why?" Debra asked, still breathless as the car hurtled down the winding road.

Aisha stared out at the ocean, the waves darkening beneath the sinking sun.

"Because this wasn't a warning," she whispered. "It was proof."

Debra met her eyes in the rearview mirror. "Proof of what?"

Aisha closed her eyes. The realization settled into her bones like ice.

"That he's close enough to kill any of us whenever he wants."

"Who are you calling?" Debra demanded, urgency sharpening her voice as Drew hastily dialed Detective Singh.

A cold tremor rippled down her spine while she listened to him explain what had happened, each word tightening the knot in her chest. She waited, breath shallow, heart pounding, for the detective's response.

"She's sending a patrol to Lexi's house right now."

Before Drew could say anything more, a siren wailed in the distance, cutting through the coastal quiet.

"My God. That was fast," Debra breathed.

"Mi amor, it's Malibu," Aisha said gently, though her pulse still raced. "There are more celebrities packed into every square inch than anywhere else. The police are always patrolling this area."

Drew lowered the phone. "Detective Singh wants us to stop by and bring her the photo."

Chapter 15
Downtown Los Angeles

The Los Angeles Police Department's downtown precinct on First Street rose in gray concrete and reflective glass, stern and imposing, the kind of building that felt official before you ever stepped inside. The front doors slid open to a spacious lobby tiled in cool white, footsteps from officers and civilians echoing across the polished floor. Beyond it stretched a maze of hallways leading to detective offices, evidence rooms, and interrogation rooms, each humming with quiet urgency.

Aisha, Drew, and Debra moved through the lobby together, Debra clutching the envelope with the photograph carefully wrapped in her scarf.

Detective Singh sat behind a cluttered desk beneath the harsh glow of a desk lamp. She looked up as they entered, her sharp eyes immediately settling on the scarf-wrapped bundle in Debra's hands. Her brow furrowed. She set down the coffee cup she had been absently stirring and gestured for them to sit. Then she opened a drawer and pulled on a pair of gloves.

"This is the same message," Singh said, her voice steady but edged with concern, "that you received, Aisha."

She slid the photograph free and examined it with meticulous care.

"That means the person who targeted Remi is still active. And they've set their sights on Aisha and Lexi."

"Yes it's the same message that was on my picture," Aisha confirmed quietly.

Singh leaned back in her chair, considering the implications. "My officers didn't find anyone near Ms. Vale's bungalow."

"Did they check on her?" Drew asked.

Singh gave a short nod. "Oh yes. They were met by an ethereal wisp who told them, 'It's in the hands of the universe.'"

"There's a shocker," Debra muttered.

"We're not looking at a random threat anymore," Detective Singh said. "This is targeted. Whoever did this is sending a pattern. Or a warning. Given the precision and the timing, they may be watching you closely."

She folded her gloved hands on the desk.

"My priority is containment and tracking. We need to determine the connection between the first crime and this stalking."

The theory was already taking shape in her mind. The repeated message suggested someone organized. Possibly obsessed. Someone who wanted recognition. Or fear.

Drew understood the importance of patterns. That was the logical path. But there was a personal dimension now. Aisha could be bait. Or worse, the next target.

"Did you find any evidence of tampering on the stunt car?" he asked. "The one that broke apart and nearly killed Aisha and her co-star, Ollie?"

"The producer filed a report flagging cable tension issues," Singh replied.

She opened the file and flipped to a tabbed section.

"In the OSHA report, there was no evidence of foul play on the equipment itself. However, there was a documented communication failure. Remi claimed he never saw a report about damaged equipment. His assistant and staff said the same. The producer was out of town the night of the shoot. So yes, communication failures across the board."

Aisha stared down at her hands, shaking her head slowly.

Singh pulled a thick case file from her drawer and began scanning surveillance stills, witness statements, prior incident reports. Her eyes moved quickly, calculating.

"Until we know more, you need to stay alert," she said. "Do not change routines abruptly, and do not do anything that could tip this person off. If they are escalating, we want them predictable."

"Well, it's a little late for that," Debra muttered.

"Aisha, we'll need you to be extremely careful. No solo moves. No surprises. Whoever this is, they're smart enough to cover their tracks."

"Don't worry, Detective. This isn't our first rodeo. We work in pairs, protect each other, and we're extremely cautious," Aisha assured her.

"No doubt. Your reputation precedes you."

Detective Singh slid the photograph into an evidence bag and leaned forward, steepling her fingers.

"Here's how we handle this," she said, her voice firm and precise. "First, we treat the photo itself as evidence. Not just the message, but the physical object. Whoever left this could have left traceable fingerprints, fibers, or even digital metadata if it was printed from a device. I'll send it to forensics immediately. We'll check for prints, DNA, and anything that might lead us to the printer or camera used."

Singh clicked her pen, her gaze returning to Aisha. Then she turned to an evidence box on the floor and used the pen to sort through several sealed bags collected from Remi's home.

"I showed you the photo with the same message at Remi's crime scene," she continued. "We need every detail you remember. Timing. Exact wording. The day it was taken. Even the smallest detail could help us profile the suspect, or at least narrow down their method. Both messages were written in red ink."

Aisha hesitated. "As I told you before, I never saw that picture. I used to sit in the director's chair on set, usually because it was closest to whatever scene I was filming at the time."

Singh nodded slowly.

"One thing we did confirm is that the Polaroid from Remi's scene was taken with his own camera. We found it in a drawer in his study." She held Aisha's gaze. "It's possible this photo of Lexi came from the same camera."

"Well, perhaps he was documenting us on set. Taking candid photos of his actors. He never told us about that," Aisha said. "Maybe the killer found these photos in Remi's files and using them as bait."

"We also found a sales contract, purchase agreement, and bill of sale for that baby blue convertible signed over to you," Detective Singh replied. "A gift from Remi?"

Drew and Debra exchanged a slow look.

"Yes. Of course," Aisha said, a dash of pride in her voice. "Remi gave me a car."

"Was that part of your contract?" Singh asked, smiling faintly.

"Of course not. He also filled my trailer with flowers when I arrived on set. I know that may seem unusual to you, Detective, but that's how a Hollywood director makes sure his cast feels valued."

"I noticed none of his other cast members received flowers. Or cars."

Drew stepped in quickly. "Detective, Aisha is a star. She's internationally known. Those are industry perks at her level."

"An action star who moonlights as a detective?"

"Art imitating life. It's a perfect fit," Debra said lightly.

"Trust me, I've got an entire binder of true crime trading cards. I'm not judging. I'm relating," Detective Singh replied.

Silence settled over the room.

"So," Singh said at last, her tone shifting, "you weren't sleeping with him?"

The silence that followed was heavier.

Aisha held her gaze. "Detective, every man with a pulse notices an attractive woman," she said, her voice calm and measured. "Did he drop subtle innuendos now and then? Yes. Make a few advances? Certainly. Ask me out more than once? Absolutely."

She let the words sit between them.

"Did I ever sleep with him?" A deliberate pause. "No. I don't mix business with desire. That's my rule."

Another beat.

"My game."

Drew caught the quiet sigh that slipped from Debra, soft but unmistakable, as if a weight he had not realized she was carrying had finally lifted.

"Well, I guess that answers that," Debra murmured.

"When someone is famous, their mistakes, failures, or scandals are magnified. So, when they fall, it's public. Painful. Ruthless," Drew deduced. "The message on the photos refer to this."

"A normal person stumbles and no one notices," Debra added. "A star stumbles and it becomes a spectacle."

"Yes," Aisha said quietly. "A poetic way of saying that the brighter you shine, the harder they wait for you to crash."

Her gaze drifted past them, unfocused, as though she were already calculating the distance to the ground.

"Writing it this way implies that stars deserve to be brought down," Drew said, thinking aloud. "That an actress has somehow sinned by being famous. That her fame is an insult. Or a betrayal."

Detective Singh nodded slowly.

"This could be a cast or crew member who feels she's receiving special treatment. Someone who thinks she overshadows others. Or believes she's due for a fall."

She flipped through the stack of interviews conducted at the party following Remi's death, scanning highlighted passages and margin notes.

"There weren't any obvious standouts," she said. Then she looked up. "But why target two different actresses from two different films?"

Her gaze settled on Aisha.

"Did either of you work on the same projects?"

"We did not," Aisha replied, her tone firm.

Drew leaned forward, considering another angle.

"Maybe a studio executive. The director. A crew member. Someone who felt her confidence needed to be manipulated. Or this is a power play. A reminder that she's replaceable. That someone else believes they control the narrative."

Aisha sank into the office chair, exhaustion catching up with her. "What are we missing?"

Detective Singh softened her voice slightly.

"Is there anyone you can think of who's been less than cordial? Anyone with a history of resentment?"

Aisha shifted in her seat.

"Detective, there will always be someone who dislikes you for the way you breathe. Or the way you look. Or the way you talk." She paused, her expression tightening. "In my experience, it usually comes down to jealousy."

"That's human nature, Detective," Drew said, stepping in. "We observe it all the time. We experience it ourselves. We see it play out in others. I witnessed a few people on Aisha's cast who were less than cordial toward her. Lexi Vale, for one. She's direct competition. And Tomás Rivas wasn't exactly warm either."

Aisha frowned. "What are you talking about?"

Drew met her eyes. "Tomás was jealous. Not just of your role, but of the attention Remi gave you. He loaned Remi money to buy those flowers for your arrival on set. I suspect he wanted to be the one giving them to you."

Aisha's forehead creased. "He never said that."

"He wouldn't," Drew replied. "He's enamored with you. Remi kept him in the shadows, so he redirected the resentment toward you. As if any of it were your fault."

"I could see that," Debra said thoughtfully.

Singh glanced at her notes. "Tomás did have an injury on his right hand. He claimed it happened while opening a champagne bottle."

Drew's expression tightened slightly.

"What about your co-star?" Singh continued, scanning the file. "Ollie Barrett?"

"He's harmless," Aisha said with a dismissive wave. "He's too busy trying to become the next Mr. Hollywood."

"He fits the general physical description," Singh said. "But he has no prints in the system and no criminal record. He was present at the party and appears to live modestly."

"And the blonde in the video," Debra pressed. "The one who went into Remi's study before his death?"

Singh looked up.

"Yes. Rather a conundrum," Detective Singh said, rustling her notes as if masking her frustration. "There were seven blondes in white floral dresses that night. Aisha. Lexi Vale. A producer from the film. Georgia Lynn. A woman who claimed she was an extra and left the party before nine. And three crew members."

"We asked Lexi about that," Drew confirmed. "She said she never saw Remi after the photo shoot earlier that evening. We also asked her about the emerald ring."

"Let me guess," Singh said dryly. "She couldn't remember. Something about the universe not offering clarity."

"Correct," Debra replied. "I can't tell if it's an act or if she's spent too many years enjoying legal herbal remedies."

Singh leaned back in her chair, unimpressed. "We received the same response."

Drew nodded. "I spoke with Georgia Lynn that night. She has a noticeable nervous tic, and she seemed unusually frazzled. Disoriented, even." He paused, replaying the evening in his mind, mentally reconstructing the sequence of events.

“I also asked her about the emerald ring,” he added. “I didn’t see anything like that on her.”

Singh stood and crossed to the large whiteboard already crowded with photographs, timelines, and scribbled notes from Remi’s case. She added a symbol representing Lexi Vale’s photograph beside the earlier evidence, then drew a red line connecting the two.

“Next steps,” she said. “We review surveillance footage near both locations. We pull phone records where possible. We look for patterns in timing, proximity, and communication.”

She capped the marker and turned to Aisha.

“We also increase protection around you. No solo outings. Any new messages go directly to us.”

Her expression left little room for argument.

Drew’s cellphone rang. He glanced at the screen and rose from his chair. “Please excuse me. It’s part of our team,” he said, stepping aside to take the call.

Aisha tried not to stare, but she couldn’t help noticing the shift in Drew’s expression as he listened. The easy composure he had worn moments earlier tightened into something more focused, more troubled. When he ended the call and returned, whatever he had heard had clearly unsettled him.

“It appears our two cases have just been linked by another common denominator,” Drew said, puzzlement threading his voice. He looked directly at Detective Singh. “Do you have a record of a Matt Valen?”

The name hit Aisha like a jolt. “Matt? Remi’s assistant?”

“Two cases?” Detective Singh repeated, studying them carefully. She turned back to her computer and entered his name into the national database. “Let’s see if there’s anything on him in RMS or NCIC.”

"We were brought to L.A. on a separate matter," Drew explained. "We were hired by the actress Vivienne LeClaire. She's being stalked."

"Stalked?" Detective Singh looked up sharply. "Why didn't she contact the police?"

"She says she has. Multiple times. Filed complaints. But she felt they were just appeasing her and not actually doing anything about it."

Debra frowned. "I'm still not seeing the connection to our case."

"Vivienne recently received another note that was left inside her house," Drew continued. "She gave it to Israel and Grace. It read: *The Death of the Author. Griffith Observatory.* 7:30 p.m." He paused, letting the words settle. "When Israel and Grace went to Griffith Observatory, they spotted Matt sitting alone on the terrace, looking out over the city. Grace recognized him from Remi's party. The moment he saw them, he ran."

Aisha felt her pulse quicken.

"They chased him down the hill," Drew said. "During the pursuit, he dropped an old film program from *Velvet Ashes*. When they picked it up, they noticed one name in the credits had been scratched out."

The room fell quiet.

Aisha leaned forward. "Whose name was scratched out?"

"They didn't say. But if Matt was the one leaving Vivienne LeClaire those threatening notes, then he's tied to both cases. But why? Why now? Why him?" Drew pressed his fingers to his temples, trying to force the pieces together. "Grace did mention that when he saw her, he said, 'She never knew who created her.'"

"Matt said that about Vivienne?" Aisha turned toward him, her voice tightening.

"What if he was just at the observatory by happenstance?" Debra asked.

"Then why run?" Detective Singh countered. She paused, the title catching her attention. "*Velvet Ashes*. That's a film?"

"It's the movie that made Vivienne LeClaire a bona fide star," Aisha replied.

"Here's something." Detective Singh rolled her chair closer to the computer and leaned in. "Matt Valen was charged with assaulting his foster mother when he was twenty-one." She scanned further down the screen. "His case worker classified him as an autistic savant."

Debra, Aisha, and Drew exchanged measured glances. It was the first solid connection they had uncovered.

"His case worker and a court-appointed therapist documented several traits," Detective Singh continued, looking up briefly before reading aloud. "Listen to this. 'Shows significant intelligence and rigidity with overt violence. Exact repetition. Rewrites the same phrase multiple times until spacing, pressure, and alignment are identical. Destroys near-perfect versions. Chronological tyranny. Organizes memories, objects, or conversations strictly by time down to the minute and becomes visibly distressed when chronology is disrupted. Spatial symmetry obsession.'"

"Okay," Aisha said, thinking back. "I could see some of that. But for the most part, he seemed so mild-mannered."

"How did he ever work in the movie business?" Debra asked. "No movie is filmed in chronological order."

"Maybe that's why he was an assistant," Drew said. "He was also twenty-one at the time of that evaluation. Maybe he's learned to manage it."

"Remi really took him under his wing. He worked for Remi for years," Aisha said, remembering a conversation she'd had with him. "Matt missed nothing. He could blend into the background, exactly where he'd learned to survive." Her mind flicked through images of him on set. "He always moved quietly, organized to a fault, always one step ahead of Remi. That's why he could handle the chaos around him with a serene professionalism that made him seem almost invisible."

"What does 'the death of the author' signify?" Detective Singh asked. The phrasing clearly meant nothing to her.

"Debra, remember when we were upstairs in Vivienne's home and we found the ledger with the same words, 'the death of the author,' written over and over?" Aisha said. "We still don't know what it refers to."

Drew cleared his throat. "There's something we have to share, Detective Singh. Vivienne LeClaire had a brother who was also a savant."

Detective Singh stopped scrolling and looked up. "I'd say that's significant. Do we know anything about the brother?"

"Jeffries LeClaire drowned in the family pool the night of Vivienne LeClaire's opening night," Drew said. "There was a lot of scandal at the time. Some claimed she killed him. Others said the father was the real suspect."

Detective Singh was already pulling up articles online. "I see his death was ruled an accidental drowning."

"Huh!" Debra blurted. Then she frowned, thinking. "Well, Matt is too young to have seen *Velvet Ashes*, let alone know who Vivienne LeClaire is," she said, more to herself than anyone else.

"This is, admittedly, speculative, but what if Matt uncovered the story from the past, found a personal connection to it, and became fixated? He dug deeper, discovered that Vivienne LeClaire was still alive and living in Hollywood, and decided to pursue the theory." Detective Singh looked to the trio, gauging their reaction.

"I remember Matt telling me he grew up in a home where perfection was mandatory and praise was rare," Aisha said. "It shaped him into someone who equated worth with usefulness. But what if those beliefs were his own, not his foster mother's?"

"It's possible," Drew said, clearly receptive. "That would further define his personality profile. I'm still considering whether he could have killed Remi, and if so, what his motive would have been."

"He generally seemed distraught about Remi's death." Aisha shook her head, finding it difficult to imagine.

"Well, I say we bring him in for questioning and see what we can learn," Detective Singh said, decision made. "I'm going to have a few words with Ms. Vale as well. I don't know if I buy that Valley girl, universal yo-yo mumbo jumbo. I'm going to see if I can jar her memory."

"But wait," Drew said, thinking aloud. "Do you have enough probable cause to bring Matt in? And even if we do, questioning him now could be a mistake."

Detective Singh raised an eyebrow. "Why?"

"Because Matt would shut down," Drew replied. "He'd get careful. Whatever he's hiding would disappear behind rehearsed answers."

Singh considered that. "What are you suggesting?"

"We let him move," Drew said. "If he's as fixated as we think, he won't stay still. He'll lead us to something. A place, a person, an object tied to the truth."

Debra frowned. "That assumes he acts."

"He will," Aisha said. "If we nudge him."

Singh's expression sharpened. "Nudge him how?"

"We leak that Vivienne LeClaire has information, or that the studio has uncovered something tied to *Velvet Ashes*," Drew explained. "Nothing concrete. Just enough to suggest the past is resurfacing."

Aisha nodded slowly. "Or we mention a detail from the film we just did with Remi. Something obscure. The kind of detail only someone obsessed would react to."

"Exactly," Drew said. "And if that doesn't work, Aisha reaches out. Plausible. Casual. No pressure."

"And we watch," Debra said, following the thread now.

"We watch," Drew confirmed. "Where he goes. Who he contacts. What he's afraid of."

A beat passed.

"If Matt knows more than he's saying," Drew added quietly, "he won't be able to resist responding."

Detective Singh turned to Aisha. "What was the biggest controversy on set?"

"It was definitely the car crash on Mulholland," Aisha said.

"Good," Singh replied. "Directors, assistants, producers, executives, they'd all know about that. Let's use it as leverage and see where it leads." She looked over at her suspect board and exhaled. "We nudge, and we watch."

Chapter 16
Hollywood Forever

Drew rolled up to the gates of Paramount Studios, anticipation written all over his face.

"Don't look so nervous, Drew. I can see it from here," Aisha said, raising her voice into the phone. On the other end, Grace fumbled with it as Aisha reacted.

"Grace, hold the phone still. This is going to work. Trust me," Aisha reassured her.

"And if it doesn't, we go home," Elena added from the back seat.

"Okay, we're here," Drew quipped as he pulled up alongside the security guard at the front gate. He lowered his window and held his phone up toward the security booth.

"Hi, Eddie. That is Eddie, isn't it?" Aisha cooed from the phone.

Eddie studied Aisha's face on the screen before responding. "Hello, Miss." His gaze shifted from the joy lighting Aisha's expression to Drew, who held the phone rigidly. Eddie briefly surveyed the interior of the car, noting Grace beside him, grinning from ear to ear, and Elena in the back seat, offering a small wave.

"Eddie, I'm filming on location today, in Vancouver. I've asked my friends to come and collect my things from the last film. Would you please allow them to pass? They know where to go." She flashed her brightest movie-star smile and hoped it would be enough.

"Of course," Eddie said quickly. "Charlie, raise the gate!"

Drew hid his surprise and tossed the phone to Grace as they passed through the wrought-iron gates of Paramount Studios, the iconic water tower looming against a washed-out Los Angeles sky.

"I told you that would work," Aisha said.

"Thank goodness," Grace replied, smiling into the phone. "All right, we're in front of the offices. We'll call you later and let you know how it went." She made a fingers-crossed gesture toward the screen as she ended the call.

"I hope we find something," Grace added to Elena, who was already surveying the studio lot. "Not sure how we're going to do this, but…"

"That never stopped us before," Drew reminded her.

Elena shot him a look. "That was before we were trespassing on a studio lot with a very specific target and absolutely no clearance."

Grace adjusted the strap of her bag and glanced back at Elena. "You say that like we haven't done worse with less of a plan."

Drew smirked. "See? Team morale remains strong."

The lot buzzed with quiet, industry chaos. Golf carts zipped past carrying clipped conversations. Background actors clustered near soundstages in period costumes. Crew members hauled equipment with the weary efficiency of people who'd done this a thousand times. The air smelled faintly of coffee, hot asphalt, and fresh paint.

Elena scanned the map posted near the entrance. "Production offices are usually tucked behind the stages. If *The Last Tango* is still wrapping post-production, their paperwork should be archived, not destroyed."

"Assuming nobody wanted it destroyed," Grace added.

Drew didn't respond. His jaw wrenched in that familiar way it did when something felt off, but he hadn't fully named it yet.

They moved deeper into the lot, blending in through sheer confidence. No badges. No credentials. Just purposeful strides and the universal language of people who looked like they belonged. It worked better than it should have.

The production offices for *The Last Tango* were housed in a squat beige building with darkened windows and a sun-faded poster still taped beside the door. The film's title scrolled dramatically across an image of Aisha and a man in shadow, promising passion and danger. Drew felt a twist of irony in his gut.

Inside, the office was dim, fluorescent lights humming overhead. Filing cabinets lined the walls. A few desks sat abandoned, their surfaces cluttered with half-empty coffee cups, call sheets curling at the edges, and uneven stacks of color-coded folders.

A lean, distinguished man occupied the front desk. Silver threaded his temples, sharpening the angles of his face as he scrolled through his phone. At the sound of their arrival, his blue eyes lifted and settled on Drew with measured attention, assessing without appearing to.

"Can I help you?"

Drew didn't hesitate. "We're with insurance review. Following up on some production safety records."

The lie tightened in Elena's chest, but her expression didn't shift.

A faint crease formed between the man's brows. "I didn't hear anything about that."

Grace stepped in smoothly. "Short notice. That's kind of our thing." She offered a small, professional smile.

Silence lingered just long enough to register.

"They let you in at the front gate?" he asked.

Drew smiled and nodded, easy, unthreatened.

The man studied them another moment before giving a reluctant shrug. "Okay. Most of the production notes are archived in the back room. Don't take anything out of the building."

"Wouldn't dream of it," Drew replied.

He gestured down the hall. "I'm J.C."

"Drew." He inclined his head toward the others. "Elena. Grace."

J.C. held their gaze a second longer than necessary, as though filing them away, then returned to his phone. "I'll be here."

The archive room felt close and forgotten, air thick with paper and dust. Just another leftover from a major motion picture. Drew thought of the mess left behind at Paramount Plaza, the binders stacked without order once the rush had passed and no one cared anymore.

Metal shelves bowed under the weight of binders labeled by department: *Stunts. Rigging. Safety. Daily Reports.*

Elena's pulse quickened.

"This is it," she said quietly. "If something was flagged, it'll be here."

They split up without discussion.

Grace took the stunt binders. Drew moved to the daily production logs. Elena headed straight for Safety, her fingers skimming the spines until she found a thin red folder labeled *Safety Notes – Week 12.*

"Guys," she whispered.

They joined her quickly.

She opened the folder. Inside were printed forms, incident reports, minor injury logs, equipment checks. Routine. Page after page of routine.

Then she turned to a report dated two days before Aisha's near fatal stunt.

The heading stopped them cold.

Cable Tension Irregularities – Immediate Review Recommended.

The air in the room seemed to compress.

Grace leaned closer. "Read it."

Elena swallowed and began. "Fluctuations in cable tension during rehearsals. Not catastrophic, but inconsistent. Enough to warrant recalibration. Enough to delay the stunt until adjustments were made."

Grace and Drew exchanged a look.

Drew's jaw tightened. "When I went to the OSHA meeting with Remi, this was mentioned but never shown. The agent only referred to it."

Elena scanned the bottom of the page. "There's a signature."

She lifted the paper slightly. "Matt Valen."

Heat crept up Drew's neck. "He signed off on it."

Grace's voice sharpened. "Which means he saw it."

"And approved it," Elena said quietly.

A voice cut through the stillness.

"Everything okay in here?"

The man from the front desk stood in the doorway.

Drew didn't miss a beat. "It's all good, J.C."

J.C. lingered for half a second, then disappeared down the hall.

Drew flipped through the remaining pages, faster now, as if urgency might change what was there. He searched for a follow-up. A correction. Any notation that showed Matt had escalated the issue.

There was nothing.

Grace exhaled slowly. "He didn't tell Remi. If he had, the stunt would've been delayed."

Elena closed the folder with deliberate care.

"So why suppress it?"

Drew's mind raced. "Matt wasn't careless. He was meticulous to the point of obsession. Missing this doesn't fit. Unless it wasn't a miss."

"Pressure?" Grace asked, reading his expression. "Budget. Schedule. Studio deadlines?"

"Or," Drew said, "he knew something else."

They stood in silence, the hum of the fluorescent lights suddenly louder, heavier.

At the end of the hall, unseen, J.C. lingered. He told himself he was just curious. Insurance review did not usually show up unannounced. And they did not usually look like that. Too intense. Too invested. He watched Drew hold the document as if it carried weight beyond paper. His phone buzzed in his hand. J.C. glanced down, hesitated, then opened his messages.

Drew heard the vibration but chose not to react. Instead of drawing attention to it, he casually shifted positions with Grace, subtly blocking the line of sight to the folder.

J.C. lowered his voice. "Do you know these people?"

No response.

He angled his phone down the hallway and snapped a photo. The sound was faint, but in the stillness, Drew caught it.

Three figures clustered around a shelf. Heads bent together. Drew's profile clear. Elena's blond hair catching the light. Grace's rigid posture unmistakable.

J.C. sent the image. "They're in the production archives. Looking at safety notes," he murmured.

Elena slipped the document back into the folder. "We should copy this."

"I already did," Grace said, tapping her phone.

Drew nodded once. "We need that document. It's the only tangible proof Matt signed off on it. It could disappear. We can't risk that."

Elena opened the folder again, removed the report, and slid it inside her jacket. "Time to go."

When they stepped back into the hallway, J.C. looked up from the desk.

This time, his smile was different. Tight. Measured.

"Find what you needed?"

"For now," Drew said.

"Are you sure you found what you needed?" J.C.'s tone was casual, but he was stalling. "I just put a fresh pot of coffee on. How about I get you some?"

"We appreciate your time," Drew said with an easy smile.

They stepped out into the sunlight. The lot suddenly felt exposed, too open, too visible.

Grace exhaled once they were clear of the building. "Matt knew. He absolutely knew."

"And he stayed quiet," Elena added.

Drew glanced back at the production office, unease settling deep in his chest. "Which means whatever he was protecting, or afraid of, was bigger than the stunt."

They headed toward the row where Drew was certain he had parked. Certain. He stopped abruptly. The space was empty. "No," he said under his breath, turning slowly in a full circle. "No. No. What happened to the car?"

Grace scanned the asphalt, her expression flinched. "This is where we came in."

Elena's stomach knotted. "Are you sure?"

Drew dragged a hand through his hair. "I… maybe I parked somewhere else?" The uncertainty in his voice betrayed him.

They walked the row again, then again. Nothing. No car. No broken glass. No sign it had ever been there.

"This doesn't make sense," Grace muttered. "Cars don't just disappear."

A cold realization slid down Drew's spine.

"Something's wrong."

They moved deeper into the lot, widening their search and cutting through the backlots where the studio felt less polished, more skeletal. Massive soundstages loomed like warehouses, their numbered doors half open. Outdoor sets sat abandoned between shoots, false building facades standing beside scattered lighting rigs. Cranes folded in on themselves like resting insects. Thick cables snaked across the ground.

The farther they walked, the quieter it became. No golf carts. No chatter. Just the echo of their own footsteps.

Elena slowed. "Do you feel that?"

Grace nodded. "Yeah."

Drew glanced back.

Two figures had emerged from between a pair of soundstages. Both wore dark clothing, their faces obscured by black masks. They were not rushing. Just following. Deliberate. Certain.

Drew's pulse spiked. "Guys," he said under his breath. "Don't look. But we're not alone."

Grace kept her eyes forward. "How close?"

"Too close."

When Drew subtly increased his pace, the men did the same. That was all the confirmation he needed.

"Walk faster," he said.

They did. The crunch of gravel behind them quickened.

"Okay," Elena whispered. "That's not paranoia."

Drew broke into a jog. "Run."

They took off, weaving between equipment carts and towering light stands. The studio lot transformed into a maze of shadows and dead ends. Footsteps thundered behind them, no longer subtle, no longer pretending.

They were being chased.

Ahead, a stone wall marked the far edge of the property.

"Drew, help me up," Elena said, reaching for his hand as he scrambled halfway up the wall, using a stack of weathered barrels for leverage.

He pulled her toward him. Below, Grace struggled to find footing against the slick wood.

“Where does this lead?” she called, bracing her foot and pushing upward.

Drew hauled himself higher, breath uneven. “I think I know,” he said, then hesitated. “I just don’t want to say it.”

“Because it leads to a cemetery?” Elena finished for him.

She swung a leg over the top and looked out beyond the wall. Rows of headstones stretched across manicured grass.

“Is this Hollywood Forever Cemetery?” she called down.

Drew climbed up beside her and looked out over the familiar expanse beyond the studio walls.

With one swift motion, Drew launched himself from the smooth white perimeter wall onto the flat rooftop of a mausoleum on the other side.

“Yes,” he called back, breathless. “Hollywood Forever.”

Before him stretched a sprawling, immaculate resting place for many of Hollywood’s most celebrated artists and performers. Pristine monuments rose in pale stone rows, tributes not only to the names etched into them but to the mythology of Hollywood itself. Nestled in the heart of Tinseltown, Hollywood Forever Cemetery unfolded across manicured acres that balanced grandeur with an almost unsettling intimacy. Willow trees stirred in the breeze. Ancient cypress stood like silent sentinels among the graves. A central lake caught the sunlight, glistening beside an ornate mausoleum.

Grace barely registered any of it. She was too busy fighting for air.

She risked a glance back toward the studio wall.

“They’re waving a gun,” she shouted.

She pulled herself up to the top of the wall and froze when she saw what lay beyond. “A cemetery?”

"Grace, focus," Elena snapped, grabbing her arm. "One foot on the wall, one on the mausoleum. Now."

A gunshot cracked through the air.

The bullet tore past Grace's head, close enough that she felt its heat slice the space beside her. She ducked instinctively and hurled herself forward, pushing off the wall with both feet. She landed hard on the mausoleum roof, knees buckling before she caught her balance.

"There are stairs," Drew said, already moving toward the far corner of the massive crypt.

They raced across the stone surface and descended the narrow metal steps on the opposite side. At the bottom, they paused only long enough to orient themselves among the maze of marble and grass.

"Do either of them look familiar?" Elena asked, her voice low.

"I don't recognize them," Grace shot back, panic edging her words. "They're wearing masks."

Drew hesitated. "I think I recognize one of them." "Come on," he said, scanning the pathways between headstones. "Let's move."

They pressed their backs to the cold wall and edged forward, Drew's eyes flicking in every direction, waiting for the next threat.

"Is it Matt?" Grace asked.

Drew didn't answer.

"This is the wall they show movies on at night," Elena said, breath tight as she tried to remember the layout.

"Movies? In a cemetery?" Grace's disbelief cut through her panic.

Elena nodded. "It's a thing here."

Drew glanced past the wall, then pointed. "You're right. The main building is just to our right."

They broke into a faster run, cutting across the well-manicured lawn and looking back over their shoulders. Ahead, a fountain sparkled, sunlight shattering into bright arcs of water. Beyond it, sculpted gardens stretched in perfect symmetry, vivid blooms and whispering palms radiating a calm that didn't belong anywhere near them. For a moment, the serenity of the grounds felt unreal, like it had been staged.

"Hey," Grace blurted, breathless and furious, "I was nearly shot!"

A sudden scream snapped through the air and stopped them mid-stride.

"What was that?" Grace whispered, chilled.

They stood still, listening. Drew held up a hand. Elena's pulse hammered in her throat.

Another scream followed, then another, high and sharp.

They edged forward.

Two peacocks wandered out from behind a tall grave marker, completely unbothered. One let out the piercing shriek again, as if offended by their presence. The other followed, slower, regal.

Their blue and green feathers fanned open in a deliberate sweep, like an ancient tapestry unfurling in the sun. Iridescent eyespots shimmered across the spread, watching without seeing.

For a beat, the trio forgot to move. They stood frozen, caught between terror and the surreal beauty of it.

The birds' calls echoed through the cemetery, a haunting sound that seemed to bounce off the stones they hid behind. The peacocks, oblivious to everything but their own slow procession, strutted past. Their tails trailed behind them like rivers of color.

"Peacocks?" Grace said, sharp with disbelief.

"They live here," Drew confirmed.

"You've got to be kidding me. What is this place?" Grace shook her head. "Only in Hollywood."

Gunfire ripped through the air.

Bullets hissed past them and slammed into the marble headstone ahead. The impact sent white shards flying, the crack splitting the quiet of the graveyard.

Grace screamed and stumbled back. Elena swore under her breath.

"Oh my God, they hit Johnny Ramone's grave," Grace gasped, fear and disbelief tangling in her voice.

Drew spun, adrenaline surging. His eyes swept the cemetery, scanning the pathways, the monuments, the shadows. The silence between shots felt thick, heavy, ladened with anticipation.

"There," Elena said, pointing. "They're on top of the mausoleum we just came from."

Drew followed her finger and spotted them. Dark figures, elevated, steady.

"Move," he said. "The Cathedral Mausoleum is up ahead."

They took off along the winding path, breaths ragged as they kept glancing over their shoulders. The two gunmen stayed on them, relentless, closing the distance with every second.

"This way," Drew urged, veering toward the looming structure ahead.

The Hollywood Cathedral Mausoleum towered before them, Gothic arches and elaborate carvings holding the space with austere beauty. They rushed up the stairs and shoved open the heavy brass doors at the top. The hinges groaned as they slipped into the cool, sunlit interior.

A central corridor stretched ahead. Two rows of life-size statues lined the hall, guiding the eye toward a stained-glass window at the far end. Vibrant light poured through it, scattering jewel-toned patterns across the marble floor.

The trio paused, glancing left, then right, searching for somewhere to disappear among the offshoot corridors that led deeper into the mausoleum.

"Which way do we go now?" Grace's voice caught, tight with panic.

For a second, the sacred space almost calmed Elena. The air smelled faintly of jasmine, as if someone had tried to soften the stone with something living.

"Left," Drew said, steering them before they could second-guess it.

They turned into the corridor. Rows of crypts lined the walls, marble facades carved with delicate detail, and fitted with brass plaques. Above them, the vaulted ceiling rose high, supported by Romanesque columns that seemed to lift the weight of the building toward domed glass panels overhead.

"They're here," Elena whispered, stopping short.

From behind them came the sound of the front doors shifting again, a low groan that rolled down the corridor.

They hurried forward. Their footsteps echoed in the calm sanctuary, each step too loud, each one giving them away.

"Tread lightly," Drew warned. "They're going to hear us."

They slipped through a set of floor-to-ceiling doors on the left into a smaller room lined with full-length crypts. Another stained-glass window watched from the far wall, flooding the space with color that made everything feel unreal.

Elena tried concealing her heavy breaths as she looked around.

"Oh no. Dead end," she said, then immediately winced. "No pun intended." She grabbed Drew by the shoulders, spun him back toward the corridor, and pushed them all out again.

"Look," Grace whispered. "There's a spiral staircase at the end of the hall."

They sprinted down the corridor and reached the stairs. A small sign hung from a chain stretched across the banister.

"Do not enter," Grace read.

Before she could say anything else, Elena unhooked the chain, to Grace's immediate shock. "Let's move, doll."

They followed the spiral downward, circling deeper beneath the mausoleum.

By the time they reached the basement level, a chill seemed to seep from the stone itself. The air grew heavier, thick with dampness. Their cellphone lights threw long, unsteady shadows across the walls, stretching and shifting like something alive.

"Are we crazy, or what?" Grace panted. "Where are we going?"

Down here, the crypts felt less like resting places and more like tombs of forgotten grandeur. Ornate marble facades, dulled with age, bore inscriptions that had lost their shine. Some were sealed behind heavy bronze doors etched with intricate designs, worn smooth by time. Others stood open, revealing rows of niches where urns sat in perfect, permanent silence.

Elena stared into the dim; her face lit from below by her phone. "This has always been one of my deepest fears," she murmured.

"What?" Drew asked, sweeping his light farther ahead. "Being chased through a cemetery?"

"No," Elena said, then let mock horror curl into her voice. "Being trapped in a mausoleum with no Wi-Fi."

"Now that's terrifying," Drew chuckled, and the sound was almost normal. "I'd take a ghost over a dial-up connection any day."

For a moment, his humor was the only thing cutting through the terror still hunting them.

Grace shot them both a look. "You two are impossible."

"Sorry. Nervous energy, doll. It's my way of coping with this stress," Elena said, wiping beads of sweat from her brow.

"You should be horrified like me," Grace shot back, taking another cautious step as if something might be waiting in front of her.

The faint glow from the sconces flickered again as they pushed deeper into the corridor. Between the crypts sat small prayer spaces, alcoves carved into the stone where mourners once knelt in solemn remembrance. Now they were abandoned, their sanctity worn down by time and neglect. Still, the air felt crowded with what had been left behind, as if the walls remembered every whispered prayer.

"All these graves are from the 1920s and 30s," Grace murmured, scanning the plaques as she moved.

"It looks like they built on top of the older crypts as the cemetery expanded," Drew said, tilting his head toward the low ceiling overhead.

Elena stopped so suddenly that Drew walked straight into her. Grace, close behind, collided with Drew.

"Did you hear that?" Elena whispered.

All three turned at once, looking back down the corridor.

For a moment, nothing moved. Nothing breathed. But the stillness felt watched. Then, faintly, a creak drifted through the dark, like a gate shifting on its hinges.

"They've found us," Grace said, panic rising fast.

"We don't know that," Drew insisted, though he didn't sound fully convinced.

They held still, listening for anything that might confirm what their nerves were already certain of. Uncertainty crawled up their spines, tightening its grip.

Drew glanced at Grace and lifted a hand, subtle. "Grace, you're shaking," he mouthed. "Breathe."

Whispers seemed to seep into the corridor, like a draft slipping through a cracked door. The three of them traded quick, fearful glances.

Then a gate slammed shut somewhere in the distance.

"I don't remember passing a gate," Grace said. "Do you?"

No one answered. They didn't have to. The looks they exchanged said enough.

They turned back the way they'd come, their steps slowing as the corridor narrowed around them. The silence felt physical, pressing against their ears, swallowing the small sounds of their breathing.

At the foot of the spiral staircase, they stopped. A gate stood there now. Solid. Unyielding. Closed.

Grace stared at it as if staring hard enough might change what she was seeing.

Then, from above, came footsteps on the stairs. Slow. Deliberate. Unhurried. Someone was climbing up, taking their time.

Elena's mouth went dry.

A faint chuckle drifted down through the spiral, thin and ugly in the dark. Not nervous. Not accidental. It was confident, like they were savoring it.

Helplessness washed over the trio. Alone. Buried under stone. No way out, and no one close enough to hear them.

Drew swallowed, the laughter still scraping at his nerves. "I'm fairly sure one of those guys was Matt."

Grace grabbed the cold metal bars and pulled. Once, hard. Then again, harder, her breath turning sharp. The gate didn't move. Only a low metallic groan answered her, echoing down the corridor as if the mausoleum itself had noticed them.

They hadn't passed this before. Had they?

Grace looked over her shoulder. The corridor behind them stretched on, unchanged, too familiar and somehow wrong. But the gate in front of them felt impossible. This gate hadn't been here.

Grace braced herself. She drew her leg back and drove a hard kick into the center of the gate, desperate for any sign of give.

"Oh my God," she gasped. "We're going to die right here and they won't even have to move the bodies. We're trapped."

They scattered into motion, searching the mausoleum for anything that might pass as an exit. Drew ran his hands along the marble beside the gate, feeling for hidden seams, a latch, a panel. Elena slipped her arm through the bars and probed for the lock mechanism on the far side. Grace moved toward a shallow niche that held a small altar, scanning the stonework for anything out of place.

Drew stepped back and studied the gate again. Then he turned to them with a decisive nod. "Together," he said. "Same spot. Same time. On my count. If one kick won't do it, maybe all three will."

He set his stance first, feet planted, squaring himself to the center of the gate. Elena moved to his left, brushing dust from her hands as she matched his position. Grace took the right, forcing her breath into something steady.

"On three," Drew said, low and controlled.

They nodded.

"One."

The silence coiled around them.

"Two."

Their muscles tightened. Weight shifted back.

"Three."

They kicked in unison. Boots hit metal with a sharp crack that echoed down the corridor. The gate shuddered, rattling in its frame. Dust shook loose from the hinges and drifted down in thin, pale clouds.

The gate held.

The impact had done nothing.

Drew reset his stance. "Again," he said, determination sharpening his voice.

They pulled back, ready to strike as one, and kicked in unison. Another hard, synchronized blow. The gate jolted. The clang ricocheted through the narrow space.

It still didn't give.

No bend. No crack. Not even the smallest hint of surrender.

Elena hissed and stepped back, shaking out her leg. "Nothing," she muttered. "Not even a wobble."

Grace pressed her forehead to her sleeve, breathing hard. Pain throbbed up her shin, but what hurt more was the gate itself. Unmoved. Unbothered. Like it could swallow anything they threw at it.

Drew ran his hand along the frame, as if pressure and willpower might find a weakness. His brow tightened. "It should've shifted," he said, quieter now. "Three people at once. It should've done something."

But the truth was right in front of them. The gate hadn't budged. Their efforts had vanished into it without leaving a mark.

The echo of the blows drained away, and the silence returned. Heavy. Suffocating. Absolute.

"We need another way out," Drew said, forcing resolve into his voice.

He took one last look at the locked gate, then turned toward the corridor stretching deeper into the mausoleum. "If we can't go back, we go forward. Let's see what's at the end of this."

They moved as a unit, keeping close to the wall as they followed the passage through the underground crypts. Each turn seemed to pull them farther into the earth. The air grew colder, dampness clinging to their skin. Somewhere ahead, water dripped in a slow, steady rhythm.

At a junction, they stopped.

"My heart feels like it's going to explode," Grace said, each word thin with effort. She bent over, hands braced on her knees.

Elena touched her shoulder, firm but gentle. "Come on, doll. Deep breaths. We're strong together. Now breathe."

Drew lifted his phone light. "There's some kind of light up ahead."

Turning the corner, they found themselves along the west wall of the crypt. Two narrow corridors stretched before them, each ending in a stained-glass window. The one at the eastern end glowed faintly, its light cool and restrained. The western window, however, flooded its corridor in rich gold.

"Will you look at that," Elena breathed.

Drawn to it, they moved toward the brighter window.

"Did someone turn the light on?" Grace whispered.

As they approached, something felt wrong. The light pouring through the stained glass was not dim or artificial. It carried a warmth that felt alive.

Drew stepped forward, brow furrowed, fingers brushing along the stone frame. “These can’t be lit by bulbs,” he said. “You’d have to replace them every few months. And how would anyone even reach them down here?”

Elena leaned closer, studying the intricate patterns woven through the glass. Then she went still.

“No,” she said slowly. “This isn’t artificial. It’s sunlight.”

Grace blinked. “Down here? That’s impossible. We’re underground.”

Drew gestured toward the window behind them on the eastern side. “Look at that one. It’s dimmer. That’s because it’s late afternoon. The sun’s farther west.”

The realization settled over Elena in a rush. Her breath caught.

“They aren’t windows,” she whispered. “They’re window wells.”

A grim smile tugged at Drew’s mouth. “Exactly. The glass sits at the bottom of a shaft. The light only reaches this one when the sun shifts far enough west.”

Grace took a step back, unease threading into her voice. “But we’re beneath the ground. How can there be a well above us?”

Drew crouched, examining the stonework more closely. “These crypts weren’t built as simple burial chambers,” he said. “They were meant to be mausoleums. The architects designed shafts to channel natural light below.”

Grace glanced down the corridor, thinking it through. “Then the sconces we passed must have been added later.”

"They must have LED lights in them. They never go out." Elena knelt beside Drew, her fingers tracing the edge of the stained glass.

"If we can remove a piece…" Drew pushed to his feet, determination settling across his face. "Let's see if any of these panes will come free."

They worked carefully, prying at the seams. The first pane resisted. The second shifted. With a final, careful tug, the glass loosened. One by one, they removed enough pieces to carve out a narrow opening.

Drew went first, bracing his hands on the stone and pulling himself through. Grace followed, then Elena. They dropped down into the well, blinking against the sudden brightness.

The late afternoon sun poured over them, its warmth a sharp contrast to the chill of the crypt below. For a moment, none of them spoke.

Then they looked up.

The stone walls rose in a tight circle around them. About seven feet overhead, a short iron ladder had been bolted into the rough stone. Its lowest rung hovered just beyond their reach.

"How are we ever going to reach that?" Grace muttered, disbelief edging her voice. "Why would they put a ladder that doesn't even touch the ground?"

They exchanged uneasy glances.

The crypt had been constructed with deliberate care. Nothing about it felt accidental. Which meant this was not an oversight. The ladder had been placed just high enough to allow access from above, but not escape from below.

"We can hoist each other up," Drew said finally, steady but thinking fast.

Elena frowned. "And what happens to the last one?"

Silence settled over them.

The ladder was the only visible way out. But if two climbed, one would remain at the bottom of the well.

No one volunteered.

Suddenly, Elena's eyes widened. "Wait," she said, her voice sharpening. "Look at the stone around the ladder. This isn't just a well. It's a shaft."

Drew and Grace squinted upward. Now that they were closer to the wall, the differences were obvious. The stone was uneven, carved with shallow grooves and narrow ledges that had not been visible from the center of the well.

"We can climb it," Drew said, the plan forming as he studied the handholds. "The ladder isn't the only way up. Okay, Grace. You're first."

Grace nodded and moved to the wall. She tested a foothold, then another, fingers searching for purchase in the grooves. Slowly, carefully, she began to climb.

"I've got it!" she cried, her voice breaking into a triumphant screech as her hands closed around the first rung of the ladder.

"Good. Keep going," Drew urged. Then he turned to Elena. "You're next."

Elena followed the same path Grace had taken, pressing herself close to the stone as she climbed. Her fingers slipped once, then steadied. When she reached the ladder, she caught the first rung and hauled herself up.

Below her, Drew mirrored her movements. He gripped the lowest rung like a pull-up bar and lifted himself high enough to wedge his foot onto the steel step. With controlled effort, he climbed after them.

One by one, they ascended the ladder until their heads neared the top of the shaft.

A metal grate sealed the opening above, its grid pattern casting shadows across their faces as sunlight filtered through.

Grace froze.

Drew glanced up. “What is it?”

Elena already understood. “Grace, there has to be a latch along the seam,” she said, steady but urgent. “Feel around the edge. There has to be a release.”

With one determined shove, Grace found the latch. The mechanism gave with a sharp metallic snap. She pushed the grate upward and hauled herself over the edge into open air, leaving the suffocating shaft behind.

Elena emerged next, scrambling over the rim. Drew followed close behind. The three of them collapsed onto the ground, chests heaving, their ragged breaths breaking the stillness. For a brief, fragile moment, the weight of what they had endured seemed to lift. They were out.

Daylight poured over them, bright and unfiltered, almost unreal after the hours spent entombed below. The sun should have brought comfort. Instead, it heightened everything.

They pushed themselves upright.

Their eyes swept the tree line, the narrow path, the scattered stones that formed walkways between burial sites. Every shadow seemed deliberate. Every patch of stillness felt staged. They searched for movement, for figures, for any sign their captors might still be nearby.

The silence unsettled them. It was too complete, too composed, as if the world itself had paused to watch what they would do next.

Drew turned in a slow circle, panic beginning to rise beneath his relief.

“Now I have to find my car,” he shouted.

Chapter 17
Venice Beach

"I told you it would work." Aisha leaned back in the chaise, filing her nails as though the night had been uneventful.

"Are you kidding?" Grace paced the length of the room. "We were almost shot and buried alive."

"Yes, but you weren't. That's a testament to how savvy you are." Aisha gave a small shrug, still focused on her nails.

Grace brushed it off. Her nerves were still humming.

"I'm almost certain one of them was Matt," Drew said. "The other guy was taller. Built like the man you, Debra, and I saw outside Lexi's bungalow." He moved between the kitchen and the living room, restless and unable to sit.

"Who was shooting at you?" Aisha asked, finally glancing up.

"The taller one. He had the gun. It's a good thing he was a lousy shot. Otherwise…" Drew let the thought die. No one needed it finished.

"So Matt was tipped off by the office guy." Elena stepped out of the kitchen carrying two cups of coffee. She handed one to Drew and the other to Grace. "Where does he fit into all of this?"

"I don't know. But he was probably the one who had my car towed," Drew said under his breath.

"Maybe he was Matt's assistant. Matt had a lot on his shoulders. The director's assistant job is about controlling information," Aisha said, her tone more deliberate now. "As Remi's assistant, Matt filtered which documents, emails, and reports reached the director. He relayed messages between Remi and the assistant directors, producers, and department heads. He kept track of what the director had been told and when." She paused, thoughtful. "Matt handled all of that for Remi. He handled it well."

"Or he had someone handling it for him," Grace murmured.

"He understood that if something went wrong, he would be the weakest link in the chain," Drew said. "That gave him room to control the situation." His expression hardened. "And manipulate it."

"But what would his motive be?" Elena took a careful sip of her coffee and sat beside Grace on the sofa.

"Matt was there on Mulholland Drive the night of the shoot," Aisha said. "He knew that car was having issues. He never told Remi. He knew Ollie and I would be in it." Her grip tightened on the nail file. "Why would he do that to me? To Remi?"

"Here's another question." Elena lifted her hand slightly. "What is Matt doing sending threatening notes to Vivienne LeClaire?"

"There has to be a savant connection," Drew said, agitation creeping into his voice. "What are the odds we have two separate cases tied together by the same threads?"

"Drew!" Francy called from the kitchen. "Your phone is ringing. It's Detective Singh."

Drew stepped away to answer. Sirens blared through the line. "Hello?"

"Drew," Detective Singh said, raising her voice over the noise. "Sorry about the background. I got your message. I'm sending a squad car to Matt's last known address. We need to bring him in for questioning."

"Good. Any other leads?"

"Nothing solid," she replied. "We're heading to the Calabasas address now. I'll let you know what we find."

"Thank you, Detective." Drew ended the call and returned to the living room. "She's sending a unit to Matt's place in Calabasas. They want to bring him in."

"Yes. So he can be charged with attempted murder and burying us alive," Grace snapped.

"Exactly," Drew said.

"Maybe he was jealous of Remi?" Aisha suggested, though she did not sound convinced. She shook her head, doubt written across her face.

"Hey, guys." Israel stepped out of his bedroom, laptop still in hand. "I just got movement on one of Vivienne's security cameras. It's Madame Arquette."

"Where?" Elena called out, already rising from the sofa.

"She's in the living room with Vivienne now. I'll keep an eye on them," Israel said, eyes fixed on his screen.

Aisha rose from the chaise and disappeared into her bedroom, raising a single finger as if she had just remembered something important. Moments later, she returned with a thick script in hand. She flipped through it quickly, stopping at the cast and crew contact page.

"It's interesting," she said. "Matt Valen lists a Venice Beach address."

Drew immediately redialed the detective. "Voicemail," he muttered. "I'll leave a message."

"Drew, why don't we just go to that address?" Elena stood, finishing the last sip of coffee before setting the cup down.

"Now you're energized," he said with a faint smile. "All right. Let's go." He turned to Grace. "You coming?"

Grace stared at them as if they had lost all sense of reason. "I was shot at and almost buried alive. Whatever happens next can happen without me getting up."

☆☆☆

Venice Beach had always been sacred ground for Drew. Summers spent learning to surf had forged his connection to the place, and his late aunt used to bring him here to while away entire afternoons along the boardwalk and the shore. Now, with Elena beside him, he moved through the crowd with a familiarity that felt almost instinctive, sidestepping rollerbladers and skateboarders who zipped past street vendors, strolling shoppers, and wide-eyed daydreamers who gave the beach its restless charm.

A lone guitarist, dressed in weathered blue jeans and a battered hat, strummed a melody that drifted like warm honey through the air. His bare, sun-bronzed torso caught the light as his golden voice poured into the afternoon. Elena gave him a slow nod of appreciation. "Great voice," she said.

Beside him stood a strong, brown-speckled horse, listening as if the song were meant for him alone. Every so often, the animal dipped its head into a bucket of straw and chewed in steady rhythm with the music.

They continued on toward the Venice Canals, a verdant refuge tucked just beyond the noise of the boardwalk. Sunlight shimmered across placid water. White arched bridges framed reflections of flowering gardens. Elegant cottages stood shoulder to shoulder with modern homes, some with kayaks or paddleboards tied to private docks. The air hummed with the soft ripple of water and the chorus of birds. Egrets, herons, and ducks glided alongside them, lending the moment something cinematic and quietly timeless.

"The address is on the left bank," Drew said, glancing at his phone.

They crossed a sloping footbridge that led to a narrow walkway. "There." He pointed toward a light blue clapboard house perched close to the canal's edge.

"Let's see if we can catch a glimpse through the side window," Drew murmured, his voice low and measured.

They moved toward the wide bay window, its glass obscured by a thin lace curtain that fluttered faintly in the breeze. The scent of damp wood and old paint clung to the air. Drew hesitated, then leaned forward, angling for a clearer view.

"There," he whispered, eyes narrowing. "The intel was right."

Elena pressed her hand against the rotting frame, her fingers grazing cracked layers of peeling paint. She leaned in beside him, focusing on the room beyond the curtain. Two men stood deep in conversation. One of them was Matt, instantly recognizable.

"Hey. That's the guy from the records office. Can you hear what they're saying?" Elena breathed, nodding toward the older man. Silver hair traced his temples. His build was lean and wiry, his posture unmistakably that of someone shaped by the ocean. Board shorts and faint streaks of purple wax along his forearm hinted at a life spent surfing.

Recognition hit her hard. "Look at them standing side by side. They could definitely be the masked men we saw at the cemetery." She glanced at Drew.

"It's them," Drew said, his voice tight. "The builds match. It's Remi's assistant, Matt. And J.C. from the office."

Elena's eyes sharpened. "Then Matt did get the message."

Drew lowered himself carefully beneath the sill, every movement controlled, cautious.

Elena shifted closer to the frame. Too close. Her elbow struck a loose pane of glass.

It rattled sharply in its casing.

They both froze.

Inside, there was a flash of movement.

In a mirror down the hall, one of the men caught their silhouettes. Faint, but unmistakable. His eyes widened.

Then he ran.

"Damn it. He saw us," Elena said, already in motion.

The man burst from the room and sprinted toward the rear exit. Elena grabbed Drew's arm. "We've been made."

"Split up," Drew shouted as he saw Matt bolt in the opposite direction through the house.

Elena tore down the side of the clapboard home and spilled onto the narrow walkway beside the canal. The suspect raced ahead, charging over a quaint arched bridge and into a maze of winding paths. Ducks scattered across the water beside him, cutting sharp lines through the surface.

Elena's pulse hammered in her throat as she chased him through the hidden oasis, her footsteps echoing against wood planks and stone.

Drew burst through the backyard gate, adrenaline spiking, and charged onto a narrow footbridge arching over the Venice Canal. The wooden planks groaned beneath his pounding steps. Ahead,

Matt wove past homes wrapped in deceptive serenity, drawing them deeper into the quiet labyrinth and deeper into danger.

“Matt!” Drew shouted, his voice ragged. “Stop! I just want to talk!”

They both saw the closed footbridge at the same instant. Neither slowed.

Drew did not register the small rowboat pulled against the grassy bank until Matt broke toward it. In one fluid motion, Matt splashed in and began paddling with his hands, scooping hard and alternating sides. His long reach gave him an advantage, and the boat cut quickly across the narrow canal.

Drew swore under his breath and sprinted past the shoreline toward the condemned bridge.

He took the broken steps two at a time and pushed onto the sagging span. Each plank shifted beneath him. The entire structure dipped and creaked as if deciding whether to hold. One wrong step could send him crashing into the murky water five feet below.

He kept his eyes locked on Matt as the boat scraped the opposite bank. Matt leapt out and bolted without looking back.

Drew hit the far side seconds later just as a child’s laughter drifted over a garden wall ahead. A family rounded the corner, enjoying an afternoon stroll.

Matt did not hesitate.

He cut straight toward them and slammed into a mother pushing a stroller, a smaller child clutching her free hand. The impact knocked her sideways. She screamed.

The stroller tipped.

For a suspended second, it balanced on the canal’s edge.

Then it rolled forward and plunged into the water.

Drew stopped cold, the world narrowing to the splash.

Rescue or pursuit.

In that heart-stopping moment, Matt slipped past and vanished through a garden gate Drew had never noticed. It was camouflaged by thick bougainvillea, nearly invisible unless you knew where to look. Beyond it, a narrow path wound down to a private dock where a fragile gondola sat tethered to a cleat.

Drew did not hesitate. He lunged for the stroller and grabbed the baby just as water began spilling over its edge. The mother and her child cried out together, their wails swallowed by the unnatural stillness of the canal.

He placed the baby safely in the mother's trembling arms, waited only long enough to see she had her footing, then turned back toward the water.

The canal lay quiet again.

Drew retraced his steps and pushed through the concealed gate. At the end of the winding path, the gondola drifted loose from its mooring, rocking gently against the dock.

Empty.

Matt was gone.

Elena burst out from the canal onto the sun-drenched boardwalk and spotted her suspect weaving through the crowd. In one swift motion, he drew a gun and fired into the air. The crack split the afternoon. People screamed and scattered in every direction.

He spun, yanked a stunned young man off his motorcycle, practically ripping it from his grasp, then gunned the engine and shot down the boardwalk.

Elena froze for half a second. There was no chance of catching him on foot.

Then she saw them. The tall steed and the golden throat singer from earlier were trying to guide the horse away from the chaos. Her pulse surged. An idea sparked.

Before she could second-guess herself, she sprinted toward the entertainers and, in one fluid motion, vaulted onto the horse's back, catching the owner completely off guard.

"Hey! What do you think you're doing?" the singer shouted.

"I'll bring him back. I promise," Elena called over her shoulder.

She seized the reins and felt the animal's powerful muscles contract beneath her. She clicked her tongue twice. "Come on, boy. You're going to help me catch a real bad man."

The stallion snorted, tossing his mane as if in answer.

They surged forward. Hooves thundered against the concrete path skimming the ocean's edge. Behind her, the horse's guardian shouted furiously in Italian, his voice fading as they gained speed.

The surf crashed alongside them, spraying salt into the air. Elena's pigtails whipped in the wind. Each breath burned her lungs, but adrenaline electrified her, sharpening everything. The sun blazed overhead. Sand and sea spray blurred at the edges of her vision.

She had never felt more alive.

The horse surged onto the sand, stretching into a harder gallop as the beach opened before them. The Pacific blurred at Elena's side. Beneath her, the brown-speckled steed moved with fierce purpose, as if it understood exactly why they had been thrown together. Elena leaned low into the wind and loosened her grip, trusting the animal to find its stride in the chase.

Ahead, the rider veered onto the Santa Monica Pier, the silhouette of the amusement park rising against the sky. Elena followed without hesitation. Hooves pounded from sand to cement, then thundered onto the wooden planks of the pier. Heads snapped toward her as the sound echoed down the pier.

The crowd split instinctively. Gasps and whispers trailed behind her, as if the stunned onlookers believed they were watching a scene unfold on a movie set.

She focused forward.

The suspect was running out of space.

At the very tip of the pier, he had nowhere left to go. Behind him loomed the towering carousel of hand-carved horses, glowing beneath carnival lights. Ahead stretched nothing but the endless Pacific.

Why would he push this far?

The suspect stiffened, panic tightening his frame. He could not slow the motorcycle in time. Elena watched as he deliberately tipped the bike sideways to avoid hurtling off the edge. Metal scraped wood. The motorcycle skidded across the planks in a shower of sparks beneath the neon lights.

He tumbled hard, rolling several feet and narrowly missing the frozen crowd.

The motorcycle lay smoking at the pier's end.

Elena reined in the horse, her heart hammering, eyes locked on the suspect.

"It's over," she called. "You have nowhere to go."

He lifted his head from where he lay sprawled on the boards, frantically searching for his gun.

Ten feet away, an elderly man bent down and picked up the firearm at his feet.

Elena caught the man's eye. "Sir, please…" Her voice faded as she watched him slowly tuck the weapon into the front of his waistband.

The suspect scanned for his next move.

Acting on instinct, Elena leaned forward in the saddle.

He lunged to run, but his pant leg snagged beneath the horse's heavy hoof. Off balance and disarmed, he stumbled and clawed at the planks, scrambling against the animal in a desperate attempt to free himself.

The crowd gasped as sirens wailed from the entrance to the pier. Bystanders shouted frantic warnings to approaching officers.

In a reckless surge of defiance, the suspect jabbed the horse's flank.

"Where do you think you're going?" Elena demanded, her voice slicing through the chaos.

He tore himself loose and staggered upright, wiping sweat and grit from his eyes, then stumbled again, veering dangerously toward the edge of the pier. A sharp yelp and a string of curses followed.

"Stop running!" Elena shouted, alarm tightening her voice. "You're going to fall. Listen, what's your name?"

A sudden, ominous creak echoed overhead.

Her gaze snapped upward.

One of the carousel's light fixtures swung wildly above them, its cable fraying, the lamp swaying like a pendulum. The earlier crash had shaken it loose. In a split second, Elena calculated the risk. One wrong move and the falling fixture could send the suspect and anyone nearby crashing into the dark water below.

She urged the horse forward, trying to angle him away from the danger.

"Listen to me. What's your name? It's J.C., isn't it?"

"J.C.!" he shouted back.

"J.C., move forward. Now!"

A sharp gasp rippled through the crowd behind her, the sound lodging deep in Elena's chest. Instinct moved faster than thought. Her eyes shot back to the swaying lamp, as if gravity itself had shifted.

The cable snapped.

The fixture broke loose in a violent burst, shattering midair. Glass and metal exploded outward.

The crash cracked like a gunshot.

Shards rained down as the railing behind the suspect splintered, bolts ripping free and fragments whipping through the air. The boardwalk beneath his feet shuddered, then buckled. Wood fractured and gave way, opening into a sudden void that swallowed his weight.

J.C. dropped despite Elena's desperate lunge toward him.

For a suspended heartbeat, fate intervened.

Instead of plunging straight into the ocean, he crashed onto a lower maintenance deck, tangled in a fishing net strung several feet above it. The mesh bowed violently under his weight, snapping tight against the dock cleats. For half a breath, it held. The net cinched around him as he lay dazed and trapped.

"Are you alright?" an officer shouted, rushing to Elena's side.

Three more officers leaned over the railing, staring down in disbelief at the scene below. The horse stood steady beside her, snorting once, unflinching amid the chaos.

Then a wave of heat washed over Elena.

It is not over.

A sharp, tearing whine split the air beneath them. The strained rope screamed as fibers began to unravel.

“Elena!” someone yelled.

She lunged over the edge, tracking the sound.

Too late.

The net split apart.

J.C. dropped.

Dock lights strobed across J.C.’s body as he fell through the torn webbing and struck the Pacific with a hollow slap. The water surged up, cold and black, swallowing the sound. He surfaced once, then again, bobbing among broken strands of rope and foam, his arms flailing in short, frantic bursts.

A swell rolled through.

His body slammed against a piling. The tide lifted him, concealed him, lifted him again. Then the surface flattened, smoothing over as if he had never been there. The last strands of rope unraveled and slipped from the dock, hissing into the sea.

Elena stood motionless, heart pounding, staring at the dark patch of water where the movement had disappeared.

A tourist’s voice shattered the stunned silence.

“Man overboard!”

The words seemed to drop straight through her.

From where she stood, she could see officers frozen along the edge of the pier, peering into the shifting black below.

Then everything snapped back into motion.

One officer seized his radio and called it in, urgency sharpening his voice. Another sprinted toward the ladder bolted to the pier. A third scanned the water, pointing to where the suspect had gone under.

Elena pushed closer, straining to see past the uniforms. The ocean answered with nothing but rolling swells and drifting scraps of rope.

"Search boats are on the way," an officer relayed through his radio.

But the water where J.C. had vanished remained empty, swallowing sound, swallowing hope.

Her attention shifted abruptly.

The elderly man.

She scanned the crowd and found him still standing there, the firearm tucked into his waistband. She motioned him forward toward the officers.

"Sir," she said firmly, "please remove the weapon slowly and keep your hands visible."

The officer nearest her gave her a long, assessing look. Then his attention sharpened.

There were questions now.

Why was there a horse on the Santa Monica Pier?

Why had a man been dangling from a fishing net?

And who, exactly, was Elena?

"Come on, boys, I'll give you the full statement." She offered a calm half-smile. "This gentleman picked up the weapon when the suspect dropped it," she added, gesturing toward the bystander.

Elena delivered her statement with precision. Calm on the surface, taut beneath it. She explained she had been working undercover on an assignment from Detective Singh. The words were simple, yet they shifted the atmosphere. The officers' posture changed, subtly but unmistakably.

One officer paused mid-note, his eyes narrowing at the mention of the name. Detective Singh.

You could almost see the calculation behind his stare. Recognition. Respect. Possibly hesitation. It was the kind of rapid assessment trained officers made. This was not hearsay. It carried weight. Singh was not just another name. Her reputation either opened doors or triggered scrutiny.

An officer stepped aside and called into dispatch to confirm Elena's account and her connection to L.A.'s well-known detective.

When he returned, his tone had sharpened with professionalism.

"Thank you, Elena. We'll search the scene for the suspect. Detective Singh can contact me at the Santa Monica precinct. I'm Officer Vasquez."

"Thank you." Elena reached into her pocket and withdrew a folded slip of paper. "I identified J.C. and an accomplice, Matt Valen, at this address." She handed it to him. "You should check it out."

She stepped back, that gentle smile resurfacing. "Now, if you'll excuse me, I have a horse to reunite with his owner."

"Only in Venice," Officer Vasquez replied.

Elena pulled her phone from her back pocket and immediately called Drew. "We've lost J.C. The cops are pulling his body out of the ocean," she said, matter-of-fact.

There was a pause on the other end. Drew struggled to process what she had just said. "That's not good," he finally managed. "I lost Matt. He got away."

"Well, I'm sure Detective Singh will want the Venice Beach house searched," Elena said. "I gave the officers my name and contact information and told them we were working with her."

"Let's head home," Drew suggested.

"I'm at the end of the Santa Monica Pier," Elena told him. "But I have to return a horse. Don't ask. Meet me in front of Muscle Beach."

"On my way," Drew replied, already sensing the explanation waiting for him would be far more complicated.

☆☆☆

Drew and Elena found Grace, Francy, and Aisha huddled around the kitchen table when they entered the apartment.

"Where are Debra and Israel?" Drew asked.

"They went back to the Griffith Observatory during daylight to see if they could find more clues," Aisha replied.

"Israel wanted to retrace the route we took through Laurel Canyon when we chased the intruder from Vivienne's mansion," Francy added. "The weather's bright and clear today, and he thought maybe something would stand out this time."

A sharp ring cut through the room.

Grace hurried to the security monitor and froze. "It's Drake."

"Buzz him up," Drew said at once.

Francy's expression tightened. "I hope nothing's wrong with Vivienne."

Moments later, Drake stood at the door. "I was hoping to find you home," he said smoothly. "Madame insisted I hand-deliver this invitation." His gaze drifted past them, taking in the apartment.

“Unfortunately, the room for this event is rather small, so Madame thought it wiser that you decide who should attend.”

Without waiting for a response, he turned on his heel and left. His coat swept behind him as he disappeared down the corridor. He offered no farewell, no explanation. Only the weight of unanswered questions lingered after him.

“Hurry, open it,” Aisha urged.

Grace turned the crimson envelope over in her hands, fumbling with the seal before finally freeing the parchment inside. Embossed in silver was a sigil of a key and crescent moon that seemed to glow beneath the light.

She inhaled sharply. “This reads like a fashion opening,” she said, scanning the page before reading it aloud.

Vivienne LeClaire
Cordially invites you to:
The Houdini Seance Chamber
Magic Castle — Los Angeles
Thursday June 21st — 8:00pm
Madame Arquette will lead.
Wear black.
"We are going to attempt my brother."

Chapter 18
Franklin Avenue

Elena adjusted her midnight silk wrap as the car rolled up the steep drive, its headlights catching the turrets of the Magic Castle in full view. The place looked conjured from smoke, part mansion, part mirage. Beside her, Grace pressed the velveteen invitation against her noir black dress.

"Well, here we go," Grace said with a small shiver. "Are you ready for this?"

Inside, the Grand Salon glowed in burgundy and gold. The air carried a faint trace of cedar and brandy. Magicians in tailored suits drifted between clusters of guests, their laughter and sleight of hand blending with the steady chime of the old grandfather clock on the landing.

Elena's gaze lingered over the glass cases of curiosities. Top hats and wands rested beside sepia photographs of men grinning next to impossible illusions.

"Feels like stepping into a memory someone else dreamed," Grace murmured. "Look. There's Madame Arquette." She gestured toward the corner of the room.

"That's her?" Elena asked.

She watched as the psychic made her way toward them. Elena had expected someone different. Madame Arquette was tall and finely boned, moving with the kind of elegance associated with old-world finishing schools. Yet something feral stirred beneath the polish, like candlelight flickering behind stained glass. She was the sort of woman who made silence feel deliberate.

"Grace, so good of you to come. Madame Vivienne was hoping you would be here. Tell me, who is this charming woman?" She lifted her hand toward Elena.

Elena immediately noticed the accent. It was a melodic hybrid, the soft, measured consonants of London threaded through the darker, honeyed vowels of Bucharest. It sounded as though two histories were negotiating every word.

"I'm Elena." She offered her hand. "It's a pleasure to meet you."

"Powerful energy you radiate, my dear," Madame Arquette said warmly.

Elena found herself without a reply. Her attention drifted instead to the cascade of silver-shot black hair gathered loosely at Madame Arquette's nape with a velvet ribbon. Around her throat rested an antique locket engraved with a sigil that seemed to shift in the light. A family crest, perhaps, or something older. The air surrounding her carried faint traces of sandalwood and ozone, as though storms followed her across continents.

They lingered at the bar, observing the curious assortment of patrons, then followed a discreet sign toward the "Magic Emporium." The retail nook gleamed under softened light. Polished wood. Glass shelves. The faint hum of hidden music. Velvet-lined cases displayed decks of cards, trick coins, and slender glass vials labeled Disappearing Powder. Grace tapped the glass lightly. "Looks theatrical," she murmured.

A concealed door disguised as a bookcase swung inward, revealing a narrow hallway lined with candle sconces. At the end, a long oak table waited. Ten chairs stood in precise arrangement; crystal glasses placed before them. At the center rested a single crystal ball on a silver stand. Their host, cloaked in a raven-feather collar, greeted them with a measured nod.

"Vivienne," Grace gasped, startled by the actress's transformation.

"Welcome to tonight's séance," Vivienne said softly. "We'll be calling on more than memory."

The Houdini Séance Chamber felt at once theatrical and sovereign, like a hoax that had claimed its own authority. Elena surveyed the other guests as they gathered, eager to take their seats. Celebrities. Socialites. Aspirants. A carefully curated cross-section of Hollywood's orbit.

The room itself felt purpose-built as an instrument of belief. Houdini's handcuffs displayed behind glass. Allan Kardec's spectacles. Weighted relics and aged letters. Each object arranged like a tuned antenna, waiting for transmission.

Madame Arquette motioned for the guests to take their seats. She gave Grace a knowing nod, as though something had already been arranged.

Elena found herself studying Vivienne. The actress sat with such rigid composure it was almost painful to witness, her spine straight, her chin lifted, every movement measured.

"This is not a conjuring," Madame Arquette began. "This is signal archaeology." She gestured for the lights to be lowered to séance protocol.

As the room dimmed, Grace felt the air compress, as though the walls had drawn closer.

Elena leaned toward her. "Vivienne is shaking."

It was nearly imperceptible. Vivienne's hands trembled a fraction, the smallest betrayal.

"Vivienne, dear, recall Jefferies' personality," Madame Arquette instructed gently.

Vivienne drew in a shallow breath. "Jefferies… my Jefferies?" A pause. "Jefferies who was doing prime factorizations at four. Jefferies who believed consciousness was a compression algorithm. Jefferies who coded languages inside languages until the day he left this earth." Her voice wavered at the last word.

"What is the last unresolved packet between you? Speak it to the universe, my dear," Madame Arquette urged.

Vivienne fixed her gaze on the table, refusing to let her composure fracture.

"If something was left unresolved," Madame Arquette continued softly, "then consciousness does not die. It simply ceases to be local."

She placed her hand on the object concealed beneath a red silk scarf before her. With deliberate care, she drew the fabric back.

A collective gasp swept through the room.

"What is that?" Grace leaned toward Elena and whispered.

"A planchette, I believe," Elena replied.

Grace shot her a perplexed look.

"It's a spiritual writing tool. The spirit is supposed to guide it to form a message."

Grace's double take needed no translation.

Madame Arquette cleared her throat. "Let us proceed. Vivienne, place only your fingertips on the planchette, along with mine," she instructed. "I ask all of our guests to concentrate. Keep your thoughts positive and true."

Grace angled her mouth toward Elena without turning her head. "Then what's that enormous crystal ball in the middle of the table for?"

"A prop?" Elena murmured.

Madame Arquette rested her fingers lightly on the planchette. Vivienne followed, slower, as if approaching something volatile.

"If the planchette moves," Madame Arquette said, addressing the room, "it is directional, not random."

The tension gathered, almost sentient. A breathless presence pooling in the corners. The nearest candle flame quivered, stretching tall, then shrinking, as though straining to speak first.

A soft creak passed through the floorboards.

The planchette twitched. Barely. Enough to draw a gasp.

"Did you feel that? He knows we're here." Vivienne's voice lifted with fragile excitement. Her hands trembled.

"Then let him speak," Madame Arquette murmured, her head tilting slowly, eyes half-lidded.

The lights flickered.

The planchette slid again, farther this time. Letters scraped beneath their fingertips, slow and deliberate.

A thread of cold air drifted across the circle, extinguishing one of the candles.

The planchette began moving toward Houdini's original handcuffs.

Grace's attention shifted from the table to the wall where the handcuffs hung framed beneath glass. But she was not looking at Houdini's signature shackles. She was staring at the mirror above them.

A shadow moved across it.

She gasped.

“Jefferies built his first compression cipher around Houdini’s escape logic,” Vivienne whispered, her voice carrying just far enough for the guests to hear.

The planchette jerked beneath their fingertips. Short. Sharp. Intentional.

Vivienne inhaled as if struck in the diaphragm.

“He is telling you what he needs from you,” Madame Arquette murmured.

Grace felt her ribcage lock in place. She lowered her gaze to the sheet of paper beneath the planchette and read in a trembling whisper. “*Do not hold me. Return to the beginning.*”

Vivienne swallowed. Tears slid down her cheeks in silence.

“He wants you to release him,” Madame Arquette continued softly. “He has already collapsed into final form.”

The Houdini trunk rattled once. A small, contained knock from within, as if confirming its presence.

Elena flinched.

Then everything stilled.

Madame Arquette lifted her hands from the planchette and leaned back in her chair, releasing a slow, measured breath.

Vivienne remained seated, motionless yet trembling, as though every calculation inside her had abruptly powered down.

Grace placed her hand gently on Vivienne’s forearm.

Vivienne whispered, not to Grace but to the room, “Thank you.”

And that was it.

No more theatrics. No spectral spectacle. Just a final, lucid message from a brilliant brother who had spent his short life compressing everything… finally reduced to one irreducible truth.

Grace and Elena sat there, stunned.

"I'm not sure what just happened," Grace murmured, glancing around the table at the other perplexed guests.

Drake stepped quietly to Vivienne's side and helped her out of the chair. He thanked Madame Arquette with measured courtesy and slowly escorted the actress from the room.

"We need to get to the bottom of this." Elena rose, scanning the chamber. "Madame Arquette, may we have a word?"

Grace hesitated, then moved to stand beside her.

Madame Arquette offered a composed smile to the remaining guests and gestured gracefully toward the door, a clear indication that she was politely dismissing them.

When the room had cleared, Elena spoke again, her tone firmer. "Madame Arquette, can you explain what just happened?"

Madame Arquette received the question with the calm of someone who had answered it countless times. "To those who believe, no explanation is necessary. For those who do not, no explanation is possible."

The girls were momentarily speechless.

Grace recovered first. "Then may I ask… could you tell us about Jefferies' living days?"

A faint shift crossed Madame Arquette's expression. "Ah. This I can explain." She gestured for them to sit.

"The LeClaire estate was not always so still, nor so shrouded in mildew and dread. Decades ago, before the windows were sealed in dust, before the gardens overgrew their boundaries like restless hands, it was a place of color, music, and indulgent wealth."

Elena found herself drawn in, captivated by the way Madame Arquette spun the story.

"And at the center of it all was Vivienne, radiant and curious, and her younger brother Jefferies, the star child."

Grace leaned back into her soft chair and nudged Elena beneath the table.

"Jefferies was the child everyone adored. Two years younger than Vivienne, he was quick with a smile and quicker with a prank. His laughter once echoed through the high halls, up the staircases, and out across the gardens, where he chased dragonflies with a net fashioned from his mother's silk scarves."

The girls exchanged a quiet smile.

"Vivienne loved him fiercely, perhaps too fiercely. Jefferies was all she had after their mother vanished into the south of France and their father retreated into his study, a phantom steeped in gin and disappointment. Vivienne read to Jefferies. She taught him French. She told him stories about ghosts and the old gods of the estate; the ones her grandmother warned them never to name in the garden after sunset."

"Let me guess. Jefferies never listened," Grace offered.

"He never did," Madame Arquette replied without hesitation. "Jefferies was a savant, brilliant, but always inhabiting his own interior world. Language fascinated him, not only its structure but its poetry. He claimed he spoke to the ghosts in the garden, in the pool house, in his bedroom, even beneath the house itself. They became his companions. He wrote them poems, notes, entire stories."

She paused.

"He was also uncompromising when it came to right and wrong. If he witnessed an injustice, he defended it with startling ferocity."

Grace and Elena slowly exchanged a knowing side glance.

"It had been a humid June evening, the kind that made even the curtains sweat. The pool had just been filled for summer, and the water was cold. Always cold." Madame Arquette shifted in her seat and leaned forward.

"That night was meant to belong to Vivienne. It was the opening of *Velvet Ashes*. But of course, things at home unraveled first. After an argument with her drunken father, who insisted she take her brother along so he would not have to deal with him, she refused and stormed out, still trembling with rage.

"The studio limousine pulled up outside the mansion gates. She did not look back. She climbed in, shut the door, and let them take her to Grauman's Chinese Theatre for the premiere.

"Jefferies slipped out during the argument. White shirt. Shined shoes. Suspenders." Madame Arquette's voice lowered. "Vivienne did not realize he was gone until she returned home and found a trail of muddy footprints leading out the back door.

"They led to the pool."

She paused.

"That is where she found her brother. Face down in the water."

Madame Arquette lifted her gaze toward the ceiling, as if offering the memory to something unseen.

"That is just horrible," Grace breathed.

"And tonight is the anniversary of his death," Elena said, the realization settling heavily.

"That is correct. But the message was not only for Vivienne." Madame Arquette fixed her eyes on the two of them and held their gaze until she saw recognition flicker in Elena's expression.

Elena stood abruptly. "Grace, we have to go. Madame Arquette, thank you for the information. Is Vivienne going home?"

Grace rose as well, sensing the shift in Elena's urgency.

Madame Arquette considered the question before replying. "Do not concern yourself with Vivienne. She will be all right now. I will see to it. Apply the second half of the message."

Elena gripped Grace's arm. "Thank you again." She pulled her toward the door. "The message has a dual meaning."

"What do you mean?" Grace asked, confusion flashing across her face as Elena hurried her down the corridor.

"Madame Arquette was trying to tell us something. Drew already figured it out. They weren't idle threats from a crazed fan. The threats were written as moral retribution, not obsession." Elena flagged the valet and slid into her car.

"From Matt? Where are we going?" Grace asked, breathless as she hurried after her.

"Drew was right. It's not a ghost haunting Vivienne," Elena said, starting the engine.

"Then what do you call what we just experienced?" Grace shot back.

"It's the revenant of conscience," Elena replied. "Manifesting through someone who refuses to let her forget. It's a ritual countdown. Each date leads back to Jefferies' death and to Vivienne's premiere. They represent moral choices."

Grace stared at her. "And Remi's house?"

"*Return to the beginning*," Elena said firmly. "That was the second half of the message. Drew needs to go back to Remi's house. That's where this started."

Chapter 19
Beachwood Canyon

Drew slammed the gearshift into third as the car knifed up Beachwood Canyon, the engine roaring along the narrow, twisting road. Night swallowed the hills. Shadows lunged from the tree-lined slopes like predators, but Drew pressed harder on the accelerator.

"We're missing something, Israel. I know it."

Israel braced one hand against the dashboard, the other gripping his phone like a weapon. His eyes stayed sharp, his breath held through every curve. They were not just racing the clock. They were racing whoever might already be inside the house at the top of the hill, the house where the murder had happened, where the truth still waited.

"Let's figure out which pieces of the puzzle haven't been accounted for," Israel said.

Remi's home loomed out of the darkness, a jagged silhouette carved against the moonlight. Drew cut the headlights and let the car roll to a quiet stop. The house that had once pulsed with parties and laughter now stood hollow and stricken.

They ducked beneath the police tape stretched across the threshold. Israel knelt at the side door and worked the lock with quick, practiced movements. The soft click seemed to echo like a gunshot in the stillness.

"That was fast," Drew murmured as he eased the door open.

They slipped inside, swallowed by darkness and the faint scent of stale beer. Beneath it lingered something metallic.

Their footsteps whispered across the polished floor as they climbed the spiral staircase, flashlights slicing thin white seams through the black.

"It feels invasive being here now," Israel said quietly.

At the top, the study door stood open. The crime scene lay before them, frozen in a grim tableau. A toppled chair. A dark smear along the wall. Papers scattered as though a storm had torn through, but only in this room.

"Gloves," Drew reminded him.

They pulled rubber gloves from their back pockets and slid them on.

Drew moved toward the window and stopped short. Fresh scuff marks scarred the floor beside the desk. They had not appeared in the police photos. He did not remember seeing them when they first walked into the scene.

A chill slid down his spine.

"Do you remember these marks?"

Israel crouched beside him. "These are new." The realization settled hard in his stomach.

He rose and crossed to the wall behind the desk. The concealed door stood slightly ajar.

It had been breached.

Israel slid it open slowly. The closet beyond had been ransacked.

"Drew. Someone came back and cleaned him out."

Drew stepped beside him, jaw tightening. "It wasn't enough to kill the man. They came back to rob him."

"Pathetic." Israel's flashlight beam caught a fractured watch face glinting on the floor. In the corner, discarded clothes sagged in a heap, items the intruder had deemed worthless.

Drew's mind flashed to the blood on the corner of the desk.

"That's the thing about blood," he said quietly. "The longer it sits and coagulates, the deeper it seeps into whatever it touches."

He stared at the antique mahogany desk.

"That's it, Israel."

"What? What is it?"

Without answering, Drew knelt beside the desk and ran his gloved hands slowly along the carved woodwork, studying the seams and joints.

"What do you see?" Israel asked. He recognized the look. Drew had found a thread.

"Remember our last case, when we found the hidden passages in City Hall?"

"I remember," Israel replied. "There was a trigger mechanism behind each door."

He was already moving, dropping to his knees beside Drew.

"Four eyes are better than two."

Their hands moved across the desk at the same time, gliding slowly over the carved wood in search of something that felt different.

Then their fingers collided.

They looked at each other.

Without speaking, they pressed down on the same spot.

A sharp click split the stagnant air. A hidden drawer sprang open with sudden force.

For a split second, they grinned at each other like kids who had just uncovered hidden Christmas presents.

Israel leaned closer and peered into the dark compartment. “It’s a script.” His brow furrowed as he lifted it carefully. “*The Resurrection of Mildred Miles*. By William Sharpe.”

“Must be important if someone went to the trouble of hiding it,” Drew said, thumbing through the manuscript.

His gaze lingered on the title. “Odd name,” he murmured.

“Do you think the killer was looking for this? Maybe that’s why there’s blood on the corner of the desk. Maybe that’s why they came back.”

“Or maybe the killer pressed a bloody hand there and had no idea about the compartment,” Drew countered. “Maybe he was just greedy enough to return for whatever valuables he missed the first time.”

“It wouldn’t be the first time a criminal made a foolish mistake,” Israel said.

Drew examined the manuscript more closely. The paper felt dense beneath his fingers, the cover marked with yellowed age spots. Several pages clung together, stiffened by time.

“This has been sitting here for a while.”

“Maybe Remi didn’t even know it was hidden,” Israel suggested.

He pulled out his phone and snapped several photos of the script. Then he opened his browser and typed in the author’s name.

“Well,” he said after a moment, scanning the results, “there are a lot of William Sharpes listed here.”

“Try William Sharpe, writer,” Drew suggested.

“There are a lot of those too.” Israel exhaled, frustration creeping in.

"Then try the script's title."

Israel typed again, scanning the screen. "Nothing. Not a single match." His shoulders sank. "Do you see anything else in the drawer?"

Drew crouched and angled his phone's light deeper into the compartment. The beam slid slowly across the inner lining. A faint scent of mahogany drifted outward.

"Wait."

His eyes caught on a thin piece of paper adhered to the inner wall, nearly invisible against the wood.

He reached in carefully and loosened it, peeling it free inch by inch. The parchment was brittle. He unfolded it with deliberate care.

"It's a receipt for the desk."

Then he froze.

His breath stalled. His pulse thudded in his ears. For a moment, he thought he had misread it. He blinked and looked again.

"That's impossible," he managed, the words barely forming.

"What is it, amigo?" Israel asked, watching the color drain from Drew's face. "What does it say?"

Recognition settled slowly over Drew's features. In this line of work, he had learned that nothing was impossible and coincidences were a luxury they could not afford.

"What does it say?" Israel pressed.

"Martha's Place," Drew said at last. "My aunt Martha. It's my late aunt's antique shop."

Israel frowned. "Seriously? That's… strange."

"The receipt has Remi's father's signature on it." Drew's voice tightened, the words barely forcing their way past the shock in his throat. "His father didn't just know about the manuscript. He bought this desk from my aunt's shop."

A bead of sweat slid down his temple as the realization struck him like a light snapping on in a dark room.

"Seriously?"

"Yes. This was my aunt's antique shop in the Valley. The address on Ventura Boulevard. Studio City." Drew nodded, still staring at the receipt as if it might rearrange itself. "It's hers."

The expression on his face unsettled Israel. He had never seen Drew look like this.

"You mean the aunt you've always talked about? The aunt who was…" Israel trailed off.

"Murdered," Drew finished quietly.

His thoughts began to race.

"That's how Remi knew those words. '*A master can instruct without doing anything. Teach without a word.*'"

"What does that mean?" Israel asked.

"My aunt used to say that all the time," Drew replied. "She'd repeat it to customers like it was scripture. Aunt Martha believed wisdom didn't need theatrics."

A faint smile flickered across his face, quickly swallowed by something heavier. The thought of her presence sent a chill across his skin. He glanced down at his arms as goosebumps rose.

"Remi said that exact phrase to me in the parking lot at OSHA the other day," Drew continued. "He told me he used to go antiquing with his father in Studio City."

Israel stood there, absorbing it, unable to respond.

Drew lowered his gaze back to the receipt.

"I wish Remi were alive so I could tell him this now."

"Well, brother, I'm sure Remi and your aunt are together now," Israel offered gently.

Drew gave a faint nod. "It's strange," he said, shaking his head. "When I met Remi in Studio City, he mentioned in passing that his father had bought a desk somewhere in that neighborhood and that he kept it in his office. I never connected the dots. The long shot didn't even seem plausible."

"Well, we've learned something about long shots," Israel replied with a small shrug. "They tend to be the most plausible explanation."

He rose and walked toward the windows, stepping carefully around the shattered crystal decanter that had once spilled dark liquor across the floorboards, now dried and tacky underfoot. He looked out toward the balcony jutting into the night.

"This was definitely the exit point. Don't you agree, Drew?"

"Yes." Drew glanced up from the script in his hands. "The boot print leads toward the window. But he must have entered another way. There's no sign of forced entry into this room before Remi came in."

Israel's mind raced. He turned abruptly and crossed back to the secret closet, sweeping his flashlight beam through the darkness. He began knocking along the inner seams in the far corner, testing for hollow spaces.

"There has to be another way into this study," he called.

Drew was already moving toward him.

"Israel… what was that?"

Running his hand along the back wall, Israel knocked again. This time, a faint hollow thud answered him.

He paused.

He pressed harder and felt the panel shift beneath his palm.

With a low groan, the wall eased open, revealing a narrow passage descending into shadow. Cool air drifted upward, carrying the scent of motor oil and concrete.

Israel's pulse quickened. A hidden staircase.

"Man, you're getting good at this," Drew called.

Israel swept his flashlight down the passage. The beam found the base of the stairs, opening directly into the garage.

"Drew," he said, his voice threaded with excitement and unease. "We've got a secret door. It leads straight to the garage."

"Well, that answers that question." Drew stepped into the closet and peered down the narrow descent.

Israel was already moving. He reached the bottom and flicked on the light.

The garage door groaned upward, revealing a wide concrete space illuminated by two humming fluorescent strips. Three vehicles sat beneath the cold white glow.

Nearest the entrance rested a silver sedan, coated in a fine layer of dust, its hood speckled with dried mud. Beside it stood a red compact convertible, parked crookedly as though someone had pulled in fast and never bothered to straighten it.

But Israel's attention locked onto the third vehicle at the back wall.

A black Ford truck.

Its glossy paint fractured the overhead light into sharp reflections. The dent above the rear wheel was unmistakable.

His chest tightened as he stepped closer.

“That’s it,” he said quietly. “The same truck Francy and I chased through Laurel Canyon. The same truck we saw outside Vivienne LeClaire’s house. I’m sure of it.”

Drew joined him, his brow lifting. “You’re positive?”

Israel nodded. “Positive. The mud patterns along the sides match. Just like the ones we saw on Francy’s car after the chase.”

“So there’s a connection to Vivienne’s case too.” Drew could barely get the words out.

Israel stood beside the truck, hands on his hips, scanning the garage in silence.

Drew circled slowly, his gaze shifting from the truck to the two cars parked along the wall. He stopped.

“…Huh.”

Israel glanced over. “What?”

Drew tilted his chin toward the nearer vehicles. “Look at that.”

Israel stepped closer. “What am I looking for?”

Drew didn’t answer. He simply watched.

Israel leaned in, studying the spacing between the vehicles. Then he paused.

“Oh. It’s parked differently.”

“Yeah.” They both looked back at the truck.

Drew lowered his voice. “That’s deliberate.”

Israel nodded slowly. “Has to be. No one does that by accident.”

Drew glanced again at the silver sedan and the red convertible. “The other two aren’t angled like that.”

Silence settled between them.

"Old habits," Drew said at last.

Israel gave a knowing nod. "The kind you don't realize you're advertising."

"...Well, that's interesting," Drew murmured.

The driver's side door of the truck hung slightly ajar.

Israel exchanged a look with Drew before pulling it open. The cab smelled faintly of gasoline and worn leather. The center console sat open and empty.

He scanned the interior carefully. "Whoever left this here wasn't expecting company. The keys are still in the ignition, Drew."

Drew stepped closer, peering through the open door.

"Israel... what's that?"

He pointed toward the far right side of the dashboard.

Israel stared at the large red button glued to the right side of the air-conditioning vent. He pressed it with his gloved finger.

"It's solid plastic," he said, frowning. "Doesn't do anything."

"Check the glove compartment," Drew suggested, leaning farther into the cab.

Israel reached across the seat and pulled it open. The contents spilled out immediately, scattering across the floor.

Among the clutter lay a small white key fob, smeared with dried blood.

"Got something," Israel muttered, lifting it carefully.

Drew reached past him and retrieved another item that had slid beneath the passenger seat. A prop knife. The rubber blade was worn and slightly bent, but convincing from a distance.

"A key fob and a fake knife," Drew said, turning it over in his hand. "Property of Paramount Studios. It's stamped on the back."

Israel's eyes swept the garage again, sharp and methodical. In the far corner, he noticed a black metal panel mounted to the wall.

"Security junction box," he said, stepping closer. "The wires have been clipped."

"That explains why the system went down right before the murder," Drew replied.

Israel's gaze shifted again, this time to the narrow electric strip embedded along the door frame behind them.

His expression changed.

"That's it," he said quietly. "The trigger for the secret entrance."

He turned and shut the concealed door that led back up to Remi's study, sealing them inside the garage. Then, with deliberate care not to disturb the blood on the key fob, he tapped the button.

A low mechanical hum filled the space.

The hidden door slid open.

"So," Drew said, thinking it through, "the killer drove the truck into the garage to conceal it. He used the key fob to access the secret passage through the closet. Then he waited for his cue, which was the woman entering Remi's study. The moment she left, he attacked."

Israel pulled a small evidence bag from his back pocket and slid the bloodstained fob inside. "Where does the plastic knife fit into that?"

Drew bagged the prop knife as well, sealing it carefully before slipping it into his backpack.

Then something clicked.

"Israel, we need to go back upstairs."

Israel quickly photographed the truck, the interior, and the license plate before following Drew up the narrow staircase, through the closet, and into the study.

Drew stopped short. “It’s gone.”

“What’s gone?” Israel scanned the room.

“The knife,” Drew said, pointing toward the desk. “The night of the murder, there was a knife sitting right there next to the script.”

Israel stepped closer and examined the surface. “There’s a faint impression in the dust.”

Drew removed the prop knife from the evidence bag and carefully aligned it with the outline on the desk.

“It’s the same shape,” he said quietly. “Exact.”

Israel looked from the desk to the bag in Drew’s hand. “So, the killer came back, ransacked the closet, and retrieved the knife from here before taking it down to the truck. Why?”

“Maybe it was a decoy,” Drew said slowly. “Or part of the staging.”

He wiped sweat from his brow.

“Tomorrow, we go to Paramount. We check the props department.”

Israel’s eyes narrowed. “You think someone there can help us?”

Drew nodded. “We met that security guard at Paramount Plaza. He said his twin brother works in props. That might be our inside connection.”

He glanced back at the desk. “That’s the only way we’re going to get answers.”

“Meanwhile, we can run these items over to Detective Singh. Maybe she can help fill in the blanks,” Israel suggested.

"Hold on." An envelope slipped free from the script and fell at Drew's feet.

The paper had faded to a weary, uneven yellow. Fine cracks veined its surface, especially along the folds. The broken seal clung to the flap, brittle and dull, leaving behind a darkened smear where it had been forced open. Drew crouched and picked it up carefully, easing the letter from its casing.

"Drew, what is it?" Israel asked, unable to read the expression settling across his face.

Drew's eyes moved slowly over the page. His jaw tightened.

"A confession," he said quietly. "A betrayal. And the last words of truth from a dying man."

Chapter 20
Woodland Hills

Debra and Francy's drive to see Darlene Sharpe carried them into Woodland Hills, where the city softened into something quieter and greener. The dense streets of Los Angeles faded behind them as they moved deeper into the San Fernando Valley.

Woodland Hills opened into wide, tree-lined roads shaded by mature oaks and aging palms. Well-kept single-family homes passed outside their windows, each suggesting space, privacy, and a settled comfort that felt far removed from downtown. They drove through the heart of the district near Ventura Boulevard and Warner Center, where storefronts, cafés, and office buildings hummed with steady activity.

"It's very quaint here," Debra commented.

"I think this is it," Francy said, leaning forward to make out the address on the mailbox through the windshield.

A small clapboard house painted bright blue stood in sharp contrast to the foothills of the Santa Monica Mountains rising behind it.

"A very sweet place to retire," Debra said softly.

They were greeted at the door by their host.

Darlene Sharpe appeared to be in her late eighties, her age visible not in frailty but in a distilled elegance, as though time had refined rather than diminished her. She was small in stature, her frame narrowed by the years, yet she carried herself with upright composure that hinted at a once-commanding presence. Her shoulders remained squared, and when she opened the door, there was a quiet expectation that she would be heard.

"Debra, Francy? Did I get that right?"

"Yes, you did," Debra replied with a gentle smile.

"Thank you so much for seeing us," Francy interjected.

"You said on the phone that you were inquiring about my father?"

Debra and Francy followed her into the kitchen, taking notice of the orderly, clean surroundings.

"You're William Sharpe's daughter?" Debra asked.

Darlene nodded, her fingers wrapped tightly around a chipped coffee mug. "Yes. My father was William Sharpe." She gestured for them to sit at the kitchen table.

Francy pulled out a chair and studied her face. "You mentioned on the phone that you never understood why your father's life unraveled so quickly."

Darlene exhaled softly. "I was thirty-two when my father died. Old enough to understand that a life's work can disappear quietly. Young enough to still believe it should not. I was living in New York then, absorbed in my own world, convinced that absence did not equal neglect."

Debra and Francy exchanged a brief glance.

"My father's life was precise. Measured. He was a writer, and my mother was a musician. So yes, they were always struggling," Darlene said, a faint crease forming between her brows.

She chose her words carefully, as though she had long ago decided that accuracy was a form of protection. She did not sound angry. She did not sound betrayed. She sounded deliberate.

“My father, William Sharpe, wrote everything down,” she continued. “Drafts. Notes. Revisions. He dated every page. He trusted paper far more than people.”

Darlene turned toward the coffee pot and gestured toward the girls. They both politely declined.

“When he died, I returned to Los Angeles to settle the house. My mother had passed years earlier, so being there again was difficult. My father had filled his days with writing. It seemed to be the only relief from his grief.”

“That must have been very hard for you,” Francy said gently.

“I was able to sell the house quickly, but not its contents. We were living in Studio City at the time, so I arranged for my father’s furniture to be sold at an antique consignment shop near our home.”

“Do you remember the name of the shop?” Debra asked.

Darlene shifted in her chair and took a measured sip of coffee. “Martha’s Place, I believe. I remember the owner. She was vibrant. A heavy smoker, if I recall correctly. She always seemed to have a cup of coffee nearby.” A faint smile touched her lips at the memory.

“Was your father published?” Francy asked.

“He had a few modest successes,” Darlene replied, brushing a strand of silver hair from her face. “But he primarily wrote scripts. None were ever picked up by a studio. When I arrived at the house, there were no manuscripts on the shelves, no drafts stacked on his desk. I assumed the work that mattered had already been preserved.”

She paused. “I was wrong.”

“Why?” Debra leaned forward.

“I found them in a burn barrel behind the house. His work, stories, drafts, and scripts. The manuscripts he had spent years writing.” Her voice remained steady, but her grip tightened around the mug.

"There were fragments of pages drifting among the ashes. That's when I understood what he had done."

She lowered her eyes briefly. "He was ill. And beyond broken. He clearly thought none of his work mattered. I only realized that after the fact."

"We're so sorry to hear that," Debra said gently.

"I know the loss of my mother, and his illness, were the greatest burdens he carried. Not to mention the string of failures he endured with his work."

Darlene rose slowly and poured herself another cup of coffee. She gestured toward the pot again, and once more the girls declined.

"Months later, I received a call from a director named Clive Harrington. He told me he had purchased my father's desk. While restoring it, he discovered a concealed compartment. Inside were pages. He said he did not know exactly what they were, only that they had been hidden with care and that the name on them was familiar."

"He wasn't clear about what he'd found?" Debra asked.

"He did not speculate," Darlene replied. "He offered no explanation. He simply wanted me to know that he had discovered the papers and that, if I wished, he could return them to me."

"And what did you think?" Francy asked.

"I assumed they were one of my father's scripts. The way he described them did not immediately mean anything to me. Pages of dialogue. Some typed. Some corrected by hand. There were gaps in the manuscript. A title I did not recognize. A date from the late forties. Nothing that clearly anchored them in context. By this point, I wasn't interested."

"How did he manage to contact you?" Debra pressed.

"He said he reached out to the owner of the antique shop. She provided my number." Darlene took another measured sip of coffee. "Harrington never contacted me again. Years later, I read in the newspaper that he had died in Spain."

She looked down at her cup. "I had often wondered what became of my father's desk."

Debra cleared her throat and folded her hands in her lap, as though bracing herself.

"Did Clive ever mention anything about a letter? A letter written to you?"

"No," Darlene replied softly. "He never mentioned a letter."

Debra pressed her lips together before continuing. "There's something we need to tell you, Darlene. It isn't easy."

Darlene's pale eyes moved from Debra to Francy, narrowing slightly. "Then don't soften it," she said evenly. "Just say it."

Francy leaned forward. "Clive Harrington's son inherited the desk after his father died."

Darlene's fingers tightened around her coffee mug. "Go on."

"Clive Harrington's son, Remi Harrington, was killed recently," Debra said carefully. "Murdered. He was found at the desk."

For a moment, Darlene did not move. The room seemed to hold its breath with her. Then she blinked slowly, as if trying to steady her vision.

"At the desk?" she repeated, her voice barely audible.

Francy nodded. "Yes. Because of that, the desk and everything inside it are now part of an active police investigation."

Darlene's mouth parted, then closed again. She placed a hand against her chest, not in pain but in disbelief.

"That desk," she whispered. "After all these years. It has found its way back into sorrow."

Debra watched her closely. "We found the same script hidden inside the desk. Pressed between its pages was a letter. A letter addressed to you, Darlene."

Darlene's gaze lifted slowly.

"The letter must have been written before your father's death and concealed with the manuscript," Francy continued gently. "We believe it was something your father intended to give you but never had the chance."

"Now, it's possible that when Clive Harrington found the script, he overlooked the letter," Debra said carefully. "But the wax seal had already been broken. We also wondered why he would have contacted you so directly."

Darlene gripped her coffee cup between damp palms, searching her memory.

"Maybe he didn't know what he had," she said slowly. "Maybe he was trying to measure how much I knew."

She let out a thin, unsteady breath.

"I spent half my life trying to be free of those memories. Trying to forget the sadness. The house. My parents' belongings. And now that desk is tangled in something like this."

Her hand fell from her chest to her lap, trembling slightly.

"A famous director. Murdered. And that desk just sitting there, as if it had been watching."

"We would like you to read your father's letter," Debra said gently, handing her the weathered envelope.

Darlene shook her head sharply at first, almost in protest. Then she exhaled and pulled the letter free. She retrieved her reading glasses from the deep pocket of her cardigan and began to read slowly.

When she looked up, her expression had shifted. "So my father wrote this script, realized it had been plagiarized, and then saw it turned into a major motion picture?"

"That's correct," Debra answered quietly.

"And he did nothing?" Darlene's voice tightened. "He just… accepted it?"

"There is no record of any lawsuit or public dispute," Francy confirmed.

"There's a portion of the letter that mentions a watermark," Francy added carefully. "Something he deliberately embedded in his writing."

"I never knew this," Darlene said, almost to herself.

Debra placed the recovered script in front of her. "What was your mother's birthday?"

"May 7, 1924."

"And her initials?" Francy asked.

"Victoria Sharpe. V.S." Darlene hesitated, her eyes widening slightly.

"He tells you in the letter that proof of his authorship always contained the V.S. symbol on pages five, seven, one, nine, two, and four," Debra explained carefully.

Darlene absorbed the words as though they had unlocked a door sealed for half a century. She lifted the script and turned slowly to page five. "Why page five?" she asked, almost to herself.

"May is the fifth month," Debra replied gently. "Seven for the day. Nineteen twenty-four for the year." She pointed to the text. "Page one has the V.S. symbol. Page five has it too. Each of these numbered pages carries your mother's initials. Your father wrote this script. It was plagiarized."

Darlene stood very still. Then, uncertain but compelled, she rose and crossed to a small desk in the corner of her living room. She opened the bottom drawer and removed a worn folder. Inside were the charred remnants and surviving pages she had salvaged from the burn barrel behind her father's house.

Debra and Francy watched in silence.

At first, Darlene moved methodically, almost cautiously. Then her pace quickened. She flipped through the fragile pages, scanning the numbered corners.

"Here," she said, her voice catching. "And here." She held up the pages, her hands trembling now. "They each have my mother's initials hidden in the text. I never saw it before."

A fragile astonishment flickered across her face.

"I think your father wrote that letter so you would know," Debra said softly. "He wanted you to understand that something he created had succeeded, even if the credit was stolen."

Francy leaned forward, her voice warm and careful. "I know this brings everything back."

"Yes," Darlene said. "That's exactly what it does."

She looked down at her hands, at the thin skin and prominent veins tracing across them. Then she lifted her gaze, her eyes bright with shock and something close to tears. "And yet, you have helped me discover something I never knew. For that, I am truly grateful." She steadied her voice. "Promise me one thing. If you learn more, anything at all, don't let it disappear into silence again. I cannot bear not knowing."

Debra nodded. "We promise."

Darlene leaned back in her chair, and for the first time she seemed every one of her years.

"I thought that part of my past was finished with me," she murmured. "It seems it never was."

☆☆☆

Drew, Aisha, and Grace stood at the front door of Vivienne LeClaire's Beverly Hills mansion, composed but tense. The weight of her phone call lingered over them, as though even the silence had been staged.

Drake opened the door slowly and stepped aside. "Madame LeClaire is waiting for you by the pool. Please, this way."

They crossed the living room, now washed in midday light. Sunlight streamed through the windows, restoring warmth to the space. Beyond the glass, the Hollywood Hills stretched golden and unguarded.

Vivienne met them before they could step outside.

She looked lighter. Not relieved. Resolved. As though something heavy had been set down, not erased.

"Please," she said, stepping aside. "Come through."

The pool lay drained and still, its pale basin exposed beneath the late afternoon sun. Deck chairs sat mismatched and slightly askew, as if no one had cared to arrange them since the day Jefferies died.

The space still held its sorrow, unmistakable and uncorrected. Yet the air felt different. Lighter. As though grief had finally been acknowledged instead of left to linger.

Vivienne remained standing. “I owe you an apology,” she said quietly. “For the fear. For the distraction. For allowing grief to masquerade as mystery.”

Drew exchanged a brief glance with Aisha but remained silent.

Vivienne walked to the edge of the empty pool and rested one hand on a chaise, steadying herself.

“For a long time, I believed my brother was trying to reach me.” Her voice didn’t break, but it wavered. “Jefferies was always dramatic. He used to say death would be an entrance, not an exit.”

Grace shifted. “But you don’t believe that anymore?”

Vivienne gave a faint, sad smile. “No.”

She turned back to them.

“When the hauntings began, I searched for comfort in what felt familiar. I blamed the dead because it hurt less than blaming the living.” She paused, holding the silence the way she once held a camera’s gaze. “And when I suspected Madame Arquette…” She shook her head. “That was desperation. She loves me. She loved my brother. That séance…”

Vivienne exhaled slowly. “It wasn’t deception. It was kindness. Her way of saying enough. It’s time to let him rest.”

Drew’s voice stayed gentle. “Then what changed?”

Vivienne crossed the terrace and leaned against the metal railing that descended into the empty pool. “The last threatening note I received,” she said. “The one that finally told the truth.”

Aisha stiffened. “The note mentioning The Death of the Author?”

Vivienne nodded. “I’ve been running from that phrase for years,” she admitted. “Treating it like a threat instead of a mirror. When I saw it written there, in that message, I understood what this was never about.”

Drew frowned. “And what was it about?”

Vivienne met his eyes. Something unspoken passed between them.

Her lips parted, then closed again. “That,” she said softly, “is something I need to say aloud. Not perform. Not dramatize. Just… confess.”

She gestured toward the hall. “May I speak with you somewhere private, Drew?”

Drew hesitated, glancing at his friends for only a beat before nodding. “Of course.”

They returned nearly half an hour later.

Vivienne’s eyes were red, but her posture was steady. Whatever she’d said had cost her something. It had freed her, too.

Drew spoke first. “It’s over.” Not a question. A confirmation.

Vivienne nodded. “It is.”

Grace let out a slow breath. “No more letters?”

“No more hiding,” Vivienne replied. “Which means no more terror.”

Drew held her gaze. “You understand what happens next.”

“Yes.” A faint smile touched her lips. “I live with it.”

The silence that followed wasn’t awkward. It was reverent.

Aisha’s expression softened, something warmer rising in her eyes. “In that case,” she said gently, “I’d like to invite you to something.”

Vivienne blinked. “Invite me?”

“My opening night,” Aisha said. “*The Final Tango*.”

Drew smiled. Grace tilted her head in approval.

“It’s about endings,” Aisha continued. “And choosing what survives them.”

Vivienne drew in a quiet breath. "I'd be honored."

Aisha extended her hand. Vivienne took it.

Outside, the mansion no longer felt haunted. It simply felt lived in.

"That was a beautiful gesture, Aisha," Drew said softly. "Inviting her to your premiere."

"When the two of you walked out of that room, I knew something had changed," Aisha replied. "I could see it. She had her epiphany. Her demons aren't running the story anymore."

"What did she say? What did she say?" Grace burst out.

"First of all, she was embarrassed," Drew replied. "She let her belief system and her emotions outrun her common sense. The weight of her brother's death marked her for life, especially because it was tangled up in her greatest success. She's carried more guilt than anyone should."

He shook his head, trying to imagine living under that kind of burden.

"And?" Grace's eyes widened.

"And…" Drew took a deep breath. "Whatever secret finally found its voice in that room will have to wait until I confirm a few more facts with Detective Singh."

Grace's disappointment showed instantly. "You've never kept a confession from us before."

"I know," Drew said calmly.

Aisha stepped in. "Grace, we have to be patient. You know how he works. He follows a clue all the way through."

Drew nodded. "I don't want to set a precedent until I verify what Vivienne told me. And besides…" He looked directly at both of them. "She was standing in front of two people who've always held her on a pedestal. She was afraid that once the words were spoken, you'd see her differently. To her, that would've been worse than any scandal."

The girls exchanged a quiet glance. They understood.

"Come on," Drew said, clapping his hands together lightly. "We're heading to Paramount to see our security guard friend, Terrell, and check in with the props department."

"And then?" Grace pressed.

"Then we meet Israel and Elena at Detective Singh's office," Drew confirmed.

☆☆☆

"I had a feeling you'd be calling," Terrell said with a knowing smile.

"Thank you for meeting us," Drew replied. "You're our lifesaving connection. Like I mentioned on the phone, we need access to Paramount Studios' props department."

"My brother Thomas is waiting for us. He's happy to help."

The gates of Paramount Studios loomed ahead like a sealed fortress, guarding its illusions within.

"The vault of dreams and lies," Terrell murmured under his breath.

As they rolled forward, Eddie, the security guard, leaned from his booth. "I see you got your car back," he observed.

"I don't suppose you had anything to do with that," Drew said, a hint of sarcasm in his smile.

"Not today," Eddie replied dryly.

"Just checking," Drew said. "We're here to see Thomas in Props."

"Let me give him a jingle," Eddie said, reaching for the phone. Then he glanced toward the back seat. "Terrell, does your brother know you're coming?"

Surprised that Eddie had spotted him, Terrell leaned forward and gave a quick wave. "Hi, Eddie. Yeah, he's aware."

"Terrell, do you miss working in Props?" Eddie teased.

"Not for a minute," Terrell shot back.

Eddie turned toward the control panel. "Alright, Charlie, raise the gate. Follow this road straight to soundstage 18. Props is right behind it. And don't park in an executive's spot this time."

Drew gave a thumbs-up and eased the car through the opening gate.

The Hollywood machine churned around them. Golf carts zipped past like impatient insects, weaving between soundstages that rose in pale, windowless blocks. Cathedrals built for illusion. Extras lingered near wardrobe trailers, half-transformed. Crew members moved with the muscle memory of long hours. Gaffers hauled cables. Production assistants clutched walkie-talkies. Producers spoke in low, urgent tones that made everything sound expensive and late.

"It's like a beehive in here," Grace said, glancing around.

"There's the building," Terrell replied.

They stepped through the wide warehouse doors and paused, momentarily overwhelmed by the scale of it all.

Endless rows of props stretched before them. Swords dulled by a hundred staged battles hung beside pristine teacups that had never held real tea. Dust-coated chandeliers loomed overhead, tagged and cataloged. Crates labeled Victorian Parlor, Hospital Generic, Alien Assorted - formed a labyrinth of borrowed realities. Somewhere deeper inside, a forklift beeped as it carried a Roman column past a stack of modern office chairs.

They moved slowly, almost reverently, aware that nothing in the space was real, yet everything had once been believed by a camera and by millions beyond it.

"There he is." Terrell lifted a hand. "This is Thomas, head of the Props Department."

Thomas had the solid build of a man accustomed to lifting and moving pieces of other people's worlds. His hair, mostly gray, was neatly trimmed, along with a matching mustache that framed his face and gave him a quiet distinction. Fine lines marked his skin, earned from long days and early mornings. His eyes were steady and observant, identical to his twin brother's, calm and focused beneath slightly heavy lids that gave him a thoughtful air.

"Hi, Thomas. We appreciate you meeting with us," Drew said in a lowered voice. "We're looking for something specific. A knife, or possibly a letter opener designed to resemble one." Drew removed the prop knife from his bag and held it out.

Thomas studied it carefully. For a moment, he said nothing. His eyes scanned the warehouse as though mentally retracing his inventory.

"Don't you have all of this on your computer?" Terrell asked.

"Yes," Thomas replied dryly. "But smaller items I document on a list until I'm sure they've been returned and labeled properly." He shot his brother a stern look.

As Thomas searched through a cabinet, Terrell leaned against a crate, arms crossed. "You still alphabetize the props wrong," he muttered.

Thomas didn't look up. "I alphabetize them correctly. You just don't understand the system."

"The system makes no sense. You've got letter openers under K."

"Because they're knives."

"They're office supplies."

"They're bladed objects."

Terrell scoffed. "You once put a fake guillotine under 'Gag Items.'"

"It was a comedy guillotine."

Drew glanced at Grace and Aisha. One of them raised an eyebrow, amused.

Terrell went on. "And don't get me started on the color coding. Red tags for danger, blue for replicas, yellow for what was it… vibes?"

"Yellow means period accurate," Thomas shot back. "Which you'd know if you ever read the labels instead of touching everything."

"I touch things because that's how humans interact with the world."

"That's how you get banned from storage rooms."

"Temporarily," Terrell huffed.

Thomas finally straightened and faced him. "If you hadn't signed out that fog machine under my name in 2019—"

"You said I could!"

"I said maybe."

Drew, Grace, and Aisha exchanged another look. One of them coughed to hide a smile.

Thomas stopped in front of a locked cabinet. The click of the key echoed in the vast room. He pulled out a slim case slowly, as if he already suspected what was inside. When he opened it, the group gathered closer.

The humor drained from the room as though someone had turned off the lights.

Terrell went quiet.

"That's not funny," he said softly.

"No," Thomas replied, his eyes fixed on the blade. "That really isn't."

The knife caught the light. It was beautiful. Polished. Real.

"This isn't the one that's supposed to be here," Thomas said quietly. "The catalog lists a replica."

They placed the real blade beside the fake one Israel had recovered from the truck. Side by side, the difference was undeniable. The fake knife was convincing at a glance, but too light, too dull. The real one carried weight. Intent. History.

"Remi Harrington," Thomas read from the engraving etched into the handle.

Drew pulled a rubber glove from his back pocket and slipped it on. He tilted the blade toward the overhead lights. A dark smear clung near the edge, dried and uneven.

"That's blood," Aisha said softly.

No one responded.

Thomas swallowed and opened the sign-in and sign-out log on his tablet. His fingers hovered for a moment before he began to scroll.

When the name appeared, Drew's face lost its color. Grace and Aisha leaned closer.

They didn't say the name aloud.

They didn't have to.

The weight of it settled deep in Drew's gut. They had stepped into a world built on illusion and uncovered the one object that refused to pretend.

"Detective Singh is waiting for us," Drew said quietly. "This changes everything."

☆☆☆

Israel leaned back against the edge of Detective Singh's desk, arms folded, his gaze drifting to the evidence board behind him. Elena noticed it had shifted since the last time. The same pieces. Different gravity.

"I've sent the blade to forensics. We should have results on the blood soon," Detective Singh said.

"You ever notice," Drew began casually, "how cases don't really explode? They compress."

Detective Singh didn't look up from the file in her hands. "That's a terrible metaphor."

"Still accurate."

She sighed and set the folder down. "Go on."

Drew gestured toward the board. "Take the truck. Black. Nondescript. Forgettable. Except it isn't. Because once you look twice, it's suddenly everywhere it shouldn't be."

Detective Singh's expression tightened, almost imperceptibly. "Israel gave me the license plate photos and the evidence recovered from inside. Vehicles don't commit crimes."

"No," Drew agreed. "But they keep appointments."

Detective Singh rose and crossed to the board, straightening a photograph that didn't need straightening. "I've got the plates running now. And the blade?"

Drew's eyes followed her. "Not the one everyone saw. The one no one thought to question. Funny thing about props. When something's meant to be fake, people stop believing it can hurt them."

"Until it does," Detective Singh said.

"Until it bleeds," Drew corrected softly.

Singh turned toward him. "It was a subtle bait and switch."

Drew picked up a pencil from her desk and used it to underline his point in the air. "The real letter opener was the weapon. The one used to cut Remi's throat. Afterward, a fake was placed on the desk so it wouldn't be identified as the murder weapon."

Singh moved to a small evidence bag pinned beneath a strand of timeline markers. "And what about this?"

"The key fob?" Drew shrugged. "Keys are intimate. They move through pockets, hands, routines. They don't end up where they don't belong unless something's gone very wrong."

Detective Singh studied the room. "Well, this one ended up with some very incriminating evidence."

"Thanks to Israel for spotting it," Drew added.

"And the script? Darlene Sharpe confirmed what we suspected?" Singh asked.

"Francy and Debra confirmed it was her father's work," Elena replied.

Singh exhaled and shifted her attention to two smaller items laid out carefully. A piece of jewelry. A strip of fabric.

"And these?"

Drew tilted his head. "Personal. Close to the body. Close enough to leave a story behind, even if no one intended to."

"I knew you'd find something on my shawl," Aisha said quietly.

Silence settled in the office.

Singh finally spoke. "We found matching hair samples on the shawl. Partial fingerprints on the earrings and the key fob."

"And?" Drew prompted gently.

"It matches the Props Department sign-out logs," Singh said.

Drew allowed himself a faint smile. "Paperwork doesn't lie. It just waits."

Singh held his gaze. "And when all of it finally says the same name?"

Drew pushed off the desk. "Then the ending writes itself."

Detective Singh didn't smile. "Endings can be dangerous. But if these clues line up, we have a perfect storm."

Drew glanced again at the board; at the way every thread now angled toward the same center. "People think the trick is hiding the truth," he said. "It's not. It's keeping it from lining up."

Singh turned to Aisha. "Tomorrow night, all of our suspects will be in the same room because of the premiere. It's the perfect opportunity to catch the killer. You understand that?"

Aisha nodded. "I have a feeling they suspect we know something. That's why we were invited backstage before the premiere under false pretenses."

Drew hesitated. "So, we still need a confession."

"That's why I need to wire you and Israel tomorrow night," Detective Singh said, looking directly at him. "It'll be easier to hide a wire under your outfits."

They both nodded.

Singh leaned back in her chair, the fatigue visible in her eyes. "This is the only move we have left," she said quietly. "If we miss this, the killer walks."

Chapter 21
Hollywood Boulevard

Grauman's Chinese Theatre was Hollywood Boulevard's jeweled dragon, where dreams swaggered down a red carpet and legends were pressed into concrete. It rose like a mirage of the Orient amid the glittering chaos of Hollywood Boulevard, a palace of illusion and spectacle swathed in crimson and gold, where the air itself seemed to shimmer with the residue of old celluloid magic.

Twin stone lions guarded the entrance, frozen mid-snarl, their eyes fixed on the crowds that surged like tides past their pedestals. Above them, the grand pagoda roof flared skyward, each tier trimmed in ornate emerald-green tile, as if conjured from the fevered dreams of a forgotten dynasty. At its peak, a slender spire pierced the California sky like a silver needle threading the coming night.

Massive red columns stood as sentinels, their lacquered surfaces gleaming in the twilight, each one lifting a piece of the myth. The myth that this place was sacred. A temple not of gods, but of fame.

The premiere of *The Final Tango* had transformed the venerable theater into a beacon, drawing fans, dreamers, and filmmakers into its orbit for one unforgettable night.

Camera crews jostled along the crimson carpet, lenses flashing beneath relentless lights. Reporters angled for position, microphones poised, waiting for the stars to emerge from polished black cars. The air vibrated with layered sound. The murmur of anticipation. The hum of generators feeding the spotlights. The distant honk of horns from the boulevard, sharp and impatient.

A few early arrivals from the film stepped onto the red carpet before the principal cast, setting the tone for the evening. Though they weren't instantly recognizable to the fans crowding the barricades, the moment their shoes touched the runner, excitement rippled through the front rows. The crowd surged forward with eager shouts, phones lifted high to capture even a passing glance. Cameras popped like a swarm of fireflies, flashing in rapid, staccato bursts.

Inside the velvet-rope perimeter, the atmosphere carried a different energy, calmer yet charged with importance. Publicists moved briskly with last-minute instructions, while ushers in crisp uniforms guided invited guests toward the theater's grand entrance. The scent of warm popcorn drifted from the lobby, mingling with the cool desert breeze sweeping in from the boulevard. Every few seconds, a fresh ripple of anticipation passed through the crowd as onlookers leaned forward, waiting for the next limousine door to open, the next star to step into the light.

Lexi Vale emerged first, stepping from her limousine with the poise of someone who understood how a single moment could shape a headline. The instant her heels touched the carpet, a sharp volley of flashes exploded along the press line. Her gown, an opalescent ivory design that shifted beneath the lights, shimmered like liquid pearl. She paused deliberately, lifting her chin just enough for the cameras to capture the diamonds at her throat, each facet catching fire under the glare.

Moments later, the atmosphere shifted again, this time with a younger, more volatile electricity.

Ollie Barrett stepped onto the carpet with awe flickering across his face, barely masking his excitement. The thunderous welcome seemed to catch him off guard, his smile widening as the noise swelled. Dressed in a sharply tailored suit threaded with subtle silver accents, he looked every bit the breakout sensation the studio had promised. The crowd's reaction sharpened, louder and more exuberant, fans calling his name with the breathless devotion reserved for new stars ascending. Ollie laughed, slightly overwhelmed, running a hand through his hair, posing for photographers before offering a proud wave and disappearing quickly through the theater doors.

In that fleeting instant of calm, an announcement crackled over the loudspeaker, asking the crowd to pause and applaud the film's late director, Remi Harrington, who was said to be with them in spirit. The stillness lasted only a heartbeat. Then the crowd erupted.

Two limousines eased to the curb in front of the gleaming theater. Klieg lights split the night sky, crisscrossing like restless comets, their beams sweeping over the massive throngs gathered along Hollywood Boulevard. Even from across the street, enthusiastic fans strained against the barricades, their voices rising into a bright, fevered chorus.

Tonight belonged to Aisha.

Her premiere shimmered with anticipation. The red carpet glowed beneath relentless camera flashes as the group emerged in effortless style. When Aisha stepped from the limousine, the reaction was immediate. A tidal wave of cheers and applause crashed against the theater's storied façade and rolled back over the frenzied crowd.

She moved into the lights draped in midnight blue, the gown drinking in the color of the sky itself. The fabric shimmered along the sculpted line of her bodice before cascading into a fluid train that whispered behind her. Diamonds flickered at her ears each time she turned toward the sound of her name, their brilliance rivaled only by the electricity in her eyes.

Even the ground beneath her heels felt sacred. The famous forecourt, its weathered concrete pressed with the immortal handprints and signatures of Hollywood legends, seemed to vibrate with expectation. Bogart. Monroe. Garland. Eastwood. Their imprints remained embedded in the earth like fossilized echoes of stardom, transforming the walkway into something closer to a shrine than a sidewalk.

Aisha felt it. The history. The weight. The belonging.

She lifted her gaze and offered the crowd a warm, perfectly measured smile, and the cheers swelled again, echoing down Hollywood Boulevard. As she advanced, her train drifted behind her in a silken hush. Reporters called from every direction, each one hungry for a quote, a glance, a moment. Bodyguards stood along the carpet, alert and immovable, ready should an overzealous admirer or ambitious reporter forget the boundaries.

But Aisha was unhurried. She waved. She posed. She absorbed it all, the flashes, the noise, the reverence, as though she had not only been born for the spotlight, but shaped by it.

Drew cut a striking figure beside her in a tailored black tuxedo; the clean lines of the jacket offset by a burgundy velvet bow tie that hinted at playful confidence. Elena followed, her silvery slip dress catching bursts of light like quicksilver. Its minimalist silhouette, paired with slicked-back hair, gave her an effortless, modern glamour. Israel added a note of creative nonchalance in a charcoal-gray suit layered over a black turtleneck, an ensemble that made him look less like an attendee and more like a director stepping away from his own film set.

Grace brought a romantic softness in blush-pink tulle that complemented her long pink braids. Embroidered flowers drifted across the airy layers of her skirt with every step, lending warmth to the electric night. Francy, ever the bold one, arrived in a sharply tailored emerald off-the-shoulder dress sculpted with dramatic curves that turned heads the moment she stepped onto the carpet. The look was daring, artistic, and entirely her own. Finally, Debra joined them in a deep plum gown accented with pearl jewelry, her calm, timeless sophistication radiating through a serene smile that grounded the swirl of excitement around them.

Together they formed a constellation of personalities and styles, each distinct yet perfectly in harmony, a brilliant tableau set against the glittering backdrop of one of Hollywood's biggest nights.

Then, almost as if summoned by the spectacle itself, a vintage 1957 Mercedes-Benz 300SL Gullwing rolled toward the edge of the red carpet. The horn gave a brief, knowing honk as the car came to a slow, deliberate stop, its engine settling into a soft purr that felt ceremonial.

For a heartbeat, nothing happened.

Then the door opened.

Vivienne LeClaire stepped out as if time itself had been waiting.

She wore a dusky twilight velvet gown that caught the lights without chasing them. Her posture was unmistakable, shoulders back, chin lifted, the quiet authority of a woman who had once taught Hollywood how to look at itself. Drake followed and offered his arm. She accepted it with a grace that made the gesture feel less like support and more like choreography.

The crowd hesitated.

Then recognition struck.

A ripple moved through the onlookers, passing across generations who had only known her through restored prints and late-night reruns. Gasps became murmurs. Murmurs swelled into shouts as the press began calling her name.

"*Vivienne*!"

Cameras snapped to life. Flashes burst like sudden stars.

"She's real," someone whispered.

She answered with a small, controlled smile, a smile shaped in another era yet landing perfectly in this one.

As she made her way down the carpet, the noise thickened, nostalgia colliding with disbelief. Even after all these years, Vivienne LeClaire did not simply arrive. She reappeared.

Then Aisha stepped forward to meet her.

The instant they entered the same frame, the paparazzi erupted. Flash after flash captured the contrast and the continuity. Vivienne, luminous and composed. Aisha, radiant and alive with momentum. The past and the present standing shoulder to shoulder.

Vivienne reached for Aisha's hands and leaned in just enough for the cameras to register the intimacy of it.

"This is your night," she said softly.

Aisha smiled, her eyes bright. "I'm so grateful you're here."

And just like that, Vivienne shifted, angling herself with instinctive precision so the lights settled where they belonged, on the woman stepping forward to open something new.

Hollywood noticed.

It always did.

The group stepped inside the theater and the velvet darkness swallowed them whole. Ornate dragons curled along the gilded proscenium arch, flickering in the half-light. Above them, the ceiling bloomed like a lotus stitched with artificial stars. Eager fans waved and snapped photos as the "Sexy Seven" slipped into their seats.

“Well, do we make our move?” Aisha whispered. “I know now this has nothing to do with the script I was offered.”

“I have a feeling this is going to be chaotic,” Debra murmured.

“We have to be ready for anything,” Israel added quickly.

“Then we do it casually,” Drew said. “We get up and make our way backstage.”

Timing it with the dim of the house lights, they rose in staggered pairs. Aisha, Drew, and Debra reached the side entrance first, a narrow door tucked beneath the curve of the proscenium. Israel, Grace, and Francy followed. Elena lingered a beat, scanning the rows behind them to make sure no one had noticed their exit before slipping through and pulling the door shut.

The backstage stairwell was tight and shadowed. The seven detectives climbed carefully, the sound of their steps muted against old concrete. Each rise felt deliberate. Each landing felt closer to something waiting.

Tension settled in like a dance. A measured advance. A calculated retreat. The space between what was real and what only appeared to be real narrowed with every step. If Hollywood had taught Drew anything, it was that people forgave fame far faster than they forgave truth, and belief tended to favor the celebrated over the factual.

He paused near the top of the stairs and lowered his voice.

“This is where we play our hand,” he whispered. “I can feel it.”

Backstage at Grauman’s Chinese Theatre was a world almost no one saw. It felt like an inverted reflection of the palace outside. The gilded dragons and glowing lanterns of the forecourt gave way, abruptly and without apology, to a narrow corridor tinged with the faint scent of dust, fabric, and the cold metallic tang of stage lights left to cool. The walls stood bare, paint worn dull by decades of hurried hands and brushing shoulders. The floorboards creaked in places, as though tired of keeping secrets.

Farther in, the corridor opened into the wings of the stage, where the audience's excited murmur pressed faintly through the heavy curtain. Up close, the theater's magic looked unmistakably mechanical. Ropes hung in disciplined rows, tied off in sailor's knots passed down from stagehands long vanished into history. Ladders disappeared into shadow where catwalks crisscrossed overhead like hidden passageways. Crates of cables and rolled backdrops stood stacked as high as ambition.

"Those steps must lead to stage level," Francy said, pointing toward a short staircase that ended just shy of the long red velvet curtains trimmed in gold fringe.

A female voice drifted toward them from behind the fabric.

"You picked quite a night to play hero, detectives. Harvey's name is on every marquee in town. The Visionary Producer. Hollywood's Golden Boy."

Drew recognized the voice instantly.

A figure stepped from behind the curtain with the careful poise of someone who had rehearsed this entrance, yet still questioned whether she belonged in it. The first glow came from the tip of a cigarette as she struck a light. The small flame briefly revealed bleach-blond hair and porcelain features warmed by faint undertones beneath the powder. Her cut was blunt and shoulder length, expertly tousled, the strands catching a muted sheen under the work lights.

She drew in, then exhaled a thin ribbon of smoke that betrayed the tension beneath an otherwise immaculate exterior.

"Surprised to see me?"

One eye twitched.

“Georgia Lynn.” Drew studied her imposing figure as she stepped fully into the light. “Surprised? Even my alarm clock has more mystery.”

“Sarcasm. Cute.” She shifted the cigarette from one side of her mouth to the other. “But golden boys like you and Harvey always forget who you stepped on to shine.”

Her gown was a sculpted column of midnight-blue silk, clinging with intention, smooth and fluid, catching the light like moonlit water. A high slit revealed one leg as she advanced, and the glint of metal flashed from a leather-strapped thigh-high holster secured tightly against her skin.

Her hand moved with deliberate calm.

She reached into the holster and drew a sleek Sig Sauer P238. The rosewood grip settled into her palm as naturally as the cigarette had. She lifted the barrel and aimed it squarely at Drew.

He froze midway up the stairs, pulse tightening. Without turning fully, he checked that the others were still behind him.

“Keep talking,” he said evenly. “Eventually something impressive might come out.”

He shifted his weight slightly, watching the subtle change in her expression. “So, I’m guessing he stepped on you?” Drew asked.

“You’re damn right he did.” She tipped her head back and exhaled, smoke drifting upward in a thin silver veil that curled along the stage curtains. “You want to know where the bodies are buried?”

She paused just long enough to feel the hook set.

“I have the answers.” A small nod. Controlled. Certain. “We don’t have much time. You need to hear the truth before Harvey gets here.”

Aisha stepped closer to Drew, her shoulder nearly brushing his back as she looked up at Georgia Lynn.

"Why don't you put the gun down."

"Harvey is your puppet master, Drew," Georgia replied coolly. "The man who's stepped on and silenced more lives in this business than anyone cares to count. And when he's arrested, the studio will need someone new to steady the ship. Someone who knows how to keep secrets from leaking into the trades."

A faint smile curved her lips, the kind that suggested layers beneath layers.

"Let me guess," Drew said, his voice calm but edged with deliberate challenge. "You're that someone."

He held her gaze.

"You spent years in Harvey's shadow. He was always one move ahead, climbing to studio chief while you were quietly absorbed back into the machinery. Just another name in the credits. Am I close?"

The words struck clean. He saw it in her eyes first. The flicker. The flare. Defiance sparking against something bruised and long simmering.

"I'll give you the confession," she said. "The accomplices. Everything."

She took a slow drag from her cigarette, using the inhale to steady herself, then adjusted her grip on the pistol. The metal caught a narrow strip of light spilling from the wings, flashing briefly before settling back into shadow.

"You hand over those few pieces of evidence you're holding," she continued, "the ones that won't mean anything once the story breaks. Do that, and you walk out of here a hero."

Smoke drifted from her lips as her expression hardened.

"Funny thing about Hollywood, Drew. It only takes one good story to make a monster fall."

"Let me guess. You practiced that in the mirror," Drew shot back.

He held Georgia Lynn's gaze without blinking.

"By 'those few pieces of evidence,' you mean the key fob with your fingerprint and Remi's blood on it? The one you stole to access his garage? Or maybe the work orders you signed for the sabotaged stunt car, then kept from Remi so you could cover your tracks?"

He took a steady breath.

"And we can't forget the rubber prop knife you swapped onto Remi's desk while arranging for him to be killed with his own letter opener."

Aisha cleared her throat, her voice precise and measured.

"You signed out the replica knife from the props department two days before the murder. Afterward, you returned the real weapon there, hoping it would disappear into inventory." She tilted her head slightly. "And your associate drove the black Ford truck registered in your name. It was hidden in Remi's garage the night he died."

Georgia's smile thinned.

"Funny," she said softly. "I didn't think you'd be smart enough to catch that."

"Funny," Drew replied, stepping forward despite the gun trained on him. "And you still can't believe we did."

She reacted instantly, raising the pistol until it aligned with his eyes. Her breath hitched, just once.

"I didn't kill Remi."

"The evidence says you were involved," Debra interjected calmly.

"I didn't kill him," Georgia repeated, a strange curve forming at the corner of her mouth. "But I know who did."

Drew stiffened. "Who are you protecting?"

Georgia's eyes flashed, something raw surfacing beneath the polish.

"No one. Not anymore."

Aisha's body went rigid.

Slowly, she turned toward the wings.

Ollie Barrett stepped from the shadows, a gun pointed directly at her.

"You can come out," Aisha said coolly, not taking her eyes off him. "I can hear your raspy breathing."

"Oy, what in the bloody hell d'you think you're up to then?" he cackled. "Proper washed up, you are. Like yesterday's kippers."

Aisha held his gaze. "Wipe that cheeky grin off that boat of yours."

"Oy, you learned me language," Ollie said, clearly amused.

"We know you were the one who murdered Remi," Aisha stated.

"You're completely daft, you are," Ollie smirked.

"Ollie, Ollie, Ollie…" Drew interrupted calmly. "You made several crucial mistakes on your so-called path to stardom. Your first mistake was in the way you crafted those threatening notes to Vivienne LeClaire."

"What?" Ollie blurted.

"You pulled letters from different newspapers and magazines to assemble the notes. Clever. Dramatic. But the detail that made me look closer was your use of the letter D." Drew's voice sharpened slightly. "In *Your days are numbered. I know what you did.* You cut the D from *The Daily Mail.* A very distinct font from the British tabloid. One I happen to recognize."

Ollie shook his head, but the movement looked less like denial and more like recalculation.

"It didn't fully click until I saw the red button you installed on the right side of Georgia Lynn's truck," Drew continued. "You used that button to remind yourself that in the US we drive on the right. For someone used to driving on the left, that adjustment doesn't come naturally."

He paused just long enough to let it settle.

"Drive right. Look left."

Ollie said nothing.

"You parked the truck in Remi's garage by reversing into the space, positioning it so the front wheels faced the garage door. As a British driver, you're used to backing into parking spaces, not pulling in head-first like most Americans. Remi, on the other hand, always parked head-in, leaving the rear of the vehicle facing the door. That immediately got me thinking…"

Drew smiled, almost devilishly.

"I went back to the boot print we found at the crime scene. It was distinctive. Unusual. Then I did some checking. The tread matched a UK-exclusive shoe brand called John Lobb. Ultra-luxury. Handmade. Not something you'd find in a mass-market shop. We already knew the print wasn't from ordinary footwear. That's what betrayed you."

Ollie's gaze drifted slowly down to his shoes.

"So, of course, we had the police run it through the UK National DNA Database. IDENT1 matched your fingerprints, thanks to that domestic violence offense you racked up years ago." Drew turned to Aisha, letting the weight of it settle.

"Your blood and fingerprints were all over the knife you used to slit Remi's throat," Aisha said evenly. "Why did you do it, Ollie? Did one of these clowns promise you a starring role in their next picture? Did they sweeten the deal with cash?"

Ollie's mood shifted instantly. The defiance hardened his posture. His jaw tightened.

"Right. And a lot more, eh? She had the hots for me." He gestured toward Georgia Lynn. "She stole Remi's key fob so I could get into his house. You told me you hid that knife where no one would find it."

His temper flared, raw and unrestrained, as he glared at Georgia Lynn.

"Traitor!" Georgia Lynn yelled. "Yes, I took Remi's key fob. I thought Ollie would use it to confront him. Instead, Ollie, belittled, hungry for power, and manipulated by Harvey, went further. He killed Remi."

For a fleeting moment, genuine remorse flickered across her face.

"I helped cover for him," she whimpered. "Driven by a toxic love and a warped need to protect him from professional ruin. And what did it get me? Betrayal." Her voice faltered as the weight of it settled in.

"And I was promised star status if I did the deed!" Ollie shot back, pausing as if savoring the confession. "Remi was always cuttin' me down. Anyways, I hated the bloke. So, I returned the favor. Plain and simple."

"There's nothing plain and simple about murder," Aisha snapped.

Now seething, Ollie stepped closer to Georgia Lynn. "Oye, let's not forget the near-fatal crash that almost killed me and Aisha!" He raised his gun and aimed it at her face. "She buried a maintenance report proving the vehicle wasn't safe."

“Why, Georgia Lynn? Why would you do that?” Drew fired back.

“Georgia Lynn wanted Aisha frightened off the film because she’d been asking too many questions on set, getting too close to the truth without even realizing it,” a voice called from the wings. “She also threatened Lexi Vale out of jealousy and panic.”

“Well, you might as well come out of hiding too, Matt,” Drew said, pointing toward the pin rail just offstage behind the curtain. “We can all see you.”

Matt slowly stood and stepped into the light. His demeanor shifted, as if he had just been reprimanded. “Dude, you think you have it all figured out,” he shouted from the wings. He lifted a pistol in his right hand and steadied it with his left as tension tightened across his shoulders.

“This little dance we’re doing is going to end badly for you,” Drew shot back.

“Then come on. Let’s dance, pretty boy.” Matt widened his stance and aimed straight at Drew. “You killed my J.C. He was the love of my life. I should take you out right now,” he warned.

Francy moved to Drew’s side. Israel stepped between Drew and Matt. “You’re going to have to go through me first,” he said, locking eyes with him.

“And me.” Grace slid into position, forming a third shield in front of Drew.

Aisha shifted forward. “Matt, what are you doing? This isn’t like you. What triggered you?”

“You’re all willing to die for him?” Matt shouted.

“Yes,” came the chorus of six.

“You see, Matt, we’re the kind of friends who lift each other up,” Drew said.

"When things fall apart, we're there for each other. We always are," Aisha added.

"Besides, Matt," Elena stepped up, "J.C. died because of his own actions, not ours. I was there."

Grace moved forward. "And I want to know why you were threatening Vivienne LeClaire."

"Harvey told me everything," he shot back. "Remi talked about Vivienne LeClaire all the time. He was fascinated by her. He told me she was still alive and that she had a famous savant brother. A savant like me. I had to know more."

"That's right, Matt. Vivienne did have a brother. A brother just like you. Smart. Efficient. One of a kind. But Harvey didn't tell you everything."

"He told me Georgia Lynn killed Vivienne's brother, and Vivienne did nothing because he was standing in the way of her fame."

"You foolish boy!" Georgia Lynn burst out. "Harvey was using you. He was using Ollie too. Playing both of you like instruments. You want to know why Remi was so fascinated by Vivienne LeClaire? Here's the first truth. When Harvey became head of Paramount, the first thing he did was fire Clive Harrington."

Drew frowned. "Remi's father?"

Georgia Lynn nodded quickly. "Yes. Clive Harrington was pushed out of the business the minute Harvey took over Paramount."

"Why would Harvey drop him?" Aisha asked.

"Well," she said with a faint smirk, "Clive directed *Velvet Ashes* the way he wanted. It was his picture, after all." She took another long drag on her cigarette.

"Clive Harrington was at the top of his game," Drew interrupted.

"Harvey was jealous of that and…" She paused. "*Velvet Ashes* was Harvey's script," she said, air-quoting the word. "So when Harvey came to power, he fired Harrington from Paramount. He thought that was the end of it." She let out a humorless laugh. "But Clive… he didn't go quietly."

Drew studied her expression, waiting for what was coming next.

"Years later, Clive discovered something. An old script buried away. Something Harvey never wanted brought into the light. Clive used it against him."

"Used it how?" Drew pressed.

Georgia Lynn looked from one detective to the next, weighing how much truth they deserved. Then her eyes settled on Drew.

"The movie that made Vivienne LeClaire a star and catapulted Harvey Goldstein to the head of Paramount…"

Drew chose his words carefully. "You mean *Velvet Ashes*?"

Georgia Lynn cut him off. "No. I mean *The Resurrection of Mildred Miles*. An original, brilliant script. Worth its weight in gold. Harvey stole it years ago. That film made him and Vivienne LeClaire famous. Every award. Every headline. All built on a stolen story." Her disdain rolled off her tongue like a curse she had been waiting years to cast. "He didn't write it. Not a single word. He stole it from a nobody."

"A nobody?" Francy shot back.

"It was a brilliant script," Georgia Lynn continued. "Buried in a stack of screenwriting competition submissions. Harvey and I were on the selection committee. We found it by accident. And Harvey, who was Vivienne's agent at the time, knew it could be the one. The one. So he stole it. Made a few minor changes. Altered the title. Rewrote the opening. And Vivienne? She sold it with her performance. She became the face of it." Georgia Lynn trembled with every word.

Drew shifted his weight. He could feel the confession tightening around them.

Georgia Lynn locked eyes with him, her voice unsteady but deliberate. "But Clive Harrington became Harvey's undoing. Clive found the original script and realized exactly what Harvey had done. So what did he do? He blackmailed him. At first, it was money. Quiet payments. Under the table. Then later, he demanded something bigger."

Aisha shot Drew a sideways glance as he leaned forward. "Bigger how?"

Georgia hesitated, then forced the words out, as if tearing off a bandage.

"He blackmailed Harvey into hiring his son. Remi got into Paramount because Clive threatened to release the original script unless Harvey secured the boy's future."

Silence settled over the room.

Georgia Lynn lifted her chin. "For your information, Remi Harrington, your wunderkind director, knew exactly what he had. Harvey's Hollywood empire was built on a stolen screenplay. Remi, loyal to his late father who uncovered the truth, used that knowledge to continue the blackmail. And that blackmail led directly to Remi's murder."

Drew's voice cut through the silence. "How?"

Before she could respond, a series of slow, methodical claps echoed from the bowels of the theater.

From the wings, a silhouette peeled itself away from the darkness.

Debra gasped, seizing Drew's sleeve with a sharp, involuntary tug.

Beneath the solitary work light, the figure stepped forward. Shadows receded, revealing Harvey Goldstein, dressed in a black tuxedo, like a spectral maestro emerging for one final, fatal performance.

“Brava, Georgia Lynn, for that riveting, Oscar-worthy performance,” he murmured.

He drew a gun from his cummerbund and advanced, unhurried. The weapon trembled ever so slightly in his grasp, but his eyes were frigid, polished shards of stone that did not waver. His finger rested lightly on the trigger.

“It seems we have an uninvited guest.” His gaze fixed on Georgia Lynn. “I really didn’t think you’d betray me.”

Drew stepped forward instinctively, shielding Aisha and Debra behind him.

Francy’s hand closed around a length of chain she had picked up from the floor and hidden behind her back, white-knuckled and ready.

Israel remained unnervingly still. With deliberate calm, he extended the collapsible baton concealed in his sleeve, studying Harvey like a predator measuring distance before the strike.

Grace and Elena flanked the perimeter, tense and silent, bodies coiled.

Harvey’s voice sliced through the quiet.

“Aisha, I knew you couldn’t resist the invitation,” he said with a faint smirk.

“Well, you know us,” Aisha said. “We hate to miss a good party.”

“And you brought your Musketeers. How sweet.” Harvey’s words dripped with disdain.

“Well, Harvey, Georgia Lynn was just about to tell us why you orchestrated Remi’s death,” Drew said evenly.

"The poor boy." Harvey shook his head. "He was going to ruin everything."

"Ruin everything?" Aisha let out a short laugh. "Didn't you already do that to the writer you stole from?"

Drew watched Harvey's hand tighten around the gun as he edged closer to Georgia Lynn, one deliberate step at a time. "Why didn't the writer come after the studio?" Drew asked, carefully keeping the tension balanced between them.

"Who knows," Georgia Lynn replied with a shrug. "He was either oblivious or realized what had been done and simply rolled over and died."

"You mean William Sharpe," Drew said. The name dropped into the silence like a stone. "The death of the author," he added under his breath.

"It was the latter," Debra said. "He rolled over and died. Once William Sharpe discovered what you had done, Harvey, he was devastated. He was a poor, struggling writer."

No one moved.

Georgia Lynn stared at Drew, perplexed. "How could you possibly know that?"

"We're detectives, remember?" Grace shot back.

"William Sharpe didn't have the means or the wherewithal to fight a major studio," Debra continued. "He never got his break in this town. He died penniless in the Valley." She searched Harvey's face for some trace of remorse, but found none. The emptiness in his expression made her doubt he was human.

"Welcome to Hollywood," Harvey replied dryly. "Success isn't about what's fair. It's about who gets there first."

“Wait a minute.” Georgia Lynn’s curiosity suddenly sharpened. “How do you know all this?”

“If it weren’t for Remi’s murder, we never would have uncovered the truth,” Drew said. “We found the smoking gun. The original evidence Clive and Remi Harrington were holding over you, Harvey. The original script. The one you stole and altered. We found it.”

He held Harvey’s gaze.

“There was more. The script contained a letter from the writer. William Sharpe wrote to his daughter before he died. A letter she never received. In it, he explained exactly what you had done to his work. The letter and the original draft were hidden inside a desk Clive stumbled upon in an antique shop.”

Drew paused, expecting a reaction.

Harvey said nothing.

“After William Sharpe’s death, his daughter cleared out his belongings. The desk was sold and eventually ended up in that antique shop. By chance, it was purchased by Remi’s father. When Clive Harrington realized what he had found, he understood the leverage he now held. Your dirty little secret.”

“Talk about fate,” Debra murmured.

“Fate?” Harvey replied coolly. “And you’re all standing here because of that script. Even you, Drew. So, there’s nothing to hide.”

Drew didn’t respond. He didn’t need to. His silence said enough.

“But there is something to protect,” Aisha said quietly.

Harvey nodded again, slower this time, deliberate. “And I am willing to protect it… at any cost.”

“Your reputation? Your fame?” Grace sneered.

“My legacy,” he said.

Georgia Lynn drew in a steady breath. "Before Clive Harrington's death, the elder Harrington confided everything to Remi. Remi had the original script of *Velvet Ashes*, along with a copy of the letter from the writer to his daughter. He held them over you like a blade, Harvey. Leverage he knew you couldn't ignore."

Drew's gaze shifted between Harvey and Georgia Lynn, searching for the truth in the spaces neither of them filled.

"That's right," Georgia Lynn continued. "Clive Harrington baited you like a fat mackerel. And when he wanted to make sure you had no cards left to play, he told you he had an accomplice."

"Accomplice?" Drew echoed.

"The shop owner he bought the desk from." Georgia Lynn winced. "Clive claimed she knew about the original script. That she could expose everything. He dangled her name over Harvey's head, another threat he didn't have to prove."

Harvey's expression hardened with something colder than anger. Resolve. He stepped closer and lowered his voice, as if even speaking the truth required caution.

"But… she never knew anything, did she?" Drew pressed.

"No." Georgia Lynn shook her head, her eyes glassy now. "She had nothing to do with it. She didn't even know the script existed. Clive just used her name. The threat of her was enough. It kept Harvey from coming after him."

Silence settled over the room.

"And Harvey believed him," Francy said.

"He did. And that's what killed her." Georgia Lynn's voice broke. "Harvey wanted to eliminate every loose end. He thought if he got rid of the woman, Clive would be the last person alive with the information and easier to control. He murdered her because of a lie Clive told to protect himself."

The words landed all at once.

Drew felt sick. Not just to his stomach. To his core.

In his heart, he knew. Right then and there, he knew. Harvey had killed his Aunt Martha. The one event that had shaped his life, that had driven him forward, that had haunted every choice he made, was tied to the man standing in front of him.

A chill spread through him, slow and paralyzing.

"The antique shop…?" His voice thinned. "Harvey, that was my aunt's store."

Harvey's jaw tightened. His eyes widened, but he didn't look away. "All I knew was that she was involved. She wasn't just selling relics. She was moving information. Artifacts. Things people would kill for."

"That's where you're wrong, Harvey." Drew's voice trembled, but it did not falter. "My Aunt Martha never knew about the hidden compartment in the desk. She never knew the script was there. Clive Harrington only found out when he stumbled onto the secret drawer after he bought it. You weren't paying attention, Harvey. You acted before you understood."

Adrenaline surged through Drew's body. He couldn't stop it. His hands shook, and the anger radiating from him filled the room. The walls seemed to tilt inward.

The memory of his aunt flooded back. Her soft voice. Her sharp eyes. The way her fingers brushed dust from forgotten objects, a cigarette balanced in the other hand. She had been many things, but careless was never one of them.

"Georgia…" His voice cracked now. "Why didn't you come forward?"

"I was an agent back then. Harvey and I both were. But Harvey was promoted to head of the studio when *Velvet Ashes* became a huge success. I didn't want to believe he was capable of something like that. I was terrified that if I said anything, I'd be next. But over time… I learned. I learned just how far Harvey would go to reach the top."

The room fell silent.

Drew tilted his head slightly, as if straining to hear something beneath the quiet. The stillness pressed in on them, deafening. A brutal reminder of everything that had just been laid bare. No one dared to move. The truth hung between them, raw and undisguised.

Drew looked at Harvey, something dark and fractured settling behind his eyes. "You killed my aunt," he said quietly. "Do you have any idea what you took from me?"

Georgia Lynn let out a low, bitter sound. "That's not all he's taken." She gestured with the gun toward Drew and his friends. "Your client on Sunset Boulevard had a similar experience."

Harvey met her stare without blinking. "You're digging your own grave," he said evenly.

"Go on, Harvey. Educate them. They deserve to know how your reign of terror began." Georgia Lynn lifted the gun higher and stepped forward, slow and deliberate.

"Several months ago, Vivienne LeClaire called me out of the blue with a warning." A deep, guttural groan rumbled in Harvey's throat. "A warning?" He scoffed. "I made that woman a star, and she thought she could threaten me? She said her psychic confirmed it. This year marked fifty years since her brother's death. It was time for her to confess her sins, or her brother's spirit would come for her."

"Is that why you threatened Vivienne?" Debra asked, guiding him forward, her voice barely above a whisper. The question was placed carefully, like bait.

"She was going to tell someone!" Harvey snapped.

"There it is," Debra said.

Drew and Israel exchanged a subtle glance, recognizing what she had just done.

"Go on, Harvey," Georgia Lynn smirked. "Tell them why you started threatening her." She shifted her stance and aimed the pistol directly at his head.

Harvey shook his head, jaw flexing. "When she told me she'd hired a group of detectives, I knew she would talk. I knew she'd blow the whole story wide open. After everything I did for her. After I made her a celebrity." His voice rose, thick with rage. "That's when I realized it was you she hired," he said, jerking his gun toward Drew. "She needed a lesson in humility."

His breathing turned ragged.

"I sent the letters to Vivienne. I made sure Matt or Ollie were inside her house. Stalking her. Teasing her. Haunting her."

Matt answered quickly. "Harvey convinced me it was Vivienne LeClaire who was threatening Remi. Remi never told me what his connection to her was, so I helped Harvey. I wanted to know why Vivienne killed the author who wrote the original *Velvet Ashes*."

"So, you used her brother's words against her. To haunt her. To terrorize her?" Grace shouted.

"Harvey told me Vivienne LeClaire and Georgia Lynn killed Remi!" Matt fired back.

"Matt, you were misled. Harvey played you," Drew said firmly.

"Ollie… I didn't know it was you who killed Remi!" Matt pivoted and raised his gun toward the Brit.

Grace gasped. Debra instinctively reached for her, then hesitated. Francy and Elena stepped closer, tension pulling them forward.

"You're leaving out an important fact, Harvey," Georgia Lynn cut in. "Don't forget to tell them the part about her brother."

A dark tension moved through Harvey as she spoke. His focus locked onto her, sharp and suffocating.

"Vivienne thought it was time to tell the world that *Velvet Ashes* was stolen," Harvey said. "She was going to tell you. All of you." He waved the gun toward the detectives, as if weighing his options. "I heard it in her voice. She was unraveling. She carried that secret for fifty years. And now she was cracking."

"Who's unraveling now?" Debra whispered, just loud enough for him to hear.

"Guilt does that to people." Drew stepped closer.

"She thought her brother's ghost was angry with her. Especially when her success failed to fill the hole his death left behind," Elena said quietly.

Israel moved forward, steady and deliberate. "So instead of coming clean, you thought a few death threats would scare her back into silence. Or scare her to death?"

"Why don't you skip ahead to the part where you killed her brother?" Georgia Lynn asked, her eyes narrowing, her voice low and controlled. "After all these years, I want to hear your reasoning."

"Vivienne's brother was a liability," Harvey replied coldly. "She stupidly confided in him. When he found out we were going to make that script our own and run with it, he threatened to go to the newspapers. He was going to tell the press I stole it."

"So, you killed him," Drew concluded.

Harvey's jaw tightened. "I showed him he couldn't swim in that pool without a life jacket."

"You drowned him," Elena said, her voice breaking.

"That's why you wouldn't pick me up for the movie premiere that night," Georgia Lynn murmured, the memory settling into place.

"Georgia Lynn." Drew looked at her directly. "Tell us what happened."

She stood there, shaking her head as the pieces came together in her mind.

"You and Mr. Keyes drove to Vivienne's house to pick her up for the premiere. You both went inside to get her. But she showed up alone that night. You stayed behind so you could kill her brother and make it look like a drowning." Her eyes fixed on him. "What about Keyes? Did he help you?"

"That coward? He didn't have the guts to protect the movie or our reputations," Harvey barked.

Drew watched Georgia Lynn closely as the realization settled into her expression. "That's why Keyes wanted nothing to do with you or the film after that night."

Aisha stepped forward. "Mr. Keyes confirmed it to me. He said he witnessed something that cost him his career."

"I dropped Keyes from our stable of rising stars," Harvey grunted. "If he behaved, I promised him behind the scenes work in exchange for his loyalty. I built my career on *Velvet Ashes*. That unstable brother of Vivienne's was going to ruin everything." His voice rose as he glanced at Georgia Lynn.

“So, you killed him too,” Georgia Lynn said quietly.

“That’s enough!” Harvey shouted, his temper fraying. “Enough of this back and forth. It’s time to take back my territory.” He turned and aimed his gun at Georgia Lynn.

Suddenly, applause erupted inside the theater. The premiere had begun.

Harvey’s name boomed through the loudspeakers, rolling like thunder across the velvet-roped entrance outside the theater. He turned back to his captives, a twisted smile forming. “You hear that? That’s my name they’re calling.”

The muffled cheers seeped through the walls, a cruel reminder that the world was celebrating while, in this room, everything was about to unravel.

“Harvey stopped at nothing to keep his secrets,” Georgia Lynn cried out.

Her voice rose, frantic and accusing, building until it seemed to circle him like a storm. Each word struck harder than the last. In the charged silence between her sentences, Harvey realized he could not endure another second of it.

He steadied the gun, suddenly conscious of the cold weight in his hand. The faint mechanical clicks sounded louder than the chaos in his thoughts. His breathing turned fast and shallow. A strange hush settled over him, the kind that comes just before something breaks.

Then he pulled the trigger.

The shot cracked through the room, sharp and deafening, like something irretrievable snapping in two. Georgia Lynn’s hand flew to her stomach. For a heartbeat, nothing moved. Her face emptied. Her breath stalled somewhere between a word and a scream. Then her knees buckled and her body gave way, folding in on itself as she collapsed. It was small. Sudden. Final.

Harvey watched her fall.

The world narrowed to fragments. The echo of the gunshot looping in his ears. The dull ache in his fingers. The air turning thick and metallic on his tongue. His heart thundered against his ribs.

Debra gasped. The only sound that dared to rise.

Harvey stood motionless, the gun still warm in his palm.

"Ladies and gentlemen," he said quietly, stepping back toward the footlights, "your investigation ends here." His smile never reached his eyes.

Drew's instincts fired a second too late. Beneath his shoes, he heard it. The faint metallic click.

"Aisha, move!" Drew shouted.

But Harvey had already signaled Ollie.

Ollie triggered the hidden mechanism.

The stage floor split open like a mouth, and the detectives dropped through it into darkness, swallowed whole by a substage chamber.

The world vanished beneath them.

For one dizzying heartbeat there was only the fall. Weightlessness. Disorientation. Air tore past their ears. Drew's stomach lurched. Debra screamed something that disappeared into the void. None of them knew how far they were plunging or what waited below. Only the cold, hollow space consuming them.

Then everything stopped.

WHUMP.

They slammed into something that gave beneath them, soft yet firm. A massive air bag ballooned and hissed, absorbing their momentum before bouncing them lightly and settling under their combined weight.

Drew lay sprawled on his back, blinking up at the square of dim stage light high above them, the trap door still open like an indifferent eye.

For a moment, no one spoke.

They stared at one another, wide-eyed, breaths ragged with equal parts fear and disbelief.

"An air bag?" Elena muttered at last.

Drew pushed himself upright, his heart still pounding hard enough to make his vision pulse.

Aisha was the first to fully recover. "What… what is this?"

Dust swirled in the stagnant air. Francy coughed and reached blindly for the nearest body. Debra, still shaken, grabbed hold of her to steady them both.

Grace was draped halfway across Drew, with Elena tangled near his legs. Israel rolled to his side, forced himself up, and quickly counted heads.

"Where are we?"

They looked up just as Harvey appeared at the edge of the open trap door. Surprise flickered across his face.

"I didn't count on that crash mat being inflated," he called down.

His disappointment hardened into calculation. His eyes scanned the chamber until they locked onto a black pipe running along the ceiling.

He fired.

The shot rang out and the bullet tore through the pipe. A violent burst of water exploded into the chamber, slamming against the walls before cascading downward in a relentless surge.

Grace gasped as the water began to rise. "He's flooding us! We have to get out. Now!"

They scanned their surroundings. The air bag sat on a platform about three feet above the concrete floor. As their eyes adjusted to the damp, shadowed space, they searched desperately for anything that could stop the torrent. There was nothing. No valve. No ladder. No visible exit.

"Harvey, this won't change anything!" Drew shouted upward.

No answer.

"Drew, the water's rising fast!" Francy yelled over the roar. The surge climbed higher, breaching the top of the air bag and spilling over their shoes.

Drew's mind raced. The air bag, once their cushion, was now a trap.

"We have to get off this thing," he ordered. "We won't find a solution standing up here. Jump into the water."

Ollie appeared at the edge of the trap door at the sound of the splash. He stared down at the detectives struggling in the fast-rising water.

"This wasn't… this wasn't the plan!" he shouted to Harvey.

Drew heard the reply.

"The plan," Harvey snarled, "is whatever I decide it is."

Ollie's eyes flickered to Aisha for a brief, conflicted moment. Then he pressed the clicker. The trap door groaned as it slid shut, sealing them in and plunging the chamber into complete darkness.

"Look for anything," Drew shouted. "Valves. Panels. Cracks." His voice sounded thin against the thunder of the water. His hands skimmed along the slick walls, searching for the slightest imperfection.

Grace and Elena switched on the flashlights on their phones at the same time, thin beams cutting through the blackness.

The water kept rising.

Drew forced himself to focus. Earlier that evening, Detective Singh had insisted on wiring him and Israel. Every confession, every threat, every gunshot, and now the roar of flooding water was transmitting directly to the LAPD. Singh and her team were stationed in vans outside the theater. They had to be hearing this.

So why had no one come?

"The walls are too smooth!" Aisha cried, slipping each time she tried to climb. "We're running out of time!"

Israel stumbled, catching himself against a metal grate that shuddered beneath his weight.

"Here!" he shouted.

Through the swirling water, he felt it. A vibration. A steady, rhythmic mechanical hum.

A pump.

"If we can jam it," Israel said, breath ragged, "the water should stop."

"Should?" Debra shot back. "Or it explodes."

"Better a chance than none at all," Francy said.

The water climbed higher, the cold biting into them, forcing their bodies into tremors.

Drew met Israel's eyes and saw it there. Determination. A refusal to let this be the end. He nodded once.

"Okay," Drew said. "We jam it. Tell me what you need."

"We have to get through this grate first," Israel replied, wiping water from his eyes.

Without another word, he ducked beneath the freezing surface and disappeared. Water crashed against the walls and rebounded into their faces, blinding and disorienting.

"Israel!" Elena screamed.

"All we have to do is stop it!" Debra shouted, though her voice wavered.

Israel burst back up for air. "Give me something solid!" he yelled over the roar. "I need leverage to pry this thing loose!"

Panic flickered across their faces. Each breath felt shorter than the last.

Francy's eyes widened. She reached instinctively for the only weapon she had carried earlier. The metal chain she grabbed backstage. She had kept it ready, just in case.

"The chain!" she shouted. "I had it in my hands, but when we fell… I don't know where it went!"

"Try the airbag," Grace called.

Francy pushed back through the water, reaching blindly for it. When her foot struck one corner, she lunged toward where she thought it had drifted.

"It might've shifted with the current," Debra warned.

Then Francy felt the chain press against her foot. She drew in a breath and dove, sweeping her hands along the submerged concrete until her fingers closed around the cold metal. She surfaced, lifting it above the water. "Will this do?"

With a sharp yank, she hurled it toward Israel.

“It’ll have to.” He inhaled deeply and plunged into the murky water. He guided the chain through the grate, working fast. As he tightened his grip, he remembered the collapsible baton hidden inside his sleeve.

He shot back up for air. The baton rested against his forearm. He snapped it open, threaded it through both ends of the chain, and began twisting. The links drew tighter with every turn, the slack disappearing.

“Help me turn this,” Israel said.

Drew grabbed the baton, and together they twisted harder and faster. The chain cinched tight around the grate, straining against the hinges until they finally tore free.

The sudden release sent both men crashing backward.

“I think we did it,” Israel cried.

He drew in a massive breath and plunged back under. Eyes open beneath the water, he searched for the source of the problem. Below the breached grate, the pump’s control panel lay exposed. He spotted it almost immediately. A small mechanical relay inside was cycling uncontrollably, forcing water through the system at full pressure. He didn’t need to destroy the pump. He only had to interrupt its motion long enough to stop the flow.

He surfaced sharply. “Amigo!” he shouted. “Pass me that baton!”

Drew dove beneath the surface, vanishing into the swirling water as he searched for the chain and baton. Seconds stretched painfully. Ten. Twenty. Then he burst upward, gasping, the baton clenched triumphantly in his fist. Without hesitation, he hurled it toward Israel, droplets spraying as it cut through the air.

Israel snatched it mid-flight, inhaled deeply, and plunged back into the frigid water. Working quickly, he wedged the baton between two moving external components, jamming the mechanism before it could complete another rotation.

The pump groaned and shuddered. Then it stalled with a heavy clunk.

Israel surfaced again. “That might do it!”

Water continued to spill for a few seconds, then slowed to a trickle as the pressure bled off.

“It’s not a permanent fix,” he said, breathing hard, “but it’s enough to buy us time.”

“Oh my God,” Debra exhaled. “Isra, you’re a genius!”

Drew wiped the water from his face. “Okay. Crisis one stopped.”

“Now we have to get out of this trap!” Aisha exclaimed.

Their focus shifted instantly. Cellphone beams swept across the chamber as they searched for a way out. Cold water swirled around their waists, and every movement sent ripples slapping against the stone walls. The air hung thick and humid, echoing with the slow, rhythmic tap of droplets falling from somewhere above. The sharp metallic scent of a ruptured pipe lingered in the darkness.

The pump Israel had jammed shuddered every few seconds but held, restricting the flow enough to stop the flooding.

Debra tilted her light upward. The trapdoor they had fallen through was sealed tight, far out of reach even if it hadn’t been locked. “We need another exit. Substage rooms usually have access to maintenance catwalks.”

“Or at least a ladder,” Grace added, scanning the perimeter.

Francy turned slowly in a circle. “These walls are too smooth. Nothing to climb. Nothing sticking out. The only things in here are water and brick.”

“Not quite,” Elena said softly.

Her beam drifted to the far corner, catching a square metal panel half-submerged beneath the rising water. One edge sat slightly raised, allowing water to slosh in and out. “That. That has to be something.”

They waded toward it, the water resisting each step.

Drew crouched carefully and tested the panel. “It’s a maintenance hatch. Probably for access to wiring or counterweights.” He gripped the exposed handle and pulled. It didn’t move.

“Locked.”

Aisha raised her light higher above the hatch. “Wait… look up.”

Set into the wall above it, nearly swallowed by shadow, was a steel rung. Then another above that. And another. A ladder, welded directly into the brick, disappearing into darkness.

“You’ve got to be kidding me,” Grace whispered. “Another ladder? What is it with L.A. and ladders?”

Elena’s eyes widened as she shook her head.

“I don’t understand,” Aisha said.

“That’s how we escaped the crypt in the cemetery,” Drew reminded her.

Francy reached for the lowest rung. It was slick but solid beneath her grip. “So… this is the way up?”

“Looks like it,” Drew said, already hoisting himself out of the water, his shoes scraping against the metal. “If we’re lucky, it leads to a maintenance loft behind the stage.”

One by one, they climbed. The ladder stretched nearly twenty feet. As they ascended, the air grew warmer, carrying the faint scent of electrical cables and rope.

At the top, Drew pulled himself onto a narrow ledge. A wooden hatch sat above him, its underside speckled with layers of paint drippings from countless set changes.

He pushed. It resisted.

He pushed again.

A crack opened, and dry air spilled through, along with the faint hum of stage lighting.

"It's backstage," he said, grinning with relief. "We're under the fly system."

Francy climbed up beside him and eased the hatch the rest of the way open. Beyond it lay a cramped space crowded with ropes, pulleys, and sandbags. The hidden superstructure behind the curtains. The distant roar of the crowd drifted toward them.

"The pre-show has started!" Aisha exclaimed.

They pulled themselves out, water dripping onto the worn floorboards.

Debra lowered the hatch and leaned against the wall, finally able to take a full breath. "Okay. We're out of the chamber."

"And nobody even knew we were down there," Elena muttered, wringing out her soaked dress.

Suddenly, Drew heard Detective Singh's voice. "Listen, they are here!" she called. She must have pieced together what had happened.

Grace let out a weak laugh. "They're going to freak out when we walk in like drowned rats."

"Let's get back to stage right," Drew said. "Then we can tell them exactly what went wrong."

Exhausted but steady, they moved along the narrow maintenance walkway. Backstage was controlled chaos. Harsh white police floodlights cut through the maze of curtains and rigging. Radios crackled. Officers moved with brisk, practiced urgency.

Drew, Aisha, Debra, Elena, Israel, Francy, and Grace were ushered past a line of LAPD uniforms, their eyes widening as the full scene came into view.

Detective Singh stood at the center of it all, her leather jacket slipping off one shoulder, her hair mussed from the headset she had just yanked away. In front of her, Harvey Goldstein slumped in handcuffs, his jaw tight, his eyes darting with anger. A few feet away, Matt and Ollie knelt with their wrists zip-tied behind their backs, both staring at the floor as if it might swallow them whole.

Behind them, paramedics crouched around a stretcher, their movements fast but precise.

Drew's eyes widened. Georgia Lynn lay on the gurney, pale, a thick bandage wrapped tightly around her stomach. Straps secured her in place, and despite the dried blood on her fingers, one wrist was cuffed to the rail.

"She survived?" Drew whispered, stepping forward before Aisha caught his arm.

One paramedic adjusted the oxygen mask over Georgia Lynn's face while another locked the stretcher legs into position. They lifted her in one smooth, practiced motion. Her eyes fluttered open just long enough to find Drew. Confusion flickered there, then fury, before she was wheeled toward the exit.

Detective Singh exhaled and turned to the group.

"We lost communication with you," she said.

"We were dropped through that trap door." Drew pointed toward the rectangular panel in the stage floor.

"Goldstein got sloppy. Real sloppy." Detective Singh jerked her head toward Harvey, who refused to meet anyone's eyes. "What made us move was the gunshot backstage."

Elena stiffened. "So, you heard it?"

"Oh yeah," Singh replied. "Heard it and saw the panic spike on every security feed we were tapping. That was our signal. We breached the theater from two access points, the catwalk entrance and the loading dock. My team intercepted Goldstein trying to drag Georgia Lynn into the utility hall. Meanwhile, the second team found these two." She nodded toward Matt and Ollie, who shrank under the attention. "Right in the middle of destroying evidence."

Debra shook her head slowly. "And Georgia Lynn?"

"Armed. Panicked. And bleeding." Singh's voice softened slightly. "We got the gun away from her before she could fire. She'll survive. And she'll be facing a long list of charges as soon as the surgeons are done with her."

The paramedics wheeled her past them, escorts clearing a path. Drew watched until Georgia Lynn disappeared through the swinging emergency exit doors.

Detective Singh straightened and brushed dust from her sleeves. "So," she said, her tone snapping back to business, "this is where we part. The trio is in custody. Everyone's safe. And I could not have solved these three cases without you. Drew, I've already reopened the cold case involving your aunt's murder. I will make sure justice is served. I will personally call Vivienne LeClaire in the morning and let her know her brother's drowning will be charged as a homicide. Vivienne was acting under fear and duress from Harvey, so she'll come out of this just fine. And thanks to all of you, Remi's murder is solved."

The group exchanged small, stunned smiles at the humility in her words.

"We're grateful for you too, Detective," Drew said, shaking her hand. "Thank you for believing in us."

"And now, your show must go on!" Detective Singh declared.

Backstage, the noise and motion carried on. But for the group, the world seemed to fall still. The night had cracked wide open, and nothing was ever going back to the way it was.

"Guys, come on, we have to get into our costumes!" Aisha urged.

They thanked Detective Singh again for all her help and hurried back to the dressing rooms.

Drew sat alone in the dim room, the truth resting in him like a second heartbeat. He'd finally learned the facts. Every detail laid out clean and undeniable. But his body hadn't caught up. It still felt like it was bracing for something, some last-minute correction that would undo it all.

The world hadn't changed. The chair still creaked when he shifted. The clock still ticked. And yet everything he was had quietly rearranged itself.

It wasn't just that his aunt had been murdered.

It was that the man who did it had stood in front of him. Named. After thirty years.

The realization peeled back memories he'd sealed shut. The night she didn't come home. The police officer's careful voice. The way adults spoke around him, as if grief were contagious. Back then, he'd told himself that if he could just understand how it happened, he could survive that it had.

Now he saw it with a clarity that hurt.

He hadn't become a detective because he believed in justice. He'd become one because he didn't believe in anything else.

Anger rose first. Hot. Reflexive. But it collapsed almost immediately into something worse: relief. Relief that the chaos had shape now. That the monster had a face. That the endless wondering could finally stop.

The relief made him ashamed.

His throat tightened as tears came, slow and unstoppable. He pressed his palms into his eyes, as if he could hold himself together by force. For years, he'd carried her death like a question he could earn the right to answer.

Now the answer was here.

And it didn't give him back a single thing he'd lost.

What it gave him was grief. Pure, unfiltered grief he'd postponed his entire life.

A quiet sob escaped him, breaking the careful discipline, he'd built his career on. He bowed forward, shoulders caving, and let the truth land fully at last: he hadn't failed her. He'd just been a child who loved her.

The door behind him opened softly.

Debra didn't announce herself. She took him in at a glance and understood enough not to rush him. She waited until his breathing steadied, until the room felt large enough again.

"Are you okay?" she asked, already knowing the answer.

He shook his head. Then, after a moment, nodded. "I don't know what I'm supposed to feel."

Debra stepped closer, her voice steady and sure. "You're not supposed to feel anything," she said. "This isn't a test. It's just the truth finally catching up to you."

Drew let that settle. The weight of it. The mercy in it.

Debra rested her head against his shoulder, grounding him.

"You spent your whole life chasing the question," she added quietly. "Now you get to be the person who survived the answer."

The words settled between them, gentle and final.

Drew closed his eyes, breathing through the ache. Not to escape it this time, but to let it be real.

And in that stillness, the chapter ended. Not with justice or closure, but with something far rarer. Permission to grieve.

☆☆☆

Drew, Aisha, Debra, Francy, Israel, Elena, and Grace gathered beneath the narrow glow of the backstage work lights, the velvet curtain trembling with the murmur of the crowd beyond it.

They stood in full tango costume, each one a blaze of color, attitude, and intention honed to a perfect edge.

Drew's jacket shimmered obsidian, stitched to his frame like a second skin. His hair was slicked back. He rolled his shoulders once, loosening the kinetic fire coiled in his spine. Aisha, wrapped in a molten red dress cut high at the leg, balanced on one stiletto as she fastened the other. Rhinestones dusted her cheekbones, catching sparks of light. Debra wore midnight blue that fell like water, her curls pinned with silver combs, her eyes steady and daring. Francy's costume was a seductive sweep of gold, open-backed, her posture tall and regal, as if she'd been carved from rhythm itself. Israel stood among them, flanked by brilliance, his vest embroidered in crimson filigree, chin lifted, ready to command and be commanded in equal measure. Elena echoed the first in sapphire, her dress a twin shade edged in black lace that hinted at mischief. And Grace, elegant and lethal in deep emerald, adjusted her long gloves with slow, deliberate precision that matched her name.

They exchanged glances. Not nervous. Electric.

The house lights dimmed. A hush rolled across the audience.

Then the announcer's voice unfurled through the theater like velvet over steel.

"As a special preview before the film begins… Ladies and gentlemen, we present: *The Final Tango*."

A single heartbeat of silence.

Then "Libertango" pulsed through the speakers, a low thrum crawling up their spines. The piano's downbeat struck like a lightning bolt. And the seven exploded onto the stage.

They moved as a single creature. Sharp legs. Quick turns. Bodies colliding and separating like sparks struck from steel. Drew and Aisha sliced the air with a whip-fast ocho. Israel dipped Debra and Elena in mirrored arcs, their dresses spilling like ink across the floor. Grace snapped into Francy's turn, the two spiraling into a perfect pivot before breaking apart in a flash of emerald and gold.

Heat rose from the stage. From the dancers. From the music itself.

Every step a declaration. Every glance a dare. Every movement a promise they had no intention of keeping tame.

It was a sexy tango, the kind that didn't ask for permission but demanded surrender. A final eruption of everything they'd trained for, everything they'd risked, everything they'd become.

When the music crashed into its final note, the seven froze in a sculpted tableau, breathing hard, shining with sweat and triumph. The curtain thundered down. Applause detonated through the theater.

In the darkness, one final line echoed, whispered like a vow:

"Some dances end… but the fire we set never dies."

Be sure to follow Drew and the Detectives
into their next global adventure in
The Curse of the Jade Dagger.

Dedication: Because I Knew Them

"When your wings are torn and you can no longer fly, these are the friends who walk with you, side by side."

To my gypsy family:

Because I knew ***Francy Muia***, dance flowed back into my life. You taught me the beauty of showing up again and again with an honest soul.

Because I knew ***Aisha Qandisha***, laughter found a softer place to land. You taught me that joy doesn't have to be loud to be real, that pride can light a whole room.

Because I knew ***Israel Loreto Diaz***, courage walked a little closer. Your strength stitched empowerment into the corners of my days, reminding me that life is an adventure and that every day is a gift.

Because I knew ***Grace Redwood***, kindness learned to speak. In quiet acts, in open hands, in the way compassion ripples through a life.

Because I knew ***Debra Arditi***, wisdom stood at my shoulder. You've shown me that understanding grows from listening deeper than words.

Because I knew ***Elena (Lani) Ford***, friendship felt natural again. Your steadfast spirit blooms like the morning sun. You see life's challenges as stepping stones, empowering newness within me.

My gratitude continues for **Vincent Dixon, Kyle Rizeq, Candela Alarcon, James Palacio, Terrell and Thomas Redwood**.

And because I knew them,
my steps are surer, my heart is fuller,
and the world, my world,
shines truer than before.
— **Andrew Pacholyk**

About the Author

Andrew Pacholyk is an American dancer, author, healer, and licensed acupuncture physician whose path into writing and holistic wellness didn't follow the traditional "creative writing to publishing" trajectory. That unconventional journey gives his work a *"grounded authenticity that feels raw, searching, joyous, and deeply human."* He bridges the "*mystical and the everyday, offering hope, healing, and meaning*" through stories that are both personal and universal.

An award-winning, international bestselling author, Andrew's work resonates with readers across the globe. As a master storyteller, he crafts deeply human narratives that blend life lessons, humor, suspense, and spiritual insight, delivering stories that linger long after the final page.

Andrew is the recipient of the Literary Titan Gold Book Award and was a 2022 Ommie Award nominee for Best Spiritual Memoir for *Barefoot: A Surfer's View of the Universe*. He received International Best-Selling Author recognition for *Lead Us To A Place: Your Spiritual Journey Through Life's Seasons*. His audiobook *The Rhythm of Betrayal* ranked among the Top 25 most downloaded mystery audiobooks of 2024.

His work has been featured in *The New York Times*, *Time Out*, *OM Times Magazine*, *The Huffington Post*, and *CBS News*. He is also the founder of the holistic healing website Peacefulmind.com.

Connect with Andrew: https://www.peacefulmind.com/about-us

The Drew and the Detective Series

Drew and his talented dancer friends are the toast of the town in Miami, captivating crowds with their electric performances at the most exclusive clubs. However, their carefree lives are shattered when a wealthy shipping tycoon is brutally murdered, sending shockwaves throughout the city. As the police investigate, suspicion falls on several family members, including Drew and his crew, after it's discovered they were seen with the tycoon's daughter shortly before the murder took place, leaving them unwittingly tangled in the web of this sinister plot.

They embark on a thrilling quest that takes them across Miami, confronting their worst fears and unearthing clues that reveal a conspiracy more twisted than they ever imagined. With their lives on the line, Drew and his friends must uncover the truth before the killer strikes again. Every second counts in *The Rhythm of Betrayal*.

When New York City's most powerful financier and his high-society wife plead for their help, Drew and his detective friends are plunged into a world of incredible wealth and deadly secrets. They quickly discover that the deceased colleague was the son of this influential couple, a brilliant young artist and dancer whose mysterious demise was no accident. Armed with the financier's wealth and influence, they uncover clues the police have missed. They follow a trail that leads from lavish penthouse parties to the underground art scene, from Broadway backstage to the secret labyrinth beneath New York.

With its pulse-pounding suspense and surprising twists, this thriller will keep you on the edge of your seat until the very last reveal. New York never sleeps, and neither do Drew and the Detectives in *Scandal Beneath the Skyline*.

www.ingramcontent.com/pod-product-compliance
Lightning Source LLC
LaVergne TN
LVHW021810120826
845149LV00026B/2040

* 9 7 9 8 9 9 8 5 5 3 5 6 1 *